MW00355881

"Rich with Celtic lore, battle, and competing magics, *Oath of the Brotherhood* is a heroic coming-of-age fantasy experience and an inspiring series opener."

SERENA CHASE
Author of Eyes of E'veria

"Carla Laureano has crafted a richly detailed dark-ages epic that will captivate fantasy lovers."

R. J. LARSON
Author of Books of the Infinite

"The Laureano world seems genuine and the lead couple a brave wonderful duo... readers will appreciate Conor as a scholar warrior defending his faith and people, and Aine leading her nation in an insurgency against the evil who took over the kingdom."

MIDWEST BOOK REVIEW

"Laureano pulls readers into this story and does not let them go. From the first page to the last readers are gripped by the multifaceted story."

RT BOOK REVIEWS

Oath of the Brotherhood

Books by Carla Laureano

MacDonald Family Trilogy
Five Days in Skye
London Tides
Under Scottish Stars

Supper Club Series
The Saturday Night Supper Club
Brunch at Bittersweet Cafe
The Solid Grounds Coffee Company

Discovered by Love Series
Jilted (novella)
Starstruck (novella)

The Song of Seare Trilogy
Oath of Brotherhood
Beneath the Forsaken City
The Sword and the Song

Oath of the Brotherhood

THE SONG OF SEARE
BOOK ONE

CARLA LAUREANO

Published by Enclave Publishing, an imprint of Third Day Books, LLC

Phoenix, Arizona, USA.
www.enclavepublishing.com

ISBN: 978-1-62184-149-4 (hardback)
ISBN: 978-1-62184-151-7 (printed softcover)
ISBN: 978-1-62184-150-0 (ebook)

Cover design by Kirk DouPonce, www.DogEaredDesign.com
Typesetting by Jamie Foley, www.JamieFoley.com

Printed in the United States of America.

For Nathan and Preston,

May you find the path God has for you and follow it fearlessly.

You are capable of greater things than you can imagine.

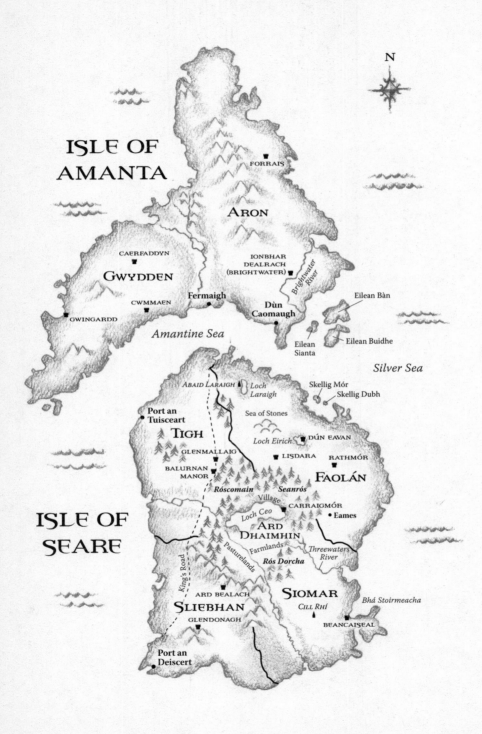

N

ISLE OF
AMANTA

FORRAIS

ARON

CAERFADDYN

GWYDDEN

IONBHAR
DEALRACH
(BRIGHTWATER)

CWMMAEN

Fermaigh

GWINGARDD

Dùn
Caomaugh

Eilean Bàn

Brightwater River

Eilean Buidhe

Amantine Sea

Eilean
Sianta

Silver Sea

Abaid Laraigh

*Loch
Laraigh*

Skellig Mór
Skellig Dubh

Port an
Tuisceart

Sea of Stones

Tigh

Loch Eirich

DÚN EAVAN

GLENMALLAIG

LISDARA

RATHMÓR

BALURNAN
MANOR

Faolán

Róscomain

Seanrós

Village

CARRAIGMÓR

Loch Ceo

• Eames

**Ard
Dhaimhin**

ISLE OF
SEARE

Farmlands

*Threewaters
River*

Pasturelands

Rós Dorcha

King's Road

Siomar

ARD BEALACH

Cill Rhí

Bhá Stoirmeacha

Sliebhan

GLENDONAGH

BEANCAISEAL

Port an
Deiscert

GLOSSARY

Abban Ó Sedna (OB-bawn oh SEN-yah)—commander of southern Faolanaigh forces

Ailbhe (AL-va)—Conor's céad mate

Ailís (AY-leesh)—Aine's mother, former queen of Faolán, now deceased

Aine Nic Tamhais (ON-yuh nik TAV-ish)—King Calhoun's half sister

Alsandair Mac Tamhais (AL-san-dahr mok TAV-ish)—Aine's father, Aronan clan chief, now deceased

Amanta (ah-MAN-ta)—the island upon which Aron and Gwydden are located

Aran (AHR-an)—mapper for the Faolanaigh forces

Ard Dhaimhin (ard DAV-in)—High City, former seat of the High King

Arkiel (ar-KEEL)—Companion who instigated the rebellion against Comdiu

Aron/Aronan (ah-RUN)—the country of Aine's birth on the isle of Amanta/its language & people

Balian (BAH-lee-an)—the faith of those who follow Balus; a follower of Balus

Balurnan (bal-UR-nan)—Lord Labhrás's estate

Balus (BAH-lus)—Son of Comdiu, savior of mankind

Beagan (BOG-awn)—Fíréin tracker

Beancaiseal (ban-CASH-el)—capital of Siomar

bean-sidhe (BAN-shee)—a spirit whose appearance is thought to foreshadow death

Bearrach (BEAR-uhk)—healer at Lisdara; Aine's instructor

Bodb (bawv)—king of Sliebhan

Cáisc (kahshk)—feast in celebration of Balus's resurrection

Calhoun Mac Cuillinn (cal-HOON mok CUL-in)—king of Faolán

Canon—the Balian Holy Scriptures

Carraigmór (CAIR-ig-mor)—fortress of the High King and the Fíréin brotherhood

céad (ked)—a company of men; literally, one hundred

Ceannaire (KAN-na-ahr)—leader of the Fíréin brotherhood

Ciaran (KEER-an)—Fíréin sentry

Cill Rhí (kill ree)—Balian monastery

Cira/Ciraean (SEER-ah) (seer-AY-ahn)—largest empire in history, now reduced to a small portion of the continent

clochan (CLO-han)—dry-stone, beehive-shaped hut

Comdiu (COM-dyoo)—God

Companions—the spirit warriors of Comdiu; angels

Conclave—the ruling body of the Fíréin brotherhood

Conor Mac Nir (CON-ner mok NEER)—son of King Galbraith

Cúan (KOO-ahn)—mapper for the Faolanaigh forces

Daigh (dy)—senior member of the Fíréin brotherhood

Daimhin (DAV-in)—first and only High King of Seare

Diarmuid (DEER-muhd)—druid; adviser to King Galbraith

Dolan (DOH-len)—Conor's manservant

Donnan (DON-uhn)—Niamh's bodyguard

Dún Eavan (doon EE-van)—crannog fortress; original seat of the king of Faolán

Eames (eems)—village near Faolanaigh camp

Eimer (EYE-mer)—housekeeper at Dún Eavan

Eoghan (OH-in)—Fíréin apprentice; Conor's best friend

Faolán/Faolanaigh (FEY-lahn) (FEY-lahn-eye)—northeastern kingdom in Seare, ruled by Clan Cuillinn / its language and people

Fergus Mac Nir (FAYR-gus mok NEER)—tanist to King Galbraith; Conor's uncle

Fionncill (fee-AHN-kill)—village outside of Lisdara

Fíréin (FEER-een) brotherhood—ancient brotherhood dedicated to the reinstatement of the High King

Forrais (FOR-rus)—Aronan town of Aine's birth, Highland seat of Clan Tamhais

Gainor Mac Cuillinn (GAY-nor mok CUL-in)—tanist to King Calhoun; Calhoun's brother

Galbraith Mac Nir (GOL-breth mok NEER)—king of Tigh; Conor's father

Gillian (JILL-yuhn)—elderly Fíréin brother

Glenmallaig (glen-MAL-ag)—seat of the king of Tigh; Conor's birthplace

Gwydden (GWIH-duhn)—a country across the Amantine Sea

Hesperides (hes-PAIR-uh-dees)—country within the Ciraean empire

Innis (IN-ish)—Fíréin sentry

Iuchbar (OOK-bar)—Balian brother and tutor at Lisdara

Kebaran (keh-BAHR-ahn)—the ethnic group into which Balus was born

Keondric Mac Eirhinin (KEN-drick mok-AYR-nin)—lord of Rathmor; battle captain

Labhrás Ó Maonagh (LAV-raws oh-MOY-nah)—lord of Balurnan; Conor's foster father

Leannan (LON-nan)—steward of Lisdara

Levant/Levantine (lev-AHNT)(lev-ahn-TEEN)—the country and language of the Kebarans

Liam Mac Cuillinn (LEE-um mok CUL-in)—Ceannaire, leader of the Fíréin brotherhood

Lisdara (lis-DAR-ah)—seat of the king of Faolán

Loch Ceo (lok kyo)—lake within Ard Dhaimhin

Loch Eirich (lok AYE-rick)—lake in which Dún Eavan is located

Loch Laraigh (lok LAR-uh)—lake in northern Faolán; site of a Balian monastery

Lorcan (LUR-cawn)—leader of Aine's guard

Lughaire (LOO-ree)—Fíréin sword master

Macha (MAH-huh)—Aine's aunt, chief of Clan Tamhais, lady of Forrais

Máiréad (MAH-red)—Conor's mother, queen of Tigh, now deceased

Marcan (MAR-kawn)—steward at Glenmallaig

Meallachán (MOL-luck-on)—bard

Melandra/Melandran (mell-AHN-drah) (mell-AHN-drahn)—country within the Ciraean Empire/ its language & people

Myles (MEE-als)—Faolanaigh warrior

Nemeton—sacred place of the Seareann druids

Niamh Nic Cuillinn (NEE-uv nik CUL-in)—King Calhoun's sister

Norin (NOR-in)—the common name of the Northern Isles; origin of the Sofarende

Odran (OH-rawn)—Fíréin tracker

Oonagh (OO-nah)—Aine's and Niamh's maidservant

Rathmór (RATH-mohr)—seat of Clan Eirhinin, a minor royal line of Faolán

Reamonn (RAH-mun)—elder Fíréin brother, overseer of fieldwork

Riocárd (rih-CARD)—lord of Tirnall, Galbraith's champion, captain of the guard

Riordan Mac Nir (REER-uh-dawn mok NEER)—Conor's uncle, senior member of the Fíréin brotherhood

Rós Dorcha (ross DEER-ka)—old forest bordering Siomar

Róscomain (ros-COM-muhn)—old forest bordering Tigh and Sliebhan

Ruarc (ROO-ark)—Aine's bodyguard

Seaghan (shayn)—commander of southern Siomaigh forces

Seanrós (SHAWN-ross)—old forest bordering Faolán

Seare/Seareann (SHAR-uh)(SHAR-uhn)—island housing the four kingdoms/its language & people

Semias (SHAY-mus)—king of Siomar

sidhe (shee)—the evil spirits of the underworld; demons

Siomar/Siomaigh (SHO-mar) (SHO-my)—southeastern kingdom in Seare/its language & people

Slaine (SLAHN-yuh)—leader of Conor's céad

Sliebhan/Sliebhanaigh (SLEEV-ahn) (SLEEV-ahn-eye)—southwestern kingdom in Seare/its language & people

Sofarende (soeh-FUR-end-uh)—seafarers from the Northern Isles (Norin)

Sualtam (SOO-alt-um)—Faolanaigh warrior

tanist—chosen successor of a Seareann king, elected by the kingdom's council of lords

Tarlach (TAR-lock)—steward at Dún Eavan

Teallach (TOL-lock)—Fíréin spear instructor

Tigh/Timhaigh (ty) (TIH-vy)—northwestern kingdom in Seare, ruled by Clan Nir/its language & people

Tor (tor)—Conor's céad mate

Treasach (TRAS-ahk)—Balian brother and tutor at Lisdara

Uilliam (WIL-yam)—Faolanaigh warrior

CHAPTER ONE

The mist hung from the branches of the ancient trees like threads from a tattered banner, though the last vestiges of sunlight still glimmered on the horizon. Conor Mac Nir shivered atop his horse and tugged his cloak securely around him, then regretted the show of nerves. He had already seen the disdain in the eyes of the king's men sent to escort him. There was no need to give them reason to doubt his courage as well.

A weathered, scarred man on a dun stallion made his way from the back of the column and fell in beside him: Labhrás Ó Maonagh, Conor's foster father.

"It's too quiet," Labhrás said, his gaze flicking to the dark recesses of the forest. "The animals have gone to ground—they sense the unnatural. Keep your eyes open."

The twenty warriors quickened their pace, battle-hardened hands straying to their weapons for reassurance. Conor gripped his reins tighter. Now he understood the comfort a sword brought. Not that it would be of any use to him. He would be no help against dangers of the human kind, let alone whatever lurked in the mist.

He felt no relief when the road broke away from the trees, revealing the first glimpse of Glenmallaig's earthen ramparts and the stone dome of the keep within. The mist had already found a foothold, wreathing the top of the walls and giving the impression they stretched unendingly skyward. The moat's stale waters lapped at the base of the walls. Glenmallaig made no pretensions about being anything but a fortress, solid and impregnable.

"Steady now," Labhrás murmured.

Conor drew a deep breath. Few knew how much he dreaded this homecoming, but Labhrás was one. Other men might have taken the honor and considerable financial rewards of fostering King Galbraith's son without a thought to the responsibility it entailed, but Lord Labhrás had raised him as he would have brought up his own child. By contrast, the king had not shown a shred of interest in Conor for his entire seventeen years.

He swallowed hard and tried to disappear into the folds of his cloak as the drawbridge descended toward the bank. The leader of their escort gave a terse signal, and the procession lurched forward amidst a thunder of hooves on timber. Conor shuddered as he passed into Glenmallaig's courtyard, a wash of cold blanketing his skin—too cold, considering the fast-approaching spring. The carts carrying Labhrás's tribute to the king clattered across behind them, and the bridge once again crept upward.

Inside the courtyard, wood smoke and burning pitch drifted on the air, stinging his nose. It should have been a welcoming vignette, but the orange firelight only cast the mist-filled courtyard in a sickly yellow glow. Conor cast a glance over his shoulder just as the drawbridge thudded shut, sealing off the life he'd left behind him.

Foolish thoughts. Conor shook them off as he dismounted and winced at the twinge in his muscles as they adjusted to solid ground. A hand on his elbow steadied him, the iron grip incongruous with its owner's graying hair and finely lined face.

"Home at last," Dolan said under his breath, a tinge of irony in his voice. More than merely a devoted retainer, the manservant had become a friend and confidant over the nine years of Conor's fosterage at Balurnan. Dolan knew better than anyone the fears Conor's return stirred within him.

A pale, skeletal man descended the steps of the double-door entry, headed for the captain. After a moment of quiet conversation, he strode in their direction with a cautious smile. Conor squinted, then drew a sharp breath. The last time he had seen Marcan, the steward of Glenmallaig had been in the bloom of good health, commanding the household with a mere word. Now his clothing hung from a gaunt frame, and shadows marked the pale skin beneath his eyes. Surely the mere passage of time couldn't have effected such a transformation.

"Welcome, my lord Conor," Marcan said with a bow, his voice as calm and capable as ever. "Your old chamber has been prepared for you. Come."

Dolan gave him a nudge, and, reluctantly, Conor followed Marcan up the front steps into the great hall. Torches threw flickering light on the cavernous room, from its rush-covered floor to the curve of the ceiling, though they could not quite dispel the shadows at its apex. Conor's gaze settled on four unfamiliar men standing before the dais that held the king's throne. From their elaborately embroidered clothing, he guessed three of them to be lords of the realm. The fourth's clean-shaven head and plain robes marked him as a cleric.

The priest turned, revealing the black tattoos that etched his neck and curled up behind his ear. Conor halted as he met the piercing blue gaze, unable to summon the will to move. The sensation of a thousand insects scrambled over his skin.

Lord Labhrás's solid form cut off his view, breaking his trance. "Take Conor to his chamber," Labhrás told Dolan. "I'll be up directly." Only when the servant took Conor by the shoulders and turned him down the adjacent corridor did he realize he was trembling.

Who was the man? And what had just happened? Conor struggled for breath as they ascended a long flight of stairs, a pang of foreboding striking deep in his gut. He gave his head a sharp shake to clear away the sluggishness. Only once he was halfway up the stairs did he regain enough clarity to survey his surroundings.

They looked completely unfamiliar.

He glanced behind him to the hall to reassure himself they hadn't detoured while he was in a daze, but no . . . this was the main staircase to the upper floor. He must have traveled this very path thousands of times, both in his early years at fosterage and in his visits back home.

Why couldn't he remember it?

Marcan stopped near the top of the stairs and pushed a door open. "Here we are, just as you left it. Your trunks are being brought up now, and I'll send the boys in to fill the tub."

Conor stepped inside, expecting a rush of recognition, but this room felt just as foreign as the stairway. Faded tapestries dampened both the chill and the echo from the stone walls. Fine woolen blankets and a wolf's pelt covered the shelf bed on one end, and a single chair with a threadbare cushion stood beside the carved oak armoire. Opposite it, a wooden bathing tub waited, already half-filled with water.

The door banged open to admit four of the keep's servants, each pair carrying a heavy wooden trunk between them. They plunked them unceremoniously near the door, then escaped into the corridor without a bow or even a nod.

Dolan scowled at their backs, then turned to the trunks and loosened the leather straps on the nearest one. He immediately began to unpack Conor's garments with practiced efficiency, shaking out the wrinkles before he hung them in the wardrobe.

Conor watched Dolan work for several minutes. "Who were the men in the hall?"

"Three of them were minor lords."

"And the fourth?"

Only the slightest pause in the servant's movements betrayed his discomfort with the question. "Unless I miss my guess, there is a druid once more at Glenmallaig."

Conor sank onto the edge of the bed, his breath catching in his throat. *A druid.* They were not uncommon in the kingdom of Tigh. Most were quiet, contemplative men, content to remain isolated in the nemetons until they were called upon to perform the rites of Tigh's gods and goddesses at the quarter year or to tender folk cures for ailments. Conor had come across their kind outside Balurnan, and while the Balians denounced their pagan ways, few could perform any magic beyond benign hearth charms.

Yet this druid's suffocating presence said he was no harmless earth wizard. Conor had grown up hearing stories of the Red Druids, blood mages of immense power that counseled kings and led men in battle. Could this man be one of them? Did the Red Druids even still exist, outside of history and bards' tales?

Before he could voice his thoughts, a light knock at the door announced the arrival of two boys with steaming buckets of water in each hand.

"Bathe," Dolan said, while the boys emptied the water into the tub. "I'll go fetch your supper. Lord Labhrás should be up soon."

Conor smiled his thanks, though food was the last thing on his mind. It was bad enough he was about to face his father and explain why he had not yet laid hands on a sword. Now he might have to contend with a Red

Druid, whose kind were notorious and ruthless inquisitors, a man who looked at him as if he already knew Conor's most dangerous secret.

He forced down his unease and stripped off his travel-stained garments. His skin prickled, but a quick glance over his shoulder assured him the door remained closed. He slid quickly into the bath's meager concealment. *Breathe. They couldn't know.* Labhrás had been careful. No books of Scripture or religious symbols had come with them, and Dolan's discretion was unquestionable.

If the king found out, it would take only a whisper to destroy Labhrás's status in the kingdom. Galbraith may have relaxed the restrictions on Balianism during his reign, but not so long ago, adherence to the forbidden faith would have landed their severed heads beside the keep's gate. Even now, Balian converts did not retain possession of their lands and titles for long.

Lord Balus, protect us, Conor prayed silently, not daring to give voice to the words. *May You be the shield between us and our enemies. May You be the Light that guides our path. May everything we do further the work of Your kingdom.*

He let out a long, shuddering sigh and sank further into the warm water, concentrating on moving his breath in and out of his lungs. Inch by inch, he forced his mind away from his worries. He could not afford to seem afraid here. To show any discomfort would only make them wonder what he was hiding.

Conor.

He sat bolt upright in the bath, sloshing water over the sides. He whipped his head around, looking for the source of the whispered voice.

I know what you conceal, Conor. Soon, they all will. I can protect you.

Gooseflesh prickled his skin, and the warm water turned cold. "Who's there? Show yourself!"

Join me, Conor. You'll be safe . . .

He jerked awake with a yelp and slid underwater before he even realized he had fallen asleep. He surfaced, spluttering, to find Labhrás watching him from the doorway.

The older man's lips twitched. "Taking a swim?"

Conor blinked. Steam still rose from the surface of the water, and the floor beside the tub was dry. A dream. Just a dream.

He shook his head with a self-conscious laugh. "Not intentionally."

He wrung water from his tangled hair and reached for the cloth beside the tub. Only once he had dried himself off and tugged a clean linen shirt over his head did he dare voice his question. "Is it true? Is there a druid at Glenmallaig?"

Labhrás nodded and sat down on the bed. "His name's Diarmuid. He's been present at court for at least a year, though I'd be surprised if he hasn't had an influence for longer than that. I don't need to tell you—"

"—the less he knows of us, the better? No. That one I figured out for myself."

Labhrás sighed. "There are things we must discuss, Conor, but they are not topics for tonight. Eat, try to get some sleep. We'll speak tomorrow."

"Aye, my lord." Conor knew better than to press him, even though there was little chance he could put any of this out of his mind tonight. He watched his foster father move to the door and then called out, "Lord Labhrás?"

"Aye, Conor?"

"I don't remember this place. Any of it. My chamber, the hall. . . . It's only been three years. I should remember something, shouldn't I?"

He expected Labhrás to reassure him, to tell him he had been grieving his mother when they last visited Glenmallaig, too young to remember anything before that. Instead, Labhrás met his eyes seriously. "Aye, you should remember something. Good night, lad."

Conor exhaled heavily and scrubbed his hands over his face. Nothing about this trip felt right. Not the escort, not the mist, not the druid's presence. He was not foolish enough to assume any of it was connected—not yet—but he knew with certainty he was far out of his depth.

CHAPTER TWO

"Conor, wake up!"

Conor jolted to alertness, his hands flying up to shield himself before he realized it was only Dolan. Bright sunlight already streamed through the bubbled glass windows of his chamber. He let out a long breath and scrubbed the sleep from his eyes while he found his voice. "What time is it?"

"Late. I let you sleep through breakfast, but now you're wanted in the hall."

"The king?"

"Indeed. Get dressed. He is not a patient man, your father."

Conor slid from bed and dressed reflexively in the clothes Dolan handed him. The moment he dreaded was almost upon him. Would his father berate him in front of everyone? Or was it to be a private audience, with no one to witness how Galbraith expressed his displeasure?

He was still struggling into his coat when Dolan shoved him unceremoniously into the chair and yanked a comb through his tangled hair. "A good thing we have no need for warrior's braids."

"Don't remind me."

When Dolan was finished, he offered a brass hand mirror, but Conor ignored it. He knew what he would see. Dolan had left his dark blond hair long and loose, as was the fashion for boys. Only men who had taken the field of battle were permitted to wear the many thin braids as a symbol of their valor. His fine wool jacket, worn over a linen shirt and pleated knee-length tunic, only served to highlight a rawboned frame that had yet to grow into a man's physique. In a court that prized appearances, this was just one more area in which he was bound to disappoint.

"Let's have this done with," Conor said, rising. With any luck, his father would only give him a quick once-over before he returned to more important matters. After all, the return of a son from fosterage was hardly a state occasion, even if it did coincide with a meeting of the king's council. Conor squared his shoulders and strode into the corridor, steeling himself for the audience below.

His steps faltered when he and Dolan entered the great hall. Men and women filled the room, pressed shoulder to shoulder and dressed in finery the likes of which Conor had never seen.

Voices rumbled at the front of the hall. Then, one boomed out, clear and deep among the rest. "Marcan, where is my son?"

Marcan appeared beside Conor and Dolan. "Right here, my lord."

Heads swiveled toward them. As Marcan led him forward, the crowd parted, and whispers rustled through the room. Conor kept his eyes fixed firmly ahead. The cloying scents of perfumed oils, straw, wool, and silk closed around him, and the press of so many bodies after the isolation of Balurnan roused his instinct to flee. By the time the throne came into view, he could barely breathe.

King Galbraith had always loomed large in Conor's memory, but he had chalked it up to a child's outsized perceptions. Now, he realized his memories were accurate. Clad in a wolf's-fur cloak with the steel crown of kingship upon his brow, the king nearly filled the throne. His waist-length hair, brown-blond like Conor's, fell in warrior's braids over his shoulder, and several plaits decorated his long beard. Beside him stood Lord Riocárd, Galbraith's champion and captain of the guard, bearing the sword of kingship. The captain was a formidable man in his own right, fierce-eyed and broad-shouldered, but even he was dwarfed in his lord's presence.

Conor looked away before his eyes could betray his anxiety—into the face of the only man he feared as much as his father. Lord Fergus, the king's tanist, was an older, paunchier version of Galbraith, and he made the king seem downright warm by comparison. He took Conor in, a slow, predatory smile spreading across his face.

Beside Fergus, a second man scrutinized him as one would observe an insect through glass, emotionless. The druid himself. Conor suppressed another shudder at the symbols of dark power tattooed on his neck and hands.

"Come here, boy," Galbraith said. "Let me see you."

Conor tore his eyes away from the observers and moved forward to kneel on the lowest step. He pressed his trembling hands together in front of him.

"Look at me!"

Conor jerked his head up and stared forward while the king's gaze roamed over him.

One corner of Galbraith's mouth twisted in displeasure. "Tell me, have you started your training yet?"

"What training would that be, sir?"

"Don't be clever with me. You know to what I refer. Sword, bow, spear."

"No, my lord." Conor's voice came out strangled, forced from his constricted throat.

"Then what exactly have you been doing for the last nine years?"

"Studying, my lord."

"Studying?" Galbraith's tone changed, a note of curiosity in it.

Conor's heart lifted slightly. "Aye, my lord. History, mathematics, literature, astronomy, law, languages—"

"What languages?"

"I can read and write the common tongue, as well as Ciraean, Levantine, and Norin. My Melandran is passable, and I know a bit of the Odlum runes."

Galbraith stared at him for a long moment. The hall fell silent but for the crackle of torches and the occasional rustle of a lady's gown, every eye riveted on the spectacle before them. Then, in one swift movement, Galbraith reached over and ripped the sword from the scabbard in Riocárd's hands. The ring of metal echoed in the hall as the blade stopped a fraction of an inch before Conor's eyes.

"The only language our enemies understand is the language of the sword." Galbraith's eyes locked unflinchingly on his son's.

Then the weapon was gone, tossed back to Riocárd. Galbraith stood, his expression thunderous as he scanned the assemblage. "Labhrás, where are you?"

"Here, my lord."

All heads turned toward Lord Labhrás where he stood at the edge of the gathering. He wore unadorned garments of fine wool, though he was easily the equal in wealth to any of the onlookers, and he remained unruffled beneath the king's furious stare. Conor would have given anything to possess even half that calm and dignity.

"I sent you a son, and you bring me back a daughter! Explain yourself."

"I did as I was asked, my lord." Labhrás's voice was soft, unchallenging. "You wished your son to be educated."

"As a warrior, not a scholar! What good is a man who cannot lift a sword to defend himself and his people? You have brought shame to Tigh."

Labhrás took a step forward, his expression hardening. "It is no shame to know of the world outside one's palace, my lord. Conor is a diligent student, and he excels in all he puts his hand to. I would think any man would be proud to call him his son."

Gasps rippled through the crowd at Labhrás's audacity, and Galbraith's face turned an unhealthy shade of purple.

"You dare—"

"I did what was agreed upon, my lord. Shall I remind you of the terms of that agreement?"

Galbraith's mouth compressed into a thin, hard line. Conor looked between the two men in amazement as the king swallowed a sharp response.

"Then you may take responsibility for what he has become. He is no son of mine." He strode down the dais and passed Conor without another glance.

Someone sniggered in the silence, but Conor barely noticed as the room wavered around him. He had been dismissed, possibly disowned, the favor that fell on an only son withdrawn as quickly and easily as Galbraith's tossed sword.

"Come, Conor." Labhrás lifted him to his feet, his hand clamped around Conor's biceps. He steered him away from the gathering toward an intersecting corridor.

The druid stepped into their path with a pleasant smile. "Allow me to introduce myself, young man. I'm Diarmuid."

Conor blinked back a wave of dizziness. "You're the druid."

"Aye. Considering your education, I suspect you understand what that means better than most."

Labhrás inserted himself between Conor and the druid, his expression hard. "It's best I return the boy to his chamber now."

Diarmuid merely smiled. "When you want answers, Conor, all you need do is ask."

Before Conor could puzzle through the cryptic offer, Labhrás ushered him past the man toward the stairs. "That could have gone worse."

"How?"

Labhrás arched an eyebrow, and Conor remembered what they strove to keep from the king and his druid. The question of religion, and the fact his education could not have been accomplished without the services of a Balian priest, had never arisen.

Conor felt stronger and clearer with every step away from the hall, and his dizziness faded. He thought back to the exchange between Labhrás and Galbraith. Was the king actually afraid of what Labhrás might say? Never would he display that kind of weakness before the lords of the realm unless what Labhrás could reveal would be far more damaging.

When they reached Conor's chamber, they found Dolan waiting. "So?"

"About what we expected," Labhrás said.

Conor looked between the men, open-mouthed. "You knew this would happen? You knew my father would disown me?"

"That was for show," Labhrás said. "Clan law doesn't allow him to disown blood. But aye, I expected his anger. As did you."

"I suppose I did." Conor focused on his foster father again. "What was that all about? What agreement?"

Labhrás and Dolan exchanged a glance, and then the servant slipped out the door. Labhrás gestured for Conor to take a seat on the bed and pulled up a chair beside him.

"Perhaps I owe you an apology. Most of that had nothing to do with you. You recall, of course, that your uncle, Riordan, sat the throne before your father."

"He abdicated in order to join the Fíréin." Conor understood the pull of the legendary brotherhood. Nearly every young boy in Seare fantasized about being one of those preternaturally gifted warriors, but only the Balian clans followed the tradition of sending the firstborn son to the Fíréin. That a king of Tigh would abandon his throne in favor of a Balian warrior-brotherhood was unfathomable.

"Galbraith was not the council's first choice as Riordan's successor,"

Labhrás said. "Several of us, myself included, looked to the minor royal branch, though a Mac Laighid has not sat the throne for generations. Riordan, however, pushed hard for Galbraith's election. He swung enough votes to win him the tanistry, and when he abdicated a few months later, he handed him the throne."

"Why not just take himself out of the succession?"

"If he did that, he couldn't influence the council's selection. Of all the candidates, Galbraith was most likely to be sympathetic toward the Balians, considering your mother was one. The king—and the rest of the council—are well aware he owes his throne to a Fíréin brother. That's why he didn't argue when Riordan returned from Ard Dhaimhin and insisted you be fostered with me."

Conor's mind whirred. "I never even met Riordan. Why would he take such an interest in me?"

"Even I don't know that," Labhrás said. "We were practically brothers, raised together in fosterage, but he always kept his own council. He was very specific, though. You were to be raised in our faith, and you were to be given an extensive education." Labhrás placed his hand on Conor's shoulder. "You see now why Galbraith would not want such a thing revealed. Should the Balians' involvement in his choices become common knowledge, the council might dethrone him."

No wonder his father was furious. Conor's scholarly pursuits and lack of fighting skill drew far too much attention to a fosterage that should never have been arranged. Yet he still couldn't fathom why Riordan would have gone to so much trouble for him.

Labhrás stood. "I've given you enough to think about for one day. But first . . ." He dipped a hand into the neck of his tunic and drew out a pendant on a long silver chain, then draped it carefully over Conor's head. "This has been with me for long enough. It's yours now."

Conor lifted the heavy pendant in his palm, his blood whooshing too fast through his veins. It was a wheel charm, a ring of ivory with three carved spokes representing the tripartite nature of Comdiu, a clear symbol of the Balian faith.

"Why are you giving this to me?"

"It's a relic of the Great Kingdom, one of the few remaining objects of power. Keep it close, and keep it hidden. It will help."

"Help what?"

"No more questions. Some things are better left unspoken." Labhrás placed a light hand atop Conor's head and then left the room.

Conor turned the charm over and studied the runes inscribed there, but his knowledge of Odlum was too rudimentary to be of any help in deciphering their meaning. He briefly considered stowing it in one of his trunks. But Labhrás did nothing idly. If he'd given Conor the charm, he'd thought he needed the protection. Conor dropped it beneath his tunic before he could examine too closely the dangers from which he was being protected.

Dolan entered and shut the door firmly behind him. "Let's see it then."

It took Conor several moments to work up the courage to draw out the charm again. "Lord Labhrás said it was an object of power."

Dolan peered at it, but he made no move to touch it. "Labhrás has worn it for years. I've always suspected Riordan meant it for you when the time was right."

"What do you know about all this?"

"I've served Labhrás since we were both children," Dolan said. "He's told me what I need to know to keep you safe, nothing else."

"And this?" Conor held up the charm. "This really has . . . magic?"

Dolan just smiled.

Conor rubbed his eyes wearily. Too much had happened in the last day to process. His dishonor before the court, the story of the kingship, the druid's presence . . . and now he wore an object, which by all accounts was imbued by some long-forgotten Balian magic. The beginnings of a headache pulsed in his temples.

"I have to think," he muttered, rising. "I'll be back in time for supper."

Dolan's brows knit together, but he didn't try to dissuade him. Conor concealed the charm and headed straight out his door. Since he barely remembered the layout of the keep, he picked a route at random and began to walk.

Iron-bound doors dotted the stone hallway, but Conor didn't try any of the handles. When he reached an intersection, he turned left down another corridor, this one decorated with moth-eaten, smoke-stained tapestries. This was part of the structure guests would never see. He trailed his fingers along the rough-hewn stone as he walked. The torch beside him guttered in an unseen breeze, yet the interior hallway had no doors or windows. He stopped as a shard of memory surfaced. Perhaps his direction had not been random after all.

Slowly, Conor pushed aside one of the tapestries to reveal a narrow wooden door. His hand trembled on the latch. *Coward.* He drew a long breath and pushed the door inward on well-oiled hinges. Hidden, perhaps, but not forgotten.

Conor stepped into blackness, the tapestry swinging back to block the torchlight. As his eyes adjusted to the dark, he could make out the dim shapes of a chair and some sort of cabinet. He stretched out his arms, and his fingers brushed stone on either side.

How could he have known this was here, but not remember the room itself?

A memory jolted him abruptly: his younger self, crouched in the corner while Galbraith shouted and a woman sobbed in the distance. His mother. He could almost hear the shouting now . . .

But no, that wasn't part of the memory. He really could hear voices. He held his breath, straining his ears for the source of the sound until he could distinguish individual words.

"—the coast of Gwydden. Some say they're making a permanent settlement."

"Sofarende don't settle. They pillage and burn and go back to their islands."

"Not this time. If they establish a permanent base—"

"Enough." Though Conor had not recognized the other voices, there was no mistaking the king's authoritative baritone. "The Sofarende are a real threat, whether they settle or not. Eventually, they'll look for richer targets, and Tigh is the first in sight."

Conor realized he was hearing a private meeting of the king's council, filtered up from the chamber below. He should leave immediately—he couldn't be the only one who knew of this room—but he couldn't pull himself away from the conversation.

"We can handle an invasion," Fergus said scornfully. "Why run to Faolán for help?"

"Because they will share the casualties. And whether you admit it or not, they command more skilled warriors in the northern territories than we have in all of Tigh. It's time to make our peace with the Mac Cuillinn."

Silence fell. Conor barely breathed.

"You know I must object to this plan, my lord," Labhrás said after a long pause. "Sending Conor to Faolán—"

"You have only yourself to blame," Galbraith said scornfully. "If you'd raised the boy in a manner befitting his station, I would never have considered such a thing. At least now Conor can be of some use to Tigh."

Blood drummed in Conor's ears. He didn't want to hear any more. He stumbled over the chair in his haste to get to the door and pushed into the corridor without considering who might be on the other side of the tapestry.

The hallway was still deserted, though, so he took a moment to catch his breath. He should never have stayed once he realized the room's purpose. How had he found it the first time? And who else knew of its existence?

Conor steadied himself with a hand against the wall while his other one reached automatically for the charm beneath his shirt. The ivory emanated a subtle but unmistakable warmth through the linen.

Only then did he realize that for the first time since returning to Glenmallaig, his mind felt completely clear.

It couldn't be a coincidence his buried memories had led him here right after he put on the charm. Was that what Labhrás meant when he said it would help? Did that mean his memory loss was due to another, darker sort of magic? If Diarmuid truly was a Red Druid, such a spell wouldn't be beyond his ability. But if that were true, what was he trying to make him forget?

Conor had to work out the details before anyone learned of his suspicions. At least it sounded as if he wouldn't have to conceal them for long.

The king was sending him to Faolán.

As a hostage.

CHAPTER THREE

Conor paced the confines of his chamber for the next two days while he waited to hear his fate firsthand. The books he brought from Balurnan held his attention for only so long, and he was too distracted to put up much of a defense in his games of King and Conqueror with Dolan. When the servant put Conor's king into check for the second time, he simply tipped the marble game piece in surrender and pushed away from the game board.

"The silence is maddening," Conor said. "I'm going for a walk."

Pacing the dim, smoky hallway did nothing to relieve the smothering sense of stillness. Labhrás's country manor was smaller and more humble than this colossal keep, but it had been alive with warmth and laughter. Right now, smells of the evening's supper would be drifting across the courtyard from the kitchen, signaling the coming night. The household warriors would eat with them in the hall before a cheery fire, while Labhrás's three daughters took turns telling tales culled from educations no less thorough than Conor's.

His chest ached at the recollection. His family was in Balurnan, regardless of the clan name he bore. He couldn't imagine King Galbraith calling for him in the evenings as Labhrás had, to mull over the day's events to the sound of the harp. The instrument had been in the Maonagh clan for generations, but they called it Conor's harp since he was the only one who could coax a melody from its aged rosewood frame. He would give anything to be back there now, his hands on the strings, instead of sitting in this oppressive keep, waiting for someone else to decide his fate.

"The harp!" Conor's feet carried him halfway down the corridor before he fully registered his intentions. He passed the secret chamber behind the tapestry, turned a corner, and stopped before a door that looked like every other entryway in the palace.

The latch gave easily, and the door opened into a large, dark room. Conor removed one of the thick candles from the iron stand inside and lit it from the torch in the hallway, then touched the flame to the other wax columns. They flared to life, bathing the room in a warm yellow glow.

Layers of dust and cobwebs covered the tapestries and darkened the colorful rug on the stone floor. Conor swept aside one of the cloths that covered the furniture and found a high-backed chair beneath it. When he lifted the flower-embellished cushion, he was rewarded with a memory of his mother, young and auburn-haired, painstakingly embroidering it by firelight.

"My mother's sitting room." How long had it been since he had set foot in this chamber? He'd last visited Glenmallaig three years ago, the same trip during which she'd had her accident, but those memories were as inaccessible as the others.

He wandered past the covered chairs and tables and stopped short before an object in the corner. Beneath the covering lay a beautiful Seareann lap harp, far finer than his instrument at Balurnan, its maple soundboard elaborately carved with mythological creatures. He touched a string, and it sprang back with a metallic hum, bringing with it a shard of memory.

He sat at his mother's feet as she held the harp in her lap. Her fingers moved nimbly up and down the strings, demonstrating the major scales and chords, which she named as she plucked them. Conor reached out to touch the instrument.

"Would you like to try?" she asked, smiling down at him.

Conor sucked in a ragged breath. His mother had played the harp? How could he have forgotten that? He tried to hold on to the image, but he could have sooner captured smoke in his hands. Tears threatened to pool in his eyes.

Instead, he settled into the chair with the instrument. He plucked each string and made minute adjustments to the pins until every note rang true. When he played an arpeggio, a shiver of anticipation rippled across his skin.

Conor began with Labhrás's favorite song, a ballad about a man who returned from war to find his family had moved on without him.

That turned into a cheerier tune Labhrás's wife favored. One by one, he played through each of his foster family's most requested songs: a mournful ballad for Morrigan, the eldest daughter; a lively reel for Etaoin, the middle child; and finally a silly jig that had something to do with a dog disguised as a bard. He smiled as he imagined eight-year-old Liadan singing along in her off-key soprano.

Then the song shifted into a melody Conor couldn't remember hearing, let alone playing. Music poured from the instrument, filling the room and reverberating through his bones while he lost himself within the notes of the song.

The door burst open with a bang. Conor's fingers slid from the strings with a discordant twang as Labhrás shut the door behind him and snuffed out the candle flames with his fingertips. "Not a sound."

Gooseflesh prickled Conor's arms, and his heart thudded in his ears. He lost track of how long he sat there in the dark, gripping the harp. Perspiration beaded on his forehead and slid down his face.

Just when Conor had reached the limits of his patience, Labhrás broke the silence. "You mustn't play here. You reveal too much. Come, quickly now; the king's summoned you."

Conor carefully set down the harp and rose, his gut twisting at the urgency in his foster father's voice. He followed Labhrás out the door and down the stairs to Galbraith's private chamber, the same chamber above which he'd eavesdropped just two days ago.

Inside the study, the king sat behind a large table, flanked by Fergus and Diarmuid. He gestured for Conor to approach.

"I'm sending you to Faolán. You're to leave with Lord Riocárd in five days."

Conor's knees almost gave way, even though he had been expecting this very announcement. "Faolán. For how long?"

"Until you're of age, at least. We've signed a treaty with King Calhoun. You're to be his hostage to ensure our good faith."

"I see. Is that all, my lord?"

Galbraith raised a hand in dismissal. Conor turned on his heel, and Labhrás opened the door for him.

"One more thing." The king's voice hardened. "Was that you earlier? The music?"

Conor's heart rose into his throat, but he composed his expression before turning back to the king. "I've been studying in my chamber most of the afternoon."

Galbraith gazed at him, his brow furrowed while he gauged his truthfulness. Then he waved him off.

As Conor turned back to the door, Diarmuid reached out and gripped the back of the king's chair. Only then did Conor notice the fine sheen of sweat on the druid's forehead.

✦ ✦ ✦

"That was very unwise of you."

Conor frowned at Dolan. He had expected the servant to reassure him about his upcoming journey to Faolán, not berate him for something he hadn't realized was prohibited. "I still don't understand why I can't play."

"After your mother died, the king decreed there was to be no music in the palace. Perhaps he couldn't bear to be reminded of her."

Conor remembered little—a fact of which Dolan was trying to take advantage—but even he knew his parents' marriage had been a political alliance, not a love match. He had seen how unwell the druid appeared. No, he was willing to bet the druid had forbidden music, not the king.

He could voice none of those thoughts, however, so he put on a humble expression. "I'm sorry. I won't do it again."

Dolan looked unconvinced, but he nodded. "We're going to Faolán then. I think you'll find some differences in the hall of a Balian king."

"Was this part of Riordan's plan?"

"I don't see how it could be. That decision was made years ago, and this was only decided in the last few days."

Conor nodded, but things were falling into line far too neatly to be coincidence.

They are not coincidence. Not everything is decided by the plans of men.

Conor shivered. He rarely heard Comdiu speak so plainly. Even though he had been raised in the Balian faith, even though he knew Balus was Comdiu incarnate, he still had a difficult time believing his God intervened so directly in the lives of believers.

"In any case," Dolan continued, "Lisdara will be a cheerier place to live than Glenmallaig, hostage or not."

Hostage. That word brought him back to reality. He was not merely a guest, nor was this a long-term alliance through marriage. Galbraith had need of Faolán's warriors, and his son's life was simply surety. Conor had been disowned and dishonored, removed from any hope of leadership. He was a sacrificial pawn. When he was no longer of any use to Tigh, his life would depend solely on his value to Calhoun Mac Cuillinn, a fierce warrior of great repute.

Suddenly, Conor's future—and his safety—looked far less certain.

CHAPTER FOUR

A tailor accompanied Dolan to Conor's chamber the next morning. Despite Galbraith's contempt for his son, it seemed he would not let him leave for Lisdara unprovisioned. It would reflect poorly on the king should Conor arrive with only one chest of plain clothing better suited to a minor landholder than a king's son.

The tailor took his measurements with his fleshy lips pursed in dissatisfaction. Conor endured the perusal in silence. His scrawny frame would not do justice to the fine clothing, so he left the selection of fabrics and trims to Dolan's judgment. He wouldn't pretend to be something he wasn't merely to avoid his father's displeasure.

You've pretended to be something you're not for years. It's the clothing that bothers you?

Conor shifted uneasily, earning a glare from the tailor. The piercing comments came more frequently now, and Conor couldn't say he was entirely comfortable with them. He voiced his disquiet to Labhrás, expecting his foster father to discount the episodes as imagination.

But Labhrás only nodded. "Until now, you've looked to me for direction, but you are practically a grown man. It's time you let Comdiu guide your decisions."

"So you don't think I'm imagining things?"

"Not at all." Labhrás placed both hands on Conor's shoulders. "Just remember, it's your choice what to believe and how much to reveal."

"Aye, my lord." Conor's throat tightened around the words. Until now, he hadn't understood all Labhrás had done for him. Though they shared no blood, Labhrás *was* his father.

"I'm proud of you, son. You will bring honor to Tigh." The older man squeezed Conor's shoulders. Then he changed his mind and pressed him into a strong embrace. "Look to Comdiu, and you won't go wrong."

Labhrás released him and moved to the door. Then he turned back, his expression sober. "If you ever need anything, and I'm not . . . available . . . remember I'm not the only one looking out for you. You'll always have a place with kin if you want it." He sent him a sad smile, then slipped out the door.

Conor sank down on the bed, the warmth he'd felt moments before squeezed out by a cold, hard knot in his middle. Surely his foster father hadn't meant the words as they sounded. Did Labhrás believe he was in danger? Was Conor in danger too?

That alone would have been unsettling, but the kin to whom his foster father referred could only be his uncle, Riordan.

If something happened to Labhrás, Conor was to join the Fíréin brotherhood.

✦　✦　✦

Once more, Conor traveled among armed, mounted men, and once more, their presence did not comfort him. A party of this size traveled slowly, with its complement of foot soldiers and mounted warriors. An endless stream of carts clattered along behind them, carrying their tents, food, and personal belongings, as well as a display of Tigh's bounty for King Calhoun. At this pace, they would spend five days on the road, most of it only a stone's throw from the ancient forest, Róscomain, and the dangers that lurked within. Even the brigandine jacket Conor wore, with its heavy metal plates sewn to boiled leather, failed to reassure him. It only reminded him how ineffective their weapons and armor would be against the threat in the mist.

But Róscomain's dark, threatening edge became tedious after a few hours, and by midday Conor began to succumb to the monotony. He marked the regular movements of the outriders as they scouted ahead for threats. He listened to the conversations of men around him and tried to guess the regions of their birth from the subtle differences in their accents. He even composed harp melodies in his head to entertain himself.

When at last the light began to fade and the first tendrils of mist twined the trees, Lord Riocárd called a stop. The servants transformed an open meadow into a canvas village with astonishing speed, setting out lavishly furnished tents for both Riocárd and Conor. Dolan brought him a bowl of stew and a chicken leg with a flask of well-watered mead, but the food could not distract him from the tree line. Boredom may have dampened his anxiety over their proximity to the forest, but the falling darkness reminded him that he had legitimate reasons for fear.

Despite his nervousness, as Conor listened to the low sounds of men and horses among the creaks of armor and the crackle of campfires, his heavy eyelids drifted down. He retreated to his tent, where he wrestled off his brigandine and stretched out fully clothed atop a plush feather bed. As soon as he tugged the blanket over himself, he fell asleep.

Until a woman's voice, low and sultry, beckoned him. *Conor.*

The sound entwined him, wrapping him in shivery fingers of pleasure. Half-sedated, Conor sat up slowly in his bed and stared toward the forest.

Lay the charm aside. You don't need it. Come to me.

Conor's hand closed around the charm, and it sent a jolt of alarm through his body. He startled awake, covered in gooseflesh despite the warmth of his blanket.

"They're out there." Dolan crouched beside Conor's cot, the low flame from the single lantern glinting in the servant's dark eyes.

"What are they?"

"Old magic from the beginning of time. The pagans call them the Folk, an ancient, half-human race that lives between our world and the next. But Balians believe they are the Fallen, the celestial beings who turned against Comdiu before time began. He gave them leave to wreak their will upon the earth. For a time, they were bound, but as Balus's gifts wane, so does the protection against them. We call them the sidhe."

In the dark, Conor trembled. Dolan had never spoken openly of the threat in the mist, and knowing the truth only heightened his fear. Until this moment, he hadn't realized exactly how sheltered he'd been at Balurnan. "Why are you telling me this now?"

"So you won't be drawn by their call. The sidhe can't harm us directly. They can only deceive us, and our faith makes us less susceptible to their lies." Dolan patted his shoulder. "Rest now. I'll keep watch."

Conor stretched out on the cot and closed his hand around the ivory wheel. Despite his efforts to sleep, disturbing questions swirled through his mind. The sidhe had beckoned him before. This time, though, the call had been harder to ignore. Would they just keep trying until he could no longer resist?

The camp stirred long before daylight without Conor finding sleep. Smells of smoke and cooking food wafted on the breeze with hushed voices and the sounds of weapons being checked and horses prepared. Then a string of curses drifted through camp.

Dolan left his side in a flash, disappearing from the tent before Conor could poke his head out the flap. When the older man returned, he wore a grim expression. "We lost three men last night. Left their horses and armor behind."

Conor's eyes went to the trees, where the mist had already begun to recede. "What did Riocárd say?"

"He's calling them deserters. They'll double the watches tonight, but it won't help."

"You sound as if this is not the first time."

Dolan glanced back at the milling camp, the tightness of his mouth betraying his concern. "Not all casualties of past campaigns have been from battle, lad. Róscomain takes its due, even if the enemy takes more."

Conor shuddered. He might have escaped the sidhe's grasp last night, but he knew how close he'd been to succumbing to the voice. Had he not been wearing the charm, he might be among the missing.

They rode well into twilight the second day, resting the horses and foot soldiers only as long as necessary and eating cold meals to avoid the time it took to light fires. The warriors eyed the tree line warily, grasping swords and spears at the slightest noise.

As Dolan predicted, Riocárd doubled the watch.

Despite his fears, Conor slept soundly, troubled only by the usual dreams of the unknown. In the morning, though, another warrior was missing, and the two dozen men on watch couldn't account for his disappearance. He had simply vanished.

"Or the others were spelled," Conor muttered as Dolan helped him into his armor.

Days melded into nights in a dreamlike fashion as they continued their progress toward Faolán. By the fifth day, when they at last broke free of the shadow of Róscomain in favor of open country, even the heartiest warriors looked drawn and anxious.

In four nights, they had lost eleven men.

They entered the meadowlands that indicated the border between Tigh and Faolán, the dark demarcation of Róscomain barely visible in the distance. The warriors drew their first easy breaths since leaving Glenmallaig. Here in the open country, the sidhe held little sway. Everyone knew the creatures of the mist clung to their dark forest, content to prey upon those who traveled the king's road.

That night, the mist blanketed the open country as thickly as it had the forest's edge. In the morning, three more men were gone.

CHAPTER FIVE

A contingent of Faolanaigh warriors met them in the meadows as the sun edged midway from its apex to the western horizon. The eight guardsmen rode powerful Gwynn stallions, each man dressed plainly in leather and plate with hammered helms. The Mac Cuillinn's green standard flapped above them in the brisk afternoon breeze.

Riocárd called a halt and waited as a single man in the center rode forward. The Faolanaigh warrior removed his helm, displaying a shock of copper hair that curled wildly out of warrior braids, and tucked it under his arm. "Lord Riocárd, on behalf of Faolán, I bid you welcome and offer you the hospitality of Lisdara."

Riocárd dipped his head in acceptance. "Mac Cuillinn, I gladly accept your offer."

Mac Cuillinn? Conor gaped at the disheveled man while Riocárd took his place alongside the Faolanaigh king and the guards shuffled themselves into order around them. Conor hung back with the other Timhaigh where he could observe their host unnoticed.

Although it was hard to judge on horseback, Calhoun Mac Cuillinn seemed to be of middling height and powerfully built, evidence of long years wielding a sword. A close-clipped red beard covered the lower half of his handsome face. His eyes, hazel-green and attentive, scanned their party and the surroundings with military discipline. Conor instantly liked him.

He was so absorbed in his study of the king he didn't notice the keep until it loomed before them. Mortared walls of gray stone rimmed a flat-topped hill, and ancient oaks, already leafing out with spring foliage, lined the interior walls. Beyond, barely visible through the greenery, rose the domed slate roof of the palace itself. Unlike Glenmallaig, with its stark lines and mist-wreathed battlements, Lisdara exuded warmth and welcome.

The road to the keep wound up a series of steep switchbacks, narrowing at times to a width barely sufficient for a cart. Conor kept his mount carefully to the inside wall and fixed his gaze straight ahead, not daring to look anywhere but the road until they leveled off before an open pair of massive timber gates.

Up close, Lisdara was even more impressive. Gray stone slabs paved the courtyard, and brilliantly colored glass windows marked the upper floor of the cylindrical keep, displaying scenes from the Balian Scriptures, as well as saints, kings, and martyrs. Conor had heard about such magnificent artistry from his tutor, but he'd never thought he would see it in person.

As the procession rattled into the courtyard, the arch-topped doors of the palace opened and spilled out a host of servants. A middle-aged man, tall and thin with bright copper hair and beard, stepped forward. He bowed first to the Mac Cuillinn, then Riocárd.

"Lord Riocárd, welcome to Lisdara. I am the Mac Cuillinn's steward, Leannan. We've prepared the guest house for you, and there is ample space in the meadow below for your men."

"I'm sure the accommodations will be adequate, Leannan," Riocárd said calmly. He dismounted and handed his reins to a stable boy, then looked to Calhoun. "I imagine you will not begrudge us a bit of rest before we come to the hall?"

Calhoun, still atop his own mount, dipped his head graciously. "Of course. My servants will see to any needs you may have."

Riocárd nodded stiffly, reminding Conor the two nations had not so long ago been enemies.

"My lord, may I take your mount?"

Conor snapped his gaze away from the men. A young boy looked up at Conor expectantly. Conor dismounted and put the horse in the boy's charge, then watched Leannan direct the chaos in the courtyard with practiced calm. Servants unloaded trunks and took horses to the stable, while the guardsmen retreated back down the hill to the meadow below. He scanned the space for Dolan and his possessions, but found neither. He'd have to find his quarters on his own, then.

Conor made it only a few steps toward the guest house—a large, thatch-covered structure on the western edge of the enclosure—before a man blocked his path. He stumbled to a halt.

The king of Faolán stood before him, surveying him with a thoughtful smile. "You must be Conor."

"Aye, my lord." Too late, Conor realized he should bow and managed only a graceless bob of his head. A flush crept up his neck. Hardly the impression he'd hoped to make on the man who controlled his future.

To his credit, Calhoun only clapped a large hand on his shoulder and turned him toward the palace. "Leannan!" The slender steward emerged from the throng immediately. "Will you show our new guest to his chamber?"

Calhoun turned back to Conor, smiling warmly. "We'll have time to get acquainted later. Right now, let Leannan take you to your quarters. If you need anything, just ask him."

Conor watched Calhoun stride back into the crowd, speechless, until Leannan caught his attention.

"This way, my lord. I've already had your things sent up."

Conor followed the steward up the front steps of the keep, still stunned by the friendly and utterly informal welcome. They passed through Lisdara's elegant hall, and the steward glanced back to make sure Conor was still following before leading him down an adjoining corridor. "I took the liberty of putting you on the family's side of the keep. The guest quarters are grander, but these are more comfortable."

Conor followed Leannan up the long flight of stairs, mentally marking their path. The palace was bigger than it looked from the outside, far bigger than Glenmallaig, which had always seemed like the largest structure in Seare. The steward turned right down an intersecting corridor at the top of the stairs, then left at another short one. Conor sensed movement out of the corner of his eye and whipped his head around in time to see the swish of skirts into one of the chambers.

He stared at the empty corridor, wondering who the girl was, until he realized Leannan was standing before an open door.

"This is your room."

Conor entered hesitantly. Sunlight streamed through another stained-glass window, casting fanciful patterns across the spacious stone chamber. Embroidered draperies enclosed a shelf bed topped with a luxurious-looking feather mattress, and a large chair sat by the window. On the other side of the room, his trunks awaited unpacking beside the tub.

"You'll want a bath before supper," Leannan said. "I'll send someone up with hot water. Would you like refreshment in the meantime?"

"Aye, thank you. Leannan . . ."

The man turned in the doorway. "Aye?"

"I've lived rather simply my whole life. You don't need to go to any trouble for me. We both know I'm a hostage."

"It's no trouble. Besides, the Mac Cuillinn gave orders you were to be treated like family. If there's a mistake, you'd best take it up with him." A smile twitched at the corners of the steward's mouth.

Conor fought his own smile. "In that case, perhaps we shouldn't bother him."

"Very well. Let me know if you need anything."

Conor stared at the closed door long after Leannan left. He'd been at Lisdara for a handful of minutes, and already he'd experienced more kindness than he'd received in his own father's keep. Was that what Dolan had meant by the difference in the hall of a Balian king?

Moments later, a procession of boys arrived to fill his tub. Dolan hadn't yet reappeared, so Conor stripped off his clothing and eased into the bath with a sigh. After five days on horseback, he'd forgotten how luxurious a tub of warm water could be.

The door creaked open, and Dolan poked his head in with a smile. "I see you wasted no time."

"I couldn't stand the road dust any longer."

Dolan entered, balancing a platter, and then nudged the door shut with his foot. "Leannan sent this up for you."

Conor's stomach rumbled at the sight of soda bread spread with butter and honey. He took the wooden mug in a dripping hand and sipped cautiously. Sweetened, heavily watered mead traced a warm line down his throat. Dolan unpacked his finest garments from his trunk and laid them on the bed.

"Where exactly am I supposed to wear those?"

"The feast tonight, of course. An alliance between Tigh and Faolán is unprecedented. All the lords of the realm have come to witness the event."

The once-comforting mead sloshed in Conor's stomach, considering a quick exit. He felt awkward enough at his own father's court, and now he was to be put on display at Lisdara?

"How many exactly?"

"Conor, relax. No one expects you to do anything but smile and nod and pretend to enjoy yourself. The attention will be on Riocárd and Calhoun anyway."

"I hope you're right." For the first time, Conor was glad for his new wardrobe. He may not be the warrior his father expected, but at least he wouldn't shame his homeland.

Minutes later, wrapped in a clean linen cloth and trying to force down the soda bread, he considered the clothing Dolan held up before him. "I'll leave it to you. I can't believe we're to feast after so long on the road. Sleep would be a far kinder welcome."

"Calhoun will treat Lord Riocárd as he would your father, and that means lavish feasts. The Mac Cuillinn may lack vanity, but he understands how this game is played."

Conor flopped back on the bed cushions with a sigh and pressed his fingers to his eyes. A game. His father had surely devised this alliance as just part of a larger plot that would benefit neither him nor Faolán. But Calhoun wouldn't consider such an agreement unless he too had a plan in which a royal hostage could be of use.

Conor stifled a yawn. As his heartbeat slowed, the tension knotting his shoulders melted away. It couldn't hurt to close his eyes for a moment, could it?

Conor woke to gentle shaking. He jerked upright and nearly collided with Dolan, who bent over him. The stained-glass windows were dark, and several thick candles now lit the room.

"The guests are already in the hall," Dolan said.

Conor's heart lurched. He looked down at his shaking hands and knew he'd be lucky to put on his own boots.

Fortunately, Dolan had no intention of letting Conor do anything on his own. The servant sat him down firmly in the single chair and began the tedious task of combing the tangles from his damp hair. Conor gritted his teeth while Dolan fashioned locks into tiny plaits. Apparently, no one was supposed to know about Conor's failures, even if the warrior braids were a blatant lie.

Dolan then dressed him in layers of fine linen, wool, and silk, all in royal Timhaigh blue. When the servant held up the mirror for him, Conor hardly recognized himself. Glenmallaig's tailor had done an admirable job in using pleats and tucks to camouflage his lack of muscle. The effect wasn't half bad.

"I look . . ."

"Like a prince." Dolan smiled and set the mirror down. "Now, enough admiring yourself. It's time to go to the hall."

On cue, a servant appeared at the door. Conor shot one last, helpless look at Dolan before following the boy down the corridor to the staircase, where he was handed off to a richly dressed page. At the entrance of the great hall, Conor halted. He had expected a few dozen lords and ladies, not this gathering of hundreds. Strains of a lute drifted over the deafening roar of voices.

To Conor's everlasting gratitude, the page did not announce him, though he hardly needed to. As soon as he stepped into the hall, all heads swiveled toward him, and their curious eyes took him in from top to bottom. He fixed his gaze on the dais and reminded himself to breathe, only to have the air whoosh from his lungs again.

Beside a man who strongly resembled Calhoun—presumably the king's younger brother and tanist, Gainor—sat the most beautiful woman he had ever seen. Pale red-gold hair fell in ringlets over her shoulders, and even from this distance, Conor could tell her eyes were the luminous gray of quicksilver. His heart took up residence in his throat. It could be none other than Lady Niamh, Calhoun's twenty-year-old sister, "the jewel in Lisdara's crown." For once, the lavish descriptions had not been exaggerated.

A moment later, the page handed him off to yet another servant, who led him to his chair. His pulse quickened when he realized he was to be seated beside her, but she did not even acknowledge his presence. Fortunately, Calhoun and Riocárd chose that moment to make their entrance. The assembled guests rose to their feet in one motion, the women applauding and the men pounding their fists on the tables. Calhoun grinned broadly as he passed through the cacophony, pausing every few steps to converse with his lords. Riocárd held himself confidently, but he knew his part, and he hung back in deference to the king.

Calhoun took his place on the dais and held up his hands. The noise ceased, and the guests took their seats amidst a rustle of silk and linen, anticipation written in their expressions.

"My lords and ladies of Faolán, it has been a generation since we have had the pleasure of hosting our Timhaigh brethren. I consider it the greatest honor to present Lord Riocárd of Tirnall, champion to the king of Tigh."

The room erupted into applause, and fists pounded on wooden tables again, as if Calhoun had announced the king himself. Riocárd stood and gave a slight bow. When the noise died down, Calhoun continued, "I also would like to welcome King Galbraith's son, Conor, whom I will have the pleasure of hosting here at Lisdara for the next several years."

The response was only slightly less enthusiastic for this announcement. Conor flushed and threw a grateful look toward Calhoun for his generous welcome, not daring to look at Niamh for her reaction.

Servants appeared at every entrance to the hallway, bearing spectacular platters of fried fish, roast pheasant, and candied vegetables. A goblet appeared at Conor's elbow. He took it and sipped the heavily spiced wine while other servants began to dish out choice morsels.

The man to Niamh's right leaned back with a friendly smile and held out his hand. "I'm Gainor, Calhoun's brother. Welcome to Lisdara."

Conor smiled in return and clasped Gainor's forearm. "Thank you, Lord Gainor. I'm certain I'll like Lisdara, if this welcome is any indication."

"Calhoun knows how to throw a feast. As you've no doubt guessed, this charming creature beside you is our sister, Niamh."

Conor bowed his head, afraid to look her in the face. "Descriptions have not done you justice, my lady."

"Nor you, my lord." The press of Niamh's lips into a thin line belied her practiced tone. Her eyes slid over him before she turned her attention back to her own wine goblet.

Gainor pushed himself away from the table and settled into the empty seat on Conor's other side. "Don't mind her. We mere mortals are beneath her notice. Now, you don't need to learn everyone's name right away, but I'll at least tell you who to hide from."

Gainor waited for the last servant to move away, then attacked the sumptuous-looking food loading his plate. Conor picked at the food while Calhoun's brother pointed out various guests.

"That right there"—Gainor indicated a handsome young man with night-black hair—"is Keondric Mac Eirhinin, lord of Rathmór, Faolán's largest holding besides the king's. His clan has always supported Mac

Cuillinn even though Clan Eirhinin has royal blood. He's the wealthiest man in Faolán besides Calhoun."

"So should I avoid him or grovel before him?"

"Don't worry. He's far too rich and important to be bothered with the likes of you."

Conor grinned. He picked out a hard-looking older man with graying hair and sharp features. He reminded Conor of Galbraith's lords. "What about him?"

"Good eye. Avoid him. He hates everyone except Niamh. He's had designs on her for years."

"But he's old enough to be her father!"

"His son's old enough to be her father. All the same, don't get cornered by him. Lord Duggan has a terrible temper."

"Duly noted."

Conor's plate looked more appetizing as his stomach unclenched, the unexpected empathy lifting his spirits.

He scanned the room again, and his eyes fell on a girl he was sure had not been there moments before. She was unremarkable but for a mane of shiny hair that fell in a sheet around her shoulders. Her pale green silk gown clearly hadn't been made for her—it hung off her small frame and clashed with the honey color of her hair. She glanced in his direction, and their eyes locked. Her gaze pinned Conor in his seat. A chill, not altogether unpleasant, rippled over his skin.

"Who's that?" he choked out, finally daring to break the connection.

Gainor followed Conor's gaze. "Aine, our half sister. I hadn't thought she would attend."

"I didn't know you had another sister."

"Our mother married an Aronan chieftain after our father, the king, died. We hardly knew Aine, but since both her parents have passed, Calhoun invited her to live at Lisdara. I'll introduce you tomorrow. You're of an age, I think."

Conor nodded mutely, his mind returning to the odd sensation that stretched between them. Was he so naive about women he could be struck speechless by two of them in the same evening? No, he had been taken by Niamh's beauty, but this was something completely different. He felt as if he knew Aine, even though he was sure he had never seen her before tonight. He dared another glance in her direction, but her place was now vacant.

For the rest of the meal, Gainor entertained him with witty stories about other feasts and carefully unnamed guests, though the chill emanating from Niamh was almost palpable. She'd probably expected far more from the son of a Timhaigh king. He could hardly blame her for being disappointed. He fell short of his own expectations most of the time.

The noise in the hall died abruptly as a man dragged a chair to the foot of the dais. He was unassuming, dressed in well-made but drab clothing, his dark hair touched with gray. Only when he produced a stunning walnut harp did Conor realize he was not a servant. Anticipation fell heavily in the hall, the silence unbroken even by the rustle of clothing.

"The bard, Meallachán of Killary," Gainor whispered.

Conor barely heard him. He had never dreamed he would be sitting a handful of feet away from the most celebrated bard in Seare.

Meallachán took his time tuning the harp, then began a plaintive melody that felt both familiar and wondrously new, his fingers flying over the strings. When he began to sing in a mellifluous tenor that enriched and deepened the ethereal sound of the harp, Conor at last understood the reason for the bard's renown. Calling both Conor and Meallachán musicians was like classifying both a raindrop and an ocean as water.

The melody washed over him as his eyes drifted closed. His heart ached at the sheer beauty of the music, and his fingers itched to take up a harp and join its voice to the harmony. He settled for committing each note to memory with the hope of later reproducing even a fraction of that wondrous sound. When the last notes died away, he opened his eyes in time to see Gainor wipe tears from his cheeks.

Conor met the gaze with his own blurred eyes, and the king's brother smiled sheepishly. Even Niamh looked moved. As the bard launched into a folk tune meant to break the melody's spell, Conor glanced down the table and saw Calhoun watching him thoughtfully.

The king gave him a slight nod, then turned his attention back to the bard, leaving Conor to wonder exactly how much of his soul he had bared on his face when he thought no one was looking.

CHAPTER SIX

"The Mac Cuillinn has invited you to breakfast in his chambers."

Conor rolled over and rubbed his eyes. He had slept deeply and dreamlessly for the first time since leaving Balurnan, but he still felt tired. Sunlight already cast kaleidoscopic patterns through the stained-glass window.

"I'm to dine with Calhoun? Why?"

Dolan fixed Conor with a hard stare. "He's the king. He needn't explain himself."

Conor threw back the blankets. "Something understated then. Best to show a full measure of humility."

Twenty minutes later, dressed in a simple tunic belted over a saffron-dyed linen shirt, he followed a servant through the maze of hallways to the opposite side of the keep. When they came to a closed door at the end of the corridor, the servant knocked lightly and pushed the door open. Conor took a halting step inside.

The king and his three siblings sat at a small, rectangular table near the windows. Calhoun glanced up and waved casually at an empty seat. "Conor, come. The tea's getting cold."

Conor wordlessly slipped into the vacant seat beside Niamh, directly across from Aine. Calhoun nudged the earthenware pot in his direction before he resumed his conversation with Gainor about the honey production in Lisdara's hives, but neither girl gave any sign of awareness of his presence.

His ears burned as he poured tepid liquid into an empty cup. He clearly didn't belong here. Why had Calhoun invited him if no one was going to even acknowledge him? To his relief, several servants chose that moment to arrive with their breakfast: warm oatcakes with honey and butter, poached fish, and fried quail eggs. At least if he was eating, he wouldn't be expected to make polite conversation.

Calhoun looked up from his conversation as if seeing him for the first time. "Conor. Have you met my other sister, Aine?"

Aine's gaze flicked to Conor's face. Her eyes were the same quicksilver gray as Niamh's, dark-lashed and intelligent. For a moment, he forgot to breathe. She was not nearly as plain as he had first thought. Then he remembered Calhoun's question and stammered out, "Uh, no, I haven't had the pleasure. My lady."

Aine dipped her head and offered a reserved smile before returning to her meal. Calhoun looked between the two of them with a thoughtful expression. The Mac Cuillinn was far too perceptive.

"I like to breakfast with my family when I'm at Lisdara," Calhoun said. "You are not obligated to join us, but know you're welcome at my table."

Conor swallowed. "Thank you, my lord. You're very generous."

"Not at all. Now, there's a matter we must discuss."

Conor's heart beat harder at the ominous statement, but he kept his expression blank.

"We value education in my household. Brothers Treasach and Iuchbar have generously come from the monastery at Loch Laraigh for that purpose, and I think you will find them as knowledgeable as your tutors back home.

"On the matter of your sword training, Gainor and I have agreed it can wait until you settle in. After that, Gainor will work with you himself until you feel comfortable joining the men in the yard."

Conor supposed he should be embarrassed by how keen Calhoun's measure of him had been, but he couldn't summon anything but relief.

"In the meantime," the king continued, "you'll have your afternoons free to pursue your own interests. I thought perhaps you might spend some time with Meallachán."

This time, Conor could not keep his shock from his face. "Meallachán?"

Calhoun arched a brow. "Did I get that wrong? I guessed you were a musician."

"No. I am. At least, I try. But Meallachán?"

"It's your choice. None of my siblings have the talent or the inclination, and it seems a shame not to take advantage of his willingness to teach."

"It would be a great honor," Conor managed at last. "Thank you, truly."

Calhoun waved off Conor's thanks. "Good, that's settled. Now, I believe Treasach is expecting you three in the library."

Niamh rose immediately, but Aine didn't move. Instead, she addressed her brother in a surprisingly deep, Aronan-accented voice. "By your leave, Calhoun, Mistress Bearrach asked me to go to Fionncill this morning."

"As long as Ruarc accompanies you," Calhoun said.

"Thank you." Aine's brilliant smile lit her entire face and once more shattered Conor's train of thought. "I'm looking forward to putting my studies into practice."

Calhoun gestured to the older sister. "Niamh, you can show Conor to the library then."

Niamh shot Conor a pointed look, and he leapt to his feet, his chair's legs shrieking against the stone floor. He gave Calhoun a hasty bow. "Thank you, my lord."

The king waved him away once more, and Conor followed Niamh back into the hallway. His awe faded with each step. Niamh might be beautiful, but she was also sullen and rude. Aine, on the other hand, merely seemed reserved.

That smile, though, had been anything but shy. Who was Mistress Bearrach to elicit that sort of reaction? And what sort of business did she have outside Lisdara?

He certainly couldn't ask Niamh. Even if she did deign to speak with him, she seemed no friendlier with her half sister than she was with him. Instead, he fumbled to fill the silence. "What exactly do Treasach and Iuchbar teach?"

"Treasach's specialty is languages, history, and geography. Iuchbar teaches mathematics and law."

"Which do you prefer?"

"Languages." A chilly half smile formed on her lips. "I wouldn't worry if you don't take to it. From what I hear, a Mac Nir needs only wield a sword."

Heat rushed to Conor's cheeks. She had obviously guessed what the delay in Conor's training meant. A surge of defensiveness propelled his next words—in Norin. "Normally, you would be right. But my education has been somewhat unconventional."

Niamh stared at him, uncomprehending.

He switched to Levantine. "The language of the Kebarans perhaps?"

Another blank stare. Finally, he said in the common tongue, "I wouldn't worry about it. From what I hear, a Faolanaigh princess need only be sweet and biddable to catch a husband."

Niamh's expression hardened. He hadn't thought it possible for her to look any colder. Inwardly, he cursed his impulsiveness when she picked up her pace, forcing him to nearly run after her.

When they arrived at the library door, Niamh looked at him pointedly, and it took a moment to understand what she wanted. He jerked the door open, and she brushed past him without a glance.

Lisdara's library was twice the size of Balurnan's, high-ceilinged and packed with books. Small square tables, each with two chairs, had been placed strategically around the room. Niamh sat at one of them, her glare warning Conor away from the empty seat beside her. He chose another spot and turned his attention to his new teacher.

One thing seemed certain about Treasach: priesthood was a recent avocation. In contrast to the soft, contemplative look of the priests he'd encountered, Treasach was built like a fighter, broad-shouldered and heavily muscled, with large, scarred hands. The scholar's queue at the nape of his neck struck Conor as a ridiculous disguise, like putting a collar on a warhorse and calling it a hunting dog.

His smile of welcome was genuine, though, and he approached Conor with an outstretched hand. "You must be Conor. Welcome. I'm Brother Treasach."

"Thank you." Conor gave him something halfway between a nod and a bow. "I'm looking forward to returning to my studies."

"Good! Let's begin then. I take it Lady Aine's not coming?"

"She had other business. The Mac Cuillinn approved."

Treasach nodded and retrieved a large tome from the table. To Conor's relief, the topic was not language, but history, specifically Ciraean social and political structure. Within minutes, Treasach had drawn Conor into a lively debate about the merits of republican and monarchical rule.

"Seareanns have combined the best of both methods," Conor said. "The Senate never could have accomplished what the emperor did because they spent too much time debating theoretical topics. Likewise,

Cira had too many tyrannical rulers for the people to ever fully embrace such a method of government."

Treasach smiled wryly. "You do realize the Seareann kingdoms are monarchies?"

"Of course. But even in Daimhin's time, the clans were free to rule themselves and elect their own kings, while having the advantage of a higher authority to settle disputes, make peace, and organize an army."

"So you're a proponent of reinstating the High Kingship?"

Conor hesitated. "I think there are some tactical advantages to centralized rule, especially in times of war. But it would take a catastrophe of unprecedented proportions to bring it about now."

"Well put, Conor." Treasach gave a satisfied nod. "Have you aspirations of politics then?"

"Certainly not, sir."

Treasach smiled and closed the book. "I think that's enough for today. I'll see you, and hopefully Aine, tomorrow."

Conor rose from his seat and moved toward Niamh. Rude or not, she deserved an apology for his harsh words. But she rushed from the room before he could reach her.

"Give her time," Treasach said softly at Conor's shoulder. "She'll come around."

Conor wasn't so sure. If he hadn't let his anger get the better of him, he wouldn't have to work twice as hard to win her over. As he left the library, though, he remembered her dismay at being seated with him at the feast. Somehow, he doubted anything he did would make her view him with less than contempt.

CHAPTER SEVEN

Aine Nic Tamhais left Calhoun's study with a distinct uneasiness in her stomach. Truthfully, the sensation had not been far from her since coming to Lisdara four months before.

Her father, Alsandair Mac Tamhais, had always spoken of Seare as a wild place, barely one step removed from its pagan roots, enmeshed in magic both dark and mysterious. Aronans thought themselves highly civilized and pragmatic, an affectation that made them closed-minded about anything that hinted at the supernatural. Lord Balus's coming had ended the need for magic, they said, and anyone who practiced it must serve a darker power.

Aine's pace quickened as she returned to the chamber she shared with Niamh. Magic hung heavy over Seare. She had felt it as soon as she set foot on the dock: the pulse of a pure, brilliant power, and beneath it, a sinuous strand of something older and much darker. That same darkness lingered in the forest beyond Lisdara, and sometimes she felt it seeking, testing the protections woven into the keep's walls. No one else seemed to notice the invisible battle that waged beyond, though, and admitting her sensitivity would only bring unwanted scrutiny. Even the ancient healer, Mistress Bearrach, did not know Aine's secrets, but the longer she studied with her, the more difficult they were to conceal.

Oonagh, the lady's maid she shared with Niamh, was folding clothes into a large oak chest when Aine entered her chamber. "My lady! I thought you were at your lessons!"

"I'm riding with Mistress Bearrach this morning. Will you send for Ruarc? I can find my riding clothes."

Oonagh curtsied in acknowledgement and hurried from the room.

Aine took her time selecting a brown wool dress and a lightweight cloak from the wardrobe. She had just pulled on the clothing when a familiar rap sounded at the door. She slid a sheathed knife onto her belt and buckled it quickly, then swept the cloak around her shoulders. When she opened the door, Ruarc lounged against the opposite wall.

Aine had known her Seareann bodyguard for so long it was hard to see him as others did, but objectively, his mere presence was enough to discourage untoward thoughts. Middle-aged, but as lean and strong as he had been in his early years, Ruarc projected restrained menace, like a viper poised to strike.

He was the gentlest soul she had ever met. He could also kill remorselessly with the proper provocation. The latter was likely why Lady Ailís, with her last breath, had passed his duty to Aine. Ruarc never questioned the matter. He had merely appeared at her side, and he had not left it since.

"You look troubled," he said, falling into step beside her. "What is it?"

"The same as always."

Ruarc fingered the dagger at his belt, a sure sign he was troubled. "Maybe it wasn't a good idea to come here. You've been unsettled since we arrived in Faolán."

"And what was there left in Aron? Mother's dead." Aine swallowed the lump in her throat. Six months was not long enough to dim her sense of loss. She steadied her voice and continued, "Aunt Macha has no use for me. She tolerated me for Father's sake. If she found out . . ."

"I know, but—"

"I'll be fine. It's just harder to ignore certain aspects of my talents here than it was in Aron."

They emerged into the bright morning sunlight and started across the courtyard to the beehive-shaped clochan, a stone remnant of a more primitive age that now served as Mistress Bearrach's residence.

"It's more than that, isn't it?" Ruarc said, his brow furrowing as he studied her. "Something else is bothering you."

"It's nothing."

But it wasn't nothing. The Mac Nir boy disturbed her. She couldn't look at him without feeling the subtle hum of energy, a stronger, brighter version of the threads underpinning Faolán. Worse yet, she had dreamed of him in Aron the night before Calhoun's invitation arrived. She had been poised to decline until she was struck with the certainty that that boy waited for her in Lisdara. Instead, the words had spilled out, "Tell my brother I'll come."

Ruarc's frown deepened. "My duty is to protect you, Aine. If you hold things back, it makes my job much harder."

Aine forced a smile and put a light hand on his arm. "I have full confidence in you." A pity his particular skills would be of no help in this situation.

Just as they arrived at the clochan, the door sprang open. An elderly, white-haired woman scowled at them from the threshold. "What took you so long?"

"Forgive us," Aine said, aware that Ruarc was struggling against a smile. He found Mistress Bearrach's ill temper more amusing than she did. Then again, he didn't bear the brunt of it. Still, the old healer knew more medicine and herb lore than a dozen of the clan's physicians, and Aine had already learned more from her in four months than in two years with her aunt's knowledgeable, but skeptical, practitioners.

Mistress Bearrach thrust a bulging leather sack at Ruarc. "There, young man, carry this for me and go get our horses. Go on, I'm not getting any younger, you know. At this rate, I'll be dead before you return."

Ruarc hid a grin and jogged back across the courtyard to where a boy waited with three blanketed horses.

"Thank you for allowing me to accompany you today," Aine said.

Mistress Bearrach harrumphed. "Just don't kill anyone. That's one mistake I can't fix."

Ruarc returned with their horses then, saving Aine from answering. He helped the healer mount first and then gave Aine a leg up onto her own mare. The horse danced nervously beneath her, obviously sensing she was a barely competent rider. Mistress Bearrach, by contrast, seemed as comfortable atop her mount as on her own feet, despite the fact horses were not common in Seare outside the palaces of kings.

The horses' hooves thudded on packed earth as they made their way down the steep switchbacks with Mistress Bearrach in the lead. At the bottom, the old woman turned due south onto a trail that was little more than a few hoof prints in the grass. Aine would have missed it had she not been following the healer so closely. After a few minutes of open meadow, the trees began to grow more thickly, forming the young forest that bordered Seanrós. Aine shivered at the touch of magic on her skin.

Mistress Bearrach cast a glance over her shoulder. "You feel it, do you? Good. You're not a total disappointment."

Aine's eyebrows lifted. Perhaps Mistress Bearrach saw more than she let on.

They traveled slowly through the border woods, breathing in the heavy scent of damp earth and vegetation. After nearly an hour, the small trail joined a larger road, and the trees again thinned into rolling countryside.

Aine drew a deep breath, and her earlier tension began to melt away in the quiet. Peat smoke drifted faintly on the breeze, wafting from the hearths of the whitewashed cottages in the distance. Ivory-fleeced sheep with black faces grazed freely, unhindered by enclosures. A cow lifted its head and lowed softly as they passed.

Up ahead, the road widened into a large area of hard-packed dirt. A square building with a shingled, peaked roof loomed before them, the lime-washed wickerwork and great three-spoked wheel identifying it as a church.

"This is Fionncill," Mistress Bearrach said.

"Only this?" Compared to Aine's birthplace, Forrais, this smattering of cottages and pastureland hardly qualified as a village.

A throng closed around them as they rode into the square. There were women in rough-spun skirts and wool shawls, tending dozens of children among them. Frail elders, propped up by daughters and grandsons. Men wrapped in bandages or wracked with coughing. Aine threw a panicked glance at Ruarc. So many patients, so many expectations. How could they possibly tend them all?

Ruarc dismounted first and helped her down from her horse. As soon as Aine's feet touched the ground, several children began tugging at her clothes.

"Are you really the king's sister?" A tow-headed girl, perhaps six years old, looked up at Aine with wide blue eyes.

"I am. My name is Aine. What's yours?"

"Mara, m'lady." The girl bobbed a curtsy and smiled shyly.

A little boy, who had been hiding behind Mara's skirts, popped to Aine's side. "Are you going to fix my mama?"

"I'm certainly going to try. Where is your mama?"

The boy grabbed her hand and dragged her across the yard to where a pale, red-haired woman cradled a tiny infant on the front steps of the church. "Mama! This is Aine! She's going to make you better."

Color bloomed in the woman's ashen cheeks. "Hush now, Donall. I'm sorry, my lady. He hasn't yet learned to hold his tongue."

"No need to apologize." Aine smiled and sat down on the steps beside her. "What's your name?"

"Caitlinn Ó Laoghaire, my lady. My husband's Donall the Elder. One of the Mac Cuillinn's tenants."

Aine nodded and turned her attention to the infant. "May I?"

Caitlinn gave the baby over to Aine without protest. Automatically, Aine extended her awareness into the boy, seeking signs of illness, but she found only a drowsy sense of well-being and the faint stirring of hunger. Whatever troubled the mother, she had not let it affect the care of her newborn.

"How old is this little one?" Aine asked.

"Born a fortnight ago, my lady."

"A difficult birth, was it?"

"Aye. The midwife barely stopped the bleeding with an application of casewort and yarrow."

"I see." Aine handed the child back to his mother. "May I examine you?"

When the woman nodded, Aine made a show of her cursory examination, though she hardly needed to. She immediately sensed the sluggishness Caitlinn hadn't been able to shake off since the child's birth. The woman had been far closer to death than she knew.

"I'll mix a tonic of yellow dock, stinging nettle, and dandelion to strengthen your blood," Aine said. "It may still be a month or two before you regain your energy, though. Try not to exhaust yourself."

Caitlinn bowed her head in relief. "Thank you, Lady Aine. You are very kind."

"Not at all." Aine smiled at Mara and Donall. "Take care of your mama, all right?"

The children beamed.

Ruarc handed her a wax tablet and stylus before she could ask. She jotted down the woman's name, her diagnosis, and the remedy and then moved on to the next patient.

None of the patients taxed Aine's skills, considering a single touch revealed what ailed their bodies. She made her examinations and assured them she could mix a remedy back at Lisdara. Soon, her wax tablet was full of names and notes, and the crowd dwindled to only a handful of petitioners.

When the last patients had been seen, Mistress Bearrach strode to Aine's side and took the tablet without asking. She scanned the notations, clucking her tongue. "Too fast. You don't spend enough time with the patients."

Aine's cheeks heated. "Do you think I got the diagnoses wrong?"

Mistress Bearrach's scowl returned, but her black eyes twinkled. "I have no doubt they are correct. But it won't do to make it look so easy. People begin to ask questions."

Aine swallowed hard. "I don't understand what you mean."

"Don't you? When you touch them, you know what's wrong with them, just as you felt the wards."

Aine tried to deny it, but her dry mouth wouldn't form the words.

For the first time, the old healer looked at her kindly. "I know how difficult it is to keep such a thing secret. There shouldn't be a need. But even here, different can be dangerous."

Then, as if the conversation had never taken place, Mistress Bearrach said, "Don't dawdle now, you two. You'd think I was asking you to carry the horse, not the other way around. We still have work to do."

Aine mounted with her guard's help and spurred her mare after the healer, concealing her smile. Apparently she was not the only one hiding her true nature.

A quick glance at Ruarc, however, showed no such amusement. In fact, he looked as troubled as she had ever seen him.

CHAPTER EIGHT

More feasting followed in honor of the Timhaigh guests, and the night after his arrival Conor dressed for a celebration again, this time in slightly plainer garments. As he made his way down to the hall, he was surprised to find only the slightest twinge of apprehension.

Far fewer guests crowded the hall, since the realm's lords had already begun to return home. Gainor and Niamh sat at their regular places, but Niamh didn't even look in Conor's direction when he took the chair beside her. Even the guests seemed to have lost interest in him.

Something else caught their attention, though. Conor followed their gazes. Aine stood in the entry, her hands fisted in her skirts, which were made of fine blue wool that suited her far better than the previous night's silk. No one in the hall moved, but whispers rustled among the tables.

Conor didn't know what he meant to do until he stood, descended the dais, and crossed the floor to her side. Surprise surfaced in those luminous gray eyes when he gave her a little bow and held out a hand. "My lady, would you permit me?"

The surprise melted into a smile. She dipped her head. "Thank you."

Aine placed her hand atop his, and Conor escorted her formally to the table. She smelled of fresh air and herbs, and the clean fragrance among the heavier scents of beeswax and rich food was almost as distracting as the insistent tingling in his palm where her fingers rested.

A servant scurried forward and pulled out the chair beside Conor's. Aine sank into it gracefully. As Conor returned to his space, Niamh shot him a poisonous look, eliciting a grin from Gainor and raised eyebrows from a number of the guests.

Their attention shifted a moment later when Calhoun arrived without

Riocárd. The king held up his hands for attention, and the lutist in the corner broke off his playing.

"I regret to inform you Lord Riocárd was called back to Tigh unexpectedly," Calhoun said. "Fortunately, we may continue to enjoy Conor's company."

Conor frowned. Even Galbraith adhered to customary courtesy. What was so important he would risk offending his new ally by recalling Riocárd so soon after their arrival?

Aine shifted in her chair beside him, drawing his attention away from one puzzle and onto another. He already had a fair read on Calhoun, Gainor, and Niamh. But Aine, with her reserved manner, brilliant smile, and secret errands, remained a mystery. Add in an ageless quality that made it hard to tell if she was older or younger than him, and it was no wonder his eyes returned to her again and again.

"What is it?" she asked, finally catching him in his perusal.

Heat crept up his neck. He could hardly tell her his thoughts. "Who is Mistress Bearrach?"

Her expression shuttered, and her body stiffened.

"I'm sorry. It's none of my business. I didn't mean to pry."

"No, it's all right." She raised her eyes to his again. "Mistress Bearrach is a healer. I'm apprenticed to her."

That explained it then. Healers always seemed slightly mysterious, as if their vast, arcane knowledge separated them from ordinary people. "I think that's admirable."

"You do?"

"Of course. You're doing something important. I haven't done anything useful my entire life." Conor flushed. Why had he said that aloud, least of all to her?

"I doubt that," she said, but she shifted her eyes back to her plate.

Conor almost groaned. She'd withdrawn again, just when he thought they were establishing a connection of sorts. He slumped in his chair, determined to return to being invisible.

When Calhoun dismissed them from the hall, though, Aine didn't immediately flee upstairs. Instead, she said, "It was thoughtful of you to escort me to the table. Thank you."

"It was my honor." Conor gave her an abbreviated bow. "It seems we are both something of strangers here."

"For what it's worth, I think you will fit in quite nicely here. Good night, Conor."

"Good night." Conor waited until she vanished from sight before he started up the stairs behind her. As he headed toward his chamber, an unfamiliar feeling settled in his chest, and it had nothing to do with magic.

✦   ✦   ✦

Aine stood outside the door of her shared chamber, wishing she could wait until her sister fell asleep. The last thing she wanted to do tonight was argue. Still, she couldn't avoid her forever. She took a deep breath and pushed the door open.

Oonagh had already helped Niamh undress down to a linen chemise, and she was brushing the girl's long hair. Niamh glanced up, but she said nothing.

Aine closed the door, relieved she wouldn't be subjected to one of her sister's tirades tonight. She undressed and washed her face and hands in the basin, then quickly climbed into bed. She thought she had forestalled a discussion, until Niamh waved a hand to Oonagh in dismissal. Aine's heart sank.

As soon as the maid left, Niamh said, "You like him, don't you?"

A flush crept up Aine's neck. "You mean Conor, I presume."

"Of course I mean Conor. I think you two have much in common. That's good."

This was not at all the direction Aine had expected the conversation to take. "Why the sudden interest in him?"

"I have no interest in Conor. But you have choices. Calhoun can't marry you off without your clan's permission, and you're not there for them to make you a match in Aron. You might even choose for yourself. And if he should be highborn, a king's son perhaps . . ."

Aine struggled to follow her sister's logic. "Is that what this is about? You think I came here to make an advantageous marriage? I assure you, I've never intended to interfere in any match Calhoun might arrange for you."

"You don't understand. I don't want to get married. Calhoun has been hearing offers for my hand this week, and I have no say in the matter. I'm a head of cattle at auction."

"I can't believe Calhoun would do something like that." But even as she spoke, Aine realized how little she actually knew her elder brother.

"It's the burden of noble birth. Look at our mother. Father in the grave no more than a year, and she's auctioned to Aron. Never mind the fact she had young children here."

The bitterness in Niamh's voice turned Aine's irritation to sympathy. Of course Niamh would resent her. Aine was a product of the union that took away her mother, leaving her with nursemaids until she was of marriageable age.

"Oh, Niamh, I am sorry. Surely it won't be so bad . . ."

"You know nothing, Aine. And I don't want your pity." Niamh climbed into bed and blew out the candle, plunging them into darkness.

Aine pulled up her own blankets and stared at the shadows the moonlight cast through the stained-glass windows. She had known coming to Seare would not just be a joyful reunion with family she'd never met. But only now did she realize, in that same deep place that recognized the isle's bright magic, that she had been brought here to meet Conor. Her dreams always had meaning, even if she didn't understand their purpose.

Like the dream she had had of Ruarc offering his sword to her. Lady Ailís had not hinted at its meaning until it was too late. Aine still didn't know how her abilities could have failed her so badly.

Or perhaps she had chosen not to notice her mother's sickness. There was nothing she could have done anyway. The tumor had been killing Ailís from the inside out.

Aine buried her face in her pillow and let her silent tears fall. What good were these gifts if she couldn't save her own mother? Why would Comdiu show her those things if she hadn't been meant to stop them?

She had asked Him that question repeatedly in the last six months, and the answer still eluded her. *You're doing something important,* Conor had said. He couldn't have pierced her more directly if he'd tried. No matter how many people she helped, it could not erase the knowledge that she'd failed the one person who meant the most to her.

Isn't it possible you weren't meant to carry this sorrow forever? Why do you insist on doing everything by your own power when there is One whose strength is greater than your own?

The last thought struck with a pang of undeniable truth. It was pure pride, this impulse to hold her problems close, instead of trusting the One whose vision was clearer than hers. Why did she think she could have stopped her mother's death if Comdiu wanted to call Ailís home?

I don't know why You took her. I don't know why You sent me here, but I know it was Your doing. Please show me my purpose.

Aine couldn't remember the last time she had settled into bed without a knot of tension in her stomach. Tonight, though, she had given her troubles to One more adept at handling them than she. She fell asleep.

✦ ✦ ✦

Conor ate alone in his room the next morning, battling the urge to see Aine. He had probably just imagined the tenuous connection between them. They had just met, after all. So why did that possibility bother him so much?

He needn't have worried, though. On his way to morning lessons, Aine fell into step with him in the corridor. "We missed you at breakfast today."

"I'm guessing Niamh is not included in that statement. No duties with Mistress Bearrach?"

"Not today. I'm sorry I missed yesterday's lessons. I heard you made quite an impression on Brother Treasach."

"Where did you hear that?"

"I spoke with him after morning devotions in the chapel."

"You have a chapel?" Conor stopped short. He had never set foot inside a Balian place of worship. It hadn't occurred to him Lisdara would have its own.

"Indeed. You're welcome to join me. I'm there nearly every morning."

Conor hesitated. He was still unsure of how much he should reveal here, even though Labhrás had told him it was his decision. "I may do that," he said slowly, and Aine rewarded him with a bright smile.

Treasach waited for them in the library. "Conor, Aine. Where's Niamh?"

"She's indisposed," Aine said. Conor wondered if Niamh's sudden illness had been timed to avoid them.

"I'm sorry to hear that. Never mind, then. Sit! We have a lot to cover."

Conor exchanged a grin with Aine at the priest's enthusiasm, and they settled at a nearby table.

"Have you ever heard about Daimhin's unseemly history?" Treasach folded himself into a chair much too small for his frame. "He was the youngest son of an unimportant clan, without lands or title, so he hired out his sword on the continent. Over time, he banded together with other men like him, and they became a formidable fighting company in great demand. Their travels took them throughout the Ciraean Empire, where they saw the abuses of the emperor's policies firsthand. Eventually, they moved south to the Levant on the Ciraean Sea, where Daimhin and his companions met a man named Balus."

Aine gasped, and Conor said, "Daimhin met Lord Balus? I've never heard that."

"Not only did he meet Him, he studied with Him. He and his men tried to fight the Levantine authorities who broke Balus on the wheel, but our Lord wouldn't allow it. They stood watch at His tomb, and when Balus was resurrected, He appeared to them."

"I know this story!" Conor said. "But the Canon doesn't name Daimhin."

"No, it doesn't. But we know he was there when Balus gave His disciples great gifts to be used for His glory and told them to spread His teachings to the ends of the earth."

"You mean magic," Aine said. "The Balian magic that has been forgotten."

"Almost forgotten," Treasach said. "Have you not wondered how the Fírein have held Ard Dhaimhin all these years?"

So it wasn't just the brotherhood's fighting skills that held off incursions into the old forest. For hundreds of years, no one but the brotherhood had laid eyes on King Daimhin's capital city, secluded behind the miles of thick, dark forest. Legend claimed that only when a high king again united the warring nations under a single throne would the Fírein relax their vigilance.

"If the gifts still exist, then why aren't they more well-known?" Aine asked, drawing Conor's attention back to the lesson.

"That's an excellent question. As Daimhin grew older, and it became time to name his heir, he realized his sons had not held true to their gifts or the teachings of Balus. He was set to announce a successor not of his bloodline, but rather than lose their inheritance, his sons murdered him and divided his kingdom. They legitimized their actions by claiming Daimhin's gifts were worthless. Tigh and Sliebhan outlawed the practice of the gifts altogether, and Faolán and Siomar actively discouraged it. Like any other ability, magic weakens without practice. Only the Fírein still exercise the gifts openly, and even among the brotherhood they have begun to fade."

Conor nodded thoughtfully. It had always seemed strange the Great Kingdom had been divided so easily. He should have guessed it related to magic.

"But this was not why I brought up the topic," Treasach said. "Daimhin was raised in the old clan government. Through his travels, he was exposed to Ciraean imperialism and occupation, Levantine religious law, and the teachings of Balus. All these influences, he brought back to Seare. Today, we will look at how the laws and structures of those governments influenced both the old Seareann kingdom and our current ones."

It was a brilliant way to teach both history and law. Still, Conor thought there was more to this lesson than a creative way to engage their interest. He would swear that what Treasach told them of Seare's origin was not written in any history book.

Despite the distracting implications, Conor found himself drawn into the discussion. Aine was at least as knowledgeable as he, and she spoke with both conviction and eloquence. Treasach sat by and grinned when their discussion about the cause of the Ciraean Empire's fall turned heated.

When Aine diverged into specific Ciraean military tactics Daimhin modified for use in Seareann terrain, Conor just stared at her, speechless. He finally managed to squeeze out, "Where did you learn that?"

Aine blushed. "All highborn children in Aron are schooled in the strategy of warfare, since women can inherit clan leadership."

"Will you someday?"

"Not likely. I'm third in line after my two uncles. They still drilled these things into my head, though. We studied the Seareann conquest in great depth."

"Can you fight, too?" Conor asked.

She shrugged. "I have some talent for archery, but I never really applied myself to it."

Conor's lips twitched at the thought of the tiny girl drawing a war bow nearly her full height, but her frown made him bury his amusement as quickly as it had come.

"Can we get back to the topic?" Treasach tried valiantly to revive the debate, but he was wise enough to know when he was defeated and dismissed them for dinner.

Conor followed Aine into the corridor. "Are you going to the hall?"

"I have to see Mistress Bearrach," she said, regret plain in her voice. "I'll see you later."

Without Aine's company, dinner in the hall seemed much less appealing, so Conor returned to his room instead. He was probably the only man who found a woman's knowledge of ancient battle tactics irresistible. Still, few boys in Tigh possessed Conor's extensive education, and the idea Aine was more than a match for him intrigued him.

When he entered his chamber, Dolan's expression said something significant had happened. "You're to meet Meallachán in the music room after dinner. He's agreed to take you on as a student."

Conor's stomach flipped. Calhoun had said he would arrange it, but when was the last time a king followed through on a promise like that? And how had Conor thought he could meet the standards of a master like Meallachán?

His anxiety only intensified as he climbed the stairs to the upper-floor music room. There Meallachán sat alone on a stool, tuning a lute and looking deceptively ordinary in his plain tunic.

Conor cleared his throat. "Master Meallachán?"

"What do you think?" Meallachán plucked a string.

"It's a bit sharp," Conor said hesitantly.

The bard gave the pin a minute adjustment and plucked it again. "Better. Come, have a seat."

Up close, Meallachán looked older than he had thought, perhaps fifty, even though his wiry build and unlined face gave him the look of a much younger man. He handled the lute with a grace and surety that somehow reminded Conor of a master swordsman.

"I hear you play?"

Conor averted his eyes. Compared to Meallachán, he could hardly claim to be a musician. "Not really. Just a bit of the harp on my own."

"We'll start with the cruit, then. It's less complicated than the harp, but no less satisfying."

Conor nodded mutely. If the man asked him to bang the cook's cauldron like a drum, he wouldn't question it. Never mind the harp in the corner beckoned to him like an old friend.

A light rap sounded at the door, and it creaked open. Aine slipped into the room, her expression sheepish. "I'm sorry I'm late."

Meallachán waved her in with a smile. "You're not late. We're just getting started."

Conor swallowed his nervousness. He hadn't expected an audience. Embarrassing himself in front of Meallachán was one thing. Failing before Aine was another.

"I have to warn you I've been pronounced hopeless," Aine said. "You may regret taking me on before it's all done."

"Nonsense. Anyone can learn given enough practice." Meallachán guided Aine to a stool beside Conor and then produced two plainly crafted cruits: pear-shaped, long-necked instruments with six strings, their soundboards burnished by years of inexperienced hands.

The bard began their lesson by naming the notes each string produced and demonstrating different scales. Then he showed them how to play the notes by plucking or strumming. Conor, though he had never touched a cruit, produced crisp, clear sounds, garnering a pleased nod from Meallachán.

"A natural, indeed," the bard said.

When it came to Aine's turn, however, she produced only a sickly twang. Meallachán adjusted her fingering until the notes sang truer, but frustration shone on her face.

Meallachán taught a simple melody next, which Conor picked up with ease. Aine still struggled. She frowned, the tip of her tongue peeking from between her lips. Then her finger slipped from a string, and she bit back an oath.

It was so out of character, Conor burst into laughter. Aine's eyes widened, her cheeks going pink. Her dismay only made Conor laugh harder.

"I told you I was hopeless! Please, Master Meallachán, may I just sit and listen?"

"If that's what you wish," the bard said with a gentle smile. "I'm still willing to teach you."

"Respectfully, I just didn't want to insult the king by rejecting his offer."

Meallachán nodded and returned to Conor's lesson, giving him progressively more difficult exercises. "Are you sure you haven't studied before?"

"Not the cruit."

By the end of the lesson, some of Conor's awe had faded. The bard was humble and utterly without artifice, genuinely pleased to share his knowledge. As Labhrás liked to say, important men demanded respect. Great men earned it.

Meallachán had earned it.

After the lesson, Aine followed Conor into the hallway. "Why did you lie to him?"

"I didn't! I've never studied the cruit. I do play the harp a little, but it seemed wrong not to learn what he wanted to teach me. Don't you think?"

"I suppose."

Conor smiled again, remembering her involuntary outburst. "After this morning, it's nice to see there's something you aren't good at. I thought Treasach was going to die of apoplexy when you started talking about flying wedges and flanking maneuvers."

"You're one to talk." Her eyes sparkled. "I'd be careful he doesn't try to bundle you back to Loch Laraigh. Besides, it seems hardly fair you know my weakness, and I don't know yours."

"Then tag along when Gainor starts my sword training. I can practically guarantee you'll have more talent at that than me. At least not being able to play the cruit won't get you killed."

Aine stopped and turned that knowing gaze in his direction. "The world doesn't need more warriors, Conor. There's quite enough fighting without you contributing to it."

"I wouldn't have expected that, given your education."

"There are good reasons to fight. I just fail to see the wisdom in forcing everyone into the warrior mold whether they fit or not."

"You sound like Lord Labhrás."

Now a mischievous light glinted in her eyes. "Lord Labhrás must be a wise man."

"Aye, he is."

They started walking again, until Aine drew up short of the staircase. Conor touched her hand, just a nudge. "Thank you."

Aine looked down in surprise. Then she nodded, her eyes finding his in a moment of wordless understanding. Conor watched her descend the steps until she disappeared from sight. He had just admitted his greatest weakness to her, and it mattered no more than a missed note on an old cruit.

CHAPTER NINE

Conor settled into life at Lisdara with surprising ease. Each morning before breakfast, he joined Aine in the stone chapel behind the keep to listen to Treasach or Iuchbar teach from the Holy Canon. Aine never asked him about his faith, but her searching looks said she suspected his attendance was not merely for show.

Afterward, they breakfasted with the king and his siblings and then moved on to their studies with the priests. Iuchbar was knowledgeable, but he favored repetition and lecture over discussion. Conor preferred Treasach's enthusiastic debates, which most often focused on ancient Seare.

Despite the pleasure he took in worship and study, though, it was Aine's presence that filled him with anticipation when he rose each morning. She was intelligent and witty, and she understood his thoughts without explanation. Yet they rarely strayed to personal topics. Conor sensed there were things she couldn't bring herself to share with him. Perhaps she was just reluctant to disturb their easy companionship, or perhaps she knew, as Conor did, his presence at Lisdara was only temporary.

On the afternoons he didn't study with Meallachán, Conor accompanied Aine to the small, walled garden beside Mistress Bearrach's clochan and helped her weed the neat rows. Here, she was in command. Conor followed her directions precisely, astounded by her knowledge of herbs and their uses, though he spent at least as much time admiring her as working. When she caught him watching her, her cheeks would color, but she'd give him a dazzling smile that made his stomach turn backflips.

Only the snippets of gossip Dolan brought back disturbed the calm, steady flow of his life. Calhoun was still officially considering offers for Niamh's hand, but once Lord Keondric presented his suit, the other men stepped back in deference. The royal bloodlines hadn't been joined in centuries, for both practical and political reasons, but Calhoun seemed to be seriously considering the union. Niamh gave no indication whether she was pleased or upset by the possibility, but at least the distraction left her with even less interest in Conor than before.

Further afield, the news was less benign. Reports of increasingly frequent Sofarende raids came from across the sea, though so far, Gwydden was holding them off. This was not necessarily good news. Should Gwydden prove too difficult to conquer, Galbraith's fears of an invasion could become a reality.

Still, Lisdara's predictable pace erased some of the wariness that had been Conor's constant companion since leaving Balurnan. Had anyone asked him, he would have said he was happy.

Then at breakfast one morning in early summer, Calhoun announced, "We've delayed long enough. It's time to begin your training. Your father expects you to show some skill with a blade, and we've neglected the matter too long."

Conor's stomach lurched. At least it would be just Gainor and not the whole guard.

As they departed for their morning lessons, Aine peered into his face. "Is it really that bad?"

"I've never even held a sword." The mere thought made Conor queasy.

"If you've never held a sword, how do you know you're no good at it?"

"I know."

Aine just laughed. "Do you want me to come? I've had some training, but I'm really terrible. It could be fun."

The idea of gentle Aine with a sword in hand made him smile. "You'd do that?"

"Of course I would!" She grinned. "Come on. We can laugh about our ineptitude at supper, and if you're still feeling bad, I'll serenade you with the cruit."

"Careful. I might take you up on that."

Conor's mood brightened, even though the tiny girl's lack of fighting ability hardly mitigated his own failures. Even if she someday inherited her clan's leadership, her personal guard would protect her. When would she ever be called to take up a sword?

Conor didn't actually expect her to come, but when he arrived at the large room Gainor had designated for lessons, she waited with a wooden practice sword in hand.

"It suits you," Conor said, grinning. "The warrior-healer."

Gainor, on the other hand, burst into laughter when he arrived. "What on earth are you doing?"

"I'm here to train," Aine said. "You don't think I can manage?"

"Oh, I think you could manage quite well. I also think Calhoun would have my head. Go have a seat out of the way if you want to watch."

Aine rolled her eyes at Conor, but she took a seat on a nearby stool. Conor shot her a smile. Surprisingly, he felt no desire to have her leave.

Gainor began by teaching stance, grip, and guard positions. They progressed to simple strikes and parries, and although Conor's movements felt stiff and awkward, he managed to complete them without falling on his face. Then they moved on to a simple, choreographed bout meant to demonstrate the flow of movements. Conor kept up admirably until he forgot to block one of Gainor's crossway slashes, and the wooden blade smacked into his neck.

"Ouch!" Conor's sword clattered to the ground.

"What did you do wrong?"

"I forgot how to parry." Conor glanced at Aine, expecting to see a grin at his poor showing. Instead, she stared at him, pale and trembling. "Aine? Are you all right?"

Aine blinked. "What? Oh, I just . . . I don't feel so well. I'm going to get some air." She slid from the stool and rushed out the door.

What was that about? For a moment, Aine had looked as if she were seeing right through him.

"Back to work," Gainor said. "Let's take it more slowly."

Conor fared no better the second time, his mind returning to Aine's odd behavior.

Gainor finally pronounced him hopelessly distracted and dismissed him for the day, though he actually seemed pleased. "We may make a fighter out of you yet."

The world doesn't need any more fighters, Conor thought, but he merely bowed and headed off in search of Aine.

✦ ✦ ✦

Aine stumbled from the keep, her heart pounding. Her excuse hadn't fooled Conor, but the truth was even more unbelievable. Only once she reached the privacy of the clochan's enclosed garden did she manage a steady breath.

Lord, what did I see?

The instant Gainor's sword had connected with Conor's neck, the practice room had disappeared, a forest scene in its place. Conor, looking much as he did now, knelt on the mossy ground, a gleaming blade at his throat. Recalling his expression sent another spasm of horror through her. It had been the terrified and resigned look of someone about to die.

Just because she saw it didn't mean it was going to happen. Maybe it was symbolic, a warning. She should tell Conor what she had seen. If he didn't go into the forest, he would never be in danger. But what if knowing of her vision actually brought it about?

Aine covered her face with her hands and drew a deep, shuddering breath. This was why she concealed her gifts. Mistress Bearrach knew about her insight into her patients, but that knowledge could bring no harm to others. If Calhoun knew she sometimes saw the future, he might be tempted to make decisions based on her imperfect visions. Kings had been led astray by far less. She could not risk anyone learning the truth.

Even if it meant Conor might die.

"Don't be ridiculous. Nothing's going to happen to him."

"Nothing's going to happen to whom?"

Aine jerked her head up. Conor stood at the garden entrance, his forehead creased in concern.

"I was just muttering nonsense," she said. "Why are you here?"

"I was worried about you." He picked his way through the rows of plants. "Don't tell me you have a headache. I know you too well for that."

Aine bit her lip, tempted to spill out the whole story. She may have only known him for a handful of weeks, but her heart told her he would never betray her.

No. She couldn't risk it. He was a Mac Nir, after all. Who knew what could happen if his father found out? She closed her eyes. "Please, Conor, don't make me lie to you."

When she opened them again, curiosity and hurt played across his expression, but he only said, "As long as it wasn't sheer horror over my ineptitude."

"No, it wasn't that at all. You made a respectable showing for your first lesson."

"Maybe." Conor smiled at her. "Come on. Let's go snatch some pastries from the kitchen."

She returned the smile and moved toward the gate. Before they could step through, he grasped her arm and tugged her back gently.

His touch seared her skin through her sleeve and sent a shiver through her entire body. He stared into her eyes, his intensity making her breath catch. "You can trust me, Aine. You know that, don't you?"

"I know." Her heart flopped over painfully in her chest.

His hand slid down her arm and squeezed her fingers so quickly she might have imagined it. "Good. Let's go back."

Aine followed him back to the keep, struggling to make sense of the sudden surge of feelings. Her world had shifted in a single instant, and she had absolutely no idea what to do about it.

✦ ✦ ✦

The cook surrendered the meat pies willingly, and they stood in a back corridor to eat them, laughing at the bits of pastry that clung to their clothing and hands. When it was time to part ways—Aine to her lessons with Mistress Bearrach and Conor to the music room—he could barely pull himself away.

As Conor climbed the stairs, though, the memory of her words in the garden resurfaced, leaving him more confused than ever. Something was wrong. He should be pleased Aine hadn't tried to deny it, but the irrational part of him only saw she didn't trust him enough to tell him the truth.

And why should she? He was Timhaigh. She'd known him for only a few months.

The music room lay empty. Once more, the harp called to him, but he ignored it and took up the cruit instead. He still couldn't bring himself to play the harp at Lisdara. To create real music in a place was like deciding to call it home. Succumbing to that desire would only make it that much harder to leave when the time came.

Conor picked out a tune of his own making, halting and imperfect and hampered by the cruit's six strings when the music in his head demanded the harp's twenty-eight. He layered the melody with counterpoints and variations until he could play something that approximated his feelings. He was so absorbed in his tune he didn't notice the man standing inside the doorway.

"That sounds like a love song," Meallachán said.

Conor broke off the song. "Almost. It's not quite what I heard in my head."

Meallachán nodded solemnly and made his way to the other chair a few feet away. "It's a gift, you know. Music. And I don't mean a gift like being able to craft a verse of poetry or construct a stained-glass window. It's a *gift*, one of the few things left of Comdiu's perfect world. One Balus gave to His believers when He restored our connection to Comdiu through His death."

"I don't understand."

Meallachán took the other cruit from the stand and began to pluck out an idle melody. Even that thoughtless, simple tune was beautiful. "Before man was created, Comdiu made the beings known as the Companions, perfect creations that lived to glorify Him. They praised Him with music and singing so magnificent mortal ears could not bear it.

"But some of the Companions were not satisfied with this existence. They coveted Comdiu's power. A Companion named Arkiel led an uprising against Comdiu, which of course failed. Rather than destroy them, Comdiu banished them from His presence.

"When Comdiu created man in His image, Arkiel desired to rule over these creatures that were so like the Master he despised. He and his followers worked subtly to turn man against his Creator.

"Arkiel's power over this world grew stronger until Comdiu sent His son, Balus, a sacrifice that broke the Adversary's hold. His death reconciled fallen man to Comdiu, and with it opened access to a small piece of His power. Music—true music, a reflection of the divine praise of heaven—is part of that power."

Conor listened raptly. He had never heard the Balian story of creation told this way. Music was a piece of a perfect world? No wonder it held so much resonance with him.

"Only a few have been chosen," Meallachán said, "to possess the gift of music in its purest form—goodness that drives away the darkness.

Daimhin himself was the greatest of them. But not all who have the gift recognize it."

Conor looked down at the cruit in his hands. "You're saying I have this gift?"

"You tell me, son."

He remembered Labhrás's reaction to his playing at Glenmallaig. "Why would He choose me? The Timhaigh adhere to the Old Ways."

"Do you not follow Balus?"

Conor had skirted the issue since coming to Lisdara, but he could avoid it no longer. He gave a single nod.

"I'll let you think on that then. And perfect your song."

Conor remained on the stool, the cruit still in his hands. He knew it was true. Perhaps he had always known it. Was that why Riordan had insisted he foster with Labhrás, so his gift could be nurtured? Had he somehow guessed Conor possessed this ability?

And how did he explain all this talk of magic and the Fíréin and gifts of the Great Kingdom? He'd been raised not to believe in coincidence, only providence. So what did Comdiu expect from him?

Meallachán and the priests joined them in the hall for supper that night. Normally, Conor relished their lively conversation, but far too much had happened that day to join in. Aine's gaze lit on him repeatedly, but whenever he glanced over, her eyes darted away.

While servants cleared the supper plates, Meallachán retrieved his harp and settled into a chair. Once again, Conor marveled at the craftsmanship of the magnificent instrument, his fingers tingling at the thought of touching those strings.

Meallachán smiled at him as if he knew his thoughts. "What shall we hear tonight? A ballad of unrequited love? A tale of heroism? Or do you fancy some dancing?"

"Play something from the Great Kingdom," Conor said.

Eyebrows rose around the table, but Meallachán nodded graciously and set his hands to the strings.

Conor had thought Meallachán's first composition was moving, but it paled in comparison to the melody that now spilled from the harp. *Music from the heavens,* Conor thought, *older than time itself.* He let the song wash over him until his heart swelled to bursting, and it took him a long moment after it ended to join the applause.

He had barely regained his composure when Meallachán asked, "What about you, Conor? Would you like to have a try?"

The blood drained from his face, and the pounding in his ears nearly drummed out his answer. "I couldn't," he heard himself say faintly. "Not after that."

Aine touched his arm gently. "Please?"

One minute, he was taking in Aine's hopeful expression, and the next he was seated in Meallachán's chair. Reverently, he accepted the harp from the bard, then sucked in his breath. The instrument throbbed with unseen energy that crackled along his skin like the warning of an impending lightning strike. Conor brushed his fingers over the twenty-eight strings that made up the full, rich sound he had so desperately missed in the cruit, and his frantic pulse calmed.

Forgetting the expectant eyes upon him, he began to play.

✦ ✦ ✦

Aine felt the yearning in Conor beside her, his eyes fixed on the bard. Apparently, Meallachán sensed it as well. When Conor wavered, she knew it would take only a quiet request to push him from his indecision.

As he prepared, he looked nothing like the perpetually uncertain boy she had come to know. His face relaxed, his eyes going distant, and he handled the instrument with both a respect and a surety she had seen only in the bard himself.

At first, he coaxed a soft, tentative melody from a few strings. A chill rippled over her skin, similar to the bolt of energy she had felt when she first saw him. The song gradually built and broadened, as he added layer upon layer of complexity. Aine closed her eyes, and images came unbidden.

Conor, a young child at his mother's knee, watching her play the harp and yearning to touch the instrument. A harsh, discordant run of notes—violence distantly remembered. Longing, loss, and at last acceptance and understanding in the strict tutelage of a man Aine guessed was Lord Labhrás. Fear and loneliness . . .

. . . and a beckoning of something darker, sinister and yet seductive, battling for his soul. She recognized the dark magic of the isle. Brilliant light battered back the shadowy tendrils, but they always remained, a counterpoint to the brighter notes.

Then came a mixture of love, fear, and longing. He was playing his present here at Lisdara, imbuing the music with a constant battle of hope and uncertainty. A repeated motif anchored the wild scattering of runs that spiraled off the melody, then drew them inexorably back. From the way it gripped her heart, Aine knew it had to symbolize her. Just when she thought she could bear no more, the music faded, the last chord reverberating with longing and inevitability.

Conor remained still, his hands on the strings and his eyes closed. Sweat beaded on his brow. Aine blinked to clear the fog from her vision and realized it was tears. A quick glance around the table showed the others fixed awestruck to their seats, all but Meallachán and Treasach, who exchanged a satisfied glance.

Conor opened his eyes. He stood, placed the harp gently on the floor, then walked unsteadily from the room without a single word.

Calhoun shook off the spell first and looked around the table. "Good night, then."

Aine rose and followed Niamh and Gainor from the room; Meallachán and the priests remained seated. She hung back just outside the hall, still too bewildered to feel guilty about eavesdropping.

Calhoun spoke so quietly she had to strain to hear. "It seems you were right. What now?"

Silence stretched. Then Meallachán spoke. "I'm afraid even I did not expect this, my lord. This boy has had next to no formal training. I daresay we haven't seen a gift this strong since Daimhin's time."

"Since Daimhin himself, you're saying," Calhoun said.

"It's a mistake to let him stay here," Meallachán continued. "The longer he plays, the more notice he is bound to draw. That could be disastrous."

"Diarmuid would never have allowed Galbraith to send him here if he knew. Someone went to great lengths to conceal him from notice," Treasach said.

Calhoun's voice held a touch of bitterness. "Well, your kind love secrets, don't they?"

"It's a dangerous time for him," Meallachán said, as if the king hadn't spoken. "The decisions he makes here will determine the future. All of our futures."

"Send him away then," Treasach said. "He'd be safe in—"

"No," the bard said firmly. "It must be his decision. You cannot tear him away from her against his will. There's a bond there that goes beyond friendship. I heard it in the music."

Aine's cheeks burned. She had been right. She expected Calhoun to sound surprised, but he only said, "I recognized it from the beginning. But there's only so much he can learn here, and the stronger he grows, the more of a target he becomes."

Aine jerked in shock. Her elbow knocked the wrought-iron candle stand across the stone floor with an ear-shattering screech. The hall went silent. A chair scraped away from the table, but she didn't stay to see who it was. Instead, she turned and fled, her heart beating so hard she thought she might faint.

Conor's musical gift marked him not just as a Balian, but something more. That put him in danger not just from his own clan, but from the darker forces at work in Seare. If they moved against him, even the protections around Lisdara might not be enough to shield him. The only place beyond the reach of the isle's dark magic was Ard Dhaimhin.

Conor must leave Lisdara. And soon.

CHAPTER TEN

After Conor played the bard's harp in the great hall, the others treated him with a mixture of hesitance and respect. Treasach and Meallachán stared at him appraisingly when they thought he wasn't looking, and even Niamh seemed less aloof. That alone would have been unsettling.

But it was Aine's manner that weighed on him most. She still smiled and bantered with him, but he glimpsed sadness behind her eyes. He yearned to tell her the night in the hall was an aberration, fueled by the emotion of Meallachán's music. He wanted to promise her he would never touch a harp again if she would just stop looking at him with those searching eyes.

He wouldn't be able to do it, though. The harp in the music room, a poor approximation of Meallachán's fine instrument, drew him each night after the others went to sleep. He tried to play quietly, but the music overtook him, and he could scarcely remember the notes when he finished.

One night, he had just taken up the harp when the door clicked open beyond the circle of candlelight. A small, shadowed figure crept into view. Aine.

She wore a dressing gown, and with her hair falling loosely around her shoulders, she looked simultaneously childlike and ageless. She pulled up a stool beside him. "I couldn't sleep. Will you play for me?"

He could no more resist her request now than he could in the hall. He put his hands to the strings and began to play the song he had first composed on the cruit.

It deserved Meallachán's harp, but this came close to the aching beauty he had heard in his mind. He now recognized the motif that had worked its way into his song days before, the one that represented this girl he loved.

When he finally set the harp on the floor and looked at Aine, he saw his feelings reflected in her glistening eyes. She rose and pressed a brief kiss to his cheek, her hair brushing his shoulders and enveloping him in the scent of lavender. Then, just as swiftly, she was gone.

Conor pressed his fingers to the spot where she had kissed him, still feeling her warm breath on his skin and the touch of her lips to his cheek. His heart thrummed in his chest, urging him to go after her and kiss her properly. To say something—anything—to convey how he felt about her.

That was ridiculous, though. He'd known her for only a few months. How could he be sure these feelings wouldn't just fade away?

But the song couldn't lie. In his hands, the harp spoke only truth.

✦ ✦ ✦

Life moved forward, even though for Conor, everything had changed. Aine didn't mention the night she had kissed him, and Conor didn't bring it up, though it was never far from his mind. He could barely stand beside her without the overwhelming desire to take her in his arms. From the look on her face in rare, unguarded moments, he knew she felt the same pull toward him. Yet she seemed determined not to be caught alone with him.

Then one night, Calhoun summoned him to his study before supper. The king sat at the table, alone, his expression somber.

"Sit down."

Conor sat. His stomach pitched when he saw the parchment lying before Calhoun, its blue wax seal broken. He swallowed several times before he managed to speak. "What is it?"

"King Galbraith is dead."

"What? How? I don't . . ."

Calhoun softened, his eyebrows knitting together. "He was ambushed on the road near Glenmallaig. He and a number of his guard were killed. Lord Fergus was wounded, but he survived."

Conor stared at the king. Surely he should feel something. Grief, anger, something other than this terrible blankness.

"There's more. Lord Labhrás has been arrested for treason."

"That can't be. He would never—"

"They claim he plotted to kill Galbraith and eliminate Fergus from the succession in order to put a Balian on the throne."

"What's going to happen to him?"

"He was to be executed tonight at sundown. It's already done." For the first time, the king's demeanor cracked, sympathy shining in his eyes. "I'm so sorry, Conor."

Conor's breath wheezed through his tight chest, and the room spun wildly. He closed his eyes, grappling for control, until a horrifying thought occurred to him. "His family? What's to be done with them?"

Calhoun shook his head. "I do not know."

Conor gripped the edge of the table and blindly pushed himself to his feet. Then he remembered himself and said hoarsely, "By your leave, my lord."

Calhoun nodded. Conor stumbled to his chamber, simultaneously numb and aching. He sat on the edge of his bed and stared at his hands.

Labhrás had known this would happen. He had warned him back in Glenmallaig, but Conor somehow never believed. Why would he? Labhrás was loyal. He simply could not have been involved in any plot to overthrow the king. Perhaps bring a grievance before the council, who alone had the power to depose Galbraith, but never kill him.

Yet another part of him was not so sure. There were too many strange coincidences. Labhrás's friendship with Riordan. Conor's unusual upbringing. The Balian charm. Conor's gift. The druid's hatred—or was it fear?—of music. And now Galbraith's assassination, for which Labhrás and a Balian conspiracy were blamed.

No. Even if Labhrás were capable of such a thing, the council would never elect a Balian king. More likely, Galbraith's tolerance of the Balians made him a target. The only person who truly benefited from this situation was Fergus, his tanist.

The door opened, and Dolan entered, his expression pained.

Even to his own ears, Conor's voice sounded distant and lifeless. "You know this wasn't an accident, Dolan. Labhrás was no traitor. Tell me what you know."

"I know nothing of this, Conor."

"It's time to stop protecting me! Tell me!"

Dolan sighed. "Labhrás did not confide in me. Perhaps he was a convenient scapegoat. Maybe they convicted him out of spite. I don't know."

Conor heard the truth in the servant's voice. He crumpled, and the fight left him in a rush. His first thought had been the safety of Lady Damhnait and the girls, but his position was no less precarious. "What happens now? Will Fergus call me back to Tigh? Or will he arrange an accident for me, too?"

"I don't know. Calhoun will act honorably, but it all depends on your uncle now." Dolan placed a hand atop Conor's head in silent commiseration and left him to his grief.

After a few minutes, Conor stood and wandered to the music room. He slumped into a corner, ignoring the harp. He couldn't bear to hear his sorrow on its strings. He imagined Labhrás being led to his execution, his head held high. Conor didn't even know if his foster father had been beheaded or hung. He did know the lord's station would not have spared him the indignity of having his head mounted beside the keep's gate.

Conor's gorge rose. No, he could not dwell on those things, not when he had a decision to make. He buried his head in his hands.

A familiar herbal scent enveloped him, and a hand touched his shoulder. He lifted his head. Aine knelt beside him, an expression of pained sympathy on her face. He steeled himself for her words of consolation, but she simply reached out and put her arms around him.

The tears Conor had safely locked away broke free in torrents, streaming down his face and dampening her hair and dress. She held him silently while he sobbed like a heartbroken child on her shoulder. When he pulled away, her cheeks were damp.

"Why are you crying?" he asked hoarsely. He brushed the tears from her face.

"I know you loved him. You can't blame yourself."

Conor wiped his eyes with the back of his sleeve. "The king was murdered, Aine. Fergus and Diarmuid killed him, and they used it as a reason to execute Lord Labhrás."

Aine's eyes widened. "Why?"

"Because Galbraith owed his throne to Balians, and Labhrás was one of them. There's more, though. I think the druid made me forget something I overheard years ago. It's only a matter of time before he comes after me."

"What if you could see what happened?"

"How?"

Wordlessly, Aine took both of his hands in hers. She closed her eyes and seemed to be concentrating, so Conor did the same.

The memory struck him with a jolt.

He was fourteen years old, and he had accompanied Labhrás to a council meeting at Glenmallaig. So far, he had only heard his mother and father fighting over him. He retreated to the secret place of his childhood, the little room behind the tapestry. He thought the chamber below would be empty, but he could hear the drone of male voices. He pressed his ear to a particular section of the wall and strained to make out the words.

"He will not yield," a deep male voice said. Not his father. Lord Fergus.

"Then convince him," an unfamiliar voice said. He had a quiet, educated tone, but he was used to being obeyed.

"And if he will not accept you as a counselor?"

"Then he will be dealt with. But let us not rush to judgment. Galbraith may be stubborn, but he has the respect of the lords. It is worth being circumspect. Replacing a king is a delicate matter."

"Conor! There you are. What—"

His mother stood in the doorway, letting a shaft of light stream into the small room. Perhaps she heard the voices below, or perhaps she just read the terror on Conor's face, but she stretched out a hand. "Quickly, we must go!"

Conor scrambled out the door. His mother's grip crushed his hand as she dragged him down the corridor toward her sitting room. Then she stopped.

A robed man stood in the hallway, smiling, but Conor did not find it reassuring. He stared at the tattoos on the man's hands and neck. Fear shuddered through him as the man began to mutter under his breath.

Lady Máiréad pushed Conor behind her. "Your spells will not work on me, sorcerer. You will be beaten from this castle. When my husband finds out—"

"He will not find out. Let's take your son back to his chamber, shall we? There's no need for him to see this."

The queen blanched, but she obeyed, moving toward Conor's chamber. He followed meekly. Lady Máiréad placed him in the chair by the armoire and kissed him softly on the forehead.

"I love you, Conor," she whispered, gripping his shoulders hard while tears trickled down her cheeks. "I'm so sorry."

She left, but he didn't watch her go. He couldn't move, speak, think. Then the sorcerer returned, minutes later. Diarmuid knelt down beside him and said, not unkindly, "Don't resist me, and this won't hurt at all."

Conor shook free of the memory as terror surged through him, as strong as it must have been in the moment he'd experienced it. He stared at Aine, wide-eyed. "What just happened?"

She averted her eyes. "You're not the only one with a gift."

He stared, trying to understand what she was saying. The scene had been too clear to be a buried memory. It could only have been a vision. But that meant his mother's death hadn't been an accident after all, not a freak tumble down the staircase as everyone claimed. Was that why he couldn't remember that part of the keep?

"The druid killed my mother. Why did he kill her and not me?"

"She was a Balian. I don't think his spells would work on her. But you were susceptible."

Conor forced air in and out of his lungs. He was the reason his mother had been killed. If he'd been stronger, resisted the spell, he might have saved her and Labhrás. The only two people he'd ever truly loved were dead because of him.

No, that was not true. A third sat beside him now.

He tried to withdraw his hands, but Aine held them fast. "Conor, it was not your fault. The druid is responsible for your mother's death, not you."

"You saw what happened. She came to find me, and because of that, she died." He shook his head. "I have to leave."

"Calhoun would protect you—"

"Even if he could, it's not me I'm worried about." He stood and helped Aine up, still holding her hands.

"Conor, grief causes people to make poor decisions. Don't act hastily."

He smiled sadly. "I'm not. Lord Labhrás knew this was going to happen, and he told me what to do."

He leaned forward and kissed Aine's cheek as she had done in this room not long ago. She rested against him for a moment, and he could feel her hesitation as she searched for something to say. Finally, she just gave his hands a squeeze and slipped out the door. Conor watched her go, his heart in his throat, but there was nothing left to say.

When he returned to his chamber, he told Dolan, "I'm leaving Lisdara tomorrow. No one must know of it until I'm well into Seanrós. Once I'm in Fíréin territory, they won't be able to touch me."

"Are you sure this is what you want? There are other ways—"

"No." Conor shook his head. "There is no other way. Will you help me?"

"Of course," Dolan said, but his brows furrowed with concern.

Conor lay in bed that night and stared at the ceiling. *Comdiu, am I doing the right thing? Labhrás told me to find Riordan if something should happen to him. He's never steered me wrong. But if that's true, why is this so difficult?*

He didn't really expect an answer, so he wasn't surprised when he got none. His swirling thoughts settled, though, and exhaustion took over. Only a single memory resurfaced before he was lost to sleep: the warmth of Aine against him and the sweet smell of her skin as he brushed his lips across her cheek.

CHAPTER ELEVEN

The following day, while Dolan made preparations for his departure, Conor opened his writing box.

To his highness, my uncle Fergus,

I heard the terrible news of my father's death. I will be coming home with all haste to mourn him properly, provided I can convince the Mac Cuillinn to give an adequate escort.

I hope we may discuss this arrangement my father made on my behalf. I cannot question his judgment, but I fear he may have been unduly influenced by those who do not have Tigh's best interests at heart.

I know the former king looked upon me with disappointment. During my time at Lisdara, I have come to see those flaws as weaknesses as he did. I beg of you the opportunity to prove myself worthy of the Mac Nir name. Perhaps I can restore some of the honor that was lost to our clan.

Please also tell Master Diarmuid I have matters I wish to discuss if he is still willing.

Humbly, your nephew, Conor Mac Nir.

He nearly choked on his disgust as he sanded and sealed the page, impressing a blob of blue wax with the Mac Nir seal. A silver coin accompanied the letter into a page's hand to ensure its speedy departure. Once the letter was away from the palace, he requested an audience with Calhoun.

"Please sit," the king said when Conor entered his chamber. He gestured to a chair. "How are you?"

Conor perched stiffly on the edge of the seat. "I'd like to see my father interred with our ancestors."

"You know why that's not possible."

"Because I'm a hostage." Conor let his shoulders slump, as if he had not expected that answer.

"Because it would be irresponsible to allow you to leave, given the circumstances. I took an oath to keep you safe at Lisdara. Nothing has changed."

Conor hardened his expression, even though his heart ached. "You'll forgive me if oaths don't mean as much to me as they once did. By your leave."

Calhoun bowed his head, his expression sympathetic. "You may go."

Conor didn't answer as he trudged from the room. Disgust churned inside him. The king didn't deserve to be treated with such disrespect, but it was necessary to his plan. Calhoun would need to offer Fergus a plausible explanation for his disappearance. By the time the king understood the reason for his behavior, he would be long gone.

Conor spent the evening pacing his room, thinking about his last and most difficult task. After the movements of the palace stilled, and the night sounds faded to silence, he crept into the music room. He lifted the harp from its spot and began to play Aine's song. The rough edges of his composition melted away as he played his emotions into the notes. All this time, he'd thought they were due to the harp, when in reality the rough edges had been his.

Aine appeared at the door within a handful of measures, cast in shadow by the candlelight. She had been waiting, just as he had hoped. He stopped in midsong and put aside the instrument.

"You're leaving?" she whispered, her voice hoarse.

He nodded.

"They're saying you argued with Calhoun, but I didn't believe it."

Conor rose from his chair. "You're going to hear a lot of things in the next few days. You know the truth."

Aine wrapped her arms protectively around herself and stared at the floor. For a moment, he considered abandoning the plan and trusting in

Lisdara's protection. But the druid wouldn't hesitate to destroy Calhoun and his family should they shield him.

He lifted Labhrás's charm from around his neck. "I want you to have this."

Her eyes widened. She touched the runes with a shaky hand. "Where did you get this?"

"Lord Labhrás gave it to me for protection. Will you wear it?"

Aine nodded, and he slipped the chain over her head. She fingered the charm reverently and tucked it beneath her shift.

"I don't know how long I'll be gone. You shouldn't wait for me."

"I would, you know." She lifted gleaming eyes to his face.

The rest of his thoughts spiraled away, and it took a moment to gather them enough to speak. "I know. But I want you to live your life. You deserve to be happy."

A single tear slid down Aine's cheek. He reached out and caught it on his finger. He should just say good-bye and be done with it, but he couldn't leave without showing her how he felt about her. He brushed her hair from her face with both hands so he could look at her one last time.

Aine rose up on her tiptoes and hesitantly pressed her lips to his. It was all the encouragement he needed. He pulled her close and felt her tremble as she melted against him, her arms sliding around his neck. Something fell into place in his heart, a sense of rightness, the deep conviction they had been brought together for a reason. This would not be their last moment together.

He broke the kiss first, but he still held her tight against him. He couldn't stop the words from spilling out. "If it's in my power, I'll come back to you."

She disengaged herself from his embrace, her cheeks flushed and her eyes shining. "I'll keep the charm safe for you until then." Before he could say another word, she was gone.

Conor let out a long breath and dragged his mind back to the final step of his plan. He blew out the candle and hurried back to his chamber, where Dolan waited with a bulging leather saddlebag. "Said your good-byes?"

Conor sighed and scrubbed his hands against his face. If he thought of Aine, he wouldn't be able to make himself leave. "It's time."

No one marked their passing as he and Dolan crept down a back staircase and made their way to the stables. When Conor began to blanket and bridle his mare, however, a stable boy poked his head from the hayloft. "Hey, what are you doing?"

"It's okay, boy," Dolan said soothingly. "An early morning errand is all. Grab a few more minutes of sleep while you can." He looked at Conor. "You know where you're going?"

"As well as I can." They had pored over the maps, determining the best place to cross the boundaries of Fíréin territory. Once there, Conor would be under the brotherhood's protection or their judgment. Conor didn't want to think about what would happen if Labhrás had been wrong.

"Ride fast and don't look back." Dolan took a breath, as if he would say more, then just clapped Conor on the back.

The servant took him as far as the gate, where he handed the guard on duty a slip of paper. Dolan had said he would take care of this part, though Conor couldn't fathom how anything short of an order from Calhoun would get him out before sunrise. The guard scrutinized the paper, then Conor, before at last giving the order to crank open the gate.

Conor mounted his mare and rode through the narrow opening. For the first time, he grasped the enormity of his undertaking. The horse sensed his nervousness and danced sideways. "Easy, girl," he murmured. "We have a steep road to travel in the dark." He cued the animal forward and began the descent from Lisdara.

By the time Conor reached the tree line, the first touch of morning light brightened the horizon. Despite Dolan's warning, he turned back to drink in the dark silhouette of the keep for the last time, and his resolve wavered. Then he imagined Labhrás, walking to his death with his head high, giving himself to his destiny without complaint.

Conor turned the horse and plunged into the trees.

+   +   +

The outer forest was young and widely spaced, and thick underbrush grew in the dappled shade. Conor threaded a path between the trees, aware of every creak and crackle in the steadily growing light. It was too quiet for a time when the birds should be awakening and the deer foraging for their breakfast.

Still, he pressed on until the slender saplings gave way to the giant trees of Seanrós, too large for a man to reach even halfway around. Here, the tangled branches formed a nearly impenetrable barrier, stopping the dawn in its progress. The light touch of magic tickled his senses, not unlike what he had felt from Meallachán's harp. A boundary of some sort, perhaps. Did that mean the Fíréin now knew of his presence?

Conor dismounted. He removed a small canvas pack containing a single change of clothing, some food, and a pouch of small coin from his saddlebag. Then he rearranged the contents so it appeared nothing was missing.

When he unsheathed the knife on his belt, he hesitated. It had to be his blood. If the druid demanded evidence of his death, he would use magic to determine if it belonged to Conor. He laid the blade across his forearm, gritting his teeth against the pain. Blood welled from the cut. He smeared it across the horse's blanket and quickly bound his stinging arm with a strip of linen.

"Sorry, girl," he murmured to the mare, stroking her soft nose. "This is as far as you go. Off with you now." He slapped the horse hard on the rump, and she took off like a carelessly loosed arrow, galloping back to her comfortable paddock at Lisdara.

With the horse out of sight, Conor became aware of how alone and vulnerable he was on foot with only a dagger at his belt. *All right, Comdiu. This is where I find out if I've understood Your wishes. Please, guide me.*

He shouldered his small pack. Even though he possessed no wildcraft, he took a heading the best he could and set off south. His footfalls thudded in the otherworldly quiet. If there were any Fíréin nearby, they could not help but notice his stumbling, crashing progress through their forest.

A breeze rustled the trees like a breath, lifting the hairs on the back of Conor's neck. He spun, but he saw only the shadowy shape of vegetation through a fine layer of mist. He shivered in a sudden chill.

Conor.

The voice. He had been foolish to think they wouldn't be waiting to devour him as soon as he left the protective circle of Lisdara's wards. He cast a panicked glance over his shoulder just before he stumbled into an object in his path.

"Are you all right?" Hands reached down and lifted him to his feet.

"I'm fine," Conor said automatically. His eyes moved to the speaker, and his mouth went dry.

He had been spellbound by Niamh's beauty when he first saw her in Lisdara's hall, but she did not compare with the woman who stood before him. She glowed in the shadowy forest, slender and pale, clad in a diaphanous green gown.

"Are you lost?"

Her voice was so melodious Conor could barely resist the urge to throw himself at her feet. He shook his head.

"Then would you mind if I walked with you?" She smiled, and Conor struggled to think clearly, enwrapped in the wonder of her beauty.

No. This wasn't right. Why would a woman be alone in the old forest?

Magic crawled over his skin, sinuous and seductive, yet somehow repellant. The voice in the mist. She had been waiting for him to leave behind the charm. She had him now. He was powerless against her.

He choked back a sob of terror.

The sidhe can't harm us. They can only try to deceive us, and we see more clearly than some.

Dolan's words cut through the spell and exposed Conor's thoughts as a lie.

"Go away," Conor said. "You won't deceive me. I am a child of Comdiu."

Her lips curled into a malicious smile. "Dear naive boy. Do you think your god holds power here? This is our forest. He gave it to us. The only power here is me."

Conor wavered. Didn't Treasach say Comdiu had relinquished the earth to the fallen Companions?

No. The only power she had over him was the power he gave her.

"Leave me," Conor said, gathering strength in his voice. "In the name of Comdiu and His son, Balus, be gone from here!"

Her expression turned feral. Then her shape shimmered, and she winked out of sight. Conor fell to his knees and began to laugh. Dolan was right. The sidhe had only the power granted to them. How close had he been to believing her lies?

Conor shouldered his bag, about to rise, when a quiet voice said in his ear, "Don't move."

Only then did he see the bright blade at his throat.

CHAPTER TWELVE

C onor did not move. He could scarcely force himself to breathe.

"Who are you?" the voice asked.

"That depends," Conor said carefully. "Who's asking?"

His captor chuckled and withdrew the sword. Conor heard an oiled hiss as he returned it to its sheath. "You've got spirit. I'll give you that."

Conor struggled to his feet, but before he could confront the speaker, four more men stepped from the shadows. No sound had indicated their presence. They all bore staves, swords, and several knives, and their dark clothing blended into the forest. Each man wore his hair bound into a single long braid.

The speaker circled around him, arms crossed over his chest. He was dark and wiry, and his voice, Conor realized now, had a distinct Siomaigh lilt.

"Fíréin?" Conor asked, more confidently than he felt.

"Aye," the leader said. "And you are . . ."

"Conor Mac Nir."

Several of the men exchanged glances, but the man before him showed no emotion. "Why are you here, Conor Mac Nir?"

"I'm looking for my uncle, Riordan Mac Nir."

"If you're delivering a message about King Galbraith's death, Brother Riordan is already aware. There was no need for you to put yourself in danger."

The man's tone grated Conor's raw nerves. Even though they could kill him where he stood, his words still came out with an irritated edge. "My message is for Brother Riordan. I must deliver it in person."

The man surveyed Conor and then turned away. "Go back to Lisdara before anyone misses you." He gave a discreet signal, and the other men melted back into the forest.

"Wait!" Conor cried. "Please. I don't have anywhere else to go. Labhrás Ó Maonagh said to come here and seek Riordan if anything should happen to him."

Why the plea should have stilled the leader's departure, he didn't know. Perhaps it was Labhrás's name or the desperation in Conor's voice, but the Fíréin brother turned back.

"Do you understand what you're asking, boy?" His gaze, sharp and predatory, pinned Conor in place. "Do you really know what this Labhrás was telling you to do?"

Conor swallowed his fear. "My uncle has answers I need. I just want to speak with him."

"Men who enter Ard Dhaimhin rarely leave. Crossing our borders means you surrender your life to the will of the brotherhood, whatever that may be. Are you willing to do that, Conor Mac Nir?"

Conor's heart rose into his throat. Once he went to Ard Dhaimhin, he might never be allowed to leave? Had Labhrás known what he asked when he sent Conor here?

"That's the price of your answers. Make your decision now. You can come with me or return to Lisdara, but you're in danger if you stay where you are."

"I'm not much of a fighter."

The Fíréin brother only stared back at him, unblinking.

Conor cast a look north, where they would soon find his horse, blood-smeared and riderless. What choice did he have?

"I'll come with you."

The man just nodded and walked away. Conor stared at his back until he realized he was meant to follow and then rushed to catch up.

"My name is Brother Odran," the warrior said when Conor fell into step beside him. "Try to keep up the best you can. It's several days' walk to the city."

Walk was a misnomer, and the exhortation to keep up might as well have been an instruction to fly. Brother Odran moved with the speed of a hunting cat, eating up long swaths of ground without leaving any sign of his passage. Apparently, the Fíréin's reputation was based in fact, not legend.

Conor pressed forward, stumbling over half-buried roots and protruding rocks. After what seemed like hours, though it could have been mere minutes, his legs began to ache, and his lungs burned. If Odran kept up this pace for two days, Conor would save them the trouble of killing him and drop dead here in the forest.

A few times, he thought the man had given up on him and left him behind, but each time, he rounded the bend to find Odran waiting. The brother said nothing, just took the lead again and set the pace faster. He might have been a spirit and not flesh and blood for the way he moved. After Conor's encounter with the sidhe, it was not a comforting thought.

Odran at last stopped beside a fallen log and passed a water skin to Conor, who gulped the cool liquid gratefully. "Not too much. You'll cramp."

Conor returned the water skin and sank down onto the log. His legs throbbed and tingled. "I tried to warn you. I'm a complete weakling."

"A scholar, are you?"

"A musician."

"Truly? Who taught you?"

"I taught myself to play, but lately I studied with the bard Meallachán."

"Master Liam will find that interesting."

Conor wasn't sure if that was a good thing or not. "Who is Master Liam?"

"The Ceannaire, our leader. He will be the one who decides what happens to you."

Conor swallowed. That didn't sound promising. "Master Liam knows Master Meallachán?"

"Aye. Can you go on?"

Conor stood and tested his aching legs. "I will do my best."

Odran moved away, leaving Conor to shoulder his small pack and hurry after him. A sick feeling crept into his middle. Why had he thought this would be simple?

By the time daylight faded from the forest, Conor wanted to die. His limbs cramped painfully, his lungs felt as if they would burst, and he could barely stagger forward in a straight line. When Odran stopped for the night, he was too tired to do anything but collapse in an aching heap on the forest floor.

"You all right?" Odran squatted to light a fire with a knife and flint. "You look tired."

Conor shot him a scathing look.

"We'll need to pick up the pace tomorrow if we're to reach Ard Dhaimhin by nightfall. We didn't cover as much ground today as I'd hoped." The tinder caught, and Odran stoked the flames until a fire crackled between them.

Conor scooted closer to the flames, not dignifying the comment with a response. He eased himself back on his elbows and closed his eyes until a booted toe nudged him.

"Here." Odran offered him a morsel of meat on the point of his knife.

Conor sat up and took the food. Odran dissected a roasted rabbit on a piece of clean-scraped bark, while a second one cooked on a spit.

"You had time to hunt? How long did I sleep?"

"An hour, perhaps." Odran gestured behind him with the knife. "We're following a trap line."

"What's a trap line?"

Odran picked up a stick and scratched a diagram into the dirt. "The forest is divided into quadrants, and each quadrant has a grid. Along each intersection of the gridlines is a trap. We follow trap lines so we don't have to hunt while we patrol the forest. The sentries are responsible for maintaining the traps on their section of the grid."

"What sentries?"

Odran smiled for the first time, a true expression of pleasure. "We've passed at least a half dozen since this morning."

Conor gulped. No wonder wanderers disappeared so easily and invisibly in the forest. "How many Firéin are there? Total, I mean, not just on guard."

"Right now, including novices? Close to four thousand."

Four thousand. That made Ard Dhaimhin the largest city outside the seaports on the Amantine, but it boasted more trained fighters than all of them put together. Tigh could probably muster only half that many.

Conor dared another question. "What will happen to me once we get to Ard Dhaimhin?"

Odran passed a portion of the rabbit meat on a shard of bark, then removed the second one from the spit. "That depends on your abilities. Every man is required to train in fighting arts and study various subjects. Not everyone is suited to becoming a warrior. Some find other occupations, like farming, fishing, or weaving."

"You do all that in Ard Dhaimhin?"

"We couldn't have remained separate all these centuries if we weren't self-sufficient," Odran said, smiling.

Conor studied Odran closely in the firelight. Perhaps he wasn't as humorless as he thought. He just didn't find much very funny. He was younger than Conor had assumed from his demeanor, too, perhaps only five-and-twenty. He didn't carry himself like warriors Conor had known, but he was dexterous and well-muscled, without a single ounce of fat on his body. "What are you?"

"What do you think?"

"You can fight, but I don't think you're a warrior, at least not in the usual sense."

"You're right. I'm a tracker."

"Like a hunter?"

Odran smiled again. "Something like that."

Conor thought of how the sword had just appeared at his throat. Odran could have killed him before he ever knew he was in danger. "You track people. People who breach the forest."

"You're quick."

"And you kill them?"

"Usually."

"Were you going to kill me?"

"What would you rather I say, aye or no?"

Conor looked down at his food, his appetite gone. "I think I'd rather not know."

"Good decision." The tracker tore meat off the skinny rabbit bone with his teeth.

Conor rolled onto his side by the fire, recalling his childhood fascination with the Fíréin. How naive he had been.

He slept fitfully, his dreams tangled with images of Lisdara and fragments of harp music. He started awake beside ashes, alone, his heart hammering wildly. When he tried to stand, his muscles cramped in protest, and he collapsed onto the dirt.

Had Odran given up on him? Had he just left him there?

The brother appeared through the trees, still moving soundlessly, as if his feet didn't touch the forest floor. He tossed Conor the newly filled water skin and scattered the remnants of their fire. "Let's go. We have a lot of ground to cover."

Conor barely restrained a moan. His legs felt like lead, if lead could feel such agony. Even his back and shoulders ached. He felt as if he'd gone a dozen rounds with Glenmallaig's house guard. And Odran expected him to move faster today?

He had no choice, though. Any sympathy Odran might have felt had dissolved overnight, and Conor had to keep up or be left behind. The brother no longer waited for him. If Conor slowed his pace, he had to redouble his efforts to catch up. Despite his alternately numb and aching body, he drew on hidden reserves of strength and matched the tracker's pace. Perhaps he wasn't so pathetic after all.

Never mind that Odran looked as if he had been out for a stroll, while Conor staggered along, sweating and panting. The brother had told him to keep up. He hadn't said he needed to look impressive while doing it.

"How much farther?" Conor asked between gasps. "Will we make it to Ard Dhaimhin tonight?"

"At this rate, we won't make it to Ard Dhaimhin for three days."

It was probably just sarcasm, but the pace increased after that.

Conor's pain increased, too, until he was one aching, quivering mass. His shaky legs threatened to give out with each step. Weak from lack of rest and food, he no longer cared if he collapsed and Odran left him behind. At least then he wouldn't have to walk anymore.

Just as Conor was about to abandon his pride and say he couldn't go on, Odran stopped. Conor stumbled to his side, silently praying for rest. Then he followed the tracker's gaze, and his mouth fell open in amazement.

CHAPTER THIRTEEN

The stories about Ard Dhaimhin left Conor unprepared for his first look. The ground sloped steeply before them to a massive loch, which spread like blue glass to each end of his vision. Half a dozen crannogs dotted the lake's surface, the small islands connected to the shore and to one another by a web of ropes and pulleys attached to bark boats. Thatched cottages and stone clochans spread from the shore. Beyond, thousands of acres of crops stretched to the distant tree line at the mountains beyond.

Then there was Carraigmór. All his life, Conor had heard tales about the impenetrable fortress on the cliff, but the traditional descriptions missed the mark. It was not a fortress built upon a cliff, but rather it *was* the cliff, carved from the sheer granite rock face that dropped hundreds of yards down into the lake. He could make out glass windows and square stone balustrades, but if he hadn't known where to look, he might have overlooked the structure entirely. It felt ancient, organic, as if it had sprung up from the land itself. He could not help but be humbled before the sight.

Odran watched him, a slight smile playing on his lips. Conor opened and closed his mouth several times before he managed to speak. "I've never seen anything like this."

"Few who aren't Fírein have," Odran said with pride. "Come, it's still a long way to the city."

Conor followed Odran down the steep, narrow switchbacks, barely wide enough for a single man to pass. Occasionally, Conor heard a birdcall he presumed came from a sentry, and Odran whistled a reply.

After nearly an hour, the switchbacks flattened into a path that bordered the marshy lakeshore. From this vantage, the lake looked more like a sea. Conor knew he was gaping like a child, but he didn't try to restrain himself. He couldn't imagine a newcomer who wouldn't be impressed by Ard Dhaimhin.

Odran paused for Conor to catch up and led him down the road into the main village, where the Fíréin's principal industries took place: blacksmithing, candle making, weaving, tanning. Ard Dhaimhin teemed with life, brimming with sights and sounds he would have imagined only in the great seaports. The clang of metal rang above conversation and the rumbling wheels of the handcarts that seemed to be the city's main mode of transport. Quenching iron drifted on the air, melding with the smells of hot beeswax, food, and wood smoke.

Odran directed Conor's attention to the expanse of fertile land beyond the craftsmen's cottages. "We cultivate all our food. Wheat, flax, and greens are grown back there. The beehives in the alfalfa fields provide honey and pollinate the orchards. We raise goats and chickens in the pasturelands beyond. As you can see, we have everything we need."

Conor quickly noted the greatest difference between the Fíréin city and those of the kingdoms: the lack of women and children. It seemed odd to see men engaged in pursuits like laundry and cooking; odder still that they all appeared trim and muscular, the kind of men Conor would expect to see displaying sword work in the practice yard. Most gave Conor's passage no notice, though a few raised hands in greeting to Odran.

After what had to be miles, they approached the massive cliff. Hundreds of narrow steps marked the side of the mountain, glistening with the water that seeped from the hillside. Conor stared at the steps. He had forgotten his exhausted body in his awe of the city, but the mere thought of traversing this staircase made his muscles quiver.

"Come on," Odran said. "You first."

He'd come this far. It was pointless to give up now. He forced his rubbery legs forward and counted the steps as he climbed, hoping to distract himself from both the dizzying view and his bone-deep weariness.

"King Daimhin was either very intelligent or very suspicious," Conor muttered after he had counted two hundred steps and still the fortress loomed high above them.

"Both, I'm sure. The climb made his lords think hard about the matters they brought before him."

Conor's chuckle dissolved into a wheeze. "That's one way to encourage men to solve their own problems."

The top of the stairs emptied through a tall, square doorway into a granite terrace only two spans deep and twice as wide. Smooth stone, polished by five hundred years' worth of foot traffic, paved the floor. Another short flight of stairs led up to a nondescript wooden door, where a single guard stood watch.

"Conor Mac Nir," Odran told the guard. "He's expected."

Odran turned to Conor. "This is where I leave you. Good luck."

Conor watched the tracker descend the steps until he realized the guard was holding the door for him. He stepped inside and once more was unable to keep the wonder from his face. A great cavern of rock surrounded him, its vaulted ceilings stretching beyond the reach of the massive, man-sized candles that lit the interior. Two long rows of oak chairs lined the sides of the hall, drawing his eye to the room's centerpiece. The famed Rune Throne was not a chair, exactly, but an interwoven tangle of ancient roots, polished to a high shine. Tendrils cradled a marble slab upon which were etched the Odlum characters that gave the throne its name. A fitting throne for a king who had carved his fortress from a cliff.

A second man met Conor inside the door. "Conor Mac Nir? Please wait here." The man disappeared down a corridor, his footsteps echoing off the rock.

He was standing in the fortress of the High King of Seare, Conor thought in amazement. Daimhin himself had walked these halls.

Footsteps reverberated off stone, and Conor turned toward the sound. He knew the man instantly, not because they'd ever met, but because it was like seeing a vision of himself in the future. Like his younger brothers, Riordan Mac Nir possessed wheat-colored hair and blue-gray eyes, but he was taller and more slender, his wiry build corded with lean muscle.

Riordan's long stride ate up the space between them, and he crushed Conor in a bone-breaking embrace. "Conor! When Brother Odran sent word back, I thought he had to be mistaken!"

Conor pulled back, recalling what had precipitated his trip. "The king is dead. Lord Labhrás has been executed."

A shadow of grief passed over Riordan's face. "I know. I'm sorry, son."

"Lord Labhrás told me to find you if something should happen to him, so I left Lisdara. They think I'm dead." He snapped his mouth shut on his ramblings.

"You look halfway there. Let's get you some food and a hot bath, and you can tell me the story from the beginning."

Conor nodded mutely, surprised by the instant affinity he felt for his uncle. Despite the obvious Mac Nir resemblance, Riordan reminded him more of Labhrás than Galbraith. Still, he could not forget that this man had orchestrated his early life. To what end he was not yet sure.

For now, he put aside those concerns in favor of more pressing questions. "Do we have to go back down the stairs?"

"No." Riordan chuckled. "There are guest chambers here at Carraigmór. You can stay here until other arrangements are made."

Conor nodded, though the mention of other arrangements stirred up nervousness. Riordan would welcome him—after all, Conor was his nephew—but would the Ceannaire?

His uncle flagged down a gray-haired man passing in the corridor. "Brother Daigh, would you show Conor to one of the guest rooms? I'm late for my evening lesson." Riordan glanced at Conor. "Don't worry, Daigh will get you settled. I'll find you later."

Conor looked at Brother Daigh, alarmed he was inconveniencing one of Ard Dhaimhin's elders. "I'm sure I can find my way if you've other things to do."

"It's no trouble. Come, it's not far."

Riordan nodded reassuringly to Conor, so he followed Brother Daigh through an arched doorway. The corridor curved upward like a tunnel and climbed a steep flight of stairs carved out of polished rock. Thick torches set in iron brackets cast intersecting pools of light and painted the ceilings with soot.

As they proceeded deeper into the fortress, Conor studied Brother Daigh. He, too, had the bearing of a fighter, despite the fact he had to be somewhere in his sixties. Why was he acting like a servant?

"Our ways will seem odd after life in the kingdoms," Daigh said. "I thought so when I came. But whether a novice or the Ceannaire himself, we are all equal in Comdiu's eyes. We all take our turns serving at Carraigmór and working the land."

"How do you keep order?"

"We have ranks. As Conclave members, Brother Riordan and I rank below only the Ceannaire himself, so we have the responsibility of giving direction to our brothers. But we value humility as much as we prize accomplishment."

Conor didn't know what to say. This communal arrangement was a foreign concept, and yet it seemed natural for men who considered Comdiu their highest authority. But how were disputes resolved? Four thousand fighting men in one place seemed like a recipe for violence, Balian or not.

"Here we are." Daigh stopped short at the top of the stairs, where the short corridor ended in a solid wall. A door stood on each side. Daigh pushed open the door on the right and gestured for Conor to enter. "Someone will bring your bath water and something to eat. Call if you need anything."

"Call who?" Conor asked, but Daigh had already gone.

Like the hall, Conor's room was a near-spherical chamber carved from granite. Minerals sparkled in the walls. A plain wooden bedstead with a rush mattress stood in the corner beside a candle stand of twisted iron and a small bath. He sank down on the bed and breathed a heavy sigh of relief.

A knock sounded at the door. It swung open to admit a dark-haired man. Even though he looked only a few years older than Conor, he already exhibited the lithe, fluid grace of Ard Dhaimhin's warriors. He held up a large bucket of steaming water in each hand.

Conor watched the young man pour the water into the tub. "Are you a novice?"

"Apprentice. My name's Eoghan. What's yours?"

"Conor."

He straightened and fixed Conor with a piercing look. "You're the Timhaigh prince."

"My father was the king," Conor said. "There's a difference."

Eoghan flashed a grin. "There is at that. Why are you up here? Aren't you going to start your novitiate?"

"I don't know. The Ceannaire has yet to make a decision."

Eoghan's eyebrows climbed toward his hairline. "That's not what I heard. It sounded to me as if Master Liam has already made up his mind."

"How could you possibly know that?"

"I'm assigned to the fortress this month. It's easy to overhear things." Eoghan moved to the door and threw him one last smile. "Good luck."

How did the Fíréin already know so much about him, when he knew so little in return? It was not as if he had planned this. Only his faith, or perhaps his desperation, had gotten him this far.

Conor removed his soiled clothing and eased into the bath. The water stung the fresh cut on his forearm, but it was a small price to pay for the way it instantly relieved his strained muscles. He unraveled his dirty braids and scrubbed his hair clean with a cake of soap, letting his mind wander.

What was Aine doing now? Supping with Calhoun and pretending to mourn him? Word of his death should have reached Tigh by now. Would Fergus even pretend his death was a loss, or would he try to work Calhoun's supposed failure to his advantage?

No, he couldn't dwell on that. Fergus could find an excuse for war, with or without his disappearance. Conor had the right to honor his foster father's wishes and ensure his own safety. Still, he had come to like and respect Calhoun Mac Cuillinn and his family. The idea of war falling upon Lisdara made him ill.

"You are not responsible for the actions of everyone in Seare," he told himself sternly. He was not that important, no matter what Lord Labhrás and his uncle had planned.

The bath water had gone cold while he ruminated, so he climbed out into the chilly air and wrapped himself in the cloth Eoghan had left. He pulled his single clean shirt from his pack, slid it over his head, and stretched out on the bed to wait.

Conor woke to near blackness, disoriented and groggy. It took a moment to remember he was at Carraigmór, a guest of the Fíréin. He squinted at the outline of the room, dimly illuminated by torchlight seeping under the door. The candles must have burned out. Exactly how long had he slept?

The latch rattled, and the door swung open, spilling light into the room.

"Uncle Riordan?" Conor squinted as his uncle lit a candle from the torch in the hallway.

Riordan moved around the room, touching the flame to the other candles until flickering golden light bathed the chamber. He ducked out and returned with a large tray.

Conor pushed himself up and groaned at his aching muscles. "I'm starving. I was afraid I missed supper."

"You did. This is breakfast. I took the liberty of bringing enough for two."

"What time is it?"

"A little past dawn." Riordan set the tray on the end of the bed and sat next to it. "Help yourself. It won't be hot for long."

Conor's stomach grumbled. It was typical Seareann fare: oat porridge with rich honey, and fried fish. He took a bowl of porridge and studied his uncle.

"Eat up. You won't get another opportunity until supper. You've a long day ahead of you."

Conor's eyebrows flew up, but porridge pasted his mouth shut.

Riordan laughed. "Relax. Nothing too taxing. I suspect you'll have a hard enough time climbing back down. I heard Odran set a quick pace."

"According to him, it was merely a crawl."

"Odran's sure-footed as they come. But he's not the quickest among us, as you'll come to find out."

Conor fervently hoped he would never have the misfortune of traveling with any of them.

Riordan turned back to his breakfast, and Conor followed suit. Difficult to believe he sat beside a legend, a man who had given up power and wealth in favor of the Fíréin brotherhood. Blood relation or not, he was a stranger. Only the high esteem of Labhrás and Dolan led him to trust him as far as he had.

When they had finished the meal, Riordan set the tray aside and fixed his attention on Conor. "Now, I suppose you better tell me why you're here."

Conor began with how he had been sent to Lisdara as a hostage and ended with news of Galbraith's murder and Labhrás's execution, omitting Aine and his musical ability. Riordan listened intently, though his expression darkened when Conor mentioned the charges against Labhrás.

"What do you think?" Riordan asked when Conor finished. "You must have an opinion."

Had any adult besides Dolan ever asked his opinion? "I think the druid and Lord Fergus killed the king and blamed Lord Labhrás because he's a Balian."

"You may be right. Galbraith was always suspicious of Labhrás, but he was bound by his oath to me. No doubt you've heard the story by now."

Conor nodded. He hesitated to ask his next question, but it would eat at him until it found voice. "What about Lady Damhnait and the girls? What happened to them? Would my uncle . . .?"

"I don't know, Conor." Riordan sighed. "If I know Labhrás, he would have made arrangements for their safety. He knew what he was risking by continuing to profess his faith openly. If there were any way to get them away safely . . ."

Please, Comdiu, let that be true. Fergus would not spare those he deemed traitors, even if they were women and children. Conor's stomach rebelled at the thought of Labhrás's family—his family—being dragged away to their deaths. That was, if they hadn't been slaughtered where they stood. A wave of dizziness passed over him.

"It's strange that Galbraith would have willingly engaged a druid as a counselor, though," Riordan continued, as if unaware of his words' effect. "He distrusted them nearly as much as Balians."

Conor recalled the vision Aine had shown him, grateful for the subject change. "Fergus arranged it. Besides, this one is different. Powerful. I think he's a Red Druid."

"Red Druid, hmm? You can feel his use of magic?"

Conor nodded.

Riordan looked thoughtful. "Interesting. Do you have any idea why Lord Labhrás told you to seek me out if something happened to him?"

"I'd assumed it was part of your plan. Yours and his, I mean."

"What plan is that?"

Conor's face heated. "I'd like to know that, too. I've never understood why you took such an interest in me."

A flicker of sadness crossed Riordan's face. "I knew your mother well. Her brother fostered at Glenmallaig for a time, and we always had much in common. Had I stayed in Tigh, she and I would be married now."

"You and my mother. Married."

"Indeed. Her clan was ambitious, and they wanted their blood joined with the royal line. When I became a Balian, though, I knew I couldn't live a lie in Tigh just to keep my throne."

"So you turned her away."

"No. I loved her." For a moment, Riordan's gaze turned distant. "I told her I was going to abdicate the throne. She agreed to leave Tigh with me."

"You loved each other? Why . . . what . . .?" Conor struggled to wrap his mind around the revelation. Then another possibility occurred to him. "Wait, you can't mean I'm . . ."

"Máiréad always maintained you were Galbraith's son. The timing was close enough no one questioned otherwise."

"But you knew." Conor's heart rose into his throat, and the room swam before his eyes. Hadn't he noticed the resemblance upon first glance? It explained so much, Galbraith's strained relationship with Máiréad, his contempt for his son. . . . "I'm a bastard?"

"No! You are not a bastard."

"You just said . . ."

Riordan reached out and touched Conor's hand. He jerked it away. "Conor, your mother and I were married by a Balian priest. You are my legitimate son."

Conor jumped up and paced in front of the bed. "I don't understand. How can that be? She married my fath—Galbraith. How could—"

"Máiréad's clan found out. They weren't about to lose their chance to have their daughter become queen, much less for love of a Balian. Since the marriage wasn't recognized by the throne, it was easy enough to make arrangements with Galbraith. It was his men that came for us." A ghostly smile twisted Riordan's lips. "I would have fought them for her, even knowing how it would end. She wouldn't let me. She went back to Glenmallaig in order to spare me."

Riordan's pain showed clearly on his face, unmitigated by the passage of years. Conor's anger faded. Riordan had done what he thought best, and he had loved Lady Máiréad. Of all the things he had said, Conor believed that most easily. "So that's why you had Galbraith send me to Balurnan."

"No. I did that because from the moment I saw you, even at a week old, I could sense you had a gift. I knew it would be extinguished at Glenmallaig, so I arranged your fosterage with Labhrás, where it would be nurtured."

Labhrás had always encouraged Conor's playing, giving him access to bards and musicians and calling for him each time he returned to

Balurnan. "I always just thought he liked music. I didn't know there was anything special about it until I came to Lisdara."

Riordan's eyebrows lifted. "Your gift is music?"

"You didn't know?"

"When you said you felt the druid's power, I assumed you could recognize magic in others, like me. Have you sensed power in anyone else?"

Conor thought of Aine. Other than the connection between them, which he attributed to a different sort of magic, he'd had no inkling of her gifts. He hadn't noticed anything unusual about Riordan, either. "The only other magic I sensed was from the charm Lord Labhrás gave me."

Riordan smiled. "He gave you the charm. I hoped he would. Do you have it with you?"

"No, I left it behind."

Riordan nodded, and his smile faded. Tears glinted in the corners of his eyes. "I know this is a lot to take in. I know you need time before . . ." He swallowed hard. "Just know I've never been happier than I am right now, seeing you stand before me."

Conor wanted to say something, but the words stuck in his throat. Riordan seemed to understand. "I'll send someone up with suitable clothing, and then I'll take you to Master Liam. After that, we'll see."

Conor watched his uncle—no, his father—leave the room, struggling to think through his shock. All these years, trying to live up to the expectations of the king, never understanding the reason for his hatred. If someone had told him . . .

What? That he was the product of an unsanctioned marriage between his mother and the king's brother? That short of Riordan's claim of paternity, Galbraith had no choice but to acknowledge him?

No, the revelation didn't make him feel any better. All it did was prove he had been rejected by two fathers, not just one. Conor had thought coming here would answer all his questions, but instead it had just created more.

A knock at the door startled him from his thoughts. Conor opened it, hoping it might be Eoghan, but it was another young man, bringing the promised clothing. Conor thanked him and shut the door quickly.

The garments were plain and serviceable, made from earth-colored linen. He pulled on the close-fitting trousers and oversized tunic and buckled on the scraped leather belt. Then he used the comb and leather thong the boy had brought to fashion his hair into a club at the base of his neck.

True to his word, Riordan appeared minutes later. "Ready?"

Conor squared his shoulders and tried to adopt Riordan's easy confidence, though he had no idea if it was successful. As they wound their way through the intersecting tunnels into the great hall, he burned every detail of his father into his brain, hoping it would lead to some sort of understanding.

In the great hall, a brother scrubbed the stone floor with a horsehair brush. Riordan stopped before him. "Master Liam, I would like to present my son, Conor."

The word *son* grated on Conor's raw nerves, but his discomfort shifted to confusion when he realized Riordan was addressing the man on his knees. This was the Ceannaire?

The man pushed himself to his feet and wiped his damp hands on his tunic. He was common-looking, of average height and muscular build, with long, reddish-blond hair bound into the customary braid. Something in his erect, yet relaxed posture made Conor think of a bowstring, the potential of power contained in stillness. His face brought back the genealogy lessons Conor should have remembered long before now.

"You're Liam Mac Cuillinn!"

Liam fixed his gaze on Conor. "Have we met?"

If Liam had seemed unassuming moments before with a brush in hand, the illusion was long gone. No doubt many a man had lost his resolve in the presence of the Ceannaire, but Conor had more at stake here than most.

"I know Lord Calhoun and Lord Gainor," he answered. "There is a distinct family resemblance."

"Aye, I understand you became quite close to my family at Lisdara."

He wasn't sure what to say. Master Liam sounded as if he was making idle conversation, but Conor was sure nothing the Ceannaire did was idle. Could he possibly know about Conor's attachment to Aine?

Liam studied him closely. "You left Lisdara to find Riordan. Did you get the answers you sought?"

"I asked the questions I meant to," Conor said. "But the answers weren't what I expected."

Unexpectedly, the Ceannaire smiled. He exchanged a look with Riordan and turned back to Conor. "What now?"

"I was hoping you might tell me, sir."

"I won't hold you here against your will. If you've satisfied your curiosity, I'll arrange an escort out of the forest."

"But Odran said—"

"Being the Ceannaire allows me to make up my own mind. What would you like to do?"

Conor glanced at Riordan, whose intense gaze belied his studied calm. If Conor left, he'd never know anything more about his father, and his presence would still bring danger to those he loved in Faolán.

"Everyone thinks I'm dead," Conor said. "I have nowhere to go."

"You wish to become a novice then?"

Conor hesitated. "Aye. I do."

"Think carefully, young man," Liam said. "When I said you could leave, it was as a guest. As a novice, you will be committing yourself to our training and our rules. They are not meant to be easy. Often they can be downright unpleasant. This is not a decision to be undertaken lightly."

Conor drew himself up straighter. "Neither was Lord Labhrás's decision to risk death to follow his conscience, or Riordan's choice to give up his throne. I understand what I'm doing."

Liam studied him with that knowing gaze, then gave a single nod. "Riordan, find him a place in Slaine's céad. Eoghan can show him the city." His smile made Conor's stomach do a somersault. "Rest up, young man. Tomorrow you begin your training."

CHAPTER FOURTEEN

"**I** should have told him long before this."

Riordan stood on one of Carraigmór's narrow granite balconies, his gaze sweeping the broad expanse of the Fíréin's domain. He sensed rather than saw the Ceannaire a few paces behind him in the doorway.

"You did what was best for the boy," Liam said. "The truth would have profited no one."

"Perhaps." The knowledge that his reunion with Conor may have come too late tempered Riordan's joy. Still, the corner of his lips twitched up in a smile when he recalled how Conor had stood his ground before Liam. "He's a remarkable boy."

Liam smiled too. "You don't know the half of it."

"You mean Conor's musical ability?"

"Aye. He has a rare gift with the harp."

As many years as Riordan had known Liam, the man's uncanny ability to see into the minds of others still discomfited him. "You read that from the meeting in the hall?"

"No, I received a message from Meallachán while you were away." Liam chuckled. "He was concerned the boy might draw the wrong attention to himself should he remain."

"Why didn't he send him here directly?"

"My youngest sister, Aine. They seem to have a significant connection, but I don't yet know how she's involved in this."

"Did Meallachán tell you that, too?"

"No, that I got from Conor directly." Liam's amusement faded. "He seems to know quite a bit about Labhrás. Did you tell him?"

"He came to tell me." Riordan swallowed as if it could push down the sudden ache in his chest. He had been among the onlookers, concealed by his cloak, when his foster brother and oldest friend had walked to the headsman.

"Then Labhrás did his job well. He educated him, he nurtured his gift, and then he sent him back here, just as we'd hoped. And now, you have your son back."

Riordan glanced sharply at Liam, but he couldn't summon any ill will toward the Ceannaire, even if he was the reason Riordan hadn't made any effort to see Conor all these years. *Things must unfold this way,* Liam had said. *If you want what's best for him, you must watch from a distance.*

It was not his place to question Liam. The burdens of the Ceannaire's visions were his to carry and his to share. That he chose to bring Riordan so much into his confidence was already an honor. Still, Riordan had the uncomfortable feeling Liam's plans for Conor went far beyond the small safeguards they had arranged.

He wasn't sure what was more unsettling: knowing what the Ceannaire saw or being protected from it.

✦ ✦ ✦

Liam knew of Riordan's discomfort as he returned to the heart of Carraigmór, but it was from long years of acquaintance rather than any exercise of his gifts. He regretted keeping him in the dark about so many details, but the fewer who knew the secrets of Ard Dhaimhin, the more secure they all were.

Liam retrieved a torch from a bracket in the wall and turned down a short, empty corridor ending in a locked door without a keyhole. He spoke a handful of words in a language long forgotten and then pushed open the door. Not even Riordan knew of this place. The password had been embedded by magic no living soul could perform and was passed down from one Ceannaire to the next, ensuring only one man could enter.

He held the torch before him as he slowly descended a flight of narrow stairs, his shoulders brushing the wall in places. The soft hiss of fire joined the scuff of his footsteps on stone. Somewhere beyond, the plink of water reverberated off rock.

The corridor seemed to end ahead in a solid wall, but Liam turned sharply into the space that angled back from the passage and stepped into the chamber.

The Hall of Prophecies. The true heart of Carraigmór, its place of secrets. Its place of purpose.

It was more of a cavern than a room, rounded like the other chambers in the fortress and lined with rows upon rows of compartments, each containing a scroll or book. Daimhin had begun to collect them in his time, and each Ceannaire over the last five hundred years had added to their number. Some of the prophecies had been recorded by brothers of Ard Dhaimhin, while others had been collected from thousands of miles away, written in dozens of languages. Not all applied to Seare: in fact, only a small portion concerned the small isle at the corner of the known world. Liam sought one particular prophecy, written by Queen Shanna herself after Daimhin's death. Few knew of it, which made the current situation that much more disturbing.

The Kinslayer shall rise, the Adversary looming treacherous over the bleeding land. Day shall be night, and the mist, unbound, shall wreak evil upon the sons of men.

In that hour alone the son of Daimhin shall come; wielding the sword and the song, he shall stand against the Kinslayer, binding the power of the sidhe, and, for a time, bringing peace.

Liam stared at the scroll that told the future of Seare. Wiser men than he had failed to decipher the full meaning of the prophecy, but now he had a better idea of what "the sword and the song" could mean and exactly what part the Fíréin might play in it.

There had been kinslayers before—bloody feuds among clans littered Seare's violent past—but this particular one was different. Never before did the one in question have a Red Druid by his side, a man who had managed to cheat death for centuries.

A man who once held the very position Liam did now.

CHAPTER FIFTEEN

A knock shuddered the door of the borrowed chamber, and Conor opened it immediately. Instead of Eoghan, a tall, whip-thin man stared back at him with barely veiled disdain.

"I'm Brother Slaine. Come with me."

Conor grabbed his pack. "Where are we going?"

Slaine fixed a steely stare on him. "To the barracks. You may be a prince in Tigh, but here you're just another novice. You will receive no special treatment."

"I don't expect any, sir," Conor said, taken aback by his tone.

"And you will not speak unless spoken to. Do you understand?"

Conor nodded mutely. Slaine narrowed his eyes and gestured for Conor to follow him.

The brother said nothing on the long descent from Carraigmór, even when Conor slid down several steps on his tailbone and thumped to a stop against his legs. He simply stared at him until he righted himself and then wordlessly continued. Some of Conor's anxiety faded. Brother Slaine might not be the most pleasant of men, but at least he didn't seem inclined to comment on Conor's shortcomings.

The village below already bustled with activity. Smoke drifted on the air with the delectable smell of frying fish and the milder aroma of oat porridge. Slaine led him down the path toward the cluster of squat clochans and stopped before an open door. He gestured for Conor to enter.

The structure was the size of Glenmallaig's hall, but round and sunken several feet below ground. An enormous stone-paved fire pit situated beneath a hole in the thatched roof provided both warmth and light.

Dozens of earthen platforms had been dug out from the exterior wall, arranged like spokes of a wheel.

"How many boys live here?" Conor asked, amazed.

Slaine scowled. "About seventy at present, between the ages of fifteen and twenty. You will do everything with your céad while you are here at Ard Dhaimhin: eat, bathe, sleep, and train. You'll meet them later. They're all at morning drills."

Conor's heart sank at the mention of drills. He had hoped not to expose his failures so soon after his arrival. Master Liam had said he wouldn't be allowed to leave, but he didn't yet know the extent of Conor's inexperience.

"Come on, boy, don't stand here gaping. You've got work to do. Brother Reamonn is waiting."

Dutifully, Conor followed Slaine up the steps and into the morning sunlight, suppressing the urge to ask about Brother Reamonn. He almost had to run to keep up with Slaine's long stride. The céad leader took a winding route through the village to where the buildings thinned into small gardens then fields in various stages of crop growth. In the farthest fields, corn and wheat already produced stalks past his waist. Nearer, root crops leafed out into neatly spaced rows, around which a dozen brothers hilled soil or pulled weeds. Slaine led him to a wide, untilled field, where at least thirty men toiled with hoes and spades.

"Brother Reamonn!" Slaine shouted.

A man in the middle of the field lifted his head and trotted toward them. Fiery-haired and covered in freckles, the bare-chested brother looked well on his way to a sunburn.

"I have another for you," Slaine said, jerking his head in Conor's direction. "Much luck may you have of him."

"Grab a hoe and find yourself a spot." Reamonn indicated a small handcart holding iron-bound farm implements.

So it was to be manual labor for him. Maybe Liam had taken his measure and deemed him unsuited to the warrior life. Conor selected a long-handled hoe from the cart. "What do I do now?"

"Get to work," Reamonn said. "We have to cultivate the whole field before we can get in the winter rye. Go on, get started."

Conor gulped and trudged out into the field past the last man.

Awkwardly, he swung the hoe and drove the metal blade into the parched ground. The impact shuddered up his arms and into his shoulders and back.

"Here, let me show you." The brother nearest him, middle-aged and already perspiring, approached him. "Put your hands here"—he adjusted Conor's grip—"and swing it like so. Use the weight of the hoe to your advantage."

Conor tried again. The tool bit into the ground far more easily. "Thank you. I'm Conor, by the way."

"Corgan. Don't worry, you'll get it."

Conor returned to work, making quicker progress this time, but before long, his arms, shoulders, and back ached as much as his legs. He took a stinging hand away from the hoe and found blood seeping from newly formed blisters. He paused to catch his breath until he noticed Reamonn's sharp gaze on him.

The row of tilled earth grew before him with agonizing slowness. Every movement sent fiery pain through his body until it hurt to even breathe. Still, he continued, forcing his mind to accept the pain rather than fight it. He still felt his aching muscles, the stinging pain in his palms, the rhythm of the hoe as it swung overhead and down into the earth, but distantly. His mind wandered to Riordan, but that only brought back the sick feeling, so he turned his thoughts instead to Lisdara. It would be midsummer soon, and Calhoun's lords would be returning for the Cáisc celebration. Longing struck deep in his chest as he imagined Aine smiling beneath a crown of wildflowers, her hair braided and twined with ribbons. In his pleasant reverie, he kissed her beneath the wide green canopy of Lisdara's oak trees.

"Brother Conor!"

Brother Reamonn's shout intruded on his daydream. Conor looked up and saw they were alone in the field, the sun beating down from its zenith. A wide swath of cultivated earth stretched before him. Reamonn waved him over.

Conor's muscles cramped, the pain nearly knocking him to his knees, but he forced himself to limp forward with the hoe.

"That's enough for today," Reamonn said. "Good work."

"Thanks." Conor gritted his teeth as his shoulder seized. "What now?"

"Slaine didn't say?"

Conor shook his head. Even his hair hurt.

Reamonn looked him over closely. "I should send you to catch up with the rest of your céad, but you might not wake up tomorrow. Take the afternoon at your leisure. Tell Slaine it was my idea."

Conor silently blessed Brother Reamonn for his mercy and limped away, too exhausted to care about what Slaine would do if he found him shirking his duties. It seemed to take hours to reach the village. Once there, his plan ended. If he lay down, he wouldn't be able to move later. Instead, he staggered toward the lake, where he perched on a rock, dragged off his boots, and dangled his aching feet in the cold water. He closed his eyes and let slow, even breaths fill his body.

"Sunbathing instead of working, I see."

Conor twisted sharply. Eoghan stood behind him, arms crossed over his chest.

"I'm sorry. Brother Reamonn—"

"Relax. Master Liam told me I should show you around this afternoon."

Conor pulled on his boots and slid from the rocks. Eoghan grinned when Conor's knees buckled beneath him.

"I tried to get to you before Brother Slaine, but he'd already put you on Reamonn's work detail. He can be harsh with newcomers."

"So I gathered. Did you get that treatment when you came here?"

Eoghan shrugged. "I was abandoned as a child. I don't remember it. Master Liam took me in, raised me here. Hard to believe he would have been a king, eh?"

"Not so hard." In a way, Liam still was a king, though his realm was a strange place, full of incomprehensible subjects. "I knew his brothers. They're cut from the same cloth. Master Liam's more intimidating, though. He looks at you like he knows what you're thinking."

"Probably because he does," Eoghan said with a smirk.

Conor halted for a moment, a question on his lips, but before he could ask it, Eoghan turned away. The older boy took pity on him and set a slow pace along the lakeshore road, pointing out the details Odran and Slaine had neglected. Conor heard the clack of wood and the clash of metal long before the training yards on the north side of the lake came into view, but even with advance warning, the sight stunned him into silence.

Nearly a thousand men and boys trained in an expansive compound, scattered across sandy training yards as far as he could see. Nearest them, boys as young as six or seven practiced with wooden swords, staffs, and spears under the watchful eyes of their drill leaders. Farther down, older boys and men trained with unsharpened steel within carefully choreographed routines. Conor paused to watch one young man work his way through a stunning sword form, his blade flashing gracefully.

"That's Iomhar," Eoghan said. "He's one of the best swordsmen at Ard Dhaimhin. He's about to take his oath of brotherhood."

They moved on to the next practice space. A dozen brothers watched as two men circled one another with wooden swords. They feinted and parried, each looking for an opening until one close miss dissolved into a flurry of strikes that ended with one man on the ground, the other's blade at his throat.

"Yield," the beaten man said. "Lucky move."

The winner withdrew his blade and hauled his opponent back to his feet. "If by lucky you mean skilled, then aye." It was evidently a long-running joke between friends. His gaze traveled to where Eoghan and Conor stood. "Eoghan! Want to give it a go?"

"Not today. I'm showing our new novice around."

The man laughed and turned his attention to Conor. "What about you? Aidan could use an opponent at his own skill level."

Aidan slugged his friend in the shoulder, and Eoghan said, "For that, Sean, I might take your challenge."

Aidan hooted with delight. "Now that's a match I'd pay to watch. What's wrong, Sean? Not so confident now?"

Conor glanced at Eoghan curiously. "What was that all about?"

"Nothing." Color rose in the older boy's face. "They're just joking. Ignore them."

Conor accepted the explanation, though he didn't believe it. The men treated Eoghan with respect, even though he was their junior. "Why aren't you training today?"

"My guide duties were in greater demand. Look ahead. There's the archery range."

Conor followed Eoghan to where a long line of men stood before dozens of straw targets. Bowstrings twanged, and arrows flew, most hitting their painted targets dead center. Was there anything those men couldn't do?

"You may start with archery," Eoghan said as the men nocked

another round of arrows. "Don't worry, you'll be onto sword and staff soon enough."

"If Master Liam hasn't already decided to make me into a farmer."

"Because you got assigned to Reamonn's work detail? Everyone has to take their turn in the fields. Besides, you're not a farmer. Even I can see that."

"Right. Maybe I can teach languages or history or something. I'm certainly no warrior."

Eoghan shook his head. "Don't be so sure. You've got the look."

"What look?"

"Like a dog with a bone. If you managed five hours with Reamonn on your first day and you're still moving, you're tougher than you think."

The boy's assessment relieved him. "I hope you're right. I'd like Fergus to see the Fírein made something out of me when my clan couldn't."

Eoghan studied him for a long moment, then turned away. "Be careful what you wish for, friend."

His dark tone made Conor's stomach lurch, but Eoghan moved on with the tour so quickly, he wondered if he'd imagined it. His guide led him to where yet another group of men practiced unarmed fighting in soft sand.

Conor watched with interest as two combatants grasped at each other's arms and attempted to throw each other off balance. One of the men kicked out, and his opponent captured his leg and drove him to the ground. After an intense struggle in the loose sand, one finally managed to snake an arm around the other's neck from behind. The pinned man turned an alarming shade of red and then made a quick gesture with his free hand. The other released him immediately, and they sprang to their feet once more.

"King Daimhin brought this style of fighting back from Hesperides," Eoghan said. "It's more effective than Seare's traditional wrestling."

"Undoubtedly." Conor couldn't imagine any of the kingdom's warriors relinquishing weapons in favor of unarmed combat, but surely there was value in knowing how to subdue an opponent empty-handed.

Another pair took the place of the first, and a second match began. Conor and Eoghan watched a bit longer before moving on. These men trained to a degree Conor had never imagined, far more than any of the king's guards. How did Eoghan think Conor could ever become one of them if he'd barely attempted the less rigorous training in the kingdoms?

"It's almost supper time," Eoghan said. "We should hurry."

They fell into a crowd of men with the same idea, all heading for the cookhouse. "How do they manage to feed so many?" Conor asked.

"Mealtimes are staggered," Eoghan explained. "They serve about five hundred at a time."

"I feel sorry for the cooks."

"Hope you never draw mess duty, then."

Conor grinned. "You should hope I don't, because I'd be a wretched cook."

When they arrived, a long line already snaked from the cookhouse, a large pavilion-like structure with a vented roof and canvas panels that could be drawn down against the weather. It housed four large fires topped with the biggest iron pots Conor had ever seen. Two brothers worked each cauldron, ladling stew into waiting bowls, while six more distributed chunks of crusty rye bread from a wooden crate the size of a wagon. Conor took his bowl and bread and followed Eoghan out to one of the dozens of tables and benches behind the cookhouse.

The soup was tasty, made from a peppery broth and filled with fish, turnips, and beans: plain fare in comparison to the king's table, but it was hot and filling.

"Not quite what you're used to?" Eoghan asked.

Were his thoughts that obvious? "I could eat this quite happily every day for years."

"You probably will. We pretty much live on beans and fish. Oh, and oats. Lots and lots of oats."

Conor chuckled. As they mopped up the last bit of soup with their bread, he noticed men heading toward a part of the city he had not yet explored. He nodded toward them in silent inquiry.

"Evening devotions," Eoghan said. "We should go, too. If we're late, we'll have to stand."

They returned their bowls to the cookhouse—Conor pitied the dishwashers even more than the cooks—and fell into the crowd. They traveled toward the tree line at the northeastern edge of the city and then down a steep path that opened into a massive granite amphitheater. Dozens of tiers ringed the bowl-shaped space, and about half of the seats were already filled. Only then did Conor begin to get a sense of how many men Ard Dhaimhin housed.

"Look, there's Brother Riordan."

Conor followed Eoghan's gaze. Riordan waved at them from one of the lowest tiers of the amphitheater.

Conor uneasily trailed Eoghan down the steps. The boy exchanged greetings with men every few steps. When they reached the bottom, Conor saw Riordan had saved a space big enough for the three of them. He took a seat between the two men.

"Evening, Eoghan," Riordan said with a nod. He turned to Conor and put a hand on his shoulder. "How was your first day?"

"Slaine got to him first and sent him to Reamonn," Eoghan said.

Riordan's eyes flicked to Conor's blistered hands. "How long'd you last?"

"All morning," Eoghan said. "Reamonn actually gave him the afternoon off."

Riordan nodded approvingly and thumped Conor's back. "Well done, son."

Master Liam appeared in the center of the amphitheater then, and the rumble of voices subsided. He called out, "Greetings to my faithful brothers."

"Greetings," the group replied in unison.

Liam lifted his hands, his eyes cast upward. Conor started as the entire gathering joined in the invocation. "Almighty Father, Maker of the Heavens and the Earth, Salvation of the Righteous, Punisher of the Wicked, Light of All Nations, and Lord of All . . ."

The Ceannaire continued alone, "May You shine Your blessings of faith, courage, and hope upon us. Let us be receptive to Your words and write Your commands upon our hearts. Blessings to Him who Is, Was, and Always Will Be. So may it be."

"So may it be," the group echoed.

Liam paused, his eyes searching the faces until his gaze met Conor's and just as swiftly moved on. "Welcome, friends, old and new. May Comdiu be with you."

"Comdiu be with you," the assembly said.

"Today I wish to tell you a story from the Second Canon of the Holy Writ, one our Lord Balus told to the Kebarans. A rich man was about to embark upon a long journey. He gave differing amounts of coin to his servants to oversee while he was gone. When the master returned, he called his servants to account for the money. The first servant had invested wisely by buying a vineyard and planting it, and he returned twice the money with which he had been entrusted. For this, the master praised him and made him the steward of all of his vineyards.

"The second servant hadn't as much money as the first, so he bought several young sheep. When those sheep multiplied, he sheared them and had the fleece woven into cloth, and sold it at the marketplace. He too returned twice the amount to his master. For his faithfulness, he was put in charge of all the master's flocks.

"The third servant was afraid to lose the money, so he buried it out of sight. When the master saw he had hidden the coin rather than using it, he was angry and threw the servant out into the night."

Conor listened in fascination. He had never heard the story before, though it reminded him of others he had learned in Balurnan's great hall. Around him, heads nodded in understanding.

"Comdiu has given us all gifts. Some men use them for their own glory. Some hide them for fear of being asked to venture beyond their experience. We will all be called to account on the Day of Judgment for what use we made of them. Those of us who used our gifts for Comdiu's kingdom will be welcomed into His presence. Those of us who squandered our opportunities in this life will have to answer for our foolishness.

"We do not choose our abilities or our circumstances. We choose only our actions. That is why Fíréin life is harsh and unyielding, filled with discipline, hard work, and study. Not so we may boast of our great strength, our courage, our knowledge, but so we may develop our gifts to their fullness and be ready for the day Comdiu calls us to His work."

Liam's eyes swept the amphitheater, and they once again landed on Conor. The directness of his gaze pierced him. Liam hadn't asked about Conor's gifts, but Eoghan implied he could read thoughts. Was this story meant for him?

No, that was ridiculous. There were at least three thousand men present. Still, Conor couldn't dismiss the sense the Ceannaire spoke directly to him.

The devotions lasted an hour, and despite Conor's attempt to focus on Liam's Scripture recitation, his mind kept wandering back to the parable. Perhaps he had read too much into it. After all, wasn't the Fíréin life based on hard work and using one's abilities to the fullest, regardless of what those were?

Conor felt guilty for his sense of inadequacy, his wish he could be something he wasn't. So what if the most important thing he did was hoe fields or haul nets? His sweat and toil would still contribute to Ard Dhaimhin.

The convocation closed with another prayer. Then the men dispersed into the dim twilight, scattering to the barracks or the bathhouses. Riordan lingered near the front and placed a hand on Conor's shoulder. "Stick with Eoghan when you can. He'll point you in the right direction."

"What about you?" The words spilled from Conor's mouth before he could consider how desperate they sounded.

Riordan's smile turned sympathetic. "We each have our own duties, Conor. I'll be here if you truly need me. But it's best you settle into your céad. Your loyalty lies there now."

Conor nodded, keeping his expression blank as Riordan climbed past him on the amphitheater's stairs. He had no right to feel disappointed. What else had he expected? Riordan might have been the man who fathered him, but he hadn't involved himself beyond whatever plans he and Labhrás had concocted.

He had been foolish to believe things would be different here.

CHAPTER SIXTEEN

Eoghan showed him the way back to their céad's barracks, and Conor's stomach clenched a little tighter with every step. Easy for Riordan to say his loyalty should lie with his céad. He already knew these boys. Or men, really. To these seventy strangers, Conor was just an outsider.

Smoke curled from the hole in the thatched roof when they arrived, light spilling from the open door along with the rumble of male voices. As Conor climbed down the steps into the cavernous space, the noise quieted.

Eoghan didn't seem to notice. "Lads, this is our new novice, Brother Conor."

Anyone who hadn't already been staring stopped what he was doing. Conor's skin prickled under the scrutiny. Was he supposed to say something?

Instead, he just gave a nod and turned to Eoghan. "Where do I sleep?"

"Choose an empty bunk."

The noise resumed around him as the men turned back to their tasks. Some swept the hard-packed floor, while others sketched or wrote with charcoal nubs on scraps of birch bark. They all looked strong, fit, and much older than Conor. A few gave him appraising glances as he passed, sizing him up and dismissing him just as quickly.

He didn't fit here any better than he had in Tigh.

He stopped at the first empty bed he found and sat on the edge of the mattress. The routine seemed to be winding down, his céad mates removing shoes and tunics and settling onto their bunks. He hesitated. It wasn't as if he could hide his thin scholar's body forever, but he wasn't sure he was ready to make a fool of himself.

Conor looked up when a pair of trousered legs came into view. The boy was about Conor's age, tall, muscular, with black hair and eyes nearly as dark.

"You're the prince."

Eoghan had said the same thing earlier, but this felt like an indictment.

Conor cleared his throat. "Not anymore, I suppose."

The boy looked him over, then his mouth tipped up in a sardonic smile. "Nice boots."

Conor looked down again, confused. Then he realized the Fíréin all wore soft, simply laced shoes. His fine, calf-high leather boots marked him as a nobleman as surely as if it had been branded on his forehead. He flushed.

"Tor, you coming? It's your turn."

Tor threw a glance at a younger boy a few bunks away, where he waited with a cross-shaped game board. King and Conqueror, Conor guessed. "Aye. I'll be right there." He turned back to Conor with a smirk. "Sleep well, princeling."

Conor frowned at the boy as he swaggered away. A few others chuckled as if they were in on the joke. He scanned the area for Eoghan, but his only friend had already been swallowed into the huge room.

Slaine strode into their midst, and the sound died instantly. He glanced around, his gaze settling on Conor just long enough to say he had noted his presence. "Lights out, lads."

Instantly, a half dozen men rose and snuffed out the rush lights, sending a waft of acrid smoke into the air even as they plunged the clochan into semidarkness. Only the small fire in the pit illuminated the rest of the céad as they settled down for the night.

Conor stripped down to his trousers, hung his tunic on the peg above his bed, and climbed beneath the scratchy wool blanket. Almost immediately, soft snores filled the room. He sighed. He would never be able to rest with the racket of seventy men snoring. Perhaps he should pray a bit first.

He only made it through the opening words before sleep took him.

✦ ✦ ✦

Sounding horns intruded on his dreams.

Conor burrowed deeper under his blankets, trying to escape the noise, until a rough but familiar voice growled, "Up now, boy!"

Conor gasped as the blanket was ripped away, the cold air hitting his bare skin, and jerked upright. He rubbed his gritty eyes and struggled to speak through his tight throat. Surely he couldn't have slept more than an hour or two. "What time is it?"

"Time to get up." Slaine grabbed Conor's tunic from the peg and tossed it at him. "Convocation, breakfast, then Reamonn. Quickly now."

Conor donned his tunic, his pulse pounding in his ears from the urgency in Slaine's orders. Most of his céad mates were already dressed, a few still combing and braiding their hair. Some headed up the steps into the gray morning.

He swung his feet over the side of the bed and thrust them into his boots.

His toes squelched into something cold and wet.

Snickers from across the room drew his attention. Tor and his game partner. Perfect. He should have anticipated something like this. No wonder the other lads had laughed at him.

He pulled his muddy feet out of his boots, marched to the cold fire pit, and emptied the lake from them. Wordlessly, he shoved his feet back in, trying not to grimace. The leather was ruined, and the sand would likely give him blisters, but he wouldn't give them the satisfaction of knowing their prank had hit its mark.

Conor lingered as long as he dared, letting the others go before him. Eoghan waited for him outside, an appraising look on his face. His eyes dipped to Conor's boots, and a smile twitched at the corners of his mouth.

"So I'm to be the new target," Conor said as they moved toward the amphitheater. "For how long?"

"Tor and Ailbhe like to test the new boys. They'll keep pressing until you put a stop to it."

"And how do I do that?"

"Beat them. At archery. At staff practice. While they sleep."

Conor chuckled at his friend's wicked grin. Then he remembered the game Tor and Ailbhe had been playing the night before. "King and Conqueror?"

Eoghan's grin widened, and he thumped Conor on the back hard enough to knock the breath out of him. "That'll do, princeling. For a start."

✦ ✦ ✦

Conor quickly fell into an unvarying routine of labor and worship: up at dawn, morning devotions in the amphitheater followed by a quick breakfast, then off to his morning work. Sometimes he tilled or planted. Other days, he hauled nets on Loch Ceo, carried water from the lake, or performed any number of other duties that left him aching and exhausted. Still, he never complained, and he never stopped, turning his mind to Aine or a harp composition he would never play. His stoicism garnered curious looks but never praise: after all, he was just doing what was expected of a Fíréin brother.

Afternoons passed with easier but no less tedious pursuits: braiding wicks for the chandlers, gutting fish in the cookhouse, or washing dishes in one of the many troughs for which he had carried water. In the evenings, he whittled small chunks of wood into the approximation of game pieces for King and Conqueror, working as quickly as he could manage to put together his own game board. So far, he'd woken up to find a frog, a centipede, and some unpleasantness from the goat pens in his boots.

"You'd better do something quick," Eoghan observed one morning. "Your footwear won't endure much more ill treatment."

Conor grinned. "This is my last piece. And it's time for a little retaliation."

He didn't have time to propose a game of King and Conqueror to Tor and Ailbhe that night. They were far too busy trying to locate the smell coming from where he'd smeared the goat dung on the undersides of their mattresses. The rest of the céad roared with laughter while they tore apart their spaces looking for the source.

And in one instant, Conor's status in the céad shifted.

Tor wasn't first to approach him for a game, though. That honor went to Larkin, one of the older of the men, soon to take his oath of brotherhood. He settled onto the bed while Conor briefly explained the rules, then asked half a dozen simplistic questions before proceeding to eliminate Conor's army in thirty-six moves.

"Never underestimate your opponent," Larkin said. "Even if he gives you reason to do so." He glanced back to where Tor watched them and gave Conor a significant nod.

The warning made him nervous, but the retaliation Conor expected didn't come.

That was the reason behind the backbreaking routine, he realized. The veneer of peace over Ard Dhaimhin was something of an illusion. Conflict and resentment still simmered beneath the surface. Most of the time, though, the men were too exhausted to do anything more than trade pranks or snide comments. Still, Conor held his breath, waiting for Tor's dislike to erupt into something more.

The first time Conor saw a man whipped bloody in front of the entire assembly for striking a brother in anger, he understood why it never would.

Physical labor and discipline might have been the life's blood of Ard Dhaimhin, but he soon learned daily devotions were its beating heart. The Fíréin required all members to attend evening convocation, but most of the oath-bound brothers attended the morning gathering as well. Sometimes Master Liam led the service, but other members of the Conclave, including Riordan, also took their turns. It was an awe-inspiring sight, all those men, all believers, gathered in one place to study the word of Comdiu. Every time they raised their voices in unison for the invocation, it sent chills across Conor's skin.

"It's something you never get used to," Riordan said. "I had to hide my faith for so long, it still seems incredible to worship openly."

Conor studied his father's profile. The convocation was the one time of day he saw him alone. They rarely spoke, but Riordan seemed to be content to just sit quietly together. "Is that why you stayed all these years?"

"I stayed because it was the one place I knew you'd always be able to find me."

Conor turned back to the rapidly emptying amphitheater. "I'm glad."

And surprisingly, he meant it.

CHAPTER SEVENTEEN

Mistress Bearrach gave Aine three days to mourn Conor before she demanded she return to her lessons in the clochan. Aine obeyed. She needed a distraction. Even though Conor was not actually dead, she still felt his loss with each breath. The knowledge he was safe and beyond the druid's reach was her only comfort.

She threw herself into her lessons at Lisdara, and Mistress Bearrach gradually gave her more responsibility for healing the sick and injured that flowed through the keep's gates. Focused on doing what little she could to contribute to her adopted homeland, she was surprised to learn she was no longer referred to as the king's Aronan sister, but "the lady healer of Lisdara."

"There hasn't been a noble healer here for centuries," Ruarc said. Never mind her clan was Tamhais, not Cuillinn. Calhoun's patronage and shared bloodline was enough for the people.

The Cáisc celebration approached with startling speed amidst Aine's duties, and the castle's servants built greenery-draped archways and wheels in the courtyard under Leannan's watchful eye. Far below the mount, pavilions and platforms sprang up to house the musicians, performers, and food stands that would entertain the masses. Cáisc marked the resurrection of Comdiu's son, Balus, after His brutal death at the hands of Ciraean authorities, and Calhoun spared no expense. It was a time to celebrate the many blessings Comdiu had bestowed upon Faolán.

Despite her sadness, Aine found herself caught up in the merry spirit. Aron celebrated far more solemnly: several days of fasting, followed by a somber feast and homily. *It's a weighty observance for a weighty occasion,*

Lady Ailís had always said. Now Aine realized the words had been at least partly tongue-in-cheek.

The lords and their families streamed into Lisdara, trailing carts of tribute to the king and retinues of servants and nursemaids. Niamh hosted the wives and grown daughters with music and embroidery and genteel female company, while Aine took charge of the children. The younger ones relished the opportunity to explore Lisdara's grounds and surrounding lands, and Aine paired picnics with scavenger hunts for healing herbs. Perhaps she might spark an interest in one of these girls. It would benefit the other clans to have skilled healers at their disposal.

"Putting them to work, I see," Gainor said with amusement.

"Look at their faces." Aine was teaching the girls how to braid lavender into swags to dry, and they attacked the task with enthusiasm. "This may be the first time they've had the opportunity to do something useful."

"Their mothers will be pleased to hear you don't think perfecting their embroidery is useful."

Aine wrinkled her nose and shooed him off to his manly duties.

On the day of the Cáisc feast, musicians, mummers, and jugglers roamed Lisdara and its environs. Servants provided a steady supply of delicacies from the kitchens, and wine, ale, and mead flowed freely, though on this day the men seemed more conscious than usual of their consumption. Aine escorted crowds of excited children around the various games set up in the meadow below. She joined them in tossing painted rings onto stakes and found herself laughing just as merrily as her charges.

At sundown, the celebration moved indoors. Once the children had been tucked safely into their beds, the adults settled into their seats with honeyed mead and cakes while Meallachán brought out his harp. Aine's heart beat faster as the bard tuned the instrument. Conor had been the last to play in the hall. She pretended not to notice the sympathetic glance Gainor sent her way.

Before Meallachán could sound the first note, the doors to the hall burst open, and the captain of Calhoun's guard strode in, his expression grim. The warrior knelt at the king's side and murmured something in his ear. Aine watched Calhoun's expression shift, and her heart plummeted.

Calhoun stood. "My lords and ladies, I'm afraid I need a word with the council."

Aine and Niamh exchanged an alarmed glance, but they rose with the wives, daughters, and minor lords who would not be privy to the discussion. Speculation rustled through the hall as it slowly drained of all but Calhoun's council members. The two girls reluctantly retreated to their chamber, but not before Aine caught a glimpse of a nervous-looking, travel-stained man.

"Do you think this has something to do with Conor?" Niamh asked when they reached their chamber, worry cracking her usual shell of disdain.

"He didn't look like an official messenger." Still, Aine hadn't liked the look on Calhoun's face.

The king summoned Aine and Niamh to his chamber early the next morning. Gainor sat with him, but their breakfast spread was conspicuously absent.

"What I'm about to tell you must not leave this room," Calhoun said. "We have learned that on Cáisc morning, King Fergus ordered the execution of over one hundred Balian villagers and their families, presumably for conspiring with Labhrás Ó Maonagh against the crown. He has made it clear he will enforce the ban on the Balian faith by any means necessary."

The blood drained from Aine's face. "Blessed Father," she whispered. Conor had been right in fearing for his life should he return to Glenmallaig.

Calhoun looked between the girls. Weariness had deepened the lines of his face, making him look far older than his years. "Our alliance puts us in a difficult position. We will attempt to address this matter with diplomacy. Should that fail . . ." He shook his head. "I cannot countenance the murder of Balian brethren."

"You would go to war over this?" Aine asked.

Calhoun looked at Gainor. "I cannot discount the new king may not react favorably to our meddling in what he considers internal matters. Until this is resolved, I want you girls to go to Dún Eavan."

"The fortress?" Aine knew only that Dún Eavan was one of several Faolanaigh strongholds.

"I want you safe before we dispatch our messengers," Calhoun said. "That gives you the rest of the day to prepare. In the meantime, I must remind you to say nothing. And prepare for a long stay."

Aine and Niamh took their leave, too stunned to speak, and walked back to their chamber. Aine drew Ruarc aside in the hallway. "Are we going to war?"

"I don't know. We should consider returning to Aron, though. There's no reason to put yourself in danger."

There was nothing for her in Aron. Still, she nodded. "I'll consider it."

Inside, Niamh paced the chamber, chewing on her thumbnail. "Calhoun promised me I would never have to go back to Dún Eavan. It's cursed."

"Cursed? How exactly?"

Niamh shuddered and refused to elaborate.

"We'll bring lots of things to do. You play the cruit passably well. Perhaps you can teach me." She stopped when she realized Niamh wasn't listening. Her sister could be dramatic, but the fact Niamh had abandoned her hostility so abruptly spoke of a bigger threat. Aine lifted up a silent, wordless prayer and tried not to acknowledge the chill that had crept into her heart.

+   +   +

While Niamh packed her necessities—embroidery, game pieces, and an extensive wardrobe—Mistress Bearrach helped Aine fill a trunk with herbs, tinctures, and salves. They would be traveling with a company of fifty men, half of whom would stay behind at the fortress. They would likely need the remedies at some point, especially if they stayed for an extended period.

Even knowing they'd be traveling with a large party did not prepare Aine for the gathering that met them the next morning. The majority were clansmen of Cuillinn and its septs, professional fighters the chiefs employed for such occasions. Calhoun must truly fear for their safety if he'd arranged this kind of escort.

Niamh looked pale when she arrived in the courtyard, dark shadows smudging the skin beneath her eyes. She had just climbed into the carriage when the curtains slid back.

"I don't suppose there's room for one more?" Meallachán asked.

Aine's heart lifted. She gestured to the enormous leather case on Meallachán's back. "For you or your harp?"

The bard smiled. "My harp and I are never separated. I'll just have to ride then."

"I'm surprised Calhoun was willing to give you up."

"I'm free to go where I please. It simply pleased me to stay at Lisdara for the last ten years. Trust me, Dún Eavan is gloomy enough with music. You don't want to experience it without."

"You've been there?"

Meallachán's expression sobered. "Aye. And if you had, you'd realize the king would not send you there without good cause."

Aine wanted to ask more about the fortress, but Niamh looked on the verge of hysterics. She would have plenty of time to question him once they arrived, though. Meallachán wouldn't be coming if it were to be a mere fortnight's stay.

A stable hand brought the bard's horse around, and Aine noted he elected to carry the heavy instrument rather than entrust it to the servants. Not that there was any room in the carts. Niamh had packed three trunks for every one of Aine's.

Shouts rose outside, and immediately, the carriage lurched forward amidst a symphony of squeaks and rattles. No one spoke, only the creak of wood and the thud of horses' hooves breaking the stillness. Niamh fidgeted in her seat. Then she rose and settled beside Aine. Silently, she twined their fingers together. Aine shoved down her shock and squeezed Niamh's hand.

When they had been on the road for some time, the curtain on Niamh's side of the carriage drew back to reveal a homely, pock-marked man on horseback. "How are you ladies faring?"

"We're fine, Donnan, thank you," Niamh said.

He nodded and let the curtain fall.

"Donnan?" Aine inquired innocently.

"My guard. Calhoun assigned him."

Aine struggled to keep the smile from her face. "He seems pleasant."

"Well, Calhoun apparently felt it was inequitable for one sister to have a guard and not the other."

"You had a guard before, I understand."

"Who told you? Gainor?"

A grin surfaced on Aine's lips. "What was his name? Brogan? I hear you could have gotten him hanged the way you were carrying on after him."

"I was twelve!" Niamh protested, coloring. "They should have known better than to assign me a young, handsome guard!"

"Well, it seems Calhoun has learned from his mistakes."

Niamh tried to look annoyed, but a smile stretched her face, and they dissolved into helpless giggles. The anxiety lifted from Aine's chest. Perhaps some good might come from the situation if it began to repair her relationship with her sister.

They stopped briefly for refreshments under strict watch at midday, then were hurried back into the carriage. Just as the sun began to sink into the horizon, they rattled to a stop. The door on Aine's side sprang open, and Donnan helped Aine, then Niamh, to the ground. "Ladies, welcome to Dún Eavan."

Aine stared, dumbstruck by her first glimpse of Loch Eirich, an expanse of water so large she could barely see the far shores. The setting sun shone beneath the canopy of clouds, reflecting brilliant shades of red, orange, and amber onto the lake's glimmering surface. In the center, the crannog and its fortress sprang from the water, its silhouette craggy and uneven against the backdrop of sky. Aine felt a stir of recognition, an acknowledgment of something ancient.

"Calhoun promised I would never have to come back here," Niamh whispered tremulously.

"It'll be all right," Aine murmured. "You'll see."

"Ladies." Ruarc ushered them to a waiting bark boat attached to a thick rope that stretched between the shore and the crannog. Aine, Niamh, and Meallachán were selected to cross first with the girls' guards. A man on the shore cranked the wheel that drove the pulley, and the boat lurched free of the sandy bank.

"The staff is expecting us," Ruarc said as the boat glided across the lake. "The king sent a rider ahead this morning."

"Does he keep staff permanently on the island?" Aine asked.

"A few. Anytime the clan comes for any length, they bring their own servants. Right now, it's just the cook, the housekeeper, and Dún Eavan's steward."

Niamh trembled. Aine grasped her sister's hand and squeezed it reassuringly, despite her own twinge of apprehension.

As the boat drew near the crannog, Aine could make out the details of the fortress, an uneven oval constructed from a haphazard jumble of stone, earth, and timber with arrow slits for windows. Smoke drifted from an outbuilding, which Aine guessed to be the kitchen.

An aging man with curling gray hair met them at the dock and gave a low bow as Ruarc and Donnan helped the girls from the boat. "My ladies, good master, welcome to Dún Eavan. I'm Tarlach, the steward here. Your rooms have been prepared, if you'll follow me."

Niamh frowned, but Aine smiled back and followed the man up the gravel path toward the entrance.

Torches lit the small hall, their sharp smell mingling with the dusty scent of the unfinished earthen floors. The room was set for a gathering with several long trestle tables and benches. Aine mistook the throne for a simple chair until she saw its worn, ancient carvings.

A plump woman Tarlach's age bustled forward to meet them. "My ladies, good master. I'm Eimer, the housekeeper. If there's anything you need, just let me know."

Niamh opened her mouth, but Aine poked her sharply in the ribs before she could put words to her sour thoughts. Eimer continued, "Master Meallachán, we have a small, private room prepared for you. My ladies, Tarlach will show you to your chamber."

The steward led the girls to one of three doorways off the hall, which Aine had assumed to be corridors. Instead, they found themselves in a tiny, windowless room no more than two spans across. Two narrow bedsteads covered with faded wool blankets took up most of the space, and a small stool held an ewer of water between them.

"Why don't you rest a while? Eimer will wake you for supper." Tarlach bowed his way out of the room and shut the door firmly behind him.

"Didn't I tell you?" Niamh moaned the second they were alone. "It's awful."

"It's rustic," Aine admitted. "At least we have a candle, not a torch. And we're certainly safe here in the middle of the lake."

"That depends on what you consider safe." Niamh flopped down on the rush mattress and plumped the pillow under her head. Stray feathers floated from the case, caught by the breeze from the arrow slit. "I'm going to take a nap. It's better than staring at these walls."

Aine stretched out on her own bed, though she didn't feel sleepy. Their belongings hadn't arrived from the shore, so she didn't even have her books to distract her. Instead, she stared at the timber roof and wondered why Dún Eavan so unsettled her sister.

A knock startled Aine from her doze. Niamh groaned and buried her face in the pillow. "Go away."

Aine rubbed her eyes. "Niamh, it's supper time."

The girl pushed herself up with a groan. "I was hoping this place was just a nightmare."

Without the fading light through windows to mark the passage of time, Aine felt as if she had slept a year. She straightened her clothing, though Niamh assured her there was no need to make an effort here. Who was there to take notice?

Out in the hall, guardsmen packed into the long trestles while Eimer set out platters of bread and bowls of stew every few feet down the board. Aine and Niamh halted, taken aback. They had never dined with so many men before.

"Ladies." Donnan appeared at their side and led them to a section of the table that had been sequestered by Ruarc and Meallachán. Gratefully, they followed him to their seats just as Eimer placed wooden trenchers before them.

Aine stole a look around the room. Compared to Aron, Seare already seemed primitive. Isolated on the crannog amidst dozens of warriors, she felt as if she was in another world entirely. No wonder Niamh hated it.

She had hoped Meallachán might play, but he too seemed affected by the fortress's gloomy atmosphere, and he returned to his chamber after the meal. When she and Niamh escaped to their own space, they found their chests had been delivered, along with a straw pallet on their floor for Oonagh. Niamh undressed for bed wordlessly and climbed beneath the covers.

"Niamh?" Aine whispered. "It will be fine. I'm sure of it."

Niamh turned over and pulled the blanket higher so only the top of her head showed on the pillow. Aine sighed. Then she blew out the candle and climbed into her own bed.

She awoke later, disoriented, her heart thrumming. The still, dark chamber gave no clue to what had awakened her.

Then she heard a low, keening wail: faint at first and then growing louder, as if it approached the fortress. Gooseflesh prickled her arms and neck.

"Niamh," she whispered. "Are you awake?"

Niamh's voice came back, shaky and thin. "I'm awake."

"What is that?"

Straw rustled on the floor. Oonagh whispered, "It's the bean-sidhe, my lady."

A cousin of the fey folk, the bean-sidhe supposedly appeared when someone was about to die. But those were just superstitions, weren't they? "It's probably the wind or an owl."

"Owls don't nest on the crannog," Niamh said as another wail pierced the silence.

"In the trees on the shore then." A kernel of cold formed in Aine's middle. This place was ancient, predating the Great Kingdom and the coming of Balianism to the island. It was not as innocuous as she had first supposed.

Automatically, Aine began to murmur an old blessing. "Comdiu protect us. Comdiu watch over us. Comdiu be at the left and the right and smooth the way before us. Comdiu stand between us and the harm of this world, and banish the darkness with the light of Your Son, Balus."

As she began again, the faint sounds of a harp took up the refrain, a soft melody that seemed meant to accompany the words, even though Meallachán couldn't possibly hear her from across the fortress. Niamh and Oonagh joined the prayer in hushed voices, repeating the words with quiet fervency. When their words faded along with the sound of the harp, they heard only silence. A weight lifted from Aine's chest.

Sleep did not return easily, though. Something greater and more sinister dwelled here, like the evil in the forest outside Lisdara, but this place did not have the keep's old, strong wards to hold it back.

Bed coverings rustled, and Aine lifted her blanket to admit Niamh into the cocoon of warmth. Lying nose to nose, her sister said, "That wasn't the wind or an owl, was it?"

Aine searched for answers that would not frighten Niamh more, but they were all lies. "No, I don't think it was."

"Comdiu protect us," Niamh murmured with a shiver.

Aine linked arms with her sister. He already had.

CHAPTER EIGHTEEN

"I wish something would happen one way or another. This waiting is unbearable!"

Aine didn't look up at Niamh, absorbed in the tonic she was mixing in the decrepit shed she had commandeered as her work space. According to the messengers that came and went in the small boats, Fergus had neither responded to the king's diplomatic overtures nor taken further action against the Balians in Tigh. Aine dared hope Calhoun's sternly worded missive had given his Timhaigh counterpart pause, but her instincts said that was just wishful thinking.

"I know," Aine answered finally. "I'd like to believe the threat of losing the alliance was enough. Maybe we'll be able to go home soon."

"I hope so." Niamh made a frustrated sound and bent her head over her sewing again. She rarely left Aine's side, even though she never seemed particularly interested in doing more than complaining. Apparently, Aine's company was a slight step up from being alone.

Three more times the bean-sidhe had returned, the wails louder and more threatening, and each time they had banished it with prayer and music. Since then, Meallachán had taken to playing his harp each night after supper. Aine wondered if she was the only one who sensed the protective cocoon created by the melody. It only strengthened her conviction about the magic she felt so strongly entwined in both Meallachán's and Conor's playing, but the bard rebuffed her attempts to discuss the matter.

Tarlach and Eimer had proved more helpful. They told her the bean-sidhe appeared only when a member of the clan arrived, as if it were drawn to Calhoun and his family. Aine didn't want to believe its influence was being felt, but the guards had suffered a string of bad luck since arriving. Chunks of rock fell from the top of the crumbling fortress walls and struck several men, and two had nearly drowned in the shallows of the lake. None of the incidents challenged Aine's healing, but at times she thought she sensed a residue of magic.

The mood at the fortress grew considerably more somber after darkness fell, and Meallachán's playing dispelled their anxiety for only so long. No one had objected when Aine had begun reading aloud from a partial copy of the Second Canon each night. The bard had watched her closely, but he hadn't commented.

"Maybe if Calhoun knew what was happening here, he'd let us come back to Lisdara," Niamh said, oblivious to the direction of Aine's musings.

Aine decanted her mixture into a small glass bottle and corked it snugly. "I'm sure he knows. They send messages twice a day."

Niamh shook her head. "They've said nothing. Captain Ó Hearn is afraid Calhoun will dismiss him. You know how our brother is when it comes to the supernatural."

"Who told you that?"

"Donnan." Niamh made a face when Aine grinned. "Fine, I'll admit it. He's pleasant, and he answers my questions, unlike all the others."

"What does he say about all this?"

Niamh pulled a string around her neck and dangled a wheel charm from her fingers. "He carved me this. I know it doesn't have any real power, but it makes me feel better."

Aine couldn't blame her, not while she wore Conor's pendant around her own neck. Her charm might contain some protective magic, but so far, it had done nothing but serve as a comforting reminder of Conor.

"I have to give this to one of the guards," Aine said, holding up the vial. "He's nearly recovered, and the captain wants him back to work."

Immediately, Niamh shoved her sewing into her basket and stood. "I'll go with you."

"Why? I'll be just a minute. I'll come right back."

"I don't want to be alone here," Niamh said. "Besides, you're the one that banished the bean-sidhe. It hasn't returned since the first night you read from the Canon. Everyone's saying so."

"That's ridiculous. It could have just as easily been Meallachán's playing."

"It hasn't come back since you began the readings."

"Come if you'd like, but enough of this nonsense about me. I haven't done anything."

Aine left the shack and crossed the earthen courtyard with Niamh at her heels. *Lord, I don't want their admiration. I don't deserve their reverence. What do I do?*

That afternoon, she joined Meallachán as he walked around the crannog. He said nothing, though he slowed his pace to accommodate her shorter stride. After a few minutes of companionable silence, he asked gently, "What's on your mind, my lady?"

Aine searched for an explanation that didn't sound embarrassingly arrogant. "The men's regard disturbs me," she said finally.

"They are reassured by your presence, my lady. They see the hand of Comdiu upon you."

"But I didn't do anything! We both know your playing is responsible for holding back the bean-sidhe."

"I know you did nothing to purposely draw their admiration. But the coming of Balus aside, Seareanns are very superstitious people, and you're their 'lady healer of Lisdara.' Is it so bad to be an example of what Comdiu can do through a willing servant?"

So much of what Meallachán said sounded right. That alone worried her. "If they look to me and not to Comdiu, then aye, it's a bad thing."

Meallachán did not reply, though he clearly disagreed. She nodded her thanks and returned to the shed, though she was too preoccupied to do more than straighten up her work space. *Lord, please show me how to act. There is so much evil in this place, and I want to be a bridge, not a barrier. They should look to You, not me.*

Aine dozed for hours that night, too unsettled to sleep soundly, until a light knock snapped her back to wakefulness.

"Aine," came a whisper. "Aine, wake up. You're needed outside."

"Ruarc?" She caught the note of urgency in his voice and squinted into the darkness. Niamh and Oonagh still slept. She thrust her feet into her shoes and quietly took her heavy cloak from its peg on the wall. The maid stirred at the creak of the door, but no one awoke.

Outside in the hall, torches guttered in their brackets, casting flickering light on the sleeping guards. The front door stood open a crack. Ruarc must have gone back outside. Was someone hurt? She crept out of the hall and into the misty night.

The yard lay still and empty, with no sign of Ruarc or the perimeter guards. Should she go back inside or should she wait?

Her breath puffed in the chilly air, and a sense of wrongness tickled her senses. Then the fog cleared, revealing the dark, prone shape of a man on the edge of the shore. She pulled her cloak around herself and hurried toward him.

"Ruarc?" Aine's heart leapt into her throat, and she fell to her knees beside him to check for life signs.

A rustle behind her alerted her to the presence of another. She assumed her calmest, most competent voice as she turned. "Get help, and bring back a light . . ."

Her voice trailed away. The ghostly shape of a woman hovered behind her, piercing black eyes staring from a skeletal face.

Aine froze, her throat almost too tight to speak. "What do you want from me?"

Malevolence poured from the specter, sending a thrill of terror through her. Aine scrambled to her feet and stumbled over Ruarc's body. Before she could regain her balance, the bean-sidhe flew at her with a horrifying screech. Aine pitched backward and tumbled down the bank into the water.

The lake seized her, her heavy cloak driving her into its murky depths. Frantically, she struggled toward the surface as her lungs screamed for air. *Don't breathe!* But the need for air overwhelmed every rational thought. Water rushed into her lungs like the touch of cold fire, searing her, crushing her from the inside.

Then, after a lifetime of agony, it no longer hurt so much. The creeping numbness was taking over, dimming her fear.

It's not so bad to die, she thought hazily.

She stretched out and succumbed to the cold embrace of Loch Eirich.

CHAPTER NINETEEN

Conor struggled in the dark, gasping for air. The cold lake water enveloped him, stealing into his lungs, draining the life from his body. He sat up in bed and clutched his burning chest, blinking away disorientation.

A few of his céad mates stirred. From the bunk beside him, Merritt lifted his head long enough to scowl at him. "Shut it, will you? I just got to sleep." He rolled to his other side and dragged his blanket over his head.

Conor clutched his pounding skull while he caught his breath. It had to have been a dream. But no, it was too vivid to be a dream. This had the startling clarity of a vision. He leapt to his feet and fled up the steps into the cool, dark night.

Footsteps followed him. "Conor, what's wrong?"

He turned. Eoghan stood in the doorway, half-dressed, his expression alarmed.

"Aine's dying." Conor's voice broke, and he gathered his thoughts with difficulty. "I have to go to her. I have to help—"

Eoghan gripped both his arms. "Tell me what happened."

Conor poured out the details of the vision, his voice shaking nearly as badly as his hands. "I have to go. If there's a chance—"

"You can't. You're a novice. You're not allowed to leave."

Conor stopped. Eoghan's statement quelled the impulse like water on a fire. "What do I do then?"

Eoghan lifted a shoulder helplessly. "Pray."

So Conor prayed while Eoghan held silent vigil. He paced a restless path around the clochan for hours until he finally collapsed helplessly against the exterior wall. When the horns woke the rest of the village, Conor blearily opened his eyes.

"You love this girl," Eoghan said softly.

Conor had never admitted it aloud—he had barely admitted it to himself—but now he said, "With everything in me. If she's gone, I have to know."

There was only one person who might be able to tell him if she was alive or dead.

Conor didn't bother to straighten his clothes or comb his hair before he started up Carraigmór's slick steps. Heedless of the danger, he took them two at a time and arrived panting and sweating at the top.

"I have to see Master Liam," he told the guard, bracing his palms on his knees while he caught his breath.

The brother looked him over doubtfully, but he allowed him inside. Another brother appeared and promised to deliver his request of an audience to the Ceannaire. Conor paced the polished stone floor for the better part of an hour before the man returned. "Master Liam will see you now. Come with me."

Conor followed him from the hall and up a flight of steep stairs that ended at a single door. The brother knocked lightly and pushed the door open. "Go ahead. He's expecting you."

Conor stepped into the tiny chamber, his heart thumping again. Stacks of books cluttered tables and the shelf-lined walls, and Master Liam sat at a large desk in the center of the room.

"Brother Conor, come in. You have a matter of urgency?"

Conor hadn't given much thought to what he would say to the Ceannaire. "I'm sorry to disturb you, sir—"

"What's on your mind?"

"Your sister, Aine." He struggled to keep his voice even. "I'm afraid she's in danger. It may already be too late—"

"Slow down. How do you know Aine's in danger?"

"I dreamed it."

Liam's eyebrows arched. "Does this happen often?"

"Never. At least not this type of dream. But I felt her drown. I'm certain of it."

Liam tented his fingers against his lips. "You have a connection with her, then."

Conor flushed and looked at the floor. It seemed presumptuous to say he loved her, that they were in love. He wouldn't have even come here had he not thought Liam might be able to do something about it.

"You may be correct."

Conor jerked his head up. "You saw it, too?"

"I'm afraid so. I don't know why you were shown that. It seems cruel. But she's in Comdiu's hands now."

Conor stared in horror. The feeling left his body, and the room spun around him. "She's dead?"

"I'm sorry, son. You must let her go. You knew you had to renounce your ties to the kingdoms, and this is perhaps the hardest link to sever. It is not easy to see Comdiu's plan in the midst of our own tragedies."

Conor barely heard Liam's words. Aine was dead. He turned and walked numbly through the door without waiting to be dismissed. The tight band around his chest squeezed the air from his lungs as surely as the water had smothered the last spark of life in Aine's body. Brothers watched him with concern as he made his way back through the fortress, but he scarcely noticed. It didn't matter. None of it mattered now.

How he managed to climb down the staircase on his numb legs, he would never know. His foot slipped once or twice, and only instinct kept him upright.

"I should have been there. I shouldn't have left."

He had only wanted to protect her, and instead she had died alone and afraid.

"Conor?"

Conor looked up at Eoghan and realized he was standing knee-deep in the lake. "She's dead."

His friend led him out of the water and back to the empty barracks. Conor barely noticed his own movements or Eoghan's reassuring words.

"I should have told her. She didn't know I loved her."

"She knew," Eoghan said. "She must have."

"I played her the song, but I didn't tell her."

Eoghan knelt to pull off Conor's boots and helped him lie back on the lumpy pallet. "Rest now. It will get easier."

"It will never be easier." Conor closed his eyes, too engulfed in grief to even weep.

When he awoke later in his own bed, he thought he must have dreamed the whole scenario, from his vision of Aine's death to Liam's sorrowful pronouncement. The puddle of water on the floor beneath his wet boots told him otherwise.

He caught his breath at the renewed rush of pain. Kind, gentle Aine. He had known her only a few short months: too short, some would say, to fall in love. After all, he was merely seventeen.

Still, he knew it to be true. Her death brought the same wrenching sense of loss he had felt when he learned of Lord Labhrás's execution, only worse. Lord Labhrás died a martyr for his beliefs. Someday his death would be avenged. But Aine? Her passing was a senseless waste, a brilliant flame extinguished too soon.

A shaft of light arced across the dim room, outlining a man's figure as he walked down the stairs. Eoghan.

"What are you doing here?" Conor mumbled.

"I brought you supper. I thought you might be hungry."

Conor turned away from the bowl of stew in Eoghan's hand. "I'm not."

Eoghan sat down on the bed adjacent to Conor's and set the bowl aside. "Do you want to talk?"

"There's nothing to talk about. She's gone." Conor lay back down on the mattress. He squeezed his eyes tightly closed and remained that way, even when his laughing céad mates returned to the barracks. Eoghan must have issued a warning, because they left him to his misery.

✦　✦　✦

The next morning, Slaine quietly but firmly directed Conor to get dressed and go to breakfast. He obeyed. He had no choice, really, nor the will to resist. What was the point? He could be just as miserable doing his duty to the Fíréin as he could lying in his bed.

He skipped morning devotions, unable to bear another sermon on finding Comdiu's will, and reported to the fields instead. Brother Reamonn had not yet arrived, so he chose a hoe from the cart and began cultivating where he left off the day before. The impact of the blade shuddered through his body, jarring his teeth and driving the breath from his lungs. He attacked the soil over and over, until something broke free inside and he collapsed weeping in the dirt.

"Why?" he sobbed aloud to Comdiu. "Why did You let them die? First

Labhrás and then Aine. They were Yours. They loved You. They loved *me*. And You took them from me!"

A hand touched his shoulder, the first indication he was no longer alone in the field, but he shook it off. He wiped his eyes with the back of his sleeve, gulped back his sobs, and rose to his feet. He lifted the hoe and returned to his task, ignoring the concerned expressions of the brothers working nearby. With every stroke, he forced his grief back down a little more.

It's not easy to see Comdiu's plan in the midst of our own tragedies, Master Liam had said. Comdiu's grand plan. Conor choked back a bitter laugh. He had never thought of their God as cruel, but why else would He show him Aine's death when he could do nothing about it? How could Liam possibly think he could ignore this tragedy and move on with his life as if nothing had happened?

Conor threw down the hoe and walked from the field, shoulders slumped. He no longer cared what his brothers would say, or for that matter, what Master Liam would say. What could they do to him that would be more painful than this?

Twilight fell before Eoghan found him on the bank of the lake, his chin propped on his bent knees. The older boy sat down a few spans away.

"I haven't thanked you," Conor said.

"I wish anything I did would make a difference."

Conor stared out at the water. "Have you ever been in love?"

"I've been here my whole life. I've never even met a woman, at least that I can remember."

"All my life, I felt that I wasn't good enough. No matter how hard I worked, I could never live up to anyone's expectations. And then I met Aine." Conor blinked away tears. "She made me feel as if who I was mattered more than what I could do. I think she actually loved me."

"Why did you leave then?" Eoghan asked.

"Because I suspected Lord Fergus, my uncle, wanted me dead, and I was afraid she'd be in danger if I stayed. Besides, I thought Riordan had answers for me."

"What kind of answers?"

"Not the ones I got." Conor picked up a stone and flung it into the lake. "Galbraith was not my father. Riordan is."

Eoghan stared, stunned. "I don't understand."

"It hardly matters now. There's nothing left for me in the kingdoms. Everyone I loved is dead."

Eoghan nodded. Conor was grateful for his restraint. Right now, he didn't want reassurances or platitudes.

"I know a little something about having limited choices," Eoghan said. "You know I was abandoned. I was two, three years old. This is the only home I've ever known."

"Would you leave Ard Dhaimhin if you had a choice?"

Eoghan's expression closed, and he pushed himself off the ground. "I don't have a choice. So I guess we're in the same boat." He extended his hand to Conor and hoisted him to his feet. "Come on. Let's go get something to eat."

Conor followed Eoghan away from the lake. He wasn't hungry, but he owed him at least that much for befriending him when he offered so little in return.

CHAPTER TWENTY

Brilliant light enveloped Aine, suffusing her body with well-being and warming her straight to her soul. She peered into the light, trying to reconcile this warm, bright place with the cold touch of water, but the lake was gone. Somehow, she knew she was only consciousness here, but the light filled her with such an inexpressible sense of joy and peace she wanted to weep.

There was another in this place, and she knew Him instantly. She yearned to throw herself at His feet, but she couldn't make out a body, only a presence so strong and joyous it overwhelmed nearly every conscious thought.

One bubbled to the surface. "Am I dead?"

The light receded somewhat, and she made out a man's shape. "In a manner of speaking," came the voice in her head, rich and melodious.

"Lord Balus! Please, I want to see Your face!"

She had the impression of a smile, though she could see no features through the light. He answered, "Your mortal mind could not behold My true brilliance."

"But I thought I was dead."

"It is not your time. I still have a task for you."

"I will do anything You ask of me," she said immediately. "But how can I do anything for You?"

"Because I choose to bless you, my daughter," He said gently. "There is a time of great sorrow coming to Seare. If left unchecked, it will spread across the world, destroying all in its path. But there are yet so many who do not know Me, who have never heard My name. It is for love of these multitudes the storm of darkness must be stopped."

Her heart overflowed with the desire to serve her Lord and Master, even if it meant her own life in sacrifice. "What can I do?"

"Have faith in Me. Seek My wisdom, accept My guidance. It is not for you to know what is to come. Only know I am with you, and there is no task for which My strength is not sufficient."

"I will do anything You ask," she said again.

"For your faith, you will be rewarded," He said softly. "Cling to that when the price seems too much to bear. Now go."

"Please! Not yet! I want to stay here with You. Please don't send me back!"

"I will be with you," came the voice, deep and resonant, as the light faded.

Aine cried out as she was wrenched from His presence, overwhelmed by the utter loneliness of the sudden distance between them. Then pain seared her lungs, and excited voices babbled around her.

Hands pressed on her chest, and a man's familiar voice pleaded, "Come back to me, Aine."

She gasped for air. Water exploded from her lungs in a rush. More hands rolled her onto her side, patted her back, held her as she gagged and choked and struggled for breath.

"She's alive," the voice said again. Ruarc. "Comdiu be praised, she's alive!"

As Aine's consciousness returned, cold set her teeth chattering and her limbs shaking. Familiar faces wore concerned expressions, but she couldn't put names to them. Someone put a blanket around her, and someone else helped her to her feet.

She was alive.

She recalled the light, but the memory was already fading.

Her feet moved on their own toward the keep while she hung her head and wept.

✦ ✦ ✦

"Can you tell us what happened?"

Aine sat in a chair in the hall, now clothed in a dry shift and covered by furs and blankets. She warmed her shaking hands around a cup of tea, while Ruarc hovered behind her protectively, one hand on her shoulder. Her mind felt clearer now, but her heart still ached.

"I heard Ruarc call me, but when I got there, he was dead."

Ruarc patted her shoulder awkwardly. "I'm right here, my lady. I wouldn't leave you."

"Perhaps you were dreaming," someone suggested. "Walking in your sleep."

"No," she whispered. "It was no dream."

Eimer pushed to the front. "Enough of this now. She needs rest, not more questions."

"If she was pushed, we need to know who did it," Captain Ó Hearn protested. "There may be a murderer among us."

"No one under your authority, Captain," Aine mumbled. "I'm so tired. I just want to sleep."

"That's enough," Eimer said. "Come, girl, we'll get you to bed."

Aine let herself be led back to her chamber and lay still in her bed while the housekeeper piled blankets atop her. Her eyelids drooped. "I saw Him," she whispered, her mind returning to that pure, joyful light. "He was beautiful . . ."

"I know," Eimer said soothingly. "Get some rest. We can talk about it when you wake up."

Reassured by the recollection of the light, Aine closed her eyes and let herself be taken by a deep, dreamless slumber.

When Aine awoke, she wasn't sure where she was—Forrais, Lisdara, or Dún Eavan. Then she saw the candlelit earthen walls and remembered the lake's deathly touch. Eimer rose from her chair in the corner and knelt beside the bed to place her hand on Aine's forehead.

"How long have I been asleep?" Speaking set off a pounding in Aine's head that momentarily blinded her.

"A day and a night. It's morning."

"Where's Ruarc? I want to see him."

"He's probably still pacing outside your door. He's been terribly worried. We all have." Eimer lowered her voice. "Meallachán said something about the bean-sidhe."

Aine recalled the specter and shuddered. It sounded like the foolish ramblings of a frightened girl. Yet she knew she had heard Ruarc's voice, knew she had seen his lifeless body before she fell into the lake. Was it her own death the bean-sidhe had been proclaiming?

When Eimer saw Aine wasn't going to speak more on the subject, she climbed to her feet. "Stay here. I'll send in Ruarc while I get you some broth."

The guard entered a few moments later, his face creased with worry, followed by Meallachán a few steps behind. She was still searching for words when Ruarc crushed her into a tight embrace.

"Thank Comdiu," he whispered. "I thought the worst."

Aine disentangled herself, touched by his emotional greeting. She had known he was fond of her, but he had never displayed his feelings so plainly. Behind him, Meallachán wore a searching expression.

Ruarc pulled the chair to her bedside. "Can you tell us what happened?"

Aine looked at the bard, who nodded. Hesitantly, she related what she remembered up to the drowning.

"This is troubling," Meallachán said.

"You don't believe me?"

"Oh, I believe you. Some Balians may believe the sidhe are merely folk superstitions, but even the Scriptures speak of powers of darkness that seek to devour the light. What's disturbing is that they should choose you."

Aine shivered beneath the blankets. She had half-hoped the bard would dismiss her tale as a hallucination.

"But that's not all, is it?" Meallachán prompted. "You died. What did you see?"

"Lord Balus spoke to me," Aine said, recognizing as she did how fantastic it sounded. In the presence of the supernatural light, what she had seen and heard seemed completely plausible. But now . . . why would Lord Balus, Master of all creation, speak directly to her? Why would He choose an insignificant Aronan girl to play a part in the future of Seare?

Aine looked at Ruarc. "Do you believe me?"

Ruarc hesitated. "I'm a simple man, Aine. What I have seen, I would not have thought possible. But the fact you are here, alive, seems proof enough without the other."

"The other?"

"I woke to someone—or something—standing in my room. He told me you were in need of help and exactly what I should do. I roused the guards, and there we found you, floating facedown on the surface of the lake."

"Surely you can't mean you were visited by a Companion!"

Ruarc said nothing, but his expression told her she had guessed right.

"A Companion," Aine whispered.

"There's something I think you should see," the bard said.

Aine pushed herself up and wrapped her dry cloak around herself. Ruarc helped her to her feet and ushered her to the keep's entrance.

"Do you recall all those nights praying for protection?" Meallachán asked. "Look."

Aine stepped out into the blinding morning light. Every last person on Dún Eavan had gathered at water's edge, staring wordlessly across the loch. She followed their gazes. Beyond the island, a roiling mass of gray mist hovered over the water and spread back toward the shore. Before it, glowing columns of golden light held it at bay. Aine could just make out vaguely human shapes holding swords of white flame at their centers.

"I don't believe it." A wave of dizziness hit her, and her knees gave way. Ruarc caught her just before she struck the ground. In that instant, both the mist and the Companions vanished from sight, leaving only clear air and the glimmering surface of the water.

"They're gone!" someone cried in dismay. As if a spell had been broken, the others began to murmur in confusion.

"They're not gone," Aine said. "Just unseen. Comdiu granted us the vision to perceive what few ever have."

The crowd gaped at her, at last registering her presence. As Ruarc helped her to her feet, Niamh pushed to the front and threw her arms around Aine. "You're awake! Did you see them?"

"I saw them." Aine's knees buckled again, and she sent Ruarc a pleading look. Wordlessly, he picked her up like a child and carried her back to her bedchamber, away from the awe-stricken looks and frantic questions rumbling on Dún Eavan's shore.

CHAPTER TWENTY-ONE

Brother Slaine brought his concerns to Riordan on the way back from morning drills. That the stern man would seek him out at all was odd enough, but for once, Slaine actually seemed concerned.

"There's something wrong with your nephew."

Riordan frowned. Slaine was not given to exaggeration. "How so?"

"Brother Reamonn said he broke down weeping in the fields and since then he's been attacking his work like a man possessed. Eoghan told me he's grieving. Over a woman."

Riordan's eyebrows flew up. "A woman?"

"That's all he'd say. He told me to ask Master Liam."

"I see." Uneasiness crept into Riordan's gut. "Thank you, Brother Slaine. I'll see what I can find out."

Riordan had been headed to the barracks, but now he switched directions and started for Carraigmór instead. A woman. Given the recent news from the kingdoms, he could guess what this was about. He proceeded directly to Liam's study and let himself in without knocking.

"What did you tell my son?" he demanded.

Liam turned from the bookshelves, a heavy folio in hand. "Good morning, Riordan."

"What did you tell him?"

"About what?" Liam took his seat.

Riordan's irritation built. "Don't be evasive. I know the news from Dún Eavan as well as you. Conor seems to think your sister is dead. How did he hear that, I wonder?"

"I didn't say she was dead. I merely said she was in Comdiu's hands, and he needed to move on."

Riordan raked his hand through his hair. "What else could he think, Liam?"

"The boy was holding onto his past. His love for Aine will keep him from devoting himself to his training."

"You mean it will keep him from fulfilling your great plan. You haven't been honest with me, and I've let it pass because I trusted you had some greater vision. But in this, I can't stay silent. It's cruel to let him believe someone he loves is dead."

Liam rose and circled the desk to stand before Riordan, his gaze steely. It was the first time the Ceannaire had ever attempted to use his considerable physical presence to intimidate him. Even though Riordan stood taller by several inches, it took effort to stand firm.

"Do you not believe the greater plan warrants what you call cruelty? Do you not think a united Seare is worth a little grief? The boy will never fulfill his true destiny if he believes it is a woman."

Riordan stared back, unflinching. "Do you believe doing harm is part of Comdiu's plan? Is our God so ineffective He needs your deception to accomplish His work?"

Each held the other's gaze for a long, tense moment. Finally, Liam returned to the desk. "You will not mention this to Conor. I had hoped for the sake of our friendship you would respect my wishes. But if that is no longer enough of an incentive, you may consider it an order."

Riordan clenched his jaw against an angry retort. Finally, he gave a terse nod and exited the study. He had spent most of his adult life at Ard Dhaimhin, and obedience to authority was as automatic as breathing. But for the first time, Riordan could not accept Liam's judgment over his own conscience. The Ceannaire was wrong to believe Comdiu's plan could be accomplished through deceit, even if he strayed dangerously close to revealing something Riordan was afraid to believe.

If Conor was to become the leader Liam believed him to be, he needed to enter into it clear-sighted, free from manipulation. The Ceannaire might have issued an order, but Riordan's loyalty was to his conscience. Whatever the consequences to him personally.

✦   ✦   ✦

Liam slumped in his chair, head in his hands. If his visions were true, their time drew ever shorter. Even now, the druid moved Tigh closer to a conquest that would consume Seare. The pressure to find and train the one who would stand against this spread of evil mounted with each passing season.

Still, he could not help feeling he had made a grave miscalculation. He had underestimated the depth of Conor's feelings for Aine, far more profound than he would have expected from one so young. In his fumbling, he may have irreparably damaged his friendship with his most trusted adviser.

Riordan had reached the limits of his loyalty. He would act according to his conscience, even if his disobedience meant expulsion from the brotherhood or worse.

Liam was counting on it.

+ + +

Conor performed his duties through a veil of grief. Outwardly, he was the perfect Fíréin novice, working without complaint and without emotion. Inside, he felt hollowed out, empty, distanced from even the movements of his own body.

Riordan was waiting for him when he returned from hauling nets with an elder brother. Conor dragged the boat onto the shore and donned the tunic and boots he had left there earlier.

"May I have a word with you?"

Conor shrugged, but he walked with Riordan away from the lake.

"I heard you went to see Liam."

Conor stiffened. He didn't want to discuss the matter. Even Eoghan had avoided the topic after their single lakeside conversation.

Riordan grabbed his arm and forced him to stop. "I've been forbidden to tell you this, Conor. Liam would have me expelled from Ard Dhaimhin."

Conor's heart beat faster at the words, but he said nothing, waiting.

"Aine is not dead. She didn't drown."

Conor lowered himself onto a boulder beneath a stand of trees. "How is that possible?"

Riordan squatted down beside him and pitched his voice low. "After you left Lisdara, Calhoun sent the girls to Dún Eavan. I've heard rumors about the old fortress, but I've never given them much thought. Something tricked Aine into going down to the lake and pushed her in."

Conor drew in a long, shuddering breath, remembering his own encounters with the sidhe.

"Her guard pulled her out in time. They say she called on Comdiu's Companions to protect her. Dozens of people saw them."

Conor didn't dare to accept what Riordan told him. He had spent days believing Aine was dead, and now he learned it was all a mistake? Could this be a cruel joke?

"Did Master Liam know this?"

Riordan averted his eyes. His father had taken a great risk in telling him, then.

"Why would he do that? Why would he lie to me?"

Conflicting emotions flashed over Riordan's face as he wrestled with his answer. "Liam does what he believes is right," he said finally. "He sees far more than the rest of us. He insists you must be trained at Ard Dhaimhin, and he fears you will leave before you're ready if you don't sever all ties to the kingdoms. He ordered me not to tell you."

"Then why did you?"

"Because I know what it's like to mourn."

Conor stared out at the lake. His piercing feeling of betrayal surprised him. If Riordan hadn't followed his conscience, would he have lived the rest of his life at Ard Dhaimhin, plodding through a colorless existence of regret and grief, until the routine sapped him of all his emotion? Was that how the Ceannaire had become so hard-hearted?

Conor turned to his father. "Thank you for telling me. I understand what it means for you to go against Master Liam."

"I'm sorry I didn't know what you were going through. I should have noticed." Riordan placed a light hand on his shoulder before he left him alone with his thoughts.

Conor scarcely noticed his departure. Aine was alive. He silently repeated the words over and over again. Ruarc had saved her. Or was it Comdiu's Companions?

Laughter bubbled up in him and turned just as quickly to sobs. He covered his face with his hands. It had been a test, an opportunity, and he had failed in the worst way. He had blamed Comdiu and turned his back on his beliefs at the first sign of difficulty. If he'd only had the slightest bit of faith . . .

I'm sorry. I failed miserably. How can You still love me when I turned away so easily? I hated You for letting her die.

The answer came with startling clarity. Comdiu had known he would fail the test long before He ever claimed him for His own. How else would Conor build his faith unless he was tested? The vision had been a lesson from Comdiu, a reminder of the narrowness of human understanding.

He rose from the boulder, and a smile broke across his face. *Thank You. Thank You for saving her. Thank You for not giving up on me. I'm sorry I didn't trust You.*

Conor's trust in Liam, on the other hand, had been badly misplaced. He had come to Ard Dhaimhin believing the Fíréin were a source of infallible judgment and knowledge, but they were merely human. Liam might have his own plans for him, but how did Conor know they were correct? Why should someone else be the judge of where Comdiu's path was leading him?

Conor went about his afternoon duties at the mill without complaint, but he couldn't hide his restlessness from Eoghan at supper. He didn't wait for him to ask.

"Aine's alive."

"But Master Liam said—"

"He lied. Or rather, he purposely misled me."

Eoghan looked stricken. "Why would he do such a thing?"

"Master Liam has plans for me," Conor said grimly. "Whatever they may be."

"I'm sorry, Conor. If I had known . . ." Eoghan stood and took his bowl. "I'll see you at devotions."

Conor watched his friend go, confused. Did Eoghan take the criticism personally? After all, Liam was as close to a father as Eoghan had ever known. How would Conor feel if he learned Labhrás or even Riordan had intentionally caused a friend such pain?

He returned his half-empty bowl to the cookhouse and started after Eoghan. Conor thought their route would take them to the amphitheater for devotions, but instead the other boy turned down an intersecting path. Conor followed at a discreet distance.

The path emptied into a secluded yard where several brothers, including Master Liam, drilled with unsharpened practice swords. The clash of metal ceased when Eoghan came into view, and voices hummed, undecipherable.

Conor peered around the corner and saw Eoghan take up a sword and face two of the older brothers. Master Liam stood aside, watching.

Conor crept closer, aware he was trespassing on a private gathering, and flattened himself against the rocks.

With the sword in his hand, Eoghan transformed, seeming to grow taller and more confident. He assumed a guard stance as he waited for an attack. When it came, he sprang into motion with a speed and fluidity that made Conor's jaw drop. The boy met each attack effortlessly, ducking in and out of range with amazing ease. Even with his unpracticed eye, Conor could see he was just toying with them, testing his skills. His opponents, on the other hand, were doing no such thing.

"He's likely to be the best swordsman Ard Dhaimhin has ever produced."

Conor spun toward the voice. Riordan stood casually behind him, his arms crossed, watching the action below. "Master Liam took him as his apprentice when he became Ceannaire. Eoghan was only four years old, but already he showed great promise."

Conor wasn't sure which stunned him more, that Eoghan was the Ceannaire's apprentice or that he had begun sword work at age four. No wonder he was so far ahead of his peers, drilling with oath-bound brothers instead of members of his own céad. "I didn't know brothers took apprentices."

"Ceannaires do. They choose their successors young, to mold them for the duty that awaits them."

So that was why Eoghan had reacted so violently to Conor's news. His connection with Liam was even more significant than Eoghan had led him to believe. He watched as the young man grew impatient with the workout and disarmed his opponents without any apparent effort.

I know something about having limited choices.

"Does he have any say in the matter?" Conor asked as Eoghan took his place in the center of the yard, this time facing three men. Even at this distance, he could see the boy's hard expression.

"It's a great honor. Why would he turn down such an opportunity?"

"Why indeed?" Conor turned back to his father, but Riordan was already gone.

CHAPTER TWENTY-TWO

A week after Aine's encounter with the sidhe, the king summoned them back to Lisdara. Fergus had neither responded to Calhoun's missive nor taken more aggressive action, so her brother must have decided they would be safer behind Lisdara's high walls than among Dún Eavan's dangers. Aine didn't complain. Comdiu's Companions might be protecting them, but that thread of sinister magic still remained.

Within days of Aine's return to the keep, the sick, injured, and curious began streaming through Lisdara's heavily guarded gates. It seemed word had traveled fast about Aine's experience. No sooner had she delivered her report to Calhoun than half the countryside arrived, clamoring for her attention.

"How many are there?" Aine asked, dismayed, when she arrived at Mistress Bearrach's clochan.

"Too many. They've come to see the lady healer of Lisdara."

Some of the cases were legitimate: sprained limbs, festering wounds, a summer lung disease that spread in the damp, warm weather. But even those patients seemed disappointed when Aine prescribed practical treatments like tisanes and poultices. Evidently, rumor said she could heal by touch alone.

Returning to Lisdara also brought Conor back to the fore of her mind. She could scarcely pass the music room without a piercing ache in her heart. The one time she dared step inside and touch the harp on which he had played his final song, she left in tears. The peace she had found at Dún Eavan deserted her.

I don't understand what You want from me! What purpose did You have in bringing us together and then tearing us apart once again?

She felt guilty, then. How could she lament the loss of Conor after Comdiu saved her life? Balus Himself had set her apart for something important. Perhaps Conor's coming had been only a cog in a larger wheel, a way of bringing about what was to come. Maybe it was just her own weakness that made her long for someone she could not have.

Yet, as time passed, she couldn't shake the feeling Conor was at the center of everything. His coming to Faolán had set something in motion she didn't understand.

She delved deeply into work and study, hoping to numb herself to the questions that plagued her waking hours. Every evening and most mornings, she withdrew to her chamber with her books, bolstering her already expansive knowledge. Afternoons she spent at the clochan, seeing the never-ending stream of patients lined up outside the door. Even those who didn't need her attention, she didn't have the heart to turn away.

When Aine wasn't thus occupied, she retreated to the stone chapel to pray or just bask in the rare moments of peace. Here she could be alone, even if her conversations with Comdiu became increasingly more anxious.

On a rainy fall evening, she lingered long past when she was expected back in the keep, too weary to even put words to her thoughts. The iron-bound door creaked open, and the breeze fluttered the candles' flames. Footsteps echoed off the vaulted ceiling, signaling Ruarc's presence even before he settled on the bench beside her.

He stared straight ahead, his profile cast in shadow by the guttering candles. "Something must change. You can't go on like this."

"I keep thinking if I can just keep going, everything will begin to make sense."

"Working yourself to exhaustion won't bring Conor back."

"I know." That Conor wasn't dead made no difference. He still haunted her. "If Comdiu has a plan for me, I'm at a loss as to what it is. I don't know what to do."

"Maybe that's because there's nothing to do."

She glanced at him. "What do you mean?"

"It seems to me if it is Comdiu's plan, you can't do much to bring it about. He's the one who must give you direction, isn't He?"

"But what if I'm not listening? What if He's telling me, and I just don't understand?"

"When has Comdiu ever had difficulty telling someone who really seeks His will what to do?"

Aine remembered her all-encompassing desire to serve Lord Balus in that other place. She wanted to know His will no less now than she had then. Why did she feel so lost?

Perhaps she'd lost sight of her true focus. She'd let her discomfort and her loneliness distract her from what He had already told her to do: pray, study, wait for guidance. Didn't Lord Balus tell her the future was not for her to know?

She rubbed her eyes wearily, exhaustion setting in again. "Everywhere I go, someone wants something from me."

Ruarc smiled gently. "You don't have to give it."

"But I was given this gift—"

"And you are using it. But would Lord Balus want you to get so wrapped up in exercising that gift that you have nothing left for Him? Perhaps He hasn't shown you His will because you haven't made time to accomplish it."

Aine stared at Ruarc, momentarily shocked. "You're right. Why would He tell me what to do when I would just find an excuse to put it off?" She placed her hand lightly on Ruarc's arm. "What would I do without you?"

"You'd get along just fine." Ruarc smiled again. "You just might figure things out later rather than sooner."

Aine unfolded herself from the bench. "Maybe. But I'm grateful all the same. Come, it's getting late."

As they stepped out into the cool night, words formed in her mind, as clearly as if they had been spoken aloud. *You have been given this gift for a reason, and you are meant to use it. But it is not all you are.*

Aine recognized the wisdom in the words. She just needed to learn what else Comdiu intended to make of her.

✦   ✦   ✦

Aine wasted no time making drastic changes in her routine. Ruarc had been right. Her obsession with her work was just an attempt to anesthetize herself from her feelings about Conor and the coming turmoil in Faolán. Her first responsibility was to spend her time in prayer and study of Scripture, to spend enough time in quiet reflection that she could hear Comdiu's whisper among the cacophony of other demands.

Not everyone accepted the change so readily. The first time Aine reported to the clochan at midday, the petitioners grumbled about her lack of consideration. The complaining increased when she went down the line and selected those with the most pressing needs first.

"You don't need me to look at a mere scratch," she chided one man, who seemed more interested in her attention than in her healing. "Your village healers can assist you."

She dismissed the curious politely but firmly. That left only a handful of patients sick enough to stay, but not so sick they couldn't wait for her attention. Aine moved through the line capably and briskly, and by the time the daylight faded to dusk, she had seen the last of them. After several days of the routine, she no longer needed to poll the waiting patients when she arrived. Word had gotten out that she no longer accommodated the gawkers.

"Thank you," she said to Ruarc as they returned to the keep. "If it weren't for you, I'd be here all night. Maybe the novelty is finally beginning to wear off."

Ruarc nodded, his expression solemn, but the corners of his eyes crinkled.

"What?"

"You haven't heard the rumors then. They're saying the lady healer of Lisdara can read men's hearts by looking at them. The gawkers are afraid to come."

Aine gaped, aghast at the thought of yet another fantastic ability added to her reputation. Then she sighed. "Very well. If it means they're staying away, they can say whatever they want. I don't have the energy to deny every new rumor."

Part of her still remained uncomfortable with her selectiveness, though. Those who sought her meant well. It was not every day they had access to someone who had been brought back from the dead, with Comdiu's Companions as proof of His protection.

Within days, though, it hardly mattered. Clouds roiled off the coast of the Silver Sea and spread westward into an angry gray ceiling. When the skies opened, they loosed ceaseless sheets of rain that sounded more like the roar of a river than a winter downpour.

The storm's cold crept through the walls and condensed on the thick glass windows. Fires burned in hearths, and servants worked through the night to keep braziers stoked with glowing coals. Aine moved her usual studies down to the hall next to the fire in an attempt to dispel her constant chill.

"No patients today?" Niamh asked as she took a seat beside her sister, her sewing basket in hand.

"The roads are flooded. It will be a miracle if anyone can get in or out of Lisdara for the next few weeks."

"Thank Comdiu for that." Niamh sighed as she withdrew the strip of embroidery she'd been working on for the last month. The gold knotwork would eventually edge her wedding dress, Aine knew. Just as she knew it was not weariness that kept her from completing it.

Aine pitched her voice below the rain. "When must you decide?"

Niamh lowered her hands to her lap, crumpling the delicate work. "It's decided. I'm to marry Lord Keondric."

"When?"

"Within the year, unless we're at war. Calhoun said he will not have me be the young widow of another man's clan."

"That's a kindness, at least."

A sardonic smile twisted Niamh's face. "Clever of our brother, is what it is. He ensures Keondric will send above and beyond the men he's required to provide for the war, and if he's killed, Calhoun can give me as a prize to another victor."

Aine wanted to argue, but she couldn't discount the idea. Calhoun was kind and honorable. But he was a king, and he looked to the safety of his crown and his people above all else. His beautiful sister was a powerful bargaining tool.

"At least you get a rest," Niamh continued. "You've done nothing but work since we've come back from Dún Eavan."

Aine shot Niamh a wry smile. "You sound like Ruarc."

"Then Ruarc is right. You haven't seemed happy."

The comment startled Aine. It had been so long since she had thought about being happy, even the word sounded foreign. She hoped for contentment, perhaps, or peace, but happiness seemed out of reach.

"Have you thought about returning to Aron? Maybe it would be easier after . . . you know."

Aine studied her sister. Sometimes it was difficult to remember Niamh knew nothing of her gift or what had really happened when she drowned in Loch Eirich. "I've thought about it, but distance won't change anything. And at least here I can do some good."

"You couldn't heal in Aron?"

"Aronans are suspicious of anything that seems too much like magic. Healers who aren't effective don't draw many patients, and those who are too effective fall under suspicion."

"I can see why you'd stay then," Niamh said. "Healing badly or not at all doesn't seem like much of a choice."

Niamh went back to her sewing, and Aine stared into the crackling flames, her book forgotten in her lap. She'd never truly considered returning to Aron, even after Conor had left. It seemed like a poor way to repay Calhoun for his welcome and his support of her studies. Besides, Lord Balus had said she was bound to Seare's future, not Aron's.

The flames leapt and twisted in her vision, mesmerizing her with their changing patterns of orange, red, and blue. The sudden roar of rain on the slate roof drummed out the fire's crackle, filling her ears and echoing in her head. Aine looked toward Niamh in alarm, but her sister seemed unaware of the storm's increased fury. Then the room went black.

Aine froze. Her heart pounded, and her frightened breath rasped loud in her ears. Water ran in rivulets down her face, plastering her hair to her head. She no longer sat in her chair at Lisdara, but instead huddled in the bushes, peering through a canopy of leaves at a coastal village. Waves churned against the rocky shoreline, threatening the boats that had been pulled up and overturned for safety.

Through the rain, she saw the waves had already caught several large vessels and pulled them out to sea. But no, the boats were moving toward shore, not away, untouched by the ocean's roiling surface. They cut through the water and bumped against the shoreline. Aine rose from her hiding place for a better view.

Men poured from the boats, and she ducked back into the bushes, her heart thudding again. They were foreign-looking, dressed in brightly dyed tunics over leather-strapped trews. They carried iron-studded bucklers and heavy broadswords, even larger than the great swords Seareanns used in battle. Sofarende.

Aine could not bring herself to loose the shout of warning lodged in her throat. She watched as half a hundred men divided into groups and descended on the thatch-roofed homes, kicking down doors. Then came the screaming. Men burst from the cottages, only to be cut down mercilessly by the warriors.

Within minutes, the scene again fell eerily silent. Instead of looting, though, the invaders gathered in the center of the village. Aine shifted for a better view.

One of the men jerked his head in her direction and then strode toward the clutch of bushes where she crouched. Aine clapped her hand over her mouth to muffle her involuntary whimper. He stopped just feet in front of her, and the bushes parted. She shrank back.

A fine-boned, angular face peered down at her from the folds of his hood. Seareann features, not Lakelander. He held out a hand. Blood smeared the black spirals tattooed across the back of it. Fear spiked through her. She knew what those meant.

"Come out, little one," he said soothingly. "I won't hurt you."

Aine crept out, drawn against her will by the thread of command in his voice, at once beckoning and repellant.

"What's your name?"

Aine opened her mouth to answer, but a young boy's voice came out instead, tremulous, frightened. "Teag."

"Teag," the druid repeated pleasantly. "Tell me, Teag, how did you know to hide out here in the rain when everyone else was inside?"

Aine—or Teag, she now realized—shrank back. She didn't want to answer, but the words came out anyway. "I saw it. No one believed me."

"Extraordinary. Well, Teag, I'm very glad I found you." The man knelt down and gestured for her to come closer. He murmured something in a language she didn't understand. Then faster than she could even see, the man drew a dagger and plunged it into her chest.

Agony blanked her vision, and Aine fell back, paralyzed by pain and terror. A second man came to the tattooed man's side.

"He told no one of consequence," the druid said.

"Good." The new warrior bent down and wrenched the knife from her chest, then handed it back to his companion. Blood gushed out of her in a warm flood. "We're done here."

They rejoined the group, leaving her behind. Now Aine knelt beside the boy, separated from his thoughts. Sorrow washed over her when she saw how young he looked, perhaps only ten, with a thatch of light brown hair and a scattering of freckles across his nose. He looked up at her with recognition. "You saw, my lady?"

"I saw." Aine's voice broke, and tears spilled down her face. "You did well, Teag. You were very brave."

"I didn't call you here. He did." He raised a trembling hand. Aine turned, but she saw only empty space. When she turned back, the boy was dead.

"Aine!"

She jerked as strong hands shook her. She blinked at the familiar sensations: the warmth of the flames, the dancing firelight, the hollow roar of rain on the roof. Ruarc knelt before her, and Niamh and Leannan hovered behind them. Her sister looked terrified.

"What happened?"

"You were in a trance," Niamh said shakily. "I got Leannan and Ruarc. I didn't know what else to do."

The details of her vision came back to Aine, so clear she could hardly believe she had not just been in a coastal village. She looked between Ruarc and Leannan, dread twisting her stomach.

"Find the king. Tigh is going to invade Sliebhan."

CHAPTER TWENTY-THREE

Conor said nothing to Eoghan about having witnessed his impressive display of sword work, nor that he knew about his status as Master Liam's apprentice. It might not be a secret, but Eoghan had obviously chosen not to mention it for a reason.

Covertly, he watched the older boy with awe. If the Fíréin were among the best warriors in the known world, and Eoghan had bested several of them without apparent effort, what exactly did that make him? Conor could see the reason for the brutal physical labor, now that he had witnessed the results of Fíréin training. How could he be expected to wield a sword if he could not even lift it?

He also understood the reason for the Fíréin's strict prohibition against idleness. With their days filled with study, work, training, and prayer, the brothers had little time to dwell on the outside world. Aine drifted to the back of his mind, but she always remained present. She made her way into his prayers at night and inspired him to press forward when he was too exhausted to stay on his feet. If she had the faith to call upon Comdiu's Companions to save her from the sidhe, he could have the faith to continue down the path Comdiu had set before him.

Then Master Liam summoned him to Carraigmór. Conor followed the messenger up the stairs, clenching his hands into fists to still their tremors. Had Liam learned that Riordan had told him about Aine? No, that matter was between Liam and Riordan. Surely there couldn't be any cause for complaint about Conor's work. He labored as diligently as ever.

When the brother showed him into Liam's private study, he stopped short. A harp stood beside a chair in the middle of the room. The

Ceannaire gestured for him to enter, but Conor could not take his eyes from the instrument.

Liam folded his hands atop his desk. "I'm told you are having some difficulty adjusting to your loss."

Conor's eyes flew to the Ceannaire's face, but he lowered them quickly, afraid of what Liam might see in his expression.

"I thought you might find some comfort in this. Will you play for me?"

Conor's chest tightened. He could not help revealing his innermost feelings once his fingers touched the strings. Yet, he couldn't deny Master Liam. He didn't want to.

Wordlessly, he sat and lifted the harp onto his lap. It was an old, beautiful instrument, its maple frame plain and graceful, the bone pins carved with delicate flourishes. Conor waited for the thrill of power he had felt from Meallachán's harp, but found nothing there but his own anticipation. Relieved, he began to play.

He was only a few bars into a traditional Seareann folk melody when Liam interrupted.

"Conor, *play* for me."

Conor understood what he asked, but even this instrument held the potential for disaster. The Ceannaire wanted to know how he felt when he thought Aine was dead? Then he would. Conor took a deep breath and began again.

The initial notes from the harp were so chilling he almost regretted his decision. He clenched his jaw and played every ounce of that crippling grief into his impromptu composition. When he was finished, he felt nauseated and wrung-out, but he lifted his chin defiantly at Master Liam.

The Ceannaire, too, appeared shaken, but he composed himself quickly. "Thank you, Conor. It's been a long time since we've had a brother with the gift of music. Even longer since we've had one who could interpret it. I had hoped . . ." He trailed off and shook his head. "Your gift deserves to be exercised, even if we have no proper teacher for you. Will you play for me again?"

"As you wish," Conor said.

"After morning drills then."

Dismissed, Conor set aside the harp and walked to the door on trembling legs. Riordan waited outside, his expression a mix of wonder and pain.

"I had no idea," he said, but Conor didn't know if Riordan referred to his gift or the emotion he had revealed. "Come, there's someone you should meet."

Conor obediently followed his father upward through a maze of corridors until Riordan stopped before a door and knocked sharply. The door opened to reveal an ancient, white-haired man with blindness-clouded eyes.

"Brother Gillian," Riordan said. "I have someone to introduce."

Gillian's face lit up. "Riordan, my boy, come in! My new acquaintance wouldn't happen to be your nephew, Conor, would it?"

"Aye, sir," Conor said immediately. "I'm pleased to meet you."

Brother Gillian opened the door wider and stepped aside to admit them. Only a bed, a chest, and a narrow desk filled the sparse chamber. A partially mended fishing net hung from a hook on the ceiling in the corner, no doubt a task Gillian could accomplish without sight.

The old man turned his face to Conor. "Are you the one responsible for the music I just heard?"

"Aye, sir."

Riordan put a hand on Conor's shoulder. "I'll leave you two to talk. Brother Gillian knows more about the magic of Daimhin's age than any man alive. He can answer your questions."

"Thank you."

"Don't mention it." Riordan's tone said he meant it literally.

When they were alone and seated on Gillian's bed, the aged brother said, "You have questions. Ask."

Conor wondered where to start. "Master Liam said it had been a long time since we've had a brother with this gift, but even longer since there was one who could interpret it. What did he mean?"

"Ah, interpretation of music," Gillian said. "Well, you see, magic possesses a language, and so does music, in its own way. Those with the gift of music have the instinctive ability to transform it into the language of magic. And some have the ability to understand what it says."

"How?"

Gillian smiled. "If we knew that, it wouldn't be magic."

Despite himself, Conor smiled back. "What about the instruments themselves?"

"You speak of Meallachán's harp? A very rare instrument, that is, one of the few remaining objects of power."

Another object of power. Conor leaned forward. "What does it do?"

"It amplifies the abilities of the player, whatever those are. Tell me, young man, what exactly is your gift?"

"I don't know. I just . . . play."

"And what do people think or feel when they hear it?"

"I tell stories, I suppose, without words."

Gillian smiled, as if he'd known what Conor was going to say. "All good stories are *true*. Even if they were completely made up by the storyteller, there is something in them that resonates with us. Courage. Love. Self-sacrifice. The storyteller makes his story real through the telling. I'll let you think on that."

Recognizing his dismissal, Conor rose. "May I visit you again, Brother Gillian?"

"Any time you like, son. I'll be waiting for you."

As Conor climbed down from Carraigmór, he mulled the elderly brother's words. How many times had he said the harp spoke truth? Yet there was far more in Gillian's statement than he could properly grasp.

An hour ago, Conor had been convinced he could be content with a life of diligent labor. Now he wasn't so sure. Gillian seemed to hold the answer for which he had been searching, even if he didn't yet know the question.

✦　✦　✦

Conor visited Brother Gillian several times a week after he finished with Master Liam, and he looked forward to the old man's teaching as much as he did the harp. Gillian's knowledge extended far beyond magic, and he taught Conor forgotten details about the history of the Great Kingdom and the aftermath of its fall.

Then Eoghan surprised him with his own news from the kingdoms. "They're calling your young woman 'the lady healer of Lisdara.' They're saying she can heal men's bodies and read their hearts."

"That's preposterous." Inwardly, though, Conor didn't doubt it. Aine had summoned his childhood memories, but she hadn't said it was the only thing she could do. "Besides, how would anyone know what's going on at Lisdara?"

"You yourself said Master Liam seems to know everything. How do you think he gets all that information? The brothers who decide not to take oaths go back to the kingdoms and pass along the news we wouldn't otherwise hear in the middle of the forest."

He supposed that made sense. Without question, Meallachán and Treasach were both Fíréin. Master Liam and his informants had far more influence than Eoghan suspected. "Will you let me know what else you hear?"

Eoghan's eyes narrowed. "Why?"

"I know I'm not meant to stay here. Master Liam already lied to me once. I can't trust him to tell me when it's time to leave."

"What exactly are you waiting for?"

"I don't know. But I don't want to be surprised by what awaits me when I go." While Conor was taking risks, he ventured, "I know you're Master Liam's apprentice. I saw you practice months ago."

Eoghan grimaced. "I'm sorry I didn't tell you myself. Everyone treats me as if I'm already the Ceannaire. I didn't want you to feel the same way."

"You're nothing like Master Liam. When it's your turn to lead the brotherhood, I hope you'll remember that."

Eoghan expression turned sad then. "Maybe it won't come to that. I'll see you at devotions."

Conor watched him leave. Great honor or not, Eoghan liked Liam's plans no more than Conor did.

After that, Eoghan no longer tried to hide the fact his existence at Ard Dhaimhin was both more privileged and more disciplined than that of his céad mates. He had unrestricted access to Master Liam and many of the Conclave members, yet the Ceannaire held him to impossibly high standards. Failure was not permitted, and Eoghan constantly had to prove his worth as Liam's successor, even if it was not a future he desired for himself.

Occasionally, between assignments, Conor stole down to the clearing to watch Eoghan practice. His friend possessed a natural gift, and even men who had spent their entire lives training at Ard Dhaimhin struggled to match him. He fought with grace and focus and a pent-up passion that spoke to the depth of his misery.

Conor knew something about expectations and just how unhappy they could make a person, but Eoghan rebuffed any attempts he made to talk about it, turning the conversation instead to Aine or to news from the outside. When not on the training grounds, Eoghan fought the restrictions on him by passing along information gleaned from the runners or the oath-bound brothers. Mostly it was just gossip, but Conor welcomed the respite from the tedium.

Then in midwinter, Eoghan learned a bit of information that went far beyond the usual gossip.

"There have been Sofarende attacks up and down the coast of Sliebhan," he whispered. They lingered at supper, alone at their table, the other boys having already departed for evening devotions. "Fergus has moved troops into the country under the guise of defending Seare, but rumor claims they've used sorcery to gain control over King Bodb."

"What about Siomar and Faolán?" Conor asked.

"They've given Fergus an ultimatum. If he doesn't move his men back across the border, they'll declare war."

War. Conor should not be surprised, considering the history of conflict among the four rival kingdoms, yet in his short life he had known only a period of tentative peace. This time, however, Fergus had a sorcerer on his side. "What's Master Liam say?"

"'The Fíréin don't involve themselves in the matters of the kingdoms,'" Eoghan said. It was an oft-repeated doctrine in the brotherhood.

"This isn't a little border dispute. This is a conquest of Seare. Fergus wants to eradicate the Balians from the island. Do you think he'll stop without attacking Ard Dhaimhin? He wants to sit the Rune Throne."

Eoghan glanced around. "We're not supposed to know this, Conor. Keep your voice down."

Conor fell silent, pushing down his sense of foreboding. This was why brothers were isolated. It was sheer torture knowing what was going to happen and not being able to do anything about it. His face twisted. Not that he could do anything about it if he were there. He'd be killed the moment he stepped onto the battlefield.

He took comfort in the fact that Faolán was more than a match for Tigh. Galbraith would not have made an alliance if he did not fear Calhoun's might. Yet there was no telling the extent of the druid's capabilities. The mere fact they had moved warriors into Sliebhan proved the balance of power had shifted.

Conor threw himself into his work, unconsciously taking out his worries and frustration on his tasks. His hard-earned contentment slipped more each day, and fear crept into his heart.

Comdiu, these are Your children. Protect them. He knew all too well from Labhrás's example that being beloved by Balus did not exempt one from tragedy.

Winter moved into spring without any news of bloodshed, and gradually Conor's fears faded into the daily routine, even if war was never far from his mind. Somehow, he neglected to notice the changes in himself that had occurred with the passing of the seasons. He was hauling nets on a boat in the loch, clad only in his trousers, when he caught sight of his reflection in the lake's glassy surface. For a second, he wasn't sure whom he was seeing: the defined muscles and broadening shoulders of the boy in the reflection didn't correlate with his memory of his own scrawny frame. He looked down at himself and realized the hours of daily labor had begun to transform him, if not exactly into a man, at least into something different than the boy he had been.

He went back to the net and realized he no longer gritted his teeth through the work, but actually enjoyed the exertion. He grinned, feeling more alive than he had in months.

"I never thought fishing was so amusing," the brother in the boat said.

Conor laughed. "Me neither."

Later at supper, Eoghan asked him, "What are you so pleased about?"

"Today I realized I'm not such a weakling anymore."

Eoghan arched an eyebrow. "You thought Tor left you alone because of your skills at King and Conqueror?"

Conor blinked. Now that he thought about it, it had been weeks since he'd been the object of more than just threatening looks. "I've been so exhausted I hadn't given it much thought."

"You're hopeless." Eoghan rolled his eyes and turned his attention back to his stew.

+ + +

"Remarkable, don't you think?" Riordan said.

Conor didn't look away from the practice yard where Eoghan drilled with the oath-bound brothers, absorbing the easy and yet precise way the boy handled the short sword. He could now see the subtleties of technique that separated his friend from the other men. "I'd be happy to have half his skill someday. Even that would make me one of the best swordsmen in the kingdoms."

"I thought you had no interest in fighting."

Conor glanced at his father, but he detected no mockery in his tone or demeanor. "I thought I had no aptitude for fighting. But it seems foolish to spend time among the Fírein and not acquire your skills, doesn't it?"

Riordan's sharp look told him his words had given away more than he intended. "I hope I didn't make a mistake, telling you about Aine."

"Master Liam made a mistake lying to me in the first place. I'm aware I'm under no obligation to stay past my apprenticeship or even my novitiate. I'm here for a reason, even if I don't know what that is yet."

"You're here to save your life!"

Annoyance bubbled up inside Conor. "That may be your plan, but Comdiu doesn't need the Fírein to protect me if that's what He wills. Aine is proof of that." He sighed and gentled his tone. "I appreciate all you've done for me, you and Labhrás and Liam. If it hadn't been for your interference, I'd never have known the truth. I might be dead now. But it changes nothing. I will do what I feel is right."

Riordan turned away without answering. Regret washed over Conor. He didn't mean to dismiss this chance to know his real father so lightly, but he couldn't allow sentiment to overshadow his greater purpose. Whatever that was.

Two days later, an unfamiliar brother summoned Conor to a meeting at Carraigmór. He left off his afternoon duties in the chandler's cottage and followed the man toward the fortress with a sinking heart. Had Liam heard his oblique criticism and decided to expel him from Ard Dhaimhin? Surely the Ceannaire wouldn't abandon his plans for Conor that easily.

The brother led him past the single guard at the door and into the hall. Conor's steps faltered when he saw Master Liam was not alone. The entire Conclave waited in a semicircle of high-backed chairs, nine unreadable men still as stone. Only Riordan betrayed any emotion, his brow furrowed.

"Thank you, Brother Eamon," Liam said to Conor's escort. "You may leave us now."

A single chair faced the Conclave, and the Ceannaire gestured for him to take a seat. Conor obeyed, holding his head high under their scrutiny.

"You are being considered for apprenticeship with the Fíréin brotherhood," Master Liam said. "Have you anything to say?"

"What?" Conor had expected expulsion, not apprenticeship. "I only began my novitiate a year ago."

Several of the men exchanged glances. Riordan spoke first. "There is some question about your suitability as an apprentice. Master Liam believes it is best addressed now."

"Do you intend to take an oath of brotherhood?" Brother Daigh asked.

Conor looked among the Conclave members. What answer did they want from him? He didn't want to lie, and the Ceannaire would probably know if he did. "At the moment, no. But I have not ruled it out, either."

A few men hid smirks.

"Then why should we accept you as an apprentice?" Master Liam asked.

Conor met the Ceannaire's gaze unflinchingly. "I should ask you the same thing. You knew my intentions before Brother Daigh posed the question. Yet here I am, an apprentice candidate."

"Brother Conor's position is not unusual," Riordan said. "We do not require apprentices to bind themselves to the brotherhood. He is just more vocal about his intentions than most."

Master Liam looked at each of the Conclave members in turn before he addressed Conor. "Brother Riordan is correct. We do not force apprentices to take oaths, nor do we require novices to undertake apprenticeships. You may leave if you wish. If you stay, you will be pledging yourself to our training for as long as we deem necessary. You may choose whether to take vows when you are put forth for full brotherhood, whenever that may be. But once you embark on this path, you are required to see it through."

Conor balked at Master Liam's words. It could take years to complete his apprenticeship. But what other choice did he have? He still had to discover his purpose in being here, and remaining a novice was not an option.

Still, he could barely force out the words. "I accept."

"Good," Liam said. "You will attend drills with your céad in the morning. Given what I understand of your exceptional education, sending you to lessons with them would be redundant, so you'll continue your current duties in the afternoon."

The Ceannaire sat back with a satisfied smile. "Your novitiate is complete. Now your apprenticeship at Ard Dhaimhin begins."

+ + +

"They accepted me as an apprentice." Conor sat across from Eoghan at a table near the cookhouse. "For a second, I thought they were going to kick me out. Master Liam did not seem pleased with me."

"Congratulations," Eoghan said, but his tone was distracted.

Conor watched his friend push a chunk of fish around his half-empty bowl. "What's wrong?"

Eoghan met his eyes and lowered his voice. "News from Sliebhan. King Fergus has seized the throne without a battle. All of Bodb's chieftains and their warriors have sworn fealty."

Gooseflesh prickled Conor's skin. Fergus had conquered the country with only minor bloodshed, and now he had all Sliebhan's warriors behind him. The situation smacked of sorcery. "When did this happen?"

"Word came last night. It's been a few days at most."

The Conclave had learned the news yesterday. And today Conor agreed to commit himself to an apprenticeship for an undefined period of time.

What had Riordan said? *He fears you will leave before you're ready if you don't sever all ties to the kingdoms.*

"They bound me here before I could hear the news." Saying it aloud only confirmed his suspicions.

Eoghan looked at him strangely. "Why would they do that? You'd have to be mad to go back to the kingdoms now."

"I don't know." But Conor felt the pull toward the turmoil of his uncle's conquest the same way he had felt the pull toward Ard Dhaimhin. He was as enmeshed in the future of the kingdoms as he was bound to Liam's plans in the High City.

Conor rubbed his arms against his sudden chill, despite the fact the evening air was mild. *Comdiu, protect me,* he thought, a ward against the unknown to come.

CHAPTER TWENTY-FOUR

Conor's first spear lesson took place the next morning. As he followed his céad mates around the lake to the practice yards, he could not shake his apprehension. Eoghan may have dismissed his concerns as mere imagination, but Conor could not rid himself of the feeling there was a bigger tapestry being woven, and he was seeing only one small part of the design.

"Delusions of grandeur," he muttered to himself.

Those delusions did not extend to his first drills as an apprentice. Their instructor, Brother Teallach, a cast-iron man in his fifties, did not consider his lack of training an excuse for not keeping up with his céad mates. Conor barely caught the spear the instructor tossed him.

"First form!" Teallach barked.

The group moved in unison into a straight thrust, and Conor stumbled forward in time to avoid getting a spear through his back.

"Second form!"

The thrust shifted to a high block, and once more, Conor followed a beat behind.

The class dragged on painfully, Conor shadowing every movement and feeling hopelessly uncoordinated. Even after the hard labor of the past year, his arms and shoulders twinged from exertion, and a bead of sweat rolled down his back. It was his first day, he reminded himself. He couldn't expect to get everything right on his first try.

Conor was relieved when Teallach split them into pairs, until he realized he had no partner. The instructor appeared before him, spear in hand. "Your attack."

How was he supposed to do that? Conor hadn't really learned the movements in the forms, though he understood they were meant to be applied against an opponent. He gripped the spear in both hands and lunged forward. Teallach knocked his spear aside and thwacked him hard on the ribs, then on the side of the head.

"Again," Teallach said.

Conor tried again with the same results, but this time the instructor's strikes were harder. His ribs stung, and his head ached.

"Again!"

How had he blocked that? The third time, he was ready to meet the instructor's counterattack. Teallach gave his own spear a quick flick of the wrist, and Conor's weapon clattered to the hard-packed earth.

A hint of a smile played on the older man's lips. "Good. It didn't take you long." Teallach hooked his foot under the spear's shaft and tossed it back to Conor. "Once more."

By the end of the session, Conor had a handful of bruises to add to his count, but he was blocking and countering simple strikes with surprising facility. His arms and shoulders burned from the new movements, but a thin shred of hope had returned.

Conor followed the rest of the group to the next lesson, archery with Brother Seamus. Seamus was more patient than Teallach had been, and by the end of the lesson, Conor was at least able to loose arrows in the direction of his target, even if most of them struck the dirt in front of it.

He approached his third and final lesson of the day with aching muscles and a feeling of dread. Hand stones were the most traditional weapons of Seare, and while swordsmanship was more highly regarded, hardly a warrior or traveler went without a pouch of stones on his belt. Still, the groans of the younger boys as they approached the target scaffolds with their painted wooden discs made it clear this was their least favorite lesson.

While Conor's céad mates selected their caches of stones and took their places in front of the targets with a combination of resignation and discipline, the instructor drew him aside. A young, fair-haired Siomaigh, Nuallain shared Eoghan's calm, approachable manner. "You've never used these?"

Conor shook his head.

The instructor showed him the proper way of holding the stone and different methods of cocking his arm for the release. It was like skipping stones on a lake, something Conor had spent hours doing on summer afternoons.

Nuallain fired a stone. It hit the target with a crack and spun the disc backward on its rope. "Give it a go."

Conor eyed a target beside the one Nuallain had just hit, about twenty paces away. He took aim and released the stone sidearm. To his shock, the projectile hit the target with as much force as Nuallain's, dead center.

Nuallain arched an eyebrow. "Try another target."

It was another ten paces back, so Conor could hardly believe it when he struck the target with equal accuracy.

"We may have found your weapon. Try this." Nuallain made a few minor adjustments to the angle of Conor's arm and his release and then handed him a larger stone. This time, the projectile hit the wooden disc with such force it cracked it in two and sent one half spinning off behind.

"That would kill a man," Nuallain said approvingly.

Conor grinned. How appropriate his natural talent lay in the least-regarded ability of the kingdoms, one requiring finesse rather than brute strength. He cast a glance down the line and received an approving nod from Merritt.

The other boys had free time between morning sessions and their lessons at the fortress, but Conor proceeded to Carraigmór as usual. He couldn't help pouring his elation over the morning's minor successes into his playing at Carraigmór, even though his arms ached so badly he could barely hold the harp.

After that, his daily routine varied only slightly. Some days, Teallach taught casting with the spear, or they worked with staffs instead. Nuallain taught them how to use hand slings and staff slings, for which Conor proved to have equal facility, even if he preferred throwing by hand. A small but shockingly strong brother named Cairbre introduced him to Hesperidian wrestling, which he took to with surprising alacrity.

Only archery remained a struggle. As Conor built strength to draw the bow, his range improved, but his aim did not. He was forced to admit he might never be a particularly proficient archer.

The only weapon with which he did not practice was the sword, and it was the one he wanted to learn most. Swordsmanship was the pinnacle of a Fírein warrior's skills, but while the other members of his céad trained with Ard Dhaimhin's sword master, Brother Lughaire, Conor continued his menial duties around the village. Most days, he worked and trained from sunup to sundown with only his daily climb to Carraigmór as rest, and many nights, it was all he could do not to fall asleep in his bowl.

"Apparently the Fíréin don't value sleep or free time," Conor told Eoghan at supper one night.

"Or maybe Master Liam is trying to keep you busy. Most apprentices are required to attend lessons rather than join work details every day."

"Maybe no one else has had my education."

"Ciannait was raised by druids." Eoghan shot him a significant look. "He probably knows more than all of us combined, and he's spending his afternoons alone in the library."

Conor didn't have much time to ponder the inequity. He had far too much training to make up, and he felt too thinly stretched to think beyond the next task at hand. He spent his few moments of free time practicing empty-handed spear thrusts or drawing an imaginary bow. He saw Eoghan less and less, but he wasn't sure if it was because of his overwhelming schedule or Eoghan's. The older boy seemed distracted whenever he was around, and sometimes he didn't appear even for supper.

Then one night before lights-out, Eoghan perched on the edge of Conor's bed. "Master Liam has asked me to take my oath."

Conor grimaced. Even if he hadn't already noted Eoghan's dissatisfaction, his friend's tone would have told him he wasn't pleased. "What are you going to do?"

"I'll take the oath. I don't have much choice, do I? I'm clanless. I've never even seen the kingdoms."

"You could become a mercenary. The Aronan clan chiefs would pay dearly to have a man of your skills."

"I don't want to spill blood as my livelihood. That means I stay here. I'm not like you, Conor. I don't speak five languages. I can't name the capitals and kings of every known country. I'm good with a sword, and that's it."

"That's no small thing," Conor said. "I would give anything to have your skill. Riordan says you're the best swordsman Ard Dhaimhin's ever produced, and he's not given to hyperbole. Can you imagine if you could train Faolán's and Siomar's warriors? Fergus would find the Balian nations a little harder to conquer than Sliebhan." The other boys threw them curious looks, so Conor lowered his voice and said, "It would be the next best thing to Liam allowing the Fíréin to fight."

"You might be right."

When Eoghan stood, Conor didn't know which decision, if any, his friend had made. Slaine extinguished the torches, cutting off any further conversation. In the morning when he woke, Eoghan was already gone.

Brother Slaine took Conor aside on his way back from morning devotions. "You're excused from drills. Meet Brother Riordan at the small dock. He'll explain."

Baffled, Conor turned down toward the lakeshore, where his father already awaited him by the boats. "What's this about?"

"Brother Eoghan's taking his trials this morning. He's asked that you be present. Come on, we'll be late."

Conor clambered into one of the smaller boats, which was attached to a pulley by a thick rope. Riordan grasped the top line and drew the craft across the hundreds of yards between the shore and the largest of the crannogs. Conor had been on the smaller of the islands, where the nets and fishing boats were kept, but the larger one was restricted to oath-bound brothers.

The vessel bumped against the steep shore, and Conor clambered out. The island, which had seemed so small from a distance, now proved to be as large as Lisdara's courtyard, sparsely dotted with trees. At the center lay the sandy testing ring.

More than a dozen men, including Master Liam and Eoghan, already waited. Conor recognized the Conclave and senior members of the brotherhood who led weaponry drills for the older men. Eoghan stood grimly in their midst, receiving last-minute instructions.

Riordan stopped Conor a few paces from the ring. "We wait here."

Across the yard, Eoghan bowed and then selected a spear from a nearby pile. Six of the brothers did the same. Even from a distance, Conor could see iron spearheads in place of the usual wood. His friend assumed a defensive stance, and the others surrounded him.

Conor held his breath as the first warrior attacked, but he needn't have worried. Eoghan met the spear thrust confidently, knocking the point wide and countering quickly. The other five moved in then, and Conor's mouth dropped open as the boy fluidly defended himself from six attackers, using the weapon as both staff and spear. His spear point stopped mere inches from the throat of one, and the defeated brother stepped away from the fray, eliminated by what would have been a killing blow. One by one, the other men fell, until Eoghan was left only with the most experienced of the group.

The two men fought, wielding their spears so quickly Conor was hard-pressed to follow individual movements. Then Eoghan misstepped, and his spear sailed from his grip. Conor gasped as the brother moved in to finish him.

Eoghan sidestepped the thrust and tackled his opponent to the ground, knocking the spear from his hand. The two men grappled in the loose sand, evenly matched in weight and strength, until it looked as if Eoghan was locked in an inescapable clinch. Then, in a blur of movement, Eoghan reversed the hold. He braced a knee on the other man's neck and held the armlock firm until his opponent submitted.

Conor gaped. He knew Eoghan's skills surpassed his own, but this went far beyond his imaginings. He had eliminated six far more experienced men in the space of three minutes. Eoghan helped his defeated opponent to his feet and retrieved their discarded spears.

Conor found his voice. "Is that the test?"

"Only part of it," Riordan said. "The easier part."

Eoghan returned the spears to the pile and moved to a stretch of canvas laid at the edge of the yard. Conor couldn't see the objects laid upon it until Eoghan chose one. A short sword.

This time, the odds were better, three against one, or so he thought until he recognized two of the men. One was Iomhar, the boy whose sword form Conor had admired on his first day. The other was Brother Lughaire, the sword master himself.

From the moment of the first attack, though, Conor could see Eoghan was in control of the match. He moved lightly and quickly, defending every attack. Almost immediately, the first man fell, struck in the neck with the flat of Eoghan's blade.

"He's only nineteen," Riordan said in a low voice. "I can't wait to see him at thirty."

Conor didn't reply, captivated by the display. Even the talented apprentice was no match for him, and Eoghan was just toying with him, prolonging the match. Iomhar lost his weapon next and slunk from the yard, leaving Eoghan and Lughaire alone.

They circled one another warily, too respectful of the other's skill to rush in. Then Eoghan sprang, driving back the sword master with a series of flawless attacks. Lughaire battled back and put Eoghan on the defensive. Swords flashed faster. Somewhere this trial had ceased to be a mock battle and ventured into a real skirmish.

Apparently, Master Liam felt the same, because he shouted, "That's enough! Stand down!"

Eoghan disengaged first, keeping his guard up until he was out of striking distance. His chest rose and fell from exertion. The men bowed warily to one another and moved back toward Master Liam.

Riordan nudged Conor forward. "We can join them now."

Conor approached the small group, more awed than ever by his friend. He had never seen anyone fight like that, not even among the Fíréin. Conor tried to catch his eye, but Eoghan's gaze was fixed on the Ceannaire.

"You more than meet the requirements for admission to the brotherhood," Liam said to Eoghan. "Will you take the oath?"

"Aye. Upon one condition."

"Oh?" Master Liam said. "What is that?"

"I wish to take an apprentice."

"That's a highly unusual request."

Beside Conor, Riordan said, "It's not without precedent. Master Fionntan took an apprentice when he accepted his commission."

"Of which Brother Eoghan is well aware." Liam smothered a smile. "Whom do you propose to mentor, then?"

"Brother Conor."

Conor's knees weakened. Eoghan was demanding to mentor him as a price of remaining with the Fíréin brotherhood?

Master Liam caught Conor's eye. "Brother Conor, what say you?"

It took him several moments to find his voice. "It would be an honor, sir."

"It will require the approval of the Conclave," Master Liam said. "We will give you an answer tomorrow."

Riordan nudged Conor toward the boats. He followed his father, too stunned to speak. They were halfway across the lake when Conor noticed Riordan's smile. "What?"

"Eoghan surprised me. I didn't think he would accept his commission."

"I don't understand."

"He could have just taken an oath of brotherhood. By requesting an apprentice, he's accepted the succession. If they vote in favor, he will be the next Ceannaire of Ard Dhaimhin. If they don't, he's free."

Conor felt sick. Last night, Eoghan hadn't wanted to even take the oath, and today he had accepted the claim to the brotherhood's leadership. "What does it mean for me?"

"He will be responsible for your training, as Liam was for his. If he wishes, he can recommend you to be his successor."

Conor's heart rose into his throat again, but Riordan wasn't finished. "He will also put you forward for your oath of brotherhood. Under Eoghan's tutelage, that's likely to be sooner than later."

Conor gripped the side of the boat, glad Riordan was working the pulley, because the strength had gone out of his trembling limbs. Somehow, Eoghan had glimpsed the pattern just as Conor had. And once more, someone had made a very large sacrifice on his behalf.

✦ ✦ ✦

The oath-binding took place at Carraigmór two days after Eoghan's trials. That morning, a brother presented Conor with a rough-spun linen robe and leather sandals. He bathed in the springhouse before pulling them on, then traversed the slippery steps up to Carraigmór.

The guard let him in without comment. Torches and candles lit the cavernous hall, and a large, flat case lay before the Rune Throne. Riordan met him inside the door, similarly garbed.

"Don't be nervous. Stand in the back until you are called, and when Eoghan asks if you will undertake training as his apprentice, you say 'aye.' The rest is for him."

Conor nodded as the Conclave members filed in, dressed in the ceremonial robes. Master Liam and Eoghan followed, conversing quietly.

Conor had expected some elaborate ritual, but Master Liam just lifted a hand, and the Conclave formed a line behind him. "Brother Eoghan, you are here today to offer your oath to the Fíréin of Ard Dhaimhin. You have already been instructed in the rights and responsibilities of this undertaking. Do you accept the offer that is extended to you?"

Eoghan's voice was clear but impassive. "Aye."

"Members of the Conclave, will you accept the oath of Brother Eoghan as admission to the brotherhood?"

In unison, the nine men said, "Aye."

Master Liam raised his hand again, and Riordan retrieved the case on the step. He offered it across his open palms to the Ceannaire. Carefully, Master Liam lifted the lid and withdrew a plain, ancient sword.

A surge of power hit Conor like a lightning bolt, humming along his skin and buzzing in his ears. It was the same magic that had created the ivory charm, the kind that emanated from Meallachán's ancient harp. He steadied himself against the wall.

Liam planted the sword point down into the stone floor. Eoghan knelt and placed his hand atop the pommel.

"Brother Eoghan, do you swear loyalty to the Fíréin brotherhood of Ard Dhaimhin?" Liam asked.

"Aye."

"Do you swear to uphold our laws and protect our traditions?"

"Aye."

"Do you forsake all other oaths and commitments to chief, clan, or kingdom, in favor of your oath to the Fíréin brotherhood?"

Eoghan's tone was wry. "Aye."

"Then rise, and be accepted as a member of the Fíréin brotherhood."

Eoghan rose and released the sword. Master Liam took it across both palms once more and laid it in the box. Conor caught his breath as the buzz died away. His heartbeat resumed its normal pace.

Riordan passed the case to another brother and exchanged places with the leader. "Liam, Ceannaire of the Fíréin of Ard Dhaimhin, do you bring forth your apprentice, Brother Eoghan, for consideration as successor to your office?"

"I do." Liam's voice echoed in the hall, clear and confident.

"Brother Eoghan, the rights and responsibilities of this commitment have been explained to you. Do you willingly commit yourself to the future leadership of the Fíréin brotherhood and the sacrifices this entails?"

Eoghan's answer came more slowly than Liam's. "Aye."

"As successor to Liam, Ceannaire of Ard Dhaimhin, you may claim the right to choose an apprentice, now or in the future. Do you wish to name an apprentice?"

"Aye. I name Brother Conor."

"Brother Conor, come forward."

Conor moved toward his father on shaky legs. He caught a hint of a smile on Riordan's face as Eoghan turned, but his friend looked appropriately solemn when he spoke.

"By accepting the apprenticeship, you submit yourself to my authority in all matters but your membership within the brotherhood. So far as my requirements do not contradict those of the Fíréin brotherhood, nor the teachings of Comdiu as fulfilled in Lord Balus, do you undertake my training and guidance, willingly and without reservation?"

"Aye."

Riordan addressed the assemblage then. "Brothers of the Conclave. Do you confirm the oaths of Brother Eoghan, successor to Liam, and Brother Conor, apprentice to Eoghan?"

"We do," they said in unison.

Master Liam surveyed the gathering, his eyes settling on Conor. "Let it be so noted in the rolls of the Fíréin brotherhood."

✦   ✦   ✦

When Conor returned to the céad's clochan that evening, Eoghan's few possessions were gone, ostensibly moved into the oath-bound brothers' barracks. He wanted to ask Eoghan why he had changed his mind, and why he had staked his future at Ard Dhaimhin on Conor's apprenticeship, but he didn't appear at meals that day or the next.

On the second morning, Eoghan caught Conor on the way back from devotions. "I asked Master Liam to excuse you from your afternoon duties four days a week. There's no way we can accomplish what I intend if you're constantly exhausted."

"Thank you," Conor said, though he wasn't yet sure it warranted gratitude. "What exactly do you have in mind?"

"You'll continue your regular drills for now. You'll train with me four days a week, starting today. The other days, we'll take what time we can find. Meet me at the docks after you finish with Cairbre."

Eoghan's casual words piqued Conor's curiosity. Why did they need to practice on the crannog? He stumbled through his morning drills, distracted, earning a few new bruises from spear practice and producing an unusually poor performance with the staff sling. When he finally arrived at the dock, he felt stretched thin by anticipation and anxiety.

Eoghan stood beside the nearest boat, a canvas-wrapped bundle beneath one arm. He gestured for Conor to take the position at the prow and clambered in after him.

Conor began the slow, difficult task of ferrying the boat across. Neither spoke for a time. Then Conor paused at the end of a long pull and turned to his friend. "Why?"

Eoghan understood. "Your path is your own. I think you should have the chance to follow it."

"I know it couldn't have been an easy decision," Conor said. "Thank you."

Eoghan didn't answer. When the boat's hull bumped against the sandy shore, Conor jumped out into the shallow water and dragged it up the beach.

Eoghan led him toward the yard where he had taken his trials only days before. "You said you would give anything to have my skill. Did you mean it?"

It felt like a trick question. "Aye."

"Good. Because you have a lot of catching up to do, and it won't be easy." Eoghan unrolled the bundle with a flourish, revealing two sets of swords, one wood, the other unsharpened steel. He took the wooden practice weapons and tossed one to Conor. "We'll start with these. They're heavier. You'll be glad for it later."

Conor caught the sword. Metal weights studded its length. It was lighter than he expected, but then again, he had just spent the last year doing little but cultivating, casting, and carrying.

"You already have the skills to be a good swordsman. You read people. You think ahead—as you proved the last five times you beat me at King and Conqueror. And according to Nuallain, you can take down a man with a stone from a hundred yards, so I'm guessing you have pretty good coordination." He grinned at Conor, who couldn't help but smile back. This was the Eoghan he remembered. "You just need strength and technique. Those are the two easiest factors to cultivate."

"How?"

"With repetition." The wicked glint in Eoghan's eye said he would be a far more exacting taskmaster than Lughaire could ever be.

Eoghan did more than drill the movements into Conor by rote, though. He demonstrated each technique and then explained every aspect of it, from which muscles should be engaged in its proper execution to its uses and weaknesses. By the time twilight fell, Conor's mind felt just as exhausted as his body.

"You might actually make a swordsman out of me someday," Conor said as they climbed back into the boat.

"Or die trying."

Conor laughed and drew the boat back along the rope to the shore, his overtaxed arms and shoulders protesting furiously. By the time they'd finished, those wooden swords hadn't felt so light.

"Same time tomorrow," Eoghan said when they parted. "Get some rest. You'll need it."

That night, Conor dreamed not of Aine or even of war, but of thrusts and parries. For the first time, his ambitions did not seem so grandiose.

The day following Conor's first lesson with Eoghan, he vowed to make up for the previous morning's distracted performance. He threw himself into his drills, garnering looks of approval from his instructors. His archery remained mediocre, but he was beginning to accept that as typical. By the time he crossed the lake with Eoghan, he was already mentally and physically spent.

Eoghan drilled parries and counters until Conor's arms and shoulders ached. Every movement had to be perfect, the angle of arm and hand just so, at least a hundred times before they could move on. Sloppy execution, whether from laziness or unresponsive muscles, earned another round of drills. Conor learned, as he had in the early days of his novitiate, to command obedience from his body even when it screamed for rest and to force his mind to accept pain and exhaustion without complaint. Unconsciously, the habit carried over into his other practices, and his work with the spear and bow leapt forward as well.

Even afternoons on the lake or in the fields did not excuse him from drills with his new mentor. Some days, Eoghan met him on the path to the village with their weapons and some food so they could drill until evening devotions, eating in the time it took to cross the lake. Other times, they took torches to the practice yard where Conor had watched Eoghan unobserved and worked into the small hours of the night.

If Eoghan was pleased with Conor's progress, he never said so. He praised perfect execution when Conor managed it, and he never berated or belittled him when he repeated his mistakes. He merely said, "Again," and launched into yet another lengthy sequence. The elation of grasping a difficult skill far outweighed any praise of Eoghan's anyway, so Conor didn't complain at the repetition, even when he practiced the same maneuver a thousand times in a row.

Still, Eoghan's training went beyond conscientiousness, and its urgency made Conor uneasy. It was as if they were racing against an unnamed deadline.

You have a lot of catching up to do, Eoghan had said on that first day, as if time weren't in abundance at Ard Dhaimhin. Perhaps Eoghan's glimpse of the larger pattern had been more comprehensive than his own.

CHAPTER TWENTY-FIVE

Aine observed the changes at Lisdara from her chamber's windows, anxiety nagging at her stomach. As soon as word of Sliebhan's capitulation arrived, Calhoun had locked down the fortress, restricting visitors to those lords and chieftains whom he specifically summoned.

Aine waited for Calhoun to announce he was sending them back to Dún Eavan, but instead he just forbade them from leaving the keep, even to walk in the courtyard. No one took the time to explain the situation to her and Niamh, but Aine could guess the reason. Fergus could never have taken Sliebhan's capital and secured the oaths of Bodb's clan chiefs with so little bloodshed if the Red Druid did not control someone on the inside. Calhoun would not let that happen to Lisdara.

Grim-faced warriors came and went at all hours, bringing promises of men and arms from Faolán's clan chiefs. Calhoun remained cloistered in his private chambers unless a full convocation of the council required the great hall, and though Aine wanted to ask him what plans they made, nothing short of another vision could gain her admission to the closed meetings.

Then the news she dreaded came on the heels of two riders bearing the red-and-black banner of Siomar. When Ruarc arrived at her chamber, his dark expression warned her of what was coming.

"Fergus engaged a small company of Siomaigh warriors near the Sliebhanaigh border. Both sides took heavy casualties, but Siomar lost more. Calhoun sent Lord Abban with several céads."

Aine's heart sank, and Niamh asked shakily, "What does that mean?"

"It means we're at war," Ruarc said. "Calhoun will not let the fighting move north into Faolán. If anyone can hold them back, it's Abban's men. They're among Seare's best warriors."

Aine said nothing. That reassurance made sense to fighting men, but even she knew skill and experience went only so far. The one thing she could do was pray.

She began to spend her free time in the small stone chapel, praying or sitting silently while lengthening shadows marked the passing hours. Ruarc stood watch over her from the back of the sanctuary, and Treasach and Iuchbar occasionally joined her, but aside from the three men, she held her vigil alone.

She missed Meallachán's presence. The bard had left with Calhoun's second contingent of men, but he didn't disclose his destination. The absence of music somehow made Aine think of Conor even more, and she replayed his nightly serenades in her mind. Sometimes, when she hummed a bar from his compositions, the ivory charm warmed against her skin. Did Conor think of her still? Did he know the threat they faced here in the kingdoms?

"Fergus is finding Siomar harder to conquer than expected," a voice said in her ear.

Aine nearly jumped off the chapel bench. She hadn't heard Treasach enter. "You've learned something?"

"He's definitely using sorcery, even though no one has identified the druid."

"Then how do they know?"

"The Siomaigh were in retreat across the Threewaters, and then like that"—Treasach snapped his fingers—"the Timhaigh stopped. Those that kept going dropped dead before they even reached the bank of the river. The rest were too afraid to try. Their captains couldn't get them to cross, and the Siomaigh archers picked them off one by one."

Aine stared in disbelief. "How is that possible?"

"Magic."

"You mean Balian magic."

Treasach nodded. "Wards used to cover the whole island, but I had no idea so many remained. Whatever sorcery Fergus is using can't abide their power. Being able to sense the wards would be a mighty big advantage for our side."

"Aye, I imagine it would." Aine's heart suddenly beat too hard in her chest, and her head felt as if it was underwater. Did Treasach know something of her abilities? Or was this all just happenstance?

No. Not happenstance. A gift. Perhaps even clear direction from Comdiu.

"I don't like that look," Ruarc said when Treasach left. He stood before Aine, arms crossed and eyes narrowed. "Calhoun will never send you to the front."

"Even if it means we can hold off Fergus indefinitely?" A feverish certainty gripped her. "Ruarc, you are a warrior. You know how important choosing the battlefield is. If we knew where the wards were, we'd have the upper hand." Aine stood, determined to march into Calhoun's chamber with her idea as soon as she could request an audience, but Ruarc's iron grip held her back.

"Until someone figures out who's identifying the wards. How long do you think it would be until Fergus and his druid sent assassins after you?"

"I'll have you to protect me," she said, but he scowled. "Ruarc, war is ugly, and men die needlessly. How could I not try to stop it if I could?"

"You don't even know you can!"

Aine recalled the tingling sensation of the wards in the forest, how the charm seemed to warm at her breast at the merest thread of magic. "I can."

"I don't like this."

She placed a hand on his arm. "I trust you to use your talents. You must trust me to use mine."

✦ ✦ ✦

"No," Calhoun said flatly.

Aine gaped at him. It was not the reaction she had expected when she forced her way into his private study. "Why not?"

"For one, it's too dangerous."

"Because I'm a woman?"

Calhoun frowned. "Because you're not a warrior."

"I'm not asking you to give me a sword and send me into battle. Just let me go to Siomar and scout the area, see what I sense!"

"What do you propose? Ride back and forth and hope you stumble over a ward? Not only is it dangerous, it's completely impractical. No. I won't do it."

Aine bit her lip. This was not going at all the way she envisioned it, and Ruarc had the nerve to look pleased. *Lord, if You want me to do this, You're going to have to make a way.*

An idea came to her. She pulled the ivory charm on its silver chain over her head and placed it on the table between them. "I have this."

Calhoun looked unimpressed. "A wheel charm?"

Aine flipped it over to reveal the carved runes. "An ancient wheel charm, made with the same magic used in the wards."

"Where did you get that?" Calhoun nudged it gingerly with his finger.

"Conor gave it to me. He didn't tell me where he got it."

Calhoun looked to Ruarc. "What say you?"

"Personally, I hate the idea. But if she's right, think of the lives it could save."

"And if it costs her own?" Calhoun asked. Ruarc averted his gaze. "That's what I thought."

"The decision is not Ruarc's," Aine said, sensing she was losing this battle. "It should be mine. If I'm willing to take the risk, and you believe it to be strategically sound, you cannot look at the situation as my brother. You are a king. You owe it to your people to protect them, whatever the personal cost."

Calhoun stared at the charm, the pulse of a muscle in his jaw betraying his conflict. Finally, he said, "I'll consider it." When she began to protest, he held up a finger. "That's all I'm willing to promise. Now I suggest you go think long and hard about what you've proposed."

Aine rose and retrieved the charm from the table. "Thank you, Calhoun."

He waved a hand. "Go. I'll let you know when I've decided."

Ruarc escorted her from the study. He remained silent the whole way back to Aine's chamber.

"Are you angry with me?" she asked, her voice small in the echoing corridor.

Ruarc touched her shoulder. "No, I'm proud of you. Your mother would be as well."

Aine reached out and quickly squeezed his hand, and she saw him smile before he left her at her chamber.

+ + +

In the end, Calhoun relented. He didn't look pleased with the idea, but it was an opportunity he could not pass up. He gave orders to prepare for a swift departure, and Aine tried not to dwell on her dangerous task as she collected the books, herbs, and implements she might need on the battlefield. Not until Ruarc met her at the door of her chamber with a leather breastplate did she fully comprehend the peril.

Seek My wisdom, accept My guidance. It is not for you to know what is to come. Only know I am with you, and there is no task for which My strength is not sufficient.

Aine let out her breath in a long, silent sigh. *Your will be done.*

She held up her arms for Ruarc to strap on the armor.

+ + +

The group that had been chosen to accompany Aine to Lord Abban's camp in northern Siomar seemed an unlikely one, even if they were all professional warriors and, as Calhoun assured her, the best of their kind. The group's leader, Lorcan, compact and brawny with white-blond hair, possessed a careful, measured manner Aine found reassuring. The red-haired twins, Myles and Uilliam, spent most of their time arguing and insulting one another. Dark and lanky Sualtam remained silent, but his comportment—a sense of violence barely reined in—made her edgy.

Only two other members of their party were not warriors: Cúan and Aran, the mappers. Their job would be to scribe the wards as Aine found them, a task for which their knowledge of Seareann topography would be essential. They looked just as uncomfortable on horseback in their armor as Aine felt.

Lorcan set a swift pace from Lisdara with the ease of a natural horseman, and he seemed to sense when the horses needed rest or the riders grew tired. Even with frequent breaks to stretch and change to their remounts, Aine's legs and back soon ached from the effort of balancing at a trot. They did not take the most direct route south, but rather avoided certain holdings while riding close to others. Some nights, they cold-camped in copses of trees or beneath hollows cut in the rolling hillsides, eschewing fires in case they drew the wrong sort of attention. When they neared the homes of Calhoun's loyal lords, two of their warriors rode ahead with letters of introduction from the king and secured the households' cooperation.

In many places, the holdings were no more than scraggly plots of farmland and thatch-roofed cottages where the lords and servants slept communally in their halls. The lords offered their hospitality with less and less enthusiasm as the group neared Siomar's border. Ruarc often slept upright beside Aine, his sword across his lap, because he didn't like the way the lord or his sons looked at her.

Their tension built further once they crossed the border into Siomar. The two kingdoms may have been at peace, united by a common enemy, but the history of warfare stretching back half a millennium wouldn't be so quickly forgotten. The party skirted all signs of habitation, camping in the open at night and doubling watches. Aine became accustomed to the hard knot of anxiety in her gut.

On the tenth day, Cúan announced they were a half day's ride from Lord Abban's last known position. Lorcan went ahead to scout the area and be sure they were not blundering into a Timhaigh trap. At midday, he rejoined the group while they rested and exchanged horses.

"They're a mile out," he said, dismounting. "They didn't see me, but I could make out the Faolanaigh banner."

Aine's stomach somersaulted. She had never met Abban Ó Sedna, but the chieftain had a reputation as a fearless leader and a fierce warrior. How would he receive her and the disruption she brought to his camp, especially once he learned her true purpose for coming? Even she could admit her claims sounded a little farfetched.

While they rested, Lorcan unfurled the green-and-silver banner and placed it atop the standard pole. Seeing the royal arms gave her a needed boost of confidence. She came on the king's authority. Lord Abban had no choice but to defer to her wishes.

They had just glimpsed the tops of the tents when a small group of riders approached them. Lorcan rode ahead, the banner streaming in the wind, and conversed with their leader. The captain skimmed Calhoun's letter of introduction and nodded.

"He was surprised to see us so soon with a woman in our party." Lorcan's voice held a wry note at the insult. "The Mac Cuillinn's messenger arrived only the day before yesterday."

"Must have been patronizing all the alehouses between here and Lisdara then," Uilliam said with a smirk. "We rode fast, but not that fast."

Myles shot his twin a warning look as they joined their escort. When they drew nearer, Aine saw it was actually two camps separated by a gulley. The nearest one flew the green-and-yellow banner of Clan Sedna below Faolán's, while the other flew two red-and-black banners of differing designs. Siomaigh.

"King Semias evidently doesn't trust the Faolanaigh on his lands without supervision," Ruarc said. "I can't say I blame him. Some things don't change so quickly."

They proceeded down a wide avenue, and Aine drew up the hood of her cloak so she could observe the camp unnoticed. A quick count numbered about three hundred men, a large contingent for countries that rarely engaged in concerted, full-scale warfare. Seareanns were known for their strike-and-retreat tactics, unlike the massive Ciraean armies that had conquered the known world not so long ago. Still, Abban had organized his camp with a precision that would have made a Ciraean general proud, cook fires marking individual campsites in a neat grid, several dozen horses picketed beyond. White canvas tents housing foodstuffs and supplies dotted the arrangement at regular intervals.

The outriders led them to a large, curtained pavilion at the center of camp, where five men pored over a stack of maps spread across a campaign table. When they stopped, one of the men detached from the group and strode out to meet them. It could only be Lord Abban.

The chieftain was a bear of a man, bigger than even the priest Treasach, his bulk emphasized by the tar-black armor he wore over his tunic. A coarse black beard punctuated with tiny plaits sprang from a square jaw, and a tangle of braid-studded hair fell around his shoulders. He hardly needed to draw a sword in battle to intimidate the enemy.

Ruarc helped Aine from her horse, and she clutched her guard's arm while her quivering legs accustomed themselves to solid ground. Then he stepped back. As Calhoun's sister, Aine was technically the leader of this party. She threw back her shoulders and lowered the hood of her cloak.

"Lady Aine," Abban said, giving her a stiff, but respectful, bow. Even his speaking voice seemed outsized. "I trust your journey wasn't too taxing?"

"Not at all, Lord Abban. I was glad to hear you were expecting us. I'm told you are not fond of surprises."

"No surprise involving Calhoun's illustrious sister-healer could be unwanted. May I offer you refreshments while we discuss matters?" He glanced at the other men, and his gaze lingered on Ruarc, who hovered protectively. "Your escort will be taken care of, I assure you."

"Ruarc will join us," Aine said, and Abban bowed his head in acknowledgement.

He led them to the pavilion, which his captains had since vacated, and let the curtains fall behind them. He gestured for them to take seats while he retrieved a pitcher and two cups from a nearby folding table.

"Blackberry wine," he said as he poured. "A goodwill gesture from our Siomaigh hosts."

Aine caught the irony in his tone. "I was surprised to see a Siomaigh camp here."

"No more surprised than they would be to see you. Semias has rather rigid ideas about women on the battlefield." By the appraising way his eyes traveled over her armor, Aine thought Abban shared those ideas. He put the cups before them and paused, his massive frame looming over them. "I could tell you how dangerous it was for you to come here, but I'm sure you've already heard it. Which leaves the question, why exactly *are* you here?"

Aine glanced at Ruarc, who produced a sealed message from inside his cloak. She passed it to Abban. "Best you hear it from the king directly."

Abban slid his thumbnail beneath the seal. Aine watched him as he read, but his expression did not hint at his thoughts. He set the letter down on the table. "You can identify the wards?"

"I believe so."

"How?"

Aine met his piercing gaze. "Does it matter?"

A muscle in Abban's jaw twitched. "Young lady, these men are my responsibility. If I'm to trust their lives to your judgment, I'll need more to go on than your word."

Aine's stomach quivered, but she was not about to let this man bully her. "You already have more than my word. You have the king's. Unless you would question his decision?"

She held her breath, expecting an angry response, but Abban just chuckled. "If I didn't know better, I'd say you have Cuillinn blood in you. Calhoun was an upstart whelp when he took the throne, but he was rarely wrong, then or now. Very well, I'll take you at your word. It doesn't sit easily, knowing if you're wrong, I'll lose some very good men."

"I admire your dedication to your warriors," she replied softly. "Be assured I do not take this responsibility lightly."

"We'll want to see the Threewaters battlefield as soon as possible," Ruarc said. "How many casualties?"

"Nearly two hundred. We outnumbered them four to one, and I'm not talking farmers and blacksmiths. These were our best men. The Siomaigh lost half in the first ten minutes. We had slightly better luck. I received sixty back, and only half of them wounded. But every man told the same story: not only did the enemy seem to know what each of its men would do, they anticipated our moves as well. Some of my warriors fought the Ciraen army, and they said even the Empire didn't have such well-directed soldiers."

"Tigh has always been known for its warriors," Aine said.

Abban looked at her over the rim of his goblet. "These were Sliebhanaigh fighters led by a Timhaigh captain."

"Seareanns fight by clan like Aronans," Ruarc explained. "Even the best leaders can barely get men from their own region to work together, let alone former enemies."

"Another indication there's sorcery involved," Aine said. "What happened then?"

"Our side retreated, but the enemy cut off our route, and we were pushed back to the Threewaters. It looked as though we were finished, but then they just stopped, as if they hit an invisible wall. The Timhaigh captain cut down his own men as an example, but they wouldn't budge. Those that made it to the bank collapsed dead. Semias's archers picked off the rest, one by one."

Aine shuddered at the image. The retelling was vivid enough. She didn't want to see it herself. Still, she had a job to do. "Can you provide directions to our mappers?"

"Of course. In the meantime, take my tent. As the only woman here, you should stay out of sight as much as you can. I'll tell the men you're here to treat the wounded. I assume you don't want the truth known."

Aine rose, sensing dismissal, and gave him a slight curtsy. "Thank you, Lord Abban. We'll leave at first light."

She stepped out of the tent and let out her breath in a rush. Her entire body sagged with relief.

"You did well," Ruarc said.

Aine nodded her thanks, but her insides twisted into knots when she recalled Abban's story. It was one thing to avow her capabilities back in Lisdara. It was another to face the reality of blood and death firsthand. What would they find when they reached the battlefield?

Ruarc placed a firm hand on her elbow and steered her to Abban's tent. The appraising stares of the warriors around them prompted Aine to lift her hood again. She had been uncomfortable at Dún Eavan surrounded by twenty-five of the clan's warriors, but somehow she didn't expect the vulnerability she felt at being among hundreds of strangers.

The following day dawned chilly and damp, and thunderclouds mounded on the horizon. Aine dressed quickly, wishing for a change of clothing that didn't smell of sweat or horse, but she abandoned that hope as futile. Ruarc appeared minutes later to help her with her armor, and then she found herself riding in the center of her seven companions again. Either she'd get used to the days on horseback, or she'd never walk again. Right now, it felt like the latter.

They skirted the Siomaigh encampment before turning south toward where the river emerged from the old forest. By the time the sun rose, glowing faintly behind the cover of clouds and mist, Cúan and Aran agreed they were less than an hour's ride from their destination.

Circling carrion birds were the first indication of their proximity to the battlefield. She steeled herself for the sight when they crested the rise, but she couldn't adequately prepare for the carnage. Bodies lay strewn across blood-soaked earth on the opposite side of the river. Those that had died on the water's edge still lay there, caught on the rocks or half-submerged in pools of blood-stained water. Hundreds of birds picked at the rotting flesh.

"Abban's men collected their dead," Sualtam said. "Apparently Fergus didn't bother."

Aine's gorge rose, but she pushed it down and locked away her revulsion. She took the lead down the hill into the shallow river valley, clapping a gloved hand over her nose and mouth at the stench. How could they have left so many men here like discarded rubbish?

She extended her awareness beyond the ever-present background hum of power, but she felt nothing. What if she couldn't do what she had so vehemently assured Calhoun and Abban she could?

No. She couldn't accept that.

"We need to cross," she said, looking up and down the river for a spot not choked with corpses.

"There." Ruarc pointed downstream to a shallow, slow-moving spot, protected by a small outcropping of rocks.

As soon as Aine's horse set its front hooves in the water, a thrill of power coursed through her. She clutched her horse's mane and rode the wave of dizziness while the mare scrambled up the opposite bank. Aine barely managed to rein her in as Ruarc splashed across behind her.

"What is it? Do you feel something?"

She nodded, her throat tight. It was undeniably Balian in origin, similar to the ones in the old forest, but this one was a hundredfold stronger than those fine, old threads of magic. It left her gasping for air, her heart hammering in her chest. The charm burned against her skin. This was not the faded remnant of a centuries-old ward.

"If I didn't know better," Aine murmured, "I would say it was new."

"How is that possible?" Ruarc asked.

"I have no idea." She slid from the mare's back and handed the reins to Ruarc. Carefully, she edged down the riverbank and knelt in the mud beside the water. Power vibrated into her bones, and she swayed in place. She closed her eyes, concentrating, and this time she sensed a faint resonance beneath the overwhelming pulse of power. As she walked upstream, the ward shuddered and vibrated, undulating with the splash and tumble of the water, then fading to barely a whisper.

When she returned to the group, they all stared, wide-eyed. "There's a new ward laid over the old one, as you'd mend a fence or darn a sock."

"Who could be doing that?" Lorcan asked.

"I don't know. But it runs the length of the river, like a natural border. I want to see how it feels where the fighting took place."

They looked at her doubtfully, but she moved upstream anyway. As she neared the battlefield, her heart started to pound. The oily stench of sorcery lay beneath the smell of rotting flesh. The ward trembled in contact with the dark magic, like liquid sizzling in a hot pan, steaming away everything but its scent.

It took supreme force of will to walk among the bodies, enveloped in the sickening smell. Ravens flapped away, squawking at her presence. She gritted her teeth and stripped off her glove, but it took several attempts before she could bring herself to kneel beside a corpse and touch its putrefied flesh.

Death and corruption spiked through her, followed by the dim echo of pain. Aine sucked in a lungful of putrid air as magic crawled across her skin, clawing its way in, desperate to find a new host. Her vision went dark.

Bright, pulsating heat flared from the charm, burning away the sorcery. She leapt to her feet and fled the scene like a startled animal. Then she collapsed on the riverbank and retched up the meager contents of her stomach.

"Aine." Ruarc's hands gripped her shaking shoulders.

"I'm all right now," she whispered, wiping her mouth with her sleeve. She let Ruarc lift her to her feet, then stumbled down to the water and scrubbed her skin raw. When she finally lurched up the bank toward the others, their expressions ranged from amazed to horrified.

Aine dried her hands on her skirt, pulled on her gloves, and took a steadying breath. "The druid's using blood magic to control the warriors. It's as if they were possessed." She shuddered, recalling the sorcery's grasping touch. "That's why they couldn't breach the ward. Their very beings would have resisted it. The magic preserves itself."

"You can sense all that?" Aran said doubtfully.

"I felt it in the corpse. The man may be dead, but the magic is still alive. It's . . ." She hesitated. "It's looking for a new host."

The men exchanged glances. The idea chilled them as much as it did her.

"This is a danger," she said. "We should burn the bodies."

Ruarc shook his head. "Abban can send men back. It's not something you need to see done."

Aine let out a slow sigh and nodded, relieved. She didn't want to spend any more time in this forsaken place than necessary. Her first mission on the battlefield had been a success, but now that she understood the evil they faced, she couldn't help but wonder if her efforts would be enough.

CHAPTER TWENTY-SIX

Eoghan demanded total commitment to every undertaking, and Conor soon understood how structured and unrelenting his mentor's early training with Liam had been. The young man possessed as great an aptitude for teaching as he did for fighting, or perhaps he had just known Conor long enough to convey information in a way he would immediately grasp. Either way, Conor's astonishing progress set Ard Dhaimhin buzzing about Eoghan's talents and those of his chosen apprentice.

Reports of war came infrequently and were sketchy at best. After Fergus's shocking conquest of Sliebhan, his newly swelled forces stalled midway into Siomar. Both sides suffered casualties without much ground gained or lost. Occasionally, Conor wondered if Eoghan censored the incoming news to keep him focused, but his mentor seemed to respect, even if he didn't understand, the ever-increasing pull Conor felt toward the kingdoms.

Fall hurtled into midwinter, a time when the Fíréin focused less on their agrarian pursuits and more on fighting. In the gap between the harvest of the winter grains and the sowing of spring crops, even the craftsmen came out to hone their skills.

"I think it's time you fight someone other than me," Eoghan said with a grin. "Let's see if you've learned anything or if you've just gotten good at reading my mind."

Conor followed Eoghan toward the practice yards, alternately excited and terrified. He had made tremendous strides in his sword work, but he hadn't yet had the chance to try himself against any other opponent.

All the younger apprentices were at their lessons at Carraigmór, so only oath-bound brothers and older apprentices practiced in the yards. Conor glimpsed Riordan sparring with a man half his age with a spear. The younger brother panted and sweated under the barrage of lightning-fast movements. The passing of years had evidently diminished none of Riordan's skills.

"You should see him and Master Liam go at it," Eoghan said. "It's practically a holiday. Half the city turns out to watch."

"I bet. Who exactly am I fighting?"

"Right this way." Eoghan led Conor to a knot of oath-bound brothers standing beside a practice yard. He stopped behind one man and clapped a hand on his shoulder. "Piran. I have a favor to ask."

Piran stepped away from the group, his expression curious. He was a lanky man in his early thirties, a few inches taller than Conor. "What is it?"

Eoghan jerked his head back toward Conor. "I need to test my apprentice's skills. You up for it?"

Piran grinned. "Absolutely. I hope you've trained him well."

Conor flushed. If he performed poorly, it would be all over Ard Dhaimhin in hours. When Eoghan returned to his side, he murmured, "Are you sure about this?"

"Don't worry. You've only been training for eight months. Hold onto your sword, and they'll be calling me a miracle worker."

Eoghan grinned, and Conor's anxiety eased a degree. Less than two years ago, he could barely lift a hoe, let alone a weapon. If Eoghan didn't care if he lost, why should he?

Conor thought he'd be able to watch a few more matches and gather his courage, but as if of one mind, the others cleared the way for him and Piran. One man tossed him a wooden sword, and he caught it as he stepped into the yard. Piran offered a friendly grin before he assumed his guard.

Five seconds into the match, Conor could see Piran was a natural swordsman. He had Eoghan's fluid quality, and he handled the blade effortlessly. Before long, Conor was breathing hard, and sweat beaded on his forehead.

Piran fought best on the attack, but his defense was not nearly as effective. Conor countered a thrust, and before Piran could react, launched his own offense. Several times, he saw his opportunity for the killing blow that would end the match, but he was not quick enough: Piran's blade knocked his aim wide each time.

Focusing too narrowly on the missed opportunity, Conor didn't anticipate Piran's block, an effective circular parry that opened his guard wide and twisted the sword from his hand. Piran smiled and delivered what should have been the decisive thrust.

Instinctively, Conor dove into a shoulder roll and grasped the sword as he popped back up into a crouch. Momentarily stunned by the unexpected move, Piran could not defend against the sweep of Conor's blade against the back of his knees. The brother stumbled, and Conor's sword came to rest just beneath his lowest rib.

Piran lowered his weapon. "I yield."

Conor stared at his opponent for several seconds before he withdrew his sword. Had he really won?

Piran clasped Conor's arm. "Well done. Quite impressive, indeed."

A smattering of applause from the others on the sidelines drew Conor's attention back to his teacher, who watched thoughtfully. Piran glanced at Eoghan with a smile. "Be careful with this one. Given enough time, he just might best you."

Eoghan's expression didn't change. "Indeed."

Conor handed the sword to the next brother and made his way to Eoghan amidst murmurs of approval. Now that the shock was wearing off, he just wanted to be as far away from those considering stares as possible. "Can we go now?"

Eoghan nodded. He looked to the others and said, "Thank you for letting us interrupt."

As they turned away, Conor glimpsed a silent watcher on the edge of the group: Brother Odran, the iron-hard tracker who had escorted Conor to Ard Dhaimhin nearly two years before. Conor's heart dropped to his knees.

Odran gave no sign of recognizing him as he acknowledged Eoghan with a nod.

"Does he pass your test?" Eoghan asked.

Odran's eyes flicked to Conor. He nodded once more.

"Test?" Conor said. "I don't understand."

"It's time to expand your training. Odran will be teaching you tracking and wildcraft. He wanted to be sure you could look after yourself."

"How long will we be gone?" Conor tried to keep the alarm from his voice but failed miserably.

"A few weeks," Odran said.

"Don't worry, we've reached a point where you can stand to be away from drills for a while. Odran will keep you sharp."

"I'm due back out in three days," the tracker said. "Eoghan will help you put together your supplies." He gave Eoghan a nod just short of a bow and shot one last appraising look at Conor before he left.

"Of all the brothers, it has to be Odran?" Conor asked.

"You don't like him?"

"It's not that." He stopped. How could he explain his rush of self-consciousness at the sight of the man who had first revealed the depth of his weaknesses?

Eoghan seemed to understand. "I know he's difficult, but when it comes to survival skills, there could be no better teacher. Trust me."

Conor nodded and fell into step with Eoghan. The older boy's mind was clearly elsewhere, but they walked halfway back to the village before Conor finally broke the silence.

"You didn't expect me to win, did you?"

Eoghan snapped his head back toward Conor, the pensive expression dissolving into a grin. "No. But don't let it go to your head. Your high block's still sloppy. If you go up against a big man like Riordan, he'll crush you."

Conor let out his breath in a rush of relief. Wherever Eoghan's mind had gone, he couldn't help but think it related to him . . . and not in a good way. But he was back, as if that dark look had never come over him. Conor returned the grin. "You still have a few days to drill the bad habit from me."

Conor's departure date arrived much too quickly, and he trudged toward the switchbacks where he was to meet Odran with uneasiness in his gut. It was the first step on a path that would take him further from Ard Dhaimhin and closer to the swiftly changing world beyond its forested borders.

"I hope you packed well," Odran said. "We're expected at the first sentry post in two days, so we'll be traveling fast."

Conor nodded. Eoghan had provided supplies from the storehouse and armory: a water skin, jerked meat, some scrap linen for bandages and straps, a sword, and a staff sling he could also use as a walking stick. He had filled his belt pouch with smooth stones the previous evening and retrieved the wool cloak he had brought from Lisdara.

Odran started up the switchbacks, and Conor followed, matching him stride for stride. He might still struggle to keep up with the skilled tracker, but at least his unceasing training had given him more stamina than he had possessed the last time.

Unlike Eoghan, Odran explained little. Instead, he expected Conor to observe him closely, only pointing out sights he would otherwise miss: a fox's den hidden by ferns, an osprey's nest high in the trees, an indentation in the forest floor that indicated a seasonal tributary. Mostly, Conor absorbed how Odran chose his footing, stepping soundlessly on a patch of moss or staying on the balls of his feet to avoid disturbing a fall of loose rocks, all while setting a pace untenable for all but the most experienced woodsman. He controlled his breathing, not allowing himself to pant, careful not to fall so far behind that Odran had to wait.

When Odran called a stop, Conor collapsed gratefully on a large rock. "Are we eating from the traps?"

"I am," Odran said. "You are going to hunt."

Conor blinked at him and pushed himself to his feet. "Any advice?"

"If you crash around like a wounded boar, you'll scare away the small game."

"Thanks. That's quite helpful." Conor took up his staff sling, and with as much care as he could muster, crept off into the surrounding trees.

In a forest teeming with life, it should not have been difficult to come across a squirrel or rabbit or even winter grouse. Once or twice, he glimpsed movement in the bushes, but in the time it took to fix his aim with a stone, the animal was gone. The light in the forest dwindled to pale gray by the time he returned to the camp, empty-handed but for a fistful of dark red berries. "Best I could do."

Odran looked up from the fire, where he turned a squirrel on a spit. "I hope you didn't eat those. They're poisonous."

Conor sighed and tossed the berries over his shoulder. The smell of roasting squirrel meat made his stomach rumble, but he had too much pride to ask Odran to share after his failure. Instead he gnawed silently on a piece of dried venison from his pack and tried not to reflect on how much it tasted like salted leather.

The next morning, Conor kept his eyes peeled for signs of life, a stone ready in his hand. He saw his chance when a fat hare hopped from the bushes. Carefully, he crept closer, took aim, and let the stone fly.

The rabbit fell over, stunned, but not dead. He hesitated only a moment before he seized it and broke its neck. He knotted a strip of linen from his pack around the rabbit's hind legs and slung it over his shoulder.

They stopped for the night a few miles short of the sentry post. While Odran checked the traps, Conor cleaned the rabbit. Skinning and gutting others' kills in the cookhouse had long since stripped his squeamishness. He spitted the meat over the fire, proud of his small accomplishment.

Odran returned with only a small game bird, but when Conor offered him a bit of rabbit meat, the tracker shook his head. "You earned that. Enjoy it."

Conor attacked the meal with enthusiasm and watched Odran gnaw the meat from the bird's slender bones. He was an odd man, but his devotion to the brotherhood was unquestionable.

"Do you ever wonder what's happening out there?" Conor asked.

"No." Odran's brow furrowed slightly. "Why would I?"

"The Fíréin are waiting for a High King to unite all of Seare. You're not curious about the kingdoms he's supposed to unite?"

"It probably won't happen in our lifetime. We're meant to live in the moment, without worrying about what is to come. Isn't that the definition of faith?"

Conor thought for a moment. He had never expected to have a theological discussion with Odran. "I think of faith as the belief things will work out the way they're supposed to, even when your path looks bleak. You can't do that if you don't look ahead."

"Perhaps your path is just different from mine. Ard Dhaimhin is my final destination. You're just passing through."

"Why do you say that?"

"Eoghan is pushing you harder than even Master Liam pushed him, and both of you show far too much interest in what's going on in the kingdoms."

Conor leaned back against a tree to finish his own meal. So he was not the only one who sensed his time at Ard Dhaimhin was growing short. But for what purpose? One man would hardly make a difference in the battle being fought between nations.

Odran volunteered for the first watch, and Conor stretched out, troubled by the direction of his thoughts. Maybe the other man's definition of faith was as accurate as his own. Right now, speculating about the future accomplished nothing, because he had no clue as to what awaited him.

CHAPTER TWENTY-SEVEN

They broke camp early the next morning amidst a damp chill that left a coating of frost on the tree limbs. Conor studied Odran as he scattered the ashes and brushed away all signs of their passing. The tracker did not acknowledge their previous night's conversation, though he seemed impatient with Conor's pace.

The sentry post lay a few miles north of their camp on the edge of Seanrós, which bordered central Faolán. It was the closest Conor had been to the kingdoms in two years, and the sight of the ancient trees intermingled with the newer growth of the border forest somehow unnerved him. Odran had found him in one of these border regions, his arrival frightening away the sidhe. Would they encounter something similar on this trip? He hadn't given thought to the things that existed outside Ard Dhaimhin's protective wards in months.

Conor would have missed the sentry's dugout had Odran not caught his attention. Tree roots overhung a low rise, undercut by ages of water, and thick foliage shielded the narrow wooden door set into the side.

The door swung inward as they approached. A stooped, elderly man peered out. "Brother Odran, you're late."

Odran gestured for Conor to follow the sentry inside. "Brother Innis doesn't waste time. Get in there."

Conor hurried after the sentry and ducked through the door. The dugout was dark and cramped, with a floor and ceiling of hard-packed earth. A candle glowed atop a rough-hewn table with its single chair, and a straw-stuffed pallet lay in the corner. The sentry shuffled to a niche stacked high with wax tablets and parchments, reminding Conor of a gnome from a bard's story.

"I'm—"

"Brother Conor, I know. You're the reason he's late. Odran loses time only when he's breaking in a new runner."

"I'm not a runner—" Conor began.

Odran shook his head and leaned casually against the wall. "Feel anything unusual lately, Brother Innis?"

"Not since the last time." Innis produced a thin wax tablet and handed it to Odran. His eyes passed over Conor as if he weren't there. Odran jerked his head toward the door, and they stepped out into tree-filtered sunlight.

"That's it?" Conor said, glancing back at the dugout.

"That's it. We have half a dozen other posts to visit in this quadrant today."

Conor fell into step beside him. "What were you asking him?"

"Nothing that should concern you."

"Did Master Liam tell you not to talk to me about it?"

"If I say no, you won't believe me. If I say aye, I still can't tell you."

Conor had come to expect Odran's evasive answers, but that made them no less irritating. "Then why would you bring it up in front of me?"

"If you're as smart as Eoghan seems to think, you don't need me to tell you."

Conor let out his breath in a frustrated whoosh. Why did everything have to be a riddle with him?

Their next several stops, only two miles apart, were just as succinct, though none of the sentries were as eccentric as Brother Innis. Nowhere else did Odran ask questions, so Conor assumed only Innis had witnessed the original incident, whatever it had been.

Halfway to their final stop of the day, Odran paused in his stride and cocked his head. "Someone breached the wards on the east edge of Seanrós. Let's go, quickly."

Conor picked up his pace, doing his best to move silently without losing sight of his guide. Maybe he would get a chance to see what a tracker did after all. Hopefully it was an innocent incursion that wouldn't involve bloodshed. Odran seemed far too comfortable with killing for Conor's liking.

They moved swiftly for at least half an hour, and the effort required to maintain both speed and silence wore on him. Three days was not long enough to master the Fíréin's deadly stealth in the woods. Odran slowed his pace, but when Conor turned to look, he saw only trees. Did the tracker sense their quarry?

Then Conor heard the soft shuffle of horses and the murmur of voices. He crouched beside Odran in a stand of giant ferns while they waited for the intruders to approach. The tracker eased his sword silently from his scabbard, and Conor palmed a stone from his belt pouch.

Horses' hooves thudded on the mossy earth, and Conor made out the distinct sounds of four voices, three men and a woman. He held up three fingers on one hand and one on the other. Odran nodded. He had probably come to the same conclusion.

A chestnut mare emerged from a thick clutch of trees, its rider small beneath a voluminous cloak. Conor glimpsed no weapons. The woman was in the lead.

Abruptly, she reined in and held up a gloved hand. Three men fanned out around her, and blades rang from sheaths.

"Who's there?" the woman called. "Show yourselves!"

Conor glanced at Odran, amazed she had perceived their silent presence, but the brother no longer crouched in the bushes beside him.

Instantly, half a dozen Fíréin brothers materialized around the intruders, swords pressed to vulnerable points in the men's armor. A tracker gripped the bridle of the woman's horse.

"What is your business here?" Odran demanded.

Conor crept around the screen of foliage for a better look. Two of the men faced away from him, and the third looked terrified, his sword hand shaking. Not a warrior, then.

"Forgive us, we didn't realize we had strayed into the old forest." The woman's voice sent a tingle across his skin, a response to an accent rarely heard in Seare. "We were tracking a ward. We meant no harm."

It couldn't be. Conor lost Odran's next question beneath the rush of blood in his ears when the woman dropped back her hood, revealing a tumble of glossy, honey-colored hair. "I am Aine Nic Tamhais, sister to King Calhoun of Faolán and Brother Liam of Ard Dhaimhin."

Conor's heart hammered against his ribcage, sending sparks of white across his vision. She'd changed immeasurably in those two short years.

Her features had matured into striking beauty, and her quicksilver eyes appraised the armed men without fear. Her commanding demeanor did not hint at her mere eighteen years.

Conor realized he was standing in plain view, gaping, but no one seemed to notice. He stepped back into the bushes and forced himself to pay attention to Odran's question. "You said you were tracking wards?"

Aine's horse shifted nervously, and she gave the brother holding the bridle a stern look. "I would let go. Fiachra is not particularly fond of strangers."

Odran nodded, and the man stepped away. Aine settled her mount and looked back to Odran. "No doubt you've felt the disturbances on the eastern wards? We're in the process of mapping them. I followed this one into the forest, but I didn't know I had crossed into Fíréin territory." She bowed her head. "I apologize."

Odran seemed unimpressed by the explanation. Conor gripped a stone, ready to throw, and then forced himself to relax. He could not hurt a fellow brother. But neither could he allow Aine to be harmed. He was about to reveal his presence when Odran spoke.

"I suggest you leave the forest with all haste. If you wander this way again, it won't matter who your relations are."

Aine dipped her head in acknowledgement. The Fíréin retracted their swords and stepped back to allow the men to turn their horses.

"Let's go," she said. The party turned back the way they had come.

Then Aine wheeled her mount around toward Odran. "Some time ago, a young man entered the northern forest, intending to go to Ard Dhaimhin. His name was Conor Mac Nir. Do you know if he ever reached the city?"

Odran looked at her blankly. "I know of no one by that name."

Aine's brow furrowed. She nodded and urged her mare into a trot toward her guards. Within moments, they disappeared into the tangle of trees.

Conor went to one knee on suddenly unsteady legs. He had thought of what he would do if he saw Aine again. Yet she had been a mere twenty spans away, and he had hidden, unable to speak or do more than stare.

Aine had asked about him, though. She had not forgotten him. If only he had revealed himself, he might have talked to her. Why had he frozen in the bushes like a frightened rabbit?

Odran strode toward him, but he passed right by. "Conor?"

"I'm here," Conor said.

Odran jerked his head toward him and blinked a few times. "How did you . . .?" He shook his head. "There are a few things you aren't telling me, I think."

+ + +

"I did what?" Conor stopped plucking the partridge beside their campfire. Odran had said nothing about the incident with Aine and her guards until they made camp for the night, and his first question was not the one he expected.

"You didn't know?"

Conor put down the bird. "I've never heard of this fading until you asked me. How would I know I could do it?"

"Nonetheless, you did. Quite well, if I walked right past you. Don't look so shocked. It's a common gift among the Fíréin. Sentries and trackers are specifically selected from those who exhibit it."

Conor could barely wrap his mind around what Odran was saying. "You mean I was invisible."

Odran chuckled, an oddly disturbing sound. "Hardly. *You* didn't change. I did. Haven't you ever been looking for something, say, your flint, and it's been in front of you the whole time? The flint didn't disappear. You just overlooked it."

"So those of us with this fading ability disappear into the surroundings?"

"Exactly."

A smile crept onto Conor's face. It explained so much: how the Fíréin just seemed to appear and disappear, how Riordan always managed to startle him, how he had watched Eoghan practice unseen all those times. It even explained why he had always won at hide-and-find as a child.

"How does it work?"

"It's different for everyone. After a while, you can just do it at will. My guess is you were concentrating on not being seen, so you made yourself nearly impossible to see."

"Nearly?"

"As I said, you're not invisible. The ability works on people's expectations. If they're looking for you, it's difficult to hide in plain view.

The bigger question is, what about the lady Aine made you so desperately want to stay out of sight?"

Conor's face heated. Odran had been setting up this question all along. He averted his eyes. "They think I'm dead. If word should get back . . ."

"The lady certainly doesn't think you're dead. And given the state of affairs in the kingdoms, I hardly think news you're alive will make an impact."

"Maybe not, but it will make Calhoun look like a liar."

Odran smiled. It was a lame excuse, and they both knew it.

Conor took the first watch, too keyed up to sleep. He wrapped his cloak around himself and tuned his hearing to the forest's night sounds, but his mind kept drifting back to Aine. She had looked like a queen in her embellished armor, confident and beautiful, commanding. Had he seen her then as he did now, he would never have had the courage to write the love song for her or to take her in his arms the night he left.

The recollection of her soft lips against his, buried in his memory the past two years, sprang to the forefront in vivid detail. His breath caught in his chest, and he shook his head as if he could shake out the memory.

Aine was not any woman. She was the lady healer of Lisdara. And evidently, she had become someone of note if she traveled with two guards and a scholar. What had she said? *We are tracking a ward. No doubt you've felt the disturbances on the eastern wards? We're in the process of mapping them.*

And Odran's question: *Have you felt anything unusual?*

The pieces fell into place swiftly and neatly. The wards that kept Ard Dhaimhin safe from incursion must extend beyond the borders of the forest. Aine was mapping them for the Faolanaigh forces. Were they merely a tool for detecting the movement of enemy warriors, or did they have a more offensive function?

The revelation gave him the direction he had been seeking. The Fíréin must understand the wards. If he could learn something of value, he could leave and offer his knowledge to Calhoun. By now, as Odran so bluntly pointed out, it hardly mattered who knew he was alive.

For the first time since coming to Ard Dhaimhin, Conor knew why he was there, and he finally had a goal fixed firmly in mind.

CHAPTER TWENTY-EIGHT

The small party of riders remained silent long after they cleared the edge of Seanrós and emerged into the meadowlands beneath a glaring sunlit sky. Perhaps the men held their peace because they knew how close they had come to engaging in a futile fight. Aine stayed quiet because she did not yet trust her voice to be any steadier than the hand holding the rein.

After a few minutes in the open, Ruarc guided his horse alongside hers. "You handled that situation very well."

"Thank you." It had been too close. The Fíréin rarely spared those who strayed across their borders without invitation, as was their sovereign right. Had Aine not identified herself as sister to both a king and a Fíréin brother, she doubted they would have been allowed to live.

Somehow, the realization did not shake her as much as her own willingness to put her men in danger. She had known the risk they faced by entering the forest, and she had trusted her connection with Calhoun and Liam would save them. The fact she'd been right did not make it any less irresponsible.

Ruarc studied her. "Did you find what you were looking for?"

A double-edged question. She nodded. "The wards we have been tracking are definitely connected to the wards around Ard Dhaimhin. Whoever is strengthening them must be Fíréin."

"Shouldn't that please you?" Ruarc asked. "At least it means it's someone on our side."

"It also means there are far more people with the ability to sense the wards than just Lady Aine," Aran said, bringing his horse alongside hers.

She gave him a nod of agreement. Cúan might still be the better scribe, but Aran had a fine mind for strategy. He grasped situations quickly and analyzed them without error. He would have made a formidable battle commander had he the remotest inclination toward warfare.

"It's only a matter of time before Fergus has one of them mapping the wards for him, and then we've lost our advantage," Aine said. "In any case, I have the evidence Gainor and Calhoun wanted. We've scoured nearly every corner of Faolán and Siomar except for the border forests, and we're unlikely to survive any more expeditions of this type."

After an hour at their brisk pace, Abban's camp came to view. Months ago, they had relocated north and west to a spot that held less strategic advantage but boasted other benefits. First, it was located at the intersection of two strong wards, which protected the camp from incursion and ensured no one infected by the druid's sorcery could enter. Second, the only way to reach it was through a gauntlet of ward-laced open land or heavily defended Fíréin territory. Aine still felt proud of her contribution to their safety, even if Aran had been the one to note the site's strategic significance.

Since then, their numbers had tripled, gathering nearly twelve hundred warriors under half a dozen banners both Faolanaigh and Siomaigh, and Aine saw at a single glance the numbers had expanded again while they were gone. The banner flying prominently above Abban's confirmed Gainor had arrived with his six hundred warriors from the north.

Shouts went up as they entered camp, passing word of their arrival back to the command pavilion at its center. Men called out greetings, as often directed toward Aine as the well-respected warriors who accompanied her.

"My lady, when you have a moment . . ." a man called out as she passed.

"Come see me tomorrow morning," she said. "I'll have some time then."

Aine spent as much time as she could attending to the medical needs of the camp, but her mapping project kept her away for days or weeks at a time, leaving long lines of patients to attend when she returned. Between the men who would gather outside the infirmary in the morning and meetings with the commanders well into the night, she was guaranteed a series of exhausting days.

Several young pages met them at the pavilion to take their horses.

Aine dismounted and handed over her reins, intending to go straight to her tent, but Lord Abban swept aside the curtains of the pavilion.

"Lady Aine, come, tell us what you found," he called.

Inside, Abban and Seaghan bent over the maps in close discussion with the two newcomers, Gainor and a man Aine recognized immediately— Keondric Mac Eirhinin.

Gainor glanced up and favored Aine with a warm smile. He moved to her side and kissed both her cheeks in welcome. "Dear sister. You have news?"

Aine stripped off her gloves and approached the table. "Lord Abban showed you our completed map?"

"He insisted on waiting for you," Abban said.

"Very well. Aran needs to make the addition anyway. We followed the Corelain Wells ward into Fíréin territory today."

"Fíréin territory?" Seaghan repeated. "And you came back?"

"The lady can be very persuasive," Ruarc said.

Aine retrieved a wide sheet of parchment from the wooden map chest and spread it atop the map they had been studying. Gainor's eyebrows lifted, and Aine smiled. Cúan had truly outdone himself with the detailed drawing, rendering Seare's eastern topography as lovingly and skillfully as any of the ancient illuminated maps. This one bore a spiderweb of crimson lines that covered all of Faolán and Siomar.

"You can see the significance," Aine said.

Gainor studied the map intently. "They all lead to Ard Dhaimhin."

"Exactly. It took perhaps a quarter of an hour before we were stopped at sword point by a half-dozen Fíréin sentries."

Keondric looked at her with a warmth that heated her cheeks. "Bravely done, Lady Aine."

Aine rushed on without acknowledging the comment. "We suspected the wards were originally created and maintained from the High City, but we had to confirm they were still active within Fíréin territory. Whoever is rebuilding the wards, though, is doing it locally." She tapped the map where the wards showed a second, dotted line.

"Do you have any ideas yet?" Gainor asked.

"Considering this is magic no one but the Fíréin remember," Seaghan said, "we should assume it's a brother. Or at least someone trained in Ard Dhaimhin."

"If it's a brother," Gainor said, "he's either afraid he will be punished for interfering with the kingdoms, or he knows it would make him a target."

"Someone with the ability to make the wards could unmake them as well," Aine said.

"That's exactly what troubles me." Gainor sank into a chair and crossed his arms over his chest. "What if this person works for Fergus? He might be trying to get us to rely on the wards' strength. If he were to break them, we would be taken by surprise."

"That's why we have rangers patrolling the wards," Abban said. "I've never been that comfortable with magic. I don't doubt Lady Aine's word, but I feel better with a few extra pairs of human eyes on our enemies' movements."

Gainor studied the map silently for a minute and then pointed to a spot several miles south of Threewaters. "I intended to encamp here. Now, it seems to me we'd be better here, at the intersection of what you call Callindor and Southbrook. We could muster warriors anywhere in Siomaigh within hours should the outriders send word Fergus is mounting an attack."

Aine glanced at Gainor. "Who's watching Faolán's borders with Tigh if you're here?"

"Lord Fliann. His men know the countryside so well a rabbit couldn't cross the border without their notice. Why?"

Aine indicated a spot along the Faolanaigh border that abutted Róscomain. "We haven't been able to map this area. There doesn't seem to be a ward here, even on the edge of the forest. Conor once hinted they encountered trouble there on their way to Lisdara. It's the only weak spot we've found."

"I'll send word to Fliann right away," Gainor said. "If there's a weakness, you can expect the druid to exploit it."

Aine nodded. "Thank you. Now if you gentlemen don't need me, I'm going to rest. I'm sure there will be a line forming at the infirmary in the morning."

Gainor and Seaghan bowed, and Abban said, "Thank you, Lady Aine. Your assistance has been invaluable."

Aine inclined her head in acknowledgement and stepped from the tent into the fading sunlight. She let out a weary sigh. Her nerves were stretched taut, and her mind whirred constantly with what-ifs. What if she was wrong about the wards? What if one of her assurances about their strength led to the deaths of these warriors she had come to know and respect? She had done her best to use her abilities for Seare, but deep down she was just a girl who had been thrown into deep water.

She'd gone no more than a few steps when a voice called out, "Lady Aine!"

She turned as Lord Keondric strode toward her. She'd always thought him handsome, with coal-black hair and brilliant, almost unnaturally blue eyes. But something about his smile made her heart beat too fast . . . and not in a pleasing way. She took a step back, and Ruarc put a steadying hand on her back.

"What you've done here is impressive," Keondric said. "I wanted to congratulate you on the accomplishment."

"Thank you, my lord." She dipped her head while searching for a way to extricate herself.

Ruarc saved her. "The lady is tired, my lord; she's just far too polite to say so. Perhaps you could speak later."

Keondric gave her a graceful bow. "Forgive me. I just wanted to convey my admiration. We will, after all, be family someday soon. Rest well, my lady."

Aine licked her lips and nodded. Why did the man unnerve her so? He'd been polite and solicitous when she had encountered him at Lisdara, but she'd never been struck with this uneasiness in his presence. Was it because there was something more than brotherly admiration in his gaze? He was betrothed to her sister, but she knew full well it was not a love match. He and Niamh had never said more than a handful of words to each other.

"You might as well get used to the admiration," Ruarc murmured behind her. "I understand Calhoun has already received a number of discreet inquiries about you."

Aine's eyes rose to Ruarc's face in alarm. "Surely, he wouldn't—"

"No. Now is not the time. But the war will eventually end, and you can't avoid the question forever."

"Conor's coming back, Ruarc." Aine poured every ounce of conviction she could muster into her voice, even though inside she wasn't nearly so sure. "Besides, we have far greater things to worry about."

Aine tossed beneath the wool blanket in her tent that night, listening to the brisk summer wind rustle and snap the canvas sides. Her confidence fell away with the tears that rolled down her cheeks. It was futile, she knew in her heart. All her work, the wards, the maps . . . they would only slow down the spread of evil that threatened to swallow Seare. Balus had told her clearly things would worsen before they improved, and now she feared her intervention would only delay the inevitable.

Or was it the unpleasant feelings dredged up by Keondric's admiration that colored her perspective? Ruarc seemed to believe she'd give up and someday marry another man, but she refused to believe the sentry's words. Conor wasn't dead. She'd know somehow. But that didn't mean he hadn't changed his mind and decided to make a home at Ard Dhaimhin.

"Foolish girl," she whispered. "Pining for someone who might never return."

She threw the blanket aside and wrapped her cloak around herself. Through the gap in the tent flaps, morning light glimmered in the gray sky. Creaks and rustles paired with the muted voices of men, signs the camp was beginning to stir. She pushed aside the canvas and stepped into the steady breeze.

Where did I lose my way, Lord? Her eyes drifted beyond the camp to the copses of ash in the distance. *I was so certain I knew what You wanted from me, and now I have no idea.*

A gust of wind whipped her unbound hair across her face, stinging her skin.

I have allowed you to succeed in this endeavor, came the answer with chill certainty, *but this was not what I asked of you.*

Aine shivered. Before she could ask the question, the answer came: *Have faith in Me. Seek My wisdom, accept My guidance.*

They were the same words Balus had given her when she was beneath the water, but somehow they only confused her more. Wasn't that what she was doing? If mapping the wards and healing were not her true purpose, then what was?

There are so yet so many who do not know Me, who have never heard My name. It is for the love of these multitudes this storm of darkness must be stopped.

The answer had been there all along. Seare might be the first battleground, but the war was far wider. Knowledge of Balus was the end goal, not peace.

A ward vibrated at the edge of her awareness like a plucked harp string. She saw the map's red lines in her mind's eye, and instantly, she knew where the disturbance had originated. She spun on her heel, intending to fetch Ruarc, but he already stood behind her.

"Something breached one of the wards," Aine said. "We need to go investigate."

"Warriors?"

"I don't think so. It doesn't feel like sorcery, but I've never been able to distinguish ordinary people crossing them before. It has to be something else."

"Have Abban send a scouting party."

"They won't know what to look for. It has to be me."

To her surprise, Ruarc didn't argue. Abban, on the other hand, resisted vehemently. He relented only when Aine agreed to add another ten warriors to her usual twenty. Once the sun rose high enough to cast shadows, Aine set out with her guard and three packhorses carrying food and shelter for their two-day excursion.

"What do you expect to find?" Lorcan asked once they cleared the camp.

"Not a pile of dead Sliebhanaigh warriors if that's what you mean."

Lorcan still looked uneasy, but the other men seemed unaware of the danger. They had traveled without incident along these wards for so long, they no longer expected battle or ambush. That alone disturbed Aine.

She identified the ward early in the day, but they rode for hours without any indication of trouble. Aine began to doubt her own certainty about the breach's location. Then, as the sun dipped behind the tree-lined horizon, she pulled up short. A kernel of cold formed in her middle, and a chill crept across her skin, as if she had passed into a pocket of winter amidst the summer warmth.

"Here." She had felt this sensation only once in her life, and it was one she couldn't mistake.

Ruarc and Lorcan closed around her protectively.

"What is it?" Ruarc asked.

"Sidhe."

"Here?" Lorcan asked. "Are you sure?"

"The last time I felt this, a bean-sidhe tried to drown me in Loch Eirich. I'm certain."

"What about them?" Ruarc jerked his head toward the guardsmen who watched her expectantly.

"Don't say anything yet." She turned to the waiting warriors and called, "There's nothing here. Whatever disturbed the ward is gone."

Relief—and perhaps disappointment—rippled through the group. She turned back to Lorcan and Ruarc and said, "I don't want to camp here tonight. I've had enough contact with the sidhe for one lifetime."

Fortunately, the men didn't ask the question that nagged at her: why would the sidhe appear in the middle of a sparsely populated region of Siomar, when before they seemed to hover around the border forests? Had their assumption that the wards repelled the sidhe been wrong? Were they somehow attracted to sources of power, whether dark or light?

That, of course, assumed this had been happenstance. There might be a far more calculated reason behind the disturbance.

Ruarc apparently had come to the same conclusion. When they made camp, he said, "We'll double the watches tonight. We'll take no chances this might be a trap of some sort."

Evening passed into deep night without any sign of danger. Still, Aine led the men in the old prayer she had said at Dún Eavan. "Comdiu protect us, Comdiu watch over us, Comdiu be at the left and the right and smooth the way before us. Comdiu stand between us and the harm of this world, and banish the darkness with the light of Your son, Balus."

She repeated it once more through, comforted by the number of voices that joined hers. The mood lightened as the men claimed Comdiu's protection. Only a few remained silent, uncomfortable with the prayer, and they were fewer than she had expected.

Weary from her sleepless nights and a string of days on horseback, Aine retreated to the simple tent. Ruarc bedded down just outside the opening. The flickering of the flames against the canvas and the snap of the fire lulled her to sleep.

Aine jolted awake in the middle of the night, her heart pounding. She poked her head through the tent opening. The fire had died, and the only light came from a crescent moon overhead. She could just make out the shapes of the sleeping men.

"What's wrong?" Ruarc whispered.

"I don't know. Something woke me." She scanned the camp with a tickle of disquiet. "Ruarc, who was on watch?"

Ruarc made his own quick assessment, and alarm broke over his face. He nudged the man nearest him with his toe. "Wake up!"

Instantly, the men sprang awake, weapons in hand. Ruarc kicked the fire's embers to life again. "We're missing men."

A quick count revealed only three of the seven men assigned to the watch. Those missing were the four who had not voiced the prayer with the rest of them.

"The sidhe," Aine whispered to Ruarc. "They must have lured them away."

"Take Aine," Ruarc said, gesturing to Lorcan.

The blond warrior hastened to her side, his sword drawn. "My lady."

Unsettled, Aine followed Lorcan into the center of the group, which quickly closed around her. Ruarc and several others lit torches and searched for the missing sentries, but she knew they would find nothing. They had gone willingly, just as Aine had when the apparition lured her to the lakeshore.

The back of her neck prickled. She started to turn, but Lorcan shoved her roughly to the ground. She hit the turf hard and pulled her dagger free from her belt just as Lorcan's blade deflected a thrust meant for her. A quick clash of metal, and the attacker lay at her guard's feet, a red stain spreading across his chest.

Ruarc appeared beside her in the chaos, his own weapon drawn, and helped her up with his free hand. "Who is it?"

"Sualtam," Lorcan said grimly. "I would have bet my life he was a loyal man."

"He probably *was* a loyal man."

All eyes turned to Aine. She still gripped her dagger in a shaking hand, and it took several tries to sheath it at her belt. "It was the sidhe."

"The sidhe lured the sentries away?" Lorcan asked. "Made Sualtam try to kill you?"

"The sidhe can make you see whatever they wish, if you don't guard yourself carefully. They exploit our weaknesses, play on our emotions, cloud our judgment. I should have expected it."

"Which means we need to return to camp," Ruarc said. "I don't think this attack was any accident."

Aine looked back to the dead man, her heart still racing. "I don't think so, either."

Hours dragged by as they waited for the sky to lighten enough to start the trip back to camp. It gave Aine far too much time to mull a new, troubling question: did the sidhe have their own agenda, or were they now doing Diarmuid's bidding?

She wasn't sure which was worse: the idea Fergus and his druid might control the sidhe, or that she had two separate enemies who wanted her dead.

✦ ✦ ✦

Aine knew something was wrong when they reached the camp. Too many sentries watched the perimeter, and they scrutinized her party suspiciously as they entered.

Abban met them outside the main tent before they could dismount. His haggard appearance told of his own sleepless night.

"What happened?" Aine asked.

"Come inside, and we'll talk there."

Aine glanced back to be sure Ruarc followed and caught Lorcan's eye. "You, too."

Lorcan followed them wordlessly into the command tent. Abban noted the second man's presence with a raised eyebrow, but he waited for Aine to speak.

"The sidhe breached the ward," she said. "We lost five men. Four disappeared, and one came back tied to his horse."

"He tried to kill Lady Aine," Lorcan said calmly, but she knew the betrayal of one of their own weighed on him.

"And you saved my life. If it were not for your attention, I would not be standing here. Both the king and I will want to see you rewarded."

Lorcan looked embarrassed. "I want no reward, my lady."

"All the same, you rendered all of us a great service," Abban said with a bow. He deflated when he turned back to Aine. "I had hoped our own problems were isolated. We too lost a number of sentries. Some of the others aren't quite in their heads."

"What do you mean?"

Abban hesitated. "They claimed to have seen things. They're saying this place is cursed. We had to restrain them to keep them from fleeing or hurting themselves."

Aine remembered the horrific visage of the bean-sidhe before it frightened her into the lake. Men who never before believed in the sidhe might certainly receive a shock to their sanity. "I'd like to talk to them. Perhaps I can help."

"Too dangerous," Abban said.

Lorcan spoke up from behind her. "I think Lady Aine has proven she doesn't frighten easily. Keep them restrained. Perhaps she can do them some good."

Aine nodded her thanks to Lorcan, buoyed by his support. "I don't know whether the sidhe are acting on their own behalf or Fergus's. Either way, they are doing the Adversary's bidding. They mean to corrupt the weaker minds and doubtful hearts. These are spiritual tactics, my lord. We have to respond in kind."

"How exactly do you intend to do that?" Abban asked.

"By fighting the darkness with light." It was exactly what she had been mulling when the disturbance on the ward distracted her. "I'll ask Calhoun to send one of the priests. The men could use some spiritual leadership."

Abban looked unconvinced, but he didn't contradict her. "If you believe it will help."

"I do. In any case, they can offer reassurance and comfort." Aine looked back to Lorcan. "I'd also like to ask the king's permission to take you into my service, if you are willing."

Lorcan gave her a deep bow. "It would be a great honor, my lady."

"It would put my mind at ease," Aine said. "And Ruarc deserves some sleep."

Ruarc and Lorcan grinned at each other. At least they were both taking to the change easily. Lorcan had time and again proven his loyalty and his skills, and it seemed only right to relieve Ruarc from the constant responsibility of looking after her.

She was beginning to think he would need every bit of help he could get.

CHAPTER TWENTY-NINE

When Conor returned to Ard Dhaimhin, he didn't mention the incident involving Aine to Eoghan. He thought Odran might comment on it, but when days passed without the subject arising, he concluded the tracker had either forgotten or dismissed it as yet another unimportant detail about the outside world.

Conor's fading ability, on the other hand, elicited more interest. He had barely been back a day when Eoghan said, "Odran tells me you've discovered a new gift."

They were back on the crannog where his training had begun, working through the drills he had neglected for the past three weeks. Conor paused, sword in hand, and grinned. "I'd hoped I could keep it quiet. I was looking forward to practicing on you."

"Too late, I'm afraid."

"You knew?"

"I suspected. You must take after Riordan. He's maddeningly difficult to track."

"I take it you've tried?"

"I trained with him as you're training with Odran. He's not so easy to follow either, if you're wondering."

Conor remembered how Odran had faded beside him and then reappeared before Aine's guards. Maybe he hadn't struggled to keep up as much as he thought.

"What do you know about the wards?"

Eoghan frowned at the change of topic. "Not much. Why?"

"There have been disturbances outside the forest. I think it has something to do with the war in Siomar."

"Odran's been holding out on me."

So Odran was Eoghan's source of information after all. "I gathered Liam forbade it."

"That's what I was afraid of. It's been too quiet for too long."

"Do you suppose Brother Gillian would know something?"

"Gillian knows something about everything. Why so much interest in the wards?"

Conor hesitated. His thoughts about Aine were private, but perhaps Eoghan could help him. "We intercepted a small party of riders on the Seanrós borders. They said they were tracking a ward from outside."

"And Odran let them go?"

"They weren't a threat," Conor said. "Just a couple of Faolanaigh scholars and their guards. I figured it had to do with the war, and I wondered what use the wards might be to them."

"I know there were far more wards in Daimhin's time, but they weren't maintained after the kingdom split. And before you ask, I don't know how maintenance is done. I'm not sure anyone does. Even the wards around Ard Dhaimhin are growing thin, or so I've heard. I can't feel them myself. I don't have the gift."

But Conor did. He had felt them each time he crossed them in the forest, just as he felt the power of Meallachán's harp, the oath-binding sword, the wheel charm. He drew on the same power each time he played.

You can do it at will, Odran had said about his fading ability.

Those with the gift of music have the instinctive ability to transform the language of music into the language of magic.

The storyteller makes his story real during the telling.

Even the wards around Ard Dhaimhin are growing thin.

His knees weakened at his sudden flash of insight. It couldn't be that simple, could it?

"Eoghan, I need to go to Carraigmór. Are we done here?"

Eoghan frowned, but he nodded. They packed their supplies and crossed back to the shore, where Conor strode off toward the keep.

A brother escorted him to Liam's study. The Ceannaire rose from his desk when he entered. "Conor. I didn't expect you for a few hours yet. Is there a problem?"

"No sir. I've just been away so long I was anxious to play. Besides, I understand Eoghan has plans for my evening."

Liam gestured to the harp in the corner. "As you wish."

Conor's hands shook as he took the harp onto his lap. He turned his mind to the wards that protected the fortress and waited, but not a single note surfaced in his mind.

"Is there a problem?" Master Liam asked.

"No, no problem." He had to play something. It was his only way back to Aine.

The music came to him, but it wasn't what he expected. His elation and confusion over seeing Aine spilled from the harp, and he turned the direction of the song with effort. He couldn't afford to reveal too much, despite Liam's claim he couldn't interpret the music. Conor tried to shape the song's direction, take it back to the wards, but instead, he managed only a discordant collection of notes. He dropped his hands from the strings, disappointment welling inside him.

"I'm sorry, Master Liam. I must still be tired from my last assignment."

"Return tomorrow then, Brother Conor."

Conor left the study, crushed by the weight of his failure. He had been so certain that if he could just focus on his objective, he could effect the transformation from music to magic and have some sort of impact on Carraigmór's wards. Yet it felt like trying to speak a foreign language of which he had no knowledge.

He was halfway across the hall when a thready voice called his name.

Brother Gillian stood in the doorway behind him, one hand braced on the wall. Conor rushed to his side and took his arm.

"Brother Gillian? What are you doing here?"

"It didn't work, did it?"

"No. How did you—"

"Not here. Help me back to my chamber, boy."

Conor could hardly suppress his questions on the way back to Gillian's chamber. When they were safely ensconced in the room, he blurted, "How did you know?"

"I could sense what you were trying to do."

"Then why didn't it work?"

"You tell me."

Conor scrubbed his hands over his face in frustration. "I have no idea. Usually I can think of something and play it."

"Ah, but there is still a difference between music and magic, isn't there? Music is a talent. Magic is a gift. Think of when you have used magic."

He thought back to the night at Lisdara with Meallachán's harp and just recently in the forest when he had faded from sight. "It was the most important thing to me at that moment."

"There's your answer then."

Conor had another question. "Why are the wards so important anyway? Other than binding the sidhe."

"They weren't made to bind the sidhe," Gillian said. "At the time, Seare was under attack from a bigger threat. After Daimhin and the coming of the truth, most of the druids retreated to the nemetons or one of the eastern isles. But a few, those you call the Red Druids, refused to give up their power. Fearing they would use their magic against the throne, Daimhin himself created the wards. The druids could not cross them. The sorcery within them is repelled by the Balian magic, and so their influence and movements were much restricted.

"While belief remained strong, the wards held. But as the influence of the darkness grew greater, the wards became weaker. They're all but gone in Tigh and Sliebhan, and somewhat intact in Siomar and Faolán."

"How do you know all this?" Conor asked in amazement.

Gillian turned his head and lifted his white hair. Faded black tattoos traced the lined skin of his neck. "You see, you must have the need to effect the wards. And you must have the tool used to create them all that time ago."

Conor knew immediately. "Meallachán's harp."

"You are a clever boy. Now run along. I have nets to mend."

Conor rose to leave. "Brother Gillian, if the wards fade where darkness holds sway, why have they begun to weaken in Ard Dhaimhin?"

Gillian opened his mouth to answer. Then he snapped it shut and gave a sharp shake of his head before he felt once more for his nets.

✦   ✦   ✦

Knowing what needed to be done made little difference to Conor's daily routine. He was still Eoghan's apprentice, and he was far from being ready to take his trials. Short of Liam's summoning Meallachán back to Carraigmór, he had no way to test his theory.

As if to temper Conor's success with Odran, Eoghan proceeded to show him exactly how far he had to go in his training. Over the next several weeks, the older boy increased the intensity of his drills, leading them with as much effort as Conor exerted and extending the length of their practice matches. Eoghan pushed him to his limits, regardless of the bruises or lacerations they inflicted on each other. Conor's time must be drawing short if Eoghan was attempting to give him a taste of a real life-or-death match. After nearly four weeks of the strict routine, Eoghan sent Conor back out with Odran to collect reports from the sentries along the southern edge of Rós Dorcha. A thrill of anticipation rippled through Conor when he realized these sentries might have direct knowledge of the war in Siomar.

Odran was no less abrupt than before, and he seemed to delight in seeing Conor fail, but he was meticulous in his teaching. Conor learned how to create different kinds of traps and snares and how to read tracks and estimate their makers' weight and speed of travel. Odran also taught him how to take and maintain a heading in the tangled thicket of ancient trees. In short, he began to impart the skills that would keep Conor alive on his own.

Odran also drilled him in close-quarters combat, an entirely different way of fighting than the open-battlefield techniques he had learned from Eoghan.

"This is about survival," he said. "In the forest, you don't have the luxury of a fair fight. Seize whatever advantage you can."

It was Odran's short preamble to ambush using his fading skills. The Fírein had perfected the strike-and-retreat tactics for which Seareann warriors were known, and this sort of fighting put Conor's strategic thinking to good use.

In between lessons, Conor and Odran took messages between posts and met up with runners who would take them back to Ard Dhaimhin. The runners were odd and solitary, and they seemed to have forgotten how to behave in human company. Conor quickly gave up trying to befriend them.

The sentries, on the other hand, welcomed the company, and Conor needed only to offer interesting stories or news from Ard Dhaimhin to elicit information in return. Their sharp eyes missed nothing, including the nuances of the shifting loyalties in the southern kingdoms.

The most interesting intelligence came from their last stop, a sentry named Ciaran. He was the polar opposite of Innis, tall and slender with the arrow-straight posture of a man too disciplined to be bent by time. He wore his long white hair in a queue away from a deeply lined face the tone and texture of fine, old leather.

Ciaran took a single look at Conor and said, "You want to ask me about the wards. Come in. I put on a pot of tea when I felt you coming."

Conor exchanged a startled glance with Odran and followed the man into his small cottage. A large table sat in the center of the room surrounded by four stools, an oddly inviting vignette for a border sentry. The interior smelled of wood smoke and fragrant herbs. Ciaran lifted the pot from the fire with a hook and produced three cups from a board above the hearth.

"Now, sit, Odran, or at least smile. Pretend this is a friendly visit." He glanced at Conor and shook his head. "Too serious, this one. But you . . . I feel music in you. What would you like to know?"

Conor sat and took the proffered cup. "You tell me. You seem to know why I'm here."

"You're here about a woman."

Conor nearly choked on his tea. "Why would you say that?"

"It's always about a woman, dear boy," Ciaran said, unfazed. "But you want to know what I've felt, don't you?"

Conor nodded, alternately intrigued and baffled. Either the sentry was completely mad, or he possessed a gift of sight not unlike Liam's and Aine's.

"Usually the wards are quiet," Ciaran said. "I can feel the comings and goings of the runners and trackers, and not long ago, a number of warriors died on the wards. But lately, someone has been rebuilding them."

Conor's mouth went dry. "Who?"

"I can't tell you that. If that's what you've come to find out, you've wasted a trip."

But Conor knew. If Meallachán's harp was the instrument used to make the wards, the bard must be rebuilding them. Why wouldn't Meallachán have simply told Aine what he knew?

Unless he had already left Lisdara.

Conor almost laughed at the bitter irony. Had he stayed at Lisdara, both the bard and his instrument would be within reach. Yet he would never have known what must be done had he not come to Ard Dhaimhin.

But why would the bard need convincing? Why would he rebuild the wards and not coordinate his efforts with Calhoun in the first place?

It was an odd inconsistency, and Conor couldn't help but wonder if the bard had plans of his own. Still, it didn't change what he knew he had to do.

When he returned to Ard Dhaimhin, Conor laid out all he had discovered in the last several weeks, expecting Eoghan to see his path as clearly as he did.

Instead, Eoghan shook his head. "I'm sorry, Conor. I can't let you go."

Conor stared at Eoghan in surprise. "It could be the key!"

"The key to what? If the bard is remaking the wards, he doesn't need your help. The matter is already well in hand."

Conor exhaled slowly and made his tone reasonable. "There's something odd about the whole thing. I can feel it. Besides, we both know I'm meant to go back. What difference does it make if it's now or later?"

"A great deal. Conor, you've made impressive progress. Astounding, actually. But you're not ready to take your trials."

"Then make me ready."

"It's been only two years, and it's never been done in less than six. Talented as you are, and I do mean that, I'd need at least two more."

Conor's hopes plummeted. "What are you talking about, Eoghan?"

"Master Liam will not allow me to petition an apprentice who has been here for less than five years. If you're right, you don't have that long. That leaves you one option."

"Please don't tell me I have to challenge you," Conor said.

Eoghan shook his head. "No. You have to challenge Master Liam. And you have to win."

CHAPTER THIRTY

Aine ducked out of her tent into the torch-lit night at the first sound of angry voices. "What's happening?"

Lorcan nodded toward a nearby scuffle already being broken apart. "An argument over dice. Treasach has it well under control."

The priest's head bobbed above the cluster of onlookers as he defused the situation in his usual calm tone. Treasach had made himself indispensable since his arrival at camp, both in spiritual matters and in controlling the numerous fights and arguments that broke out on a daily basis. No one seemed anxious to strike a priest, especially one with hands that could crush a man's head like a gourd.

The men were talking now, and they clasped forearms, the argument apparently forgotten. Treasach extracted himself from the group and made his way toward Aine.

"Only the third one tonight," he said lightly, "and this one didn't even end in bloodshed."

Aine shivered. Lorcan ducked into the tent to retrieve her cloak before she could tell him the sensation had nothing to do with the night air. She didn't sense the presence of the sidhe, but she knew they were near. Sometimes, they came in the form of a seductive voice or a beckoning figure, luring men away from the camp in the night. Other times, they fomented distrust and anger over matters as small as a dice game. Already, six men had been killed in such arguments, their murderers shackled and sent back to Lisdara for trial.

"The waiting is getting to them," Aine said. Lorcan returned with her cloak, and she shrugged it on as if it could protect her from the invisible threats. "These are not men given to idleness. I'd hoped the daily drills and devotions might have improved matters."

"This is a subtlety I would not have expected from Fergus," Treasach said.

"It's exactly what I expected from the druid, though. I doubt Fergus is in control any longer, if he ever was." Aine glanced at Lorcan. "It may be time to take a closer look at those wards. Be sure we haven't missed anything."

Aine had felt tugs on the wards several more times since the night Sualtam tried to kill her, and each time, the intensity of the dissent increased. Siomaigh flags no longer flew alongside Faolanaigh in the same camp. Seaghan and Abban maintained an amicable accord as commanders, but the sidhe had done a thorough job stirring up buried distrust and old animosity among the warriors.

"What exactly could you do if we did?" Lorcan asked.

"I suppose there's nothing to be gained by investigating further if the wards hold. I just hate idleness as much as the men do." Aine hugged her arms to herself and chewed her lip.

"Get some rest, my lady," Lorcan said. "You've been working yourself to exhaustion."

Aine gave the men brief smiles before ducking back into her tent. Thank Comdiu for Ruarc, Lorcan, and Treasach. They buffered her against the worst of the camp's conflict, even if they all dreaded the moment the sidhe decided to plant murderous thoughts in the heads of half a dozen men at once.

"Lord, I need direction," she murmured as she settled onto the rickety campaign cot. Since the attacks on the wards began, she had done little but pray for faith and guidance. It was all within His plans, she knew, but she still waited for some indication of her next move.

The charm warmed against her skin, and Aine's stomach erupted into butterflies. It had to be related to Conor. She turned the charm over in her hands. He was not dead. The more she thought about it, the more certain she was that the Firéin sentry had misled her.

"Where are you now?" she whispered, pressing the charm between her hands. "Are you coming back to me?"

She laughed bitterly at her own foolishness and dropped the ivory wheel beneath the neckline of her shift. She should not wish for it. Conor was safer in Ard Dhaimhin, separate from the problems of the kingdoms. He was probably happy playing his harp and poring through old tomes of history. Perhaps he had even learned to fight a little. Why would she wish on him this sick, creeping sense of uncertainty, the inevitability of defeat even as they vowed to fight to their last breath? This was no place for him. It was no place for her.

"I need to sleep. I'm driving myself mad." Aine tossed aside her cloak and climbed beneath her blanket without bothering to take off her boots. Within moments, she plunged into a sea of troubled dreams, tossed relentlessly among images of war, the bean-sidhe at the lake, Conor, and half a dozen other times and places that made no sense to her. The images built with ever-increasing dread into a crescendo—

Aine gasped awake, her blood pulsing in her ears. Only the occasional muffled voices of the perimeter patrol broke the camp's silence. What had awoken her? Was it merely the dream?

She was about to dismiss her anxiety as a product of her troubled dreams when she felt a deep, discordant vibration, like the snap of a harp string midnote. She struggled to identify the source until it came a second time with dizzying nearness.

"Oh, dear Comdiu, please," she whispered. Then panic took over, pumping blood through her veins. She grabbed her cloak and darted from the tent.

Lorcan bounded to his feet from where he sat on guard outside. Before he could ask, Aine said, "Wake Abban. Find Ruarc. The wards have snapped."

Horror crossed Lorcan's face, and for a moment, he too stood immobilized. Ruarc appeared almost immediately. "I'll wake him. Lorcan, stay with Aine."

Within minutes, they gathered in the command pavilion, the map of the wards spread out before them. Aine's hand shook as she pointed to several intersecting lines. "They've unmade Callindor, Southbrook, and Threewaters. I used to be able to feel them, and now . . . I feel nothing." Her voice broke on the last word, but she gathered herself before tears could come.

"We'll rouse the camp and send a rider to Seaghan. Just because they've broken the wards doesn't mean they've attacked yet. They could be biding their time."

"Send riders to Gainor, too. They might be able to fall back behind Westfalen. It's one of the reinforced wards." It was a futile hope, though. A strong ward could be broken just as easily as a weak one.

The camp churned in barely controlled chaos. Abban sent two riders to Gainor's camp, as did Seaghan. The Siomaigh were more familiar with the terrain and had a greater chance of arriving safely. Each camp readied two hundred men. Too few, but they were only meant to cover Gainor's retreat should the Faolanaigh warriors be taken unaware.

"I want to go," Aine said.

Abban shook his head. "I'll be leading one of the forces south, so I need you here. The men know and respect you. Prepare for casualties."

"But the injured men—"

"The ones who survive the trip back are the ones you can help. The others will be beyond your skills. I've been fighting my whole life, Lady Aine. If I thought you could help, I'd send you. You are of more use here."

When Abban wrote his message to Calhoun, Aine added a few lines of her own, urging him to rely on Lisdara's physical defenses rather than the compromised wards. Ensorcelled warriors or not, the fortress was built to withstand a siege.

Ruarc took her aside once the message had been dispatched to Calhoun. "If we have to fall back, I'm taking you to Lisdara. Lorcan is organizing a party of riders now."

Aine started to protest, but Ruarc cut her off. "No arguments. If we see battle, we return. You are too valuable to risk being taken as a hostage. I assure you, you will be imprisoned and forced to aid their side, until they need you no longer. It will not be a pleasant end."

Aine shivered. If he had been trying to frighten her, he had succeeded. Besides, she could hardly argue when it made good strategic sense. No king would want his commanders to be captured and tortured, and Aine's knowledge was more damaging than what most battle captains could give up.

She paced the confines of the command pavilion for the next two days, clutching the ivory charm and murmuring prayers while Lorcan and Ruarc alternated guard duty. Half of her prayed for a vision of the battlefield, even as the other half resisted it. What good was it to know what was happening when she could do nothing about it?

On the third day, two riders appeared on lathered horses, bearing separate messages. Despite the fact she was not technically in charge, they sought her out.

"Ruarc, fetch Lord Mavin, please. He'll need to hear this." Aine poured water for the exhausted messengers with shaking hands. Before they even had a chance to finish their drinks, Mavin appeared in the tent. The pale-haired captain was only a few years older than her, and Aine knew nothing about him other than that Abban trusted him.

"I was on my way. What news?"

The messengers began to rise, but Mavin waved them back down. "You can tell us just as easily seated."

One of the men, whom Aine recognized as Abban's messenger, spoke first. Aine realized he was probably younger than her. "They're in retreat. Lord Abban says to hold this position as long as the last ward remains. Otherwise, remove to the border camp."

"Casualties?" Aine and Mavin asked in unison.

"Heavy. I left two days ago, and Abban had already lost half of his men. Lord Gainor was in retreat with a hundred warriors, but they were fighting admirably."

"And you?" Aine asked the second messenger.

"I left right after Keene, my lady. Lord Abban wanted you to know they weren't attacked by Sliebhanaigh. They were Siomaigh."

The tent fell silent. Mavin's jaw flexed convulsively. "I'll go speak with Seaghan."

"I'll go," Aine said. "Lord Seaghan won't lie to me. He won't see me as a threat."

Mavin considered only a moment. "Take ten men. Send someone ahead, and meet him on neutral ground. If there's any sign of aggression, send a rider back. I'll ready our warriors."

Aine nodded. "Thank you."

She kept her demeanor calm, but inwardly, she felt sick. Siomaigh attacking Faolanaigh could mean only one thing. Diarmuid had gotten to Semias as he had to Bodb. Fergus would now have the combined forces of three kingdoms behind him, nearly ten thousand warriors. Faolán could muster perhaps two thousand more if Calhoun took men from the villages. Without some sort of intervention, their resistance would be short-lived.

Less than an hour later, Aine's party crossed the half mile of meadow to the Siomaigh camp, beneath the Mac Cuillinn's banner and a threatening gray sky. Aine stopped the men at a safe distance and dispatched the bannerman to take her request for parlay to Seaghan. She held her breath, praying they would not receive the messenger's head in reply.

She felt faint when the bannerman came back, the green flag snapping above him in the gusty wind. The warriors around her let out a collective sigh of relief. "He'll see you. He's coming out."

A party of six riders rode from the camp beneath a red-and-black banner just as raindrops began to spatter around them. Seaghan himself carried his standard. They reined in a safe distance away, and the commander rode forward.

Aine glanced briefly at Ruarc and Lorcan before she separated from her own party to meet him.

"Lady Aine. I'm encouraged to see you."

"Lord Seaghan."

Seaghan studied her for a moment, his blue eyes sharp in spite of the fatigue that lingered around the edges. "We've received orders to attack any Faolanaigh on Siomaigh land."

Aine swallowed the lump in her throat, but she kept her voice strong. "I see. Are you informing us of your intentions or giving us an ultimatum?"

Seaghan considered before he heaved a sigh. "Neither. Semias has betrayed us. He no longer commands my loyalty." He tossed the standard to the ground between them, the red-and-black banner a wound on the green earth. "We'll fight with Faolán if you'll grant us asylum."

Aine stared hard at him, pretending to weigh his sincerity while her thoughts whirled. This was not what she had expected. Did she even possess the authority to speak on Calhoun's behalf? "I would venture to say the Mac Cuillinn would welcome your warriors. If you swear an oath."

"Your king would require our fealty?" Seaghan's eyes narrowed. "We are Siomaigh. We fight for Siomar."

"I require your oath you will fight with and not against Faolán, and you will not seek to take Faolanaigh lands and titles as payment for your service." Her conviction built with every word. She straightened atop the horse and made her voice hard. "Otherwise, we will consider you and your warriors enemies. If you had not noticed, we now outnumber you two to one."

A wry smile crossed Seaghan's face. "Do you wish anything else from me, my lady? My firstborn son, perhaps?"

Aine stared back, unsmiling. "Do not mock me, Lord Seaghan. I ask nothing unreasonable. In this, I do speak for my king. I doubt you will receive as good an offer from yours."

Seaghan bowed his head. "You have my oath, Lady Aine. My men and I will not fight against Faolán . . . unless your king should throw in his lot with Fergus, in which case, my oath is void. We will not seek lands or titles, but we will expect reasonable provender and shelter once we enter Faolanaigh lands."

"Fair enough." Aine worked to keep the satisfaction from her face. "Expect retreating forces in the next several days. We may need to fall back behind the border should this ward break like the others."

Seaghan gave her a tight bow from horseback and wheeled his mount. Aine watched him leave before she called to her own party, "Let's go deliver the good news."

They had ridden a few minutes when Lorcan said, "I don't remember securing an oath being one of our goals when we came here."

"It seemed like a good idea," Aine said. "I can't imagine Calhoun wanting six hundred Siomaigh on Faolanaigh lands without some assurance they won't turn and join their countrymen."

Lorcan's smile held more than a hint of admiration. "I pity anyone who has to negotiate with you, my lady."

Aine summoned a weak smile in return, but her hand still trembled on the reins. She had done well, better than Mavin could have managed, but it felt like a bandage on a gushing wound. This quick solution would not hold forever.

As if on cue, she felt a deep vibration, followed by a snap that struck her like a physical blow. The last ward protecting Abban's camp had broken.

CHAPTER THIRTY-ONE

The skies opened up over Ard Dhaimhin, sheeting rain and sending anyone without urgent business rushing for cover. The two men in the practice yard, however, hardly seemed to notice, locked in the intensity of an evenly matched contest. The older of the two, dark-haired and muscular, seemed to have the upper hand, handling his short sword with the assurance of a born warrior, the heavy blade no weightier in his hand than a reed. His opponent, tall and blond, waited for something, unwilling to take the offense. Then he lunged, a move so quick and unexpected his opponent barely had time to parry.

"He's got Mac Nir reflexes," Liam said approvingly.

"He hasn't won yet," Riordan said. From the sheltered outcropping above the yard, he could see the way the young man saved his energy for the killing blow, not risking exposing himself to such an experienced opponent. The men they watched could have bested the most skilled swordsmen in the four kingdoms. At times, it was still hard to believe one of them could be his son, Conor.

That skill was hard-won. While Eoghan had had the chance to develop his abilities gradually, Conor had lived the sword for two years, drilling and fighting six or eight hours a day. Had Riordan not seen it with his own eyes, he would have deemed the outcome impossible. They should not have been able to turn a scrawny seventeen-year-old boy into an able warrior in only three years.

"Eoghan's preparing Conor to fight me," Liam said. "Watch. That's my move."

Now that Liam had drawn his attention to it, Riordan saw the subtle change in Eoghan's usual style, the way he shifted to his offhand side, a certain rhythm of parry and counterattack. He hadn't realized the young brother was such a gifted mimic. Entranced by the similarities, he did not immediately register the Fíréin leader's words. "Why would he do that?"

Liam produced a wrinkled sheet of parchment and handed it to Riordan. His heart sank at the contents. "This is confirmed? Siomar has fallen?"

"Along with half the old wards. The druid found someone who knows the binding magic." Liam sighed. "I knew it would happen. I just didn't expect it so soon. I thought we'd have another year with him at least."

"You orchestrated it all, didn't you?" Riordan asked, not taking his eyes from the match. "You never planned on keeping him here."

Liam cast him a sidelong glance. "I know you disagree with my methods, but had I not arranged the pieces, Conor would still be shoveling dirt in a field somewhere."

Riordan swallowed down a sharp answer at the realization Liam had manipulated him rather than trusting him with the truth. "So you'll accept Eoghan's petition?"

"I'll still make Conor fight me."

"Can he win?"

Liam shrugged, an eloquent movement that said he knew but would not divulge his secrets. He took the letter back and turned away.

"Aren't you going to watch the rest of the match?"

"I don't need to," Liam said over his shoulder.

Riordan turned back to the scene below. Conor's sword cut through the sheets of rain, moving so quickly Riordan barely saw the motion that disarmed Eoghan and set the tip of the blade against his chest. The two men stood unmoving for a moment. Then Conor withdrew the sword and extended a hand to his mentor.

Riordan turned away. He didn't know what the future held for his son, or even what Liam had sought to bring about, but Conor's time at Ard Dhaimhin was drawing to a close.

✦   ✦   ✦

"Well done, my friend." Eoghan squinted in the rain and made a face at his sodden clothing, now plastered to his body. He bent down to retrieve his fallen practice sword. "I saw it coming, I just wasn't quick enough."

"Lucky move," Conor said, even as elation over his victory coursed through him.

"Luck had nothing to do with it. I've been working you hard for months. It's paid off. Just in time, too."

"Have you heard something?"

Eoghan hesitated, but at last he nodded. "Siomar has fallen. Semias's men have attacked the Faolanaigh. They must be under Fergus's control."

"The wards?"

"Broken."

Conor swore under his breath. "I'm too late then. They have Meallachán."

"I'm sorry, Conor. I feel responsible, even though I don't think you could have done anything to stop it."

"It's not your fault. And you're right. I probably couldn't have done anything to stop it." He hesitated over the next question. "Have you heard anything—?"

"About Aine? No."

Good. If Liam's sister had been hurt or killed, news would surely have made it back to Ard Dhaimhin. Only Faolán stood between Fergus and complete domination of the isle now. How long before he declared himself High King and invaded Ard Dhaimhin? With the wards failing, the Fíréin had no choice but to get involved. Should the war come to the city, there would be much more at stake than just their way of life.

"What are you going to do?" Eoghan asked as they started up the path toward the village, now slick from the rain.

"I'm going to Carraigmór."

Eoghan shook his head. "You beat me today, Conor, but that doesn't mean you can take on Master Liam. If you challenge him before you're ready, you'll lose your only opportunity—"

"I'm not going to challenge him. I'm going to make a case to the Conclave for why they should get involved in this war. I want them to send a party after Meallachán."

A slow smile spread over Eoghan's face. "The Conclave could overrule Liam with a majority vote. If you make a good enough case for yourself, it might work. I'll back you."

"No, don't get involved. Once I'm gone, you may still have some influence with Master Liam. Maybe you can change his mind if I can't."

"And if you can't?" Eoghan asked.

"Then I'll fight him. If I lose, I'll worry about the consequences then." And trust he knew the sentries and runners well enough to make it out alive when he deserted. Hopefully it wouldn't come to that.

Conor had not told Eoghan about his dreams of Aine. He had felt her emotions—her exhaustion, her terror, but most of all her determination to do all she could to hold back the forces that threatened Faolán. Since then, he could swear she had called to him on more than one occasion. *Where are you now?* she had pleaded. *Are you coming back to me?*

His heart beat faster at the recollection. It was not his imagination, even if he could not precisely name the magic that allowed him these glimpses of her. Perhaps it was the charm. Or perhaps it was just the indefinable connection they had forged in his short time at Lisdara. Whatever the reason, he knew even if he could do nothing to halt the storm of war from overtaking Faolán, he wanted to spend those last days by her side.

Tell me if I'm doing the right thing, he pleaded skyward as he made his way back to the barracks. *Please give me some indication of how I'm supposed to go about this.*

Comdiu remained silent.

Then I'll trust You to stop me if it's the wrong choice. I just don't intend on making it easy.

Now that he contemplated leaving Ard Dhaimhin to join a war that would almost certainly mean his death, the city seemed a world apart. It would be so easy to stay here and pretend none of what he knew really existed.

Until the last of the wards broke, and thousands of men streamed into Ard Dhaimhin, determined to seize Carraigmór's throne for Fergus and his druid.

Somehow, he had to convince the Conclave to get involved, before their stubbornness killed thousands and ended the Fíréin brotherhood once and for all.

That night, Conor requested a meeting with the Conclave and the Ceannaire. To his surprise, Liam agreed immediately, granting him an audience the next morning.

After devotions, of which he comprehended only a handful of words, he climbed the stairs to the fortress. The brother on guard let him into the hall where ten men sat in a semicircle, Liam in the middle. Another chair sat opposite, facing them. It felt like a trial.

"Brother Conor," Master Liam said, sweeping a hand toward the chair. "Please, have a seat, and share why you requested an audience with the entire Conclave."

"It's a matter than concerns all of the Fíréin," Conor said. "And if you don't mind, I'd rather stand."

"Very well. What is on your mind?"

Conor took a deep breath. "No doubt you know Siomar has fallen to the Mac Nir's army. You also know the wards that extend from the forests throughout Seare have begun to fail. I wished to ask the Conclave, and you, Master Liam, what you intend to do about it."

"Why should we do anything?" Liam asked calmly.

Conor hadn't expected that response. Evasion, perhaps, or annoyance, but not indifference. "I understand the Fíréin's policy of noninterference, but the breaking of the wards affects Ard Dhaimhin. There can be no question Fergus means to control all of Seare and declare himself High King."

Riordan looked at him sympathetically. "Surely you're not suggesting Fergus will be able to conquer four thousand trained brothers."

"He will have at least twice that number. It hardly matters if he can conquer Ard Dhaimhin or not. He will destroy it in the attempt. You know there is one who can create or unmake the wards. Find him, and bring him back here. The age of the brotherhood will end unless you intervene."

"You make a compelling argument, Brother Conor," Liam said with a bare smile. "But you are forgetting we have vowed only to hold the city and Daimhin's throne until the return of the High King, whoever and whenever that may be. If we abandon that, we abandon the vows that have kept us strong for five hundred years."

Conor looked at the Conclave in disbelief. "When I first came to Ard Dhaimhin, Master Liam, you told the parable of the man who entrusted his money to his servants. You said the Fíréin life is harsh and disciplined so we would be ready when Comdiu called us to His work.

"When is that time, if not now? Men have lived and died here for centuries, training for some glorious purpose that never comes to pass. And now that time is at hand, and you refuse to act? All that is good in the kingdoms is threatened. We alone have the ability to end this evil, to restore good to our land. If you cannot see this is Comdiu's work, then you are no better than the unfaithful servant who hid his master's gold and was thrown out into the dark as punishment."

The members of the Conclave stared, stunned by his boldness. His heart raced wildly, and he struggled to maintain his composure while he waited for Liam's answer. Had he been successful in startling him from his complacency?

"I commend your passion on the subject, Brother Conor," Liam said. "But we have taken oaths. I will remind you that you have as well. Would you abandon your honor so easily?"

"I take my vows seriously. But honor demands I act. You may choose to hold the brotherhood back from a fight that is right and just, but I will not be part of that decision. I will leave Ard Dhaimhin to find the bard Meallachán and his harp. Failing that, I will fight with Faolán."

"You agreed to remain until you fulfilled the requirements of your apprenticeship," Brother Daigh said, his voice hard. "You are not eligible for petition for two more years."

Conor drew a deep breath. He felt as if he watched the exchange from the outside now. "I understand. I am exercising my right of challenge."

The Conclave burst into amazed murmurs, all except Riordan and Liam. The Ceannaire smiled. "Since you are my apprentice's student, I have first right to the challenge. However, I will cede that right to another member of the Conclave if you wish."

Conor looked around the circle. The men seemed as shocked as he felt. Any of them would be an easier opponent than Liam, even his father, who was the largest and strongest of the ten. Liam had given him a way out, and Riordan's expression urged him to take it. There was more at stake here than release from his apprenticeship, though. They had dismissed his pleas to join the war. They saw him as a foolish boy who knew nothing of battle, who was ready to throw his life away in a futile fight.

"Thank you, but I extend my challenge to you, Master Liam."

The Ceannaire's smile broadened. "Very well. I accept. The match will take place on the large crannog tomorrow after morning devotions. Tell Brother Eoghan he will witness his apprentice's trials."

Conor gave Master Liam a short bow. "Aye, sir. Thank you."

He escaped Carraigmór as quickly as he could, his heart squeezed painfully in his rib cage. What had just happened? He'd gone before the

Conclave to make a reasoned case for their involvement. Instead, he'd ended up challenging a man who, rumor said, had never lost a match. Conor wasn't even sure of the rules of the challenge. He might have forfeited his life should he lose.

"Your challenge, your terms," Eoghan told him. "You can choose to fight to the death or merely to first blood, though no one has chosen the former in centuries."

"Do I have any hope of winning?"

"You beat me," Eoghan said, but it was hardly the resounding assurance he'd hoped for.

Conor's foolishness mocked him through sleepless hours. What had he been thinking? He'd extended the challenge, which was bad enough, but then he'd refused to take the easier course offered him. It was as if someone else had inhabited his body and spoken on his behalf. He hardly remembered doing it.

That was ridiculous. He had no one to blame but himself.

Or did he? Hadn't he dared Comdiu to stop him? He'd even said he wasn't planning on making it easy, as if he could concoct any plan that could challenge the Almighty Creator. Perhaps his own foolishness meant rather than a quiet tap on the shoulder, Comdiu would stop him in a sensational and humiliating manner.

Or maybe Comdiu just needed to make it clear he couldn't get out of this through his own power.

It sounded like his own thought, but it was too rational to have come from his churning head. His heart lifted, hope blossoming. Maybe he had just been given a shove in the right direction.

I'll leave this up to You then. You know better than I that three years cannot compete with a lifetime of training. If it's Your will I leave Ard Dhaimhin, You'll have to make it happen.

CHAPTER THIRTY-TWO

The morning of the challenge match dawned under a bright blue sky, without sign of the rain that had plagued Ard Dhaimhin for days. Conor took it as a good omen, even though his stomach began its somersaults when the first of the curious glances fell on him. So word had gotten around already.

He put his head down and strode toward the amphitheater, hoping that his posture would deflect most of the questions. He stifled a groan as Ailbhe fell into step beside him. True, it was Tor who had taken a dislike to him, but Ailbhe hardly did anything without his friend's permission.

"You think you can win?" the boy asked, his tone more curious than challenging.

Conor flicked a glance at Ailbhe, forcing down a surge of defensiveness. "What do you think?"

Ailbhe studied him. "You fight like Brother Riordan. He's the only one who's ever beaten Master Liam."

"You think so?"

"I hope so. If you lose, I have to do all Tor's chores in the barracks for a month. Don't let me down." Ailbhe gave him a grin, the first real expression of solidarity, followed by a heavy thump on the shoulder. "Good fortune, Brother Conor."

"Fortune," Conor repeated numbly. He wasn't sure which was more surprising: the fact that the boy had broken the Fíréin prohibition against gambling, or that he'd bet against his friend. On him.

A smile spread across Conor's face. Perhaps he could do this after all.

When Eoghan slid onto a bench across from him, he was trying to steady his nerves and force down enough breakfast to sustain his energy through the match. He glanced up long enough to catch his mentor's eye. "Do you have any advice for me?"

"Don't think," Eoghan said. "You have the training and the instincts. Don't let your brain get in the way."

"If that were a problem, I wouldn't be in this situation." Conor hadn't meant to be funny, but when he caught Eoghan's gaze, they both broke into nervous chuckles. "Whatever happens today, thank you. I know what you sacrificed to take me as an apprentice."

"Some good it did you. I'd hoped to avoid this scenario. You ready?"

The words jolted Conor's system and caused his heart to ricochet in his chest. He gave Eoghan a sober nod, every trace of humor vanishing. One way or another, in a few short hours, his life would take a dramatically new direction.

Eoghan let him save his energy and ferried him across the lake to the crannog. At least Conor was comfortable with the location, the site of much of his training. If he could just convince himself this was another practice match and keep his mind off the stakes, he might actually have a chance. *Don't let your brain get in the way.* Very well. He'd already determined Comdiu would have to intervene in this one.

When they arrived at the yard, Master Liam waited with all nine Conclave members. Apparently, the Conclave stood with their leader. Conor didn't look at them. He felt intimidated enough without reading the pity in their faces.

"Don't let them rush you," Eoghan whispered as they approached the yard. "Take as much time as you need. Work some forms. It's your challenge."

Eoghan handed Conor the bundle containing his weighted practice sword and the sharpened weapon for the challenge. He moved to the corner of the yard, feeling the other men's gazes upon him. After a moment of hesitation, he chose the steel.

The practice weapon had been a good approximation of the real thing, but it still took several forms before Conor ceased to be aware of the sword in his hand. By then, he had worked up a sweat, and his muscles felt fluid and warm. He turned and saw Master Liam had done the same thing. At least he was taking Conor's challenge seriously.

Now came the formalities. Conor stepped into the yard and called, "Liam, Ceannaire of the Fíréin brotherhood, I challenge you."

Liam stepped forward. "Conor, apprentice to Eoghan of the Fíréin brotherhood, I accept."

Brother Daigh entered the yard and gestured for them to approach. Riordan was not judging the match as was his privilege as first seat on the Conclave? Conor scanned the area and saw his father had joined Eoghan opposite the Conclave members. The sight warmed him.

Daigh was speaking now, and Conor turned his attention forward. "Brother Conor, the challenge."

"Short swords to first blood."

Liam nodded his agreement. "I accept."

"You will fight to the first sign of blood, drawn intentionally by the opponent's sword," Daigh said. "If either should withdraw prior to that point, he shall forfeit the decision. Any questions?"

Conor shook his head. Liam smiled, not unkindly. Daigh continued, "Very well, then. Brothers, take your positions."

Conor moved back several steps and assumed a guard stance. Liam raised his sword, completely at ease, as if they were chatting rather than fighting. Conor focused on his opponent's eyes and used his peripheral vision to watch for a shift in stance that would indicate an attack.

Liam leapt forward, his sword a blur of offensive strikes. Only Conor's instincts kept the bright blade from his flesh. *Blessed Comdiu, he's fast!*

Liam paused, and Conor countered with a low thrust. The Ceannaire brushed it aside as he might swat a gnat. His elbow was low, part of Conor's mind noted, filing the fact away for future use. He'd be weak countering an overhand slash . . .

Conor tried it, but Liam parried and countered easily. He leapt out of the way as the tip of the Ceannaire's sword sliced open his tunic. There was a collective indrawn breath as the witnesses waited for the slow blossom of red beneath, but it never came. That had been far too close.

Don't think. You have the training and the instincts. Conor forced himself to relax and met the next onslaught with more confidence, but his blade got nowhere near Liam. Unless Conor developed the miraculous ability to draw blood from several inches away, he was going to wear down long before the Ceannaire.

Back and forth they went, circling for better position, each meeting the other's blade before it could strike home. Sweat trickled down Conor's face and dripped onto his tunic, more from anxiety than exertion. At least

Liam no longer looked so fresh. He, too, was having to work harder to keep the equilibrium of the match.

The air seemed to thicken then, time slowing by just a fraction. The tension melted from Conor's body and the scene turned soft around the edges. He found himself parrying just a bit faster, countering a split second quicker. He was acutely aware of the movement of air currents around them, the sound of the sand beneath their feet, the rasp of breath in his lungs. Details began to register in the back of his mind: the shift of weight to Liam's offhand side, the slightest flicker of an eyelash when he was about to feint, the way he held his breath before delivering a particular strike.

Then time sped up again, and Conor was fighting faster than he had thought himself capable, moving without conscious thought. Before he could even register his intention, he saw his opening and took it.

Pain seared Conor's throat. He halted and realized the tip of Liam's sword had broken the skin just above his collarbone. It was a masterful show of control: a mere fraction more and Conor would be dead, or at the very least, mute. Blood slowly trickled down his chest.

Liam was breathing hard. "Well done, Brother Conor. Another minute, and you might have had me."

Only then did the other details—and the reason for the shocked silence—seep in. A slight smile stretched Conor's lips.

Liam followed his gaze downward to his chest, where the tip of Conor's blade lay against his ribs amidst a slowly spreading red stain.

"It's a draw!" Daigh announced in shock.

Their eyes met, and cautiously, they withdrew their weapons. It took all Conor's willpower not to reach up and touch the wound. Instead, he asked, "What does a draw mean?"

"The decision is Liam's," Daigh said.

Conor's heart fell to his stomach. All his hard work was for naught?

"Bravely fought, Brother Conor," Liam said. "I haven't had a match like that in years. You should be proud of what you have accomplished, as should Brother Eoghan."

"Thank you, sir," Conor said, but he felt only the heavy weight of failure.

"I am satisfied you have met all the requirements of our training and then some. If you still wish it, I release you from your apprenticeship. Leave Ard Dhaimhin with my blessings."

Conor stared for what felt like a full minute. "I can leave? Even though I didn't win?"

"The fact you risked this challenge when you were given an alternative shows both character and purpose. You've proven you have your own path to follow."

Conor bowed his head, humbled by the praise. "Thank you, sir. But I believe it means Comdiu will not allow His plans to be thwarted by either of us."

Liam offered his hand, and Conor clasped his forearm. "Enjoy your accomplishment for now, and come to the fortress when you're ready. We have some matters to address before you go."

"Aye, sir."

Conor felt oddly serene in the aftermath of the match, as if he had merely watched the challenge. Tomorrow he would walk from the peace of Ard Dhaimhin and into the roiling uncertainty of a kingdom under siege, where he would face battles that would make his challenge match with Liam seem like idle play. Somehow, in this bubble of calm, the idea did not frighten him. It paled in comparison to the sudden thrill of hope that shot through him.

Aine, I'm coming.

+ + +

Liam and Riordan remained on the crannog long after the others left, staring at the gently rippling surface of the lake.

"You were right," Riordan said finally.

"About what?"

"About everything. I'm sorry I doubted you."

"You had the right to doubt," Liam said. "I think Comdiu worked things out in spite of me, not because of me."

Riordan turned, studied Liam's profile. "I don't understand."

"Conor was correct. The age of the brotherhood will come to an end, and there's not a thing I can do about it. It's how it's meant to end. I saw that today."

There were far too many layers in the statement to peel back, so Riordan went for the most obvious question, the one that had nagged him since the match. "It wasn't a draw, was it? Conor was just a little quicker than you today."

Liam only gave his mysterious smile and turned to the waiting boat. Riordan shook his head and followed, but he knew he was right. Conor had somehow managed to beat the Ceannaire in a fair match, a fact disturbing in its symbolism. He climbed into the boat behind his leader, pushed away from the shore, and forced back a shiver of foreboding as they glided into deep water.

✦ ✦ ✦

After evening devotions, Conor and Eoghan made their way to Carraigmór. Every few feet, brothers stopped them with questions. Had it really been a draw? Had Conor actually managed to bleed a man who had never lost a match?

Conor put them off the best he could and kept moving toward the fortress. Eoghan kept his eyes fixed on Carraigmór's imposing bulk, a muscle pulsing in his jaw. It was a sure sign he was struggling not to speak his mind. But why? Was it the brothers' sudden attention on Conor? Or did Eoghan sense, as Conor did, that there was far more involved in that match than a simple challenge?

"It wasn't me," Conor said finally.

"What do you mean it wasn't you?" Eoghan frowned, finally looking at Conor. "I just watched you."

"Something happened back there. And don't say I just managed to get out of my own way. It was more than that. I'm not that good."

"Today you were."

"Today Comdiu wanted me to win my freedom." Conor studied his friend. Eoghan kept his thoughts close, but even he couldn't hide the emotion roiling beneath the surface. Was it resentment? "I thought you would be pleased. This is a victory for you, too. Isn't this what we've been working toward?"

"Of course I'm pleased!" Eoghan stopped. "You should have seen yourself. You were incredible. I'm proud to claim even the smallest bit of credit. It's just that . . ." He shrugged. "You're my only real friend. I wouldn't be human if I didn't want you to stay."

Conor gripped Eoghan's arms, his gaze boring into his friend's.

"You're my brother, Eoghan. I don't just mean in Fíréin terms. If we survive this, we'll cross paths again."

"That's a big if." Eoghan pulled out of Conor's grip and started back down the path. "The Conclave is naive if they believe Ard Dhaimhin will hold out against Fergus and the Red Druid indefinitely."

"I'm not sure they do. They just can't let go of their traditions. Promise me you won't throw your life away."

"I could ask the same of you." Eoghan stopped at the base of Carraigmór's steep upward climb. "This is where I leave you. I'll go see to your provisions."

"Thank you, Eoghan." Conor wanted to say more, but they had already expressed too much sentiment for one day, so he turned and began the ascent for the last time.

At the top, the brother at the door admitted him without question. Riordan waited for him inside the cavernous hall with oddly bright eyes. "I never thought I would see this day, Conor."

Conor followed Riordan down the corridor toward Master Liam's study. "You thought I would lose."

"That's not what I meant. Labhrás would be proud of you."

"Do you think so? He never wanted me to be a warrior."

"We wanted it to be your choice. We knew you would seek your own way."

"An awful lot of my path has been orchestrated from right here." For the first time, though, Conor could look on the Fíréin's interference without resentment. The plans of men succeeded only where Comdiu allowed it.

"Whatever you may think of our actions, we did what we believed was right. If mistakes have been made, they were made out of ignorance, not malice."

Conor sensed the apology in the statement, the closest he would receive from any members of this proud brotherhood, even his own father. He extended his hand, and Riordan gripped his forearm for a long moment before turning to rap sharply on Liam's door.

"Go on. I'll wait here."

The Ceannaire stood by a bookshelf, thumbing through a heavy volume. A familiar case lay on the desk. Conor shut the door behind himself and stood quietly, unwilling to speak first.

At last, Liam turned. "Conor. Right. We have some business here."

"I'm swearing an oath?"

"A formality. As you know, few brothers leave Ard Dhaimhin once they enter, but from those who do, we require some assurances." Liam moved to the table and lifted the latch on the case. Conor braced himself for the rush of power, but instead, he felt only the low, pleasant hum of energy. The magic drew him as Liam removed the sword from the case and planted the tip into the ground.

This close, Conor saw the details he had missed at the oath-binding: the gold-chased basket-weave design in the grip, the four-looped shield knot emblazoned on the pommel. He could just make out the fine etching of runes down the length of the blade.

He placed his palm atop the pommel, its iron smoothed and burnished by generations of oaths. Magic enveloped him immediately, spreading through his body like warm honey. He heard the faint whisper of voices, too many to distinguish individually, but he sensed the meaning of the words clearly. The oaths of thousands of men. His fingers flexed convulsively on the metal. The oath-binding was not simply symbolism?

"Conor?" Liam looked at him quizzically, and he realized the Ceannaire had been talking to him.

"I'm sorry?"

"I asked if you were ready. You need only answer the questions."

Conor swallowed hard and nodded.

"Do you swear to uphold the sanctity, privacy, and safety of the Fíréin brotherhood outside of Ard Dhaimhin?"

"I do." As Conor spoke the words, he felt a tug in his chest, followed by the whispered echo of his own voice. *I do.*

"Do you swear to comport yourself with honor and dignity as befits your training and education at Ard Dhaimhin?"

"I do." The echo grew louder, and Conor almost released the sword.

"Do you swear to never raise weapons against a Fíréin brother except in defense of your own life?"

"I do."

Liam nodded to Conor, and he released the sword abruptly, expecting to find the shield knot burned into his palm. Of course it wasn't.

"Then go with the blessing of the brotherhood. May Comdiu go before you in all your endeavors."

Conor gave a deep bow. "Thank you, Master Liam."

"One more thing." Liam opened a small box on his desk and withdrew a wooden coin embossed with the same shield knot emblazoned on the sword.

"What is this?"

"The symbol of the brotherhood. It will identify you to others like you in the kingdoms. Where you see this mark, you can be assured of assistance. Go now. Follow the path Comdiu has set before you."

Conor turned the coin over in his hand, struck by sudden, unexpected regret. "Somehow I didn't expect leaving would be this difficult."

"'The path of the faithful is perilous and fraught with sorrows as well as blessings,'" Master Liam quoted.

Conor closed his hand around the wooden coin and gave the Ceannaire another low bow. "Thank you, Master Liam. For everything."

When he emerged, Riordan waited for him on the stairs. "Done?"

"It wasn't what I expected. Did you hear it, too?"

Riordan's brow furrowed. "Hear what?"

Conor's thoughts now seemed foolish and fanciful. Perhaps he had just imagined the whispers, fueled by stories of heroes and enchanted swords. It was an unsatisfying explanation, though, and Conor knew magic when he felt it. But it hardly mattered now. He was leaving behind this strange brotherhood with its oaths and strictures and magic-imbued swords for the far more frightening reality of war in the kingdoms.

"Tell me the truth," he said suddenly. "Let's assume the match against Master Liam was an aberration, or maybe even a miracle. You've seen me fight. Can I survive in the kingdoms?"

Riordan seemed to consider his answer before speaking. "Conor, you are an extraordinarily gifted swordsman. Eoghan's skill and your hard work notwithstanding, you should have never been able to accomplish what you did in such a short period of time. I've seen few who can match you, here or in the kingdoms."

Conor swallowed his protest, stunned by the praise.

"But I will caution you," Riordan said. "You are still very young. As many men will resent you for your skill as respect you for it, and it won't always be readily apparent which is which. Politics in the kingdoms do not favor those who threaten the established order. Don't lose your focus on what is important."

"You sound as if I'm returning to seize the throne from Fergus," Conor said.

"You may think of yourself as a dishonored clansman with Fíréin training, but you are still a Mac Nir. Some will seek to use you for that. Just be wary."

Later that night, Conor and Eoghan shared a small jug of mead on the crannog where they had spent so many evenings drilling.

"Some people won't believe you're there just to fight," Eoghan said, "especially when you've been thought dead for the past three years. You might be mistaken for a spy."

"It's a poor spy who draws so much attention to himself," Conor said wryly. "Besides, Calhoun knows me. He wouldn't believe I would align myself with the man who killed Lord Labhrás."

"These are strange times. I take it you're going to find Aine?"

"I am."

"Will you sweep in and declare your undying love?" Repressed laughter underpinned Eoghan's tone.

Conor rolled his eyes. "Don't be ridiculous."

"I'm not the one who's been killing himself to be worthy of a king's sister. Don't pretend you haven't wondered what she'll think of you now."

He had, but he wasn't about to admit it aloud. "Knowing Aine, she'll be utterly unimpressed."

"Don't be so sure. After a few years on the front, she probably has a new perspective on warriors."

"How do you know she's on the front?"

Eoghan bowed his head. "Odran told me you saw her in the forest. I know she's been mapping wards for the king for almost two years."

Conor wasn't sure whether to feel guilty he hadn't told Eoghan the truth or angry his friend had kept the knowledge from him. "She'll have a map of the wards, and her captain will know where Fergus and his army are. They'll be able to give me an idea of where I should seek Meallachán."

"She's at Abban's camp, wherever that might be," Eoghan said. "One of the border sentries could tell you where they've gone. After what we heard about Semias, they may already be in retreat."

Conor set aside the mead jug, his head now aching nearly as badly as his body. It was far too easy to forget the reality of what awaited him.

"It's going to be a long journey," he said, pushing himself to his feet.

"I should take advantage of a soft bed and a roof over my head while I still can."

They returned to the shore in silence, Eoghan's discomfort plain in his stiff movements as he drew them back across the water. Conor couldn't reassure him. They all made their decisions, for good or bad. Even Eoghan, his closest friend, his brother, had held back information, and Conor had done the same. It was time to strike out on his own, follow his own path.

How strange that in the end, Master Liam seemed to understand best of all.

✦ ✦ ✦

Conor slept soundly on his last night in Ard Dhaimhin, but it stemmed more from exhaustion than from peace of mind. He woke automatically before the bugles roused the city. He had already said his good-byes, and now he just wanted a quiet departure.

He had nothing to take with him but his good wool cloak, serviceable if a bit too short, the clothes on his back, and the small pouch of coins he had brought from Lisdara. He'd never before realized how little he actually owned.

When he crept from the barracks into the pale morning, Riordan and Eoghan were waiting for him.

"You didn't think we'd miss seeing you off, did you?" Riordan said with a hint of a smile.

Conor returned it. "I'm glad you're both here."

"Especially since we have your weapons," Eoghan said. "Let it not be said the brotherhood sent you away defenseless."

Eoghan held up a sheathed sword on a leather baldric. Conor took it and drew the blade from the scabbard. It was plain, well-made steel, with a leather-wrapped grip and a brass pommel, meant for use and not for show. He shrugged on the baldric and adjusted the buckle so the sword rested comfortably across his back, an easy draw from his right shoulder. "Thank you."

"We're not done."

The two men also presented him with a staff sling, a leather pouch for his hand stones, and a small parcel of food.

"No bow?" Conor asked.

"We thought about it," Eoghan said, "but it would just be useless weight. You couldn't hit a man with an arrow if you threw it at him."

Conor laughed. "Sadly, that's true."

"There's one last thing." Riordan produced a dagger from beneath his tunic and handed it to him, hilt first.

Conor's eyes widened. The dagger was a lovely old piece with a slender, silver-chased handle and stamped leather sheath, as much for display as for service.

"This was the only thing of value I took from Tigh when I joined the brotherhood," Riordan said softly. "I'd like you to have it."

Conor examined it closely. Unexpectedly, his throat constricted, and he fought back tears. "I wish . . ."

"I know. These three years have been an unexpected blessing, Conor. I never thought to see you become a man." Riordan pulled Conor into a warm embrace, the kind Labhrás would have given him. "Trust Comdiu to guide you, and your path will become clear."

It was nearly the same thing Labhrás had said that last day at Glenmallaig—the last time Conor had ever seen him. Tears rose again and threatened to spill over. He cleared his throat. "Thank you, Father."

He quickly turned to Eoghan, who looked uncomfortable. "I'll see you soon, brother."

Eoghan nodded and gripped his arm. The long look they shared told Conor more of his friend's thoughts than he'd ever say. Had it not been for Conor, this departure might have been his.

Conor started toward the long set of switchbacks that would take him up and out of the city. He felt eyes on him until he reached the top, but when he turned back to wave a last farewell, the two men were gone.

CHAPTER THIRTY-THREE

Conor chose his route through the forest deliberately, following the trap lines and avoiding sentry posts. The trackers would notice his presence on the wards, but they would be too far away to intercept him. Not coincidentally, his path took him to the one sentry who would demand little in return for information.

He arrived at Brother Innis's post while the sun was still high on the second day. The old man waited outside his dugout when Conor stepped into view.

"I thought you might come." Innis turned and disappeared inside.

"These preternatural abilities of yours disturb me," Conor said as he followed him into the damp earthen hut.

The sentry laughed, a sound like the rustle of dried leaves. "Preternatural, no. Odran brought news of your victory against the Ceannaire as soon as it happened. I'm surprised you didn't see him."

"Odran can be seen only when he wants to be. Besides, it wasn't a victory; it was a draw."

"That is a victory. But you're not here to boast."

"No." Conor rummaged through his bag, drew out a ripe stone fruit, and set it on the table. "I'd hoped for a favor."

Innis eyed the fruit hungrily. It hadn't taken long to discover the old man's weakness. The sentries' diets were nutritious but unvarying, and they rarely included the more delicate of Ard Dhaimhin's produce.

Innis took the fruit and inhaled its fragrance like some men savored wine. "What is the favor?"

"Do you know the location of the Faolanaigh camps in Siomar? I understood they might be falling back."

"Behind the Faolanaigh border. Most of the Siomaigh wards were broken."

"I've heard. Where is Lord Abban now?"

"In a place we call the Triangle, where three strong wards intersect at the edge of the young forest. Near a village called Eames."

"I know it." The village must have sprung up with the wards, because it was one of the few on Ard Dhaimhin's ancient maps that still existed. "How about the others?"

"Lord Gainor will be joining them with what's left of his men."

Conor did not need to ask what had happened. Even if Gainor had seen the Siomaigh coming, he would not have known Semias was no longer an ally.

He swallowed, struggling to maintain his impassive tone when he felt anything but. "What about Calhoun's sister?"

"The healer? Alive. In fact, most of Abban's camp is alive because of her. She sensed the wards break and called the retreat."

The specificity of the information gave Conor pause. Those were details one could have only if there were a Fíréin informant in Abban's camp. But that was not his current concern. Aine was alive. He sagged with relief.

"Thank you," he said. "Enjoy your fruit."

"I will." Innis once again examined the gift closely, his visitor forgotten. Conor shook his head and slipped out the door into the forest.

He got his bearings and struck out due north. If his calculations were correct, he could arrive in Abban's camp in fewer than two days. The mere thought of seeing Aine sent his heart beating double-time and his thoughts skittering off in unproductive directions, but he forced his mind back to his surroundings. He could not forget he would soon be leaving Fíréin-protected territory and entering an area where wards were failing and enemy forces sought a foothold.

He camped beneath a stand of alder, eating Eoghan's provisions cold so he wouldn't have to light a fire. Even though he was still on Fíréin lands, he dared not draw attention to himself. He slept sitting upright against the trunk of one of the great trees, his sword beside him, his ears attuned to any unusual sounds, even in sleep. Nothing larger than an owl ventured near all night, though, and Conor departed before first light.

He knew the instant he left Seanrós, even without the wards. Younger trees mingled with the old, and the interlaced canopy of branches overhead let in more light. In places, he could see patches of blue sky above him. Here, he took even more care to move soundlessly. The Fíréin were not the only skilled trackers in these woods.

Still, he saw no sign of any other human. Throughout the morning, he smelled smoke, probably from the trappers who lived in the border woods, eking out a paltry living from small animal pelts, but he kept his distance. The forest thinned further, and midafternoon sunlight slanted into his eyes through the gaps in the canopy overhead. He would reach open land long before nightfall.

Then he noticed the silence. The songbirds should have been trilling their chorus. Conor stopped, ears trained on the forest sounds, and faded into the foliage around him.

The nearby call of a red-throated warbler raised the hairs on the back of his neck. Warblers should not be this far from their roosts in the western mountains. In fact, Conor hadn't seen or heard one since leaving Tigh. Silently, he fished several hand stones from his pouch and loosened the dagger at his belt.

He crouched among the ferns for several moments, watching and waiting. He hadn't imagined the sound, had he? No, the birds were still silent. There was someone out there.

A flash of white caught his eye, and Conor whipped his head around in time to see a man melt into the trees. A skilled woodsman, but not Fíréin. They knew better than to wear such conspicuous colors. Conor waited a moment and then plunged silently from his hiding place.

He followed the man by ear and let distance stretch between them. Ahead, he saw another flash, perhaps sunlight catching steel. The signal's recipient?

When they came within a hundred yards of where forest thinned into open land, the two men stopped. Conor faded into a stand of saplings, measuring his breathing, every muscle controlled. What were they waiting for?

Leaves rustled around him, but the day was still. He scanned the trees and saw three more men. His ears told him there were more behind him. If they had glimpsed him before, they couldn't find him now, or they assumed he was one of their party. After all, what were the chances a stranger would wander into their midst?

Perhaps it was not merely coincidence that brought him here. Conor scanned the trees again.

Five more men. Nine total. The glint of metal indicated weapons. An ambush? And for whom?

Conor lost track of the time he spent in concealment, but the shadows had lengthened when he at last heard the soft thud of hooves beyond the tree line. The men must have cut across the forest's edge to intercept a party of riders.

The warbler called again, and the man in the lead moved forward. Conor moved with him, counting on his fading ability to hide the fact he wasn't one of them. The sound of horses drifted closer, this time with the low drone of voices. An errant breeze threw a few clear, Faolanaigh-accented words his way.

Conor closed on the man to his right, aware of the others nearby. He would have to do something quickly, or it would not just be the Faolanaigh riders in trouble. He readied a stone in his hand and waited for an opportunity.

There. The man had stopped behind a screen of foliage. Conor launched the stone, and it connected with the back of the stranger's head with a crack. He went down with a soft thud.

Conor did not allow himself to dwell on the thought he may have killed him. Instead, he pressed toward the edge of the forest, trying to get a glimpse of the riders.

Six men atop fine, mud-splattered horses followed the tree line closely. A red-haired man slumped atop a large bay, swathed in bloody linen. When he turned to speak to the black-haired warrior beside him, Conor drew in his breath sharply. Was that Gainor Mac Cuillinn?

He studied him a moment longer. It was unmistakably Calhoun's younger brother. Was this small party all that remained of Gainor's forces?

The urgency of the situation struck him. There did not seem to be a whole man among them. They would be no match for a fight they saw coming, let alone a surprise attack. He had to do something.

He shifted forward, seeking the leader of the ambush. Whether he made a mistake or it was pure bad luck, the man chose that exact moment to look in his direction. His expression changed when he realized Conor was not one of his band.

Conor calculated his options in a split second. He couldn't silence the man before he sounded the alarm. Instead, he rushed for the tree line. "Gainor, go!"

For a single moment, all six men turned, too startled to even draw their weapons. Then the first arrow flew, and the ambushers burst from cover.

Gainor hesitated only a moment before digging in his heels and kicking the horse into a gallop. Arrows flew thick around him, but the powerful charger carried him quickly out of range. Conor was vaguely aware the others had followed, but he had no time to check if he was alone. He fitted a stone to his staff's sling and aimed at the nearest archer. It caught the man solidly in the chest, and he dropped like a sack of grain. The second stone flew just as true, taking down another bowman.

That left the swordsmen, and there were far more of them than Conor had estimated. He left his sword sheathed and gripped his staff with both hands. The first man rushed him, a second close behind. Conor sidestepped an attack and countered with a well-aimed strike to the midsection, then drew his staff free in time to deflect the arc of the second man's blade. Surprise registered on his opponent's face, giving Conor the opportunity to brush aside the sword and swing the staff into his head.

As he turned, he glimpsed the dark-haired rider, now engaged in a pitched battle with a skilled swordsman.

Four men closed around Conor, two in front and two behind. He parried one thrust in time to whirl and block another attack from behind. He needed to get out of this deadly circle. Gouges already weakened the staff, and he could not continue to meet their blades as if it were steel. He defended himself furiously from two, sometimes three attackers at once, desperately looking for an opening. Finally, he saw a flaw in the rightmost attacker's guard and drove the end of the staff into the center of his chest. The man went down, unable to breathe through his paralyzed diaphragm.

Conor circled into the gap left by the felled man so he could face the others one at a time. A second man feinted skillfully, but Conor waited until he overcommitted himself and delivered a vicious strike to the head.

The remaining two pressed forward, working like a pair of hunting wolves. One harried him while the other looked for an opportunity to take him down. Conor resisted the urge to draw his sword. In the seconds it took him to trade weapons, they would descend on him.

He shifted to the offense and pressed the first man back. A sharp blow to the wrist broke the bones and sent his weapon flying. Another strike to the head dropped him, unconscious, to the turf. Before the second man could comprehend what had happened, Conor swung the staff full force into his midsection. His opponent's ribs gave a sickening crunch, and he pitched to the ground.

Conor whirled, looking for the next attack, but he and the dark-haired man stood alone. The other warrior's four opponents lay dead, but Conor's still lived, some unconscious, others writhing in pain.

Relief flooded into the space left by adrenaline, and Conor bent forward, bracing his palms on his knees. Somehow, he had survived his first test unscathed.

"Are you wounded?" the other man asked.

"No." Conor straightened and shook off a wave of dizziness. "I'm fine. You?"

"No worse than before." The warrior took in the scene matter-of-factly, unperturbed by the men he had slain. "That was some display. Why didn't you kill them?"

Why didn't he? Conor cast about for a reasonable explanation. "I figured they'd need to be questioned."

"I know who sent them." The man walked to one of Conor's disabled opponents and wordlessly thrust the sword into his chest.

Conor clenched his jaw and pushed down nausea as the warrior executed the men he had so painstakingly kept alive. When he thought he could speak neutrally, he asked, "Did Lord Gainor get away?"

"Aye, and four of his bravest guards as well." The man walked to Conor and offered his hand. "Keondric Mac Eirhinin."

So that's why he recognized him: he was the young lord Gainor had pointed out during his first feast at Lisdara. Conor clasped his forearm. "Conor."

"Brother Conor?"

"Just Conor will do."

Mac Eirhinin nodded and pushed no further. "We're indebted to you. As you can tell, we were in no shape to meet an ambush."

"You've seen battle already." Conor nodded towards the man's bandaged thigh.

"If you can call it that. It was a massacre." Mac Eirhinin wove through the bodies, collecting weapons and tossing them into a pile. "How did you come to intervene?"

"Just passing through. I tracked the men here. I didn't expect to see Gainor."

"How do you know Lord Gainor?" The warrior's bland tone didn't quite cover his intense interest.

"We met some years ago."

Mac Eirhinin only nodded and gestured to the weapons. "Take what you like. Ó Sedna will send men back to collect the rest."

Conor didn't need anything beside his sword and staff, but the nobleman watched him, assessing, so he took his time looking through the pile of weapons. Finally, he chose a serviceable knife with a sharp, thin blade.

"How far is the camp?" Conor asked, anxious to leave the bloody scene behind.

"Three miles or so. With any luck, my man's on his way back with horses already."

Mac Eirhinin's limp became more pronounced as they walked toward camp, but he kept a quick pace.

"What happened before I got here?" Conor asked. "Lord Gainor looked badly hurt, and those men did not happen onto you by accident."

"I could say the same about you."

Conor chose his words with care. "I was headed to Lord Abban to offer my assistance. Just in the right place at the right time, I suppose."

"From what I saw, he'd be happy to have you. Comdiu knows we can use all the skilled fighters we can get." Mac Eirhinin broke off, perhaps realizing he trailed into topics best not discussed with a stranger. "To answer your question, the battle nearly cost us our entire company. Some of us stayed behind with Lord Gainor to cover the retreat. We're all that's left. Seems they weren't content to let us go after all."

"Looks to me they were seeking hostages. So far, Fergus hasn't fought unless he needed to. Probably thought he could force the Mac Cuillinn's hand."

"You're well-informed," Mac Eirhinin said slowly. "Your accent sounds Timhaigh."

Now they were getting to the heart of the matter. Conor wondered if the chieftain was beginning to put together the pieces. He had, after all, seen him briefly at Lisdara three years before. "I was born there, but I wouldn't call it home. Does it matter? There's us, and there's them. You said yourself, you can use all the help you can get."

Mac Eirhinin did not answer. Conor followed his gaze to the small party of horsemen approaching in the distance.

"Bless Balus," Mac Eirhinin murmured. "I've had enough walking for one day."

Conor glanced at the man's leg, where a trail of blood seeped from the bandage into his boot. His estimation of the chieftain rose another notch.

The riders closed the distance rapidly: a different trio of men, led by a bulky, disreputable-looking warrior. Mac Eirhinin grinned as they approached. "Are those horses for us to ride, or did you just mean to bring back the bodies?"

"Bloody cowards," the leader grumbled. "You'd think one man could have seen to Lord Gainor and the rest stayed to fight. Under orders, they said. Who's this?"

"Conor," Mac Eirhinin answered immediately.

"Brother Conor?"

Conor almost laughed. "No."

Mac Eirhinin gestured toward the leader. "This is Dearg. Behind him, Taicligh and Uvan."

Conor nodded to them and introduced himself to one of the two riderless geldings. The warriors' eyes followed him as he vaulted onto the horse's back and rested his staff against his shoulder. He made sure he stayed close to Mac Eirhinin and Dearg as they turned back toward camp, aware their gratitude did not automatically translate to trust.

"How is Lord Gainor?" Conor asked.

"Alive," Dearg said. "Barely."

He would be dead, had Conor not happened along. The others as well. This was no coincidence, even if he still felt conflicted about the first real test of his skills.

The camp appeared over the next rise, much larger than Conor had expected. Banners of varying colors, Faolanaigh and Siomaigh, flew above the sprawling site. "Not all the Siomaigh sided with Fergus?"

"They were safe behind the wards when it happened, so they weren't infected," Mac Eirhinin said. Apparently, much more had happened than the broad strokes of the Fíréin reports had let on.

Shouts broke out across the camp, announcing their arrival. Conor took a deep breath and prepared himself for the inevitable barrage of questions. Still, that nervousness could not compare with the realization he might soon come face to face with Aine.

CHAPTER THIRTY-FOUR

Aine was kneeling beside one of her patients in the infirmary tent, checking his stitches for signs of infection, when she heard a commotion of hooves and shouts outside.

Lorcan poked his head inside. "It's Gainor. He's hurt. Badly."

Aine jumped to her feet and followed Lorcan to where four guards lifted her unconscious brother from his horse. Fear pierced her midsection. Wounded badly was an understatement.

"Put him in his tent," she said. "I'll be right there."

She paused long enough in the infirmary to collect two large sacks filled with supplies and followed the men to her brother's tent. Dozens more had already gathered, and she had to push a path to his bedside.

"Everyone but Lorcan, out now."

All but the guard immediately beat a hasty retreat. Aine knelt beside her brother's pallet to survey his condition. Bruises and filth mottled his pasty skin, and blood-soaked bandages bound him from head to toe. She inhaled deeply, closed her eyes, and placed a hand on his chest.

Gainor's pain assailed her, and it took a moment to distinguish the injuries from one another. She sorted through the sensations, cataloging each injury with as much detachment as she could manage. Broken bones everywhere: hand, leg, ribs, collarbone, nose. Wounds from spear and sword in his shoulder, beneath his collarbone, in his side, in his leg. Part of his right ear was missing, and his left eye was swollen shut, hiding damage that could mean permanent blindness. Yet none of the wounds had been mortal.

Aine swallowed her horror. She could not think of him as her brother now. He was simply another patient. "Lorcan, I'll need your help."

With Lorcan's assistance and some creative use of wood and linen, Aine managed to set the broken bones and tend the worst of the flesh wounds. Still, it would be a miracle if Gainor walked again, and the anesthetics at her disposal would do only so much to dull the pain.

"A physician could have done a better job," she said, pushing her damp hair from her face. "He can't make the journey back to Lisdara, though. If he survives the next day and night, we'll write Calhoun and have him send someone."

"You underestimate your abilities, my lady," Lorcan said. "I'll go fetch a servant to sit with him so you can rest."

Aine pushed herself to her feet, despair stealing the strength from her limbs as she wandered outside into the rapidly fading light. The wind had picked up, and the air smelled of rain. Were there others like Gainor, left for dead on the battlefield, without guardsmen to carry them to safety? She pressed her fists to her eyes and willed back tears. She couldn't break now. Of the thousand warriors in camp, nearly a third of them were injured, half of those seriously. Without her attention, they would likely die. No, she had far too much responsibility to let herself fall apart.

Ruarc appeared beside her. "You look exhausted."

"I am exhausted. Did you learn what actually happened?"

"Each man has a different story. Best I can tell, they saw him fall but stayed with the retreat. Mac Eirhinin and his men went back for him."

The mention of Lord Keondric usually summoned uneasiness, but now she felt only gratitude. "Has he returned?"

"They were pursued from the battlefield. Mac Eirhinin stayed behind to fight while the others fled with Gainor."

Aine understood what he left unsaid. It was the guards' responsibility to bring the king's tanist back safely, but it didn't sit well to leave a man behind. She rubbed her temples. "Maybe I will go lie down. Lorcan should be back in a minute with someone to tend to Gainor."

Ruarc delivered her to her tent on the other side of the command pavilion, but she had no sooner stepped inside than she heard more shouts from the perimeter. Her heart leapt into her throat. She darted out as someone shouted, "Mac Eirhinin's back!"

"Blessed Comdiu. He's alive?"

Five men rode up the wide center aisle, Lord Keondric in the lead. The chieftain's clothing was tattered and stained, and the bandage around his thigh barely staunched the flow of blood from a new wound. Still, he looked a far sight stronger than Gainor. She owed him a sincere word of thanks.

Then Aine noticed the stranger in the party. He dismounted lightly and handed his reins to a servant. He was not one of Abban's or Gainor's men, but he seemed familiar nonetheless. His lean, muscular build said he was a warrior, and he wore old-fashioned clothing with his hair in a single braid. Fíréin?

Then he turned and met her gaze, and her knees nearly buckled. He may have changed in three years, but she knew him all the same. A shock of recognition passed between them.

Keondric was making some sort of introduction to the assemblage, but Aine barely heard him over the drumming of her heart. She took a halting step forward, and her shock turned to fierce joy that felt more like pain than pleasure.

"I can't believe it," she whispered. "Conor."

+ + +

Conor hardly expected to see Aine in the group that greeted them at the center of camp. His brief glimpse in the forest had only hinted at the stunning woman she had become. When she stepped forward, he stood immobilized, his heart rising into his throat. Hope swelled within him at her expression, a mixture of amazement, joy, and something he feared to name.

Conor started toward her, but before he could take more than a few steps, a bulky warrior with silver-blond hair positioned himself between them. "The lady may know you, friend, but we don't."

The threat in the man's voice was clear, as was the challenge in his eyes. Aine stepped forward and placed a hand on the man's arm. "Conor is an old friend, Lorcan. It's all right."

Lorcan bowed his head in acknowledgement and stepped away with obvious displeasure. Conor realized the entire group was watching the exchange with open interest. Apparently, so did Aine, because she stiffened and said formally, "This is such a surprise. How exactly did you come across Lord Mac Eirhinin?"

"I'd like to know that as well," came a booming voice. A bearded giant pushed to the front. "We feared the worst when you didn't return, Mac Eirhinin."

"It would have been, if not for Conor. He warned us of the ambush. Conor, this is Abban Ó Sedna."

Conor bowed slightly. "Lord Mac Eirhinin exaggerates."

"I'm sure," Abban said wryly. "Come, let's discuss this in private."

Conor dared not glance at Aine as he followed Abban into the large canvas tent. Despite their polite phrasing, the words were an order, not an invitation. Mac Eirhinin may have accepted Conor as a friend, but this mountain of a battle commander might not be so easily convinced.

Inside, Abban gestured to a chair near a large table spread with maps. The topmost one caught Conor's attention, a fine rendering of Siomar and Faolán overlaid with a web of red lines. He read the legends on several—Callindor, Northglenn, Eavenwood—before the commander swept it out of view.

The tent flap opened, admitting Mac Eirhinin with Aine and Ruarc steps behind. Abban gestured for them to approach, but only the young lord joined Conor at the table.

"You are not under guard here because Mac Eirhinin calls you a friend," Abban said. "Your Timhaigh accent, however, immediately puts your motives under suspicion. So that leaves two questions: who are you and how did you happen upon Lord Gainor's party?"

Conor briefly considered lying, but too many people had witnessed Aine's reaction. It was only a matter of time before they puzzled out the truth. Too bad the truth would put no one at ease.

"My name is Conor. Once, my clan name was Mac Nir."

Abban seemed surprised, but whether by his identity or his transparency, Conor couldn't guess. "It *was* Mac Nir? You claim it no longer?"

"My forebears have hardly done it honor."

Abban glanced at Aine. "Is this true? Is he who he claims?"

Aine cleared her throat, but she didn't look at him when she said, "It's true."

"You're in remarkably good health for a man who has been dead three years. Care to explain?"

Conor surveyed the commander. Lord Abban would continue to press as long as he answered his questions. "Suffice it to say I had my reasons for disappearing as I did. I've spent the last three years at Ard Dhaimhin, and now I've come back to offer assistance."

"The Fíréin deign to send one man to help in our war?" Abban flashed a sardonic smile. "How kind."

"I come of my own accord. The brotherhood stays out of the kingdoms' affairs, even in these dire times." Conor kept his sudden pang of concern from surfacing on his face. The commander would be within his authority to have him summarily executed as a spy. "Are you so confident in your victory that you would turn down another skilled fighter?"

Mac Eirhinin spoke up. "We were ambushed. Conor alerted us and took down eight men himself with only a staff and a sling. Had it not been for his intervention, we would all be dead, including Lord Gainor. I'd say he's proved his intentions rather thoroughly."

Abban turned back to him. Before the chieftain could speak, Conor said quietly, "The simple fact is this: I am a Balian. Fergus and his druid seek to destroy all that is good in Seare. I could not stand by in Ard Dhaimhin and watch it happen. I have some information that can be of use if you will allow me to join you."

Abban nodded slowly, still wary, but the worst of the suspicion had disappeared from his expression. "We can discuss the matter over supper. I expect you'll want to wash first. Mac Eirhinin, have Lady Aine look at that leg before you lose any more blood."

The dark-haired lord struggled to his feet.

"Come to the infirmary," Aine said. "You'll need stitches. If you'll excuse us, my lords." Her eyes settled on Conor and flitted away again. She followed the young chieftain from the tent, Ruarc a step behind them.

Abban watched them go. "She's something, isn't she? I would have said a lady in this camp would be a disaster, but the men regard her as a lucky charm. She's saved us all more than once."

"The lady healer of Lisdara," Conor said. "She's something of a patron saint."

"Indeed." Abban fixed his eyes on Conor. "Son, you might as well be honest with me. You're here because of her. I know the two of you became close when you were at Lisdara."

"She is part of the reason I'm here," Conor said. "But that won't keep me from my duty, should it come to it."

"I believe you." Almost to himself, Abban added, "I just hope it makes a difference."

CHAPTER THIRTY-FIVE

Conor scrubbed the grime from his face and hands and did his best to make himself look presentable. Abban had not yet returned, but since he wasn't anxious to face the scrutiny of the camp, he sat down in one of the chairs and began to check over his weapons.

The tent canvas rustled, and Conor looked up, expecting the commander. It was Aine.

He set aside his sword and rose. Behind her, the twilight had succumbed to night, and the light from the pavilion's oil lamps turned her hair to burnished gold. She had changed her dress, and the simple wool clung to curves he didn't remember her having.

Aine took a step toward him, then halted. Her eyes locked with his, but he could read nothing of her thoughts in their depths.

His stomach back-flipped. Could he have been wrong about her reaction? After all, she was no longer the shy girl he'd met at Lisdara, but a confident woman who commanded the respect of an entire camp. How could he blame them when his own heart hammered so hard in his chest he could barely breathe?

Then the barest hint of a smile lifted her lips. She crossed the pavilion in a few swift steps, and he enfolded her in his arms. The sense of rightness he'd felt at Lisdara settled over him, as if he'd reclaimed a piece of himself he'd forgotten was missing.

"I wasn't sure you would come back," she whispered into his tunic.

He stroked her hair. "I heard you call for me. It just took me a while to make my way here."

Aine pulled away and stared up at him, her cheeks wet with tears, her gray eyes wide. He smoothed a lock of hair away from her face, and she inhaled sharply at his touch. The transparent longing in her expression made his knees weak.

She caught his hand and ran her fingers over the calluses on his palm and his fingertips, the marks of the sword and the harp. "You've been playing."

"Every day." He closed his fingers around hers, his eyes never leaving her face. "That's why I'm here. I found the answers I sought at Ard Dhaimhin."

Ruarc slipped into the tent, unsurprised to see them standing so close. "Ó Sedna and Mac Eirhinin are on their way back."

"Thank you." Aine tried to pull away, but Conor held her fast. Ruarc cleared his throat, and Conor released her an instant before the two noblemen entered the tent.

Abban barely gave them a glance as he crossed to the table. "Good. You're both here. We have much to discuss. I've invited Lord Keondric to join us."

Conor found himself seated beside Abban, facing Aine and Mac Eirhinin, just as the servants arrived with pots of venison stew and trays of crusty rye bread. His eyes kept returning to her while the servants placed the food before them. When he managed to tear his gaze away, Mac Eirhinin was watching him, his expression hard. A hint of unease rippled through Conor.

They ate in silence. When the servants returned to remove the bowls and refill their ale, Conor cleared his throat and addressed the table. "What can you tell me of our situation here? I've received only the broad strokes."

"The situation is we've lost a third of our men in the south," Abban said. "We've holed up behind the last strong wards we can find, much good that will do us. Calhoun has another five hundred men on the Timhaigh border, just in case. Meanwhile, we can't engage our enemy for fear the sorcery will infect us."

"Fergus is using blood magic to control his men," Aine explained. "It's like a parasite. When the victim dies, it looks for another host."

"The infected can't cross the wards?" Conor asked.

"No, but Fergus has someone who can unmake them," Abban said. "He's using the wards to control our movements, place us where he wants us. Eventually those will fail, and there's nothing we can do about it."

Conor saw the reality of the situation in the expressions of those around the table. "That's not entirely true. We can find the ward-breaker."

"It would take time," Abban said. "Time to discover who this person is, time to reach him."

"I know who it is. It's the bard Meallachán."

Aine gasped. "Meallachán? Why would he help our enemy?"

"I don't know. Perhaps he's being forced. Maybe he's infected. Besides, we don't need *him*. We just need his harp."

"You learned how the wards are made?" Aine asked, breathless. "You could rebuild them?"

"If that were possible," Mac Eirhinin mused, "the ensorcelled warriors would be trapped between the wards, unable to move."

They exchanged glances, afraid to give in to sudden hope.

"We'll need to tell Calhoun," Abban said. "I don't trust the message to be sent by rider. Aine, you will go to Lisdara and speak with him. We can have a party ready in two days."

"I'm not leaving the camp! Who will see to the men?"

"Gainor needs a physician," Mac Eirhinin said. "Your replacement can see to them. You'll be safer at Lisdara, behind walls and wards."

Aine leapt to her feet and looked at each of them in turn. "Do you understand what you are saying? It sounds easy enough—just find Meallachán and his harp and bring them back here. *If* you can find him, and *if* you can reach him, he'll be guarded." She appealed to Conor. "It's a suicide mission. Do you know how little chance there is for success?"

"If not me, then who?" Conor asked quietly. "I'm Timhaigh. I can blend in. I've been well-trained by the Fíréin. And I'm the only one who can use the harp. It's the sensible move."

Aine blinked back tears, but she said nothing.

Conor sought to lighten the mood. "Who knows? I already came back from the dead once."

Her eyes flashed. "How dare you make light of it! You have no . . ." She closed her eyes and reined in her anger. "I need to see to Gainor. Excuse me."

Conor glanced at Abban. "Should she—"

"Ruarc or Lorcan will be outside. They're never far. In the meantime, get some rest. Ask one of the captains for an extra blanket. Unfortunately, we have plenty now."

"Thank you." Conor rose and nodded to each. "My lords."

After the stifling tension of the tent, the air felt gloriously cool, the faint smell of summer rain just discernible beneath wood smoke and cooking food. He drew in a deep breath and attempted to quiet his mind, but Aine's stricken, accusing stare refused to leave him.

There was no other way. He had been prepared for this very mission, his life saved, his path guided, so he could accomplish this task. And yet now that he was back, now that he knew Aine had not forgotten him, how could he bear to leave her again?

He searched the camp for Aine's tent, trying to convince himself he actually sought Ruarc to discuss plans for her departure. Within minutes, he had exhausted all the possibilities. He was about to give up and seek a place to bed down for the night when he caught sight of two silhouettes at the edge of camp beyond the supply tents: one tall and imposing, the other slender and cloaked.

Ruarc turned as he approached. He relaxed visibly when he recognized Conor and moved off a few paces to give them their privacy.

"It's not fair," Aine said hoarsely. Tears streaked her cheeks again. He reached for her, and she moved into his embrace without hesitation. "I don't want to lose you again. I've prayed for this moment for three years. To think it might have only been so you could leave and do this . . . it's cruel."

"You must commit me to Comdiu again. I'm alive only by His will." He rested his chin atop her head, surprised by how naturally they fit together, how little shyness he possessed around her. "I felt you die in Dún Eavan. When I thought you were gone, it broke me. I believed Comdiu must be unspeakably cruel to take you away. When I learned you still lived, I realized how little I understood of Comdiu's plans and how quick I was to dismiss Him. If this is why He brought us here, I have to trust things will unfold according to His will."

Aine tilted her head back to look at him. "While I was in the lake, Lord Balus spoke to me. He told me there were dark days ahead for Seare and I must be faithful. I've tried, but this . . . I don't want to believe I was spared just to be a part of this."

The anguish in her voice tore at Conor's heart. He searched for words to reassure her, but they all felt inadequate. Instead, he slid one hand behind her neck and kissed her gently. Aine melted into the embrace, her hands moving up his back as she gave herself to the kiss, and the warmth he'd felt flared into something more. He disentangled himself with effort and stepped back.

"I should have told you how I felt before I left," he said.

She smiled. "I knew. I heard it in your song."

"I have loved you from the moment I took your hand in the hall. Do you remember?"

"Of course I remember. I dreamed of you before I ever came to Lisdara. Somehow I knew I would love you."

Her words made him giddy. She loved him. The fears that had haunted him for three years vanished. "And now? Have you since come to your senses?"

She shook her head, mischief surfacing in her expression. "I'm afraid those are long gone."

"Good." He sobered and took her hands again. "Because if I come back, I want to marry you. If you'll have me."

Tears sprang to her eyes again, but she was smiling. "Of course I will. Nothing would make me happier."

He laughed, and she threw her arms around his neck. Then he kissed her again until they were both breathless and trembling. Ruarc cleared his throat, and Aine jerked away to a safe distance. Conor threw a sheepish glance at the guard, expecting to see warning in his expression, but Ruarc struggled against a smile.

Conor grinned. "She's just agreed to marry me."

"So I gathered." Ruarc said. "I suggest we all return to camp—separately—before you draw unwanted attention to yourselves."

Aine threw an embarrassed look at her guard, but she stretched up on tiptoe to steal one last kiss from Conor. "Good night."

"Good night, my love." Conor squeezed her hand and smiled as she disappeared back into camp with Ruarc.

She still loved him. She wanted to marry him.

If he came back alive.

At the thought, the joy he had felt moments before turned cold. What were the chances he'd actually live to follow through on that promise? Had he just condemned Aine to even more heartache?

Lord, have I just done a terrible thing?

The first fat drops of rain stung his face as they spattered down around him. If it was an answer, he didn't know what it meant.

CHAPTER THIRTY-SIX

The days before Aine's departure for Lisdara passed far too quickly. Conor stole any moment he could to hold her and reassure himself he was not merely dreaming her presence, but those moments were few and far between. She darted around the camp, ensuring her patients would be cared for in the short time between her departure and the arrival of the king's physician. Gainor continued to worsen despite her tireless efforts, and Conor saw how the possibility of losing him pained her.

"I know what's killing him; I just can't stay ahead of the infection." Aine wrapped her arms around Conor's waist and pressed her head against his chest, as if he was all that stood between her and disaster. "What use is my gift when I know what must be done, but I can't do it fast enough?"

Conor kissed the top of her head, but inwardly, her words mirrored his own thoughts. The messengers that would bring vital intelligence on the enemy's movements were late, and with each passing day, his opportunity to find Meallachán's harp waned.

To distract himself, he joined sword drills with the other men. He sensed them sizing him up, and he knew he did not fall short in the comparison. He had spent more time with a sword in the last two years than many of the younger men had in their entire lives. Still, he knew they were far more comfortable with the idea of taking lives than he. He wasn't yet sure if that was good or bad.

Treasach waited for him after one such drill. Conor had known the priest was in camp, but their paths hadn't yet crossed.

"The warrior-bard," Treasach said with a hint of laughter in his voice. "I never thought to see you as comfortable handling a sword as a harp."

"That makes two of us. Your kind does their work well."

The priest didn't try to deny it. "Our kind, you mean. Still, if I hadn't seen it with my own eyes, I wouldn't have believed it."

Conor struggled with words for a long moment. "I couldn't kill."

"You see that as a weakness?"

"I see it as a liability. What if I can't do what needs to be done?"

"You should thank Comdiu you had the choice. Taking a man's life when it is justified and necessary is nothing to be ashamed of, but it is not to be celebrated. When it is time, you will do what needs to be done. Just know there is a cost."

Conor nodded. So far, he'd been able to avoid being directly responsible for anyone's death, but he couldn't fool himself into thinking that would last forever, especially if he were to go after the harp.

The morning of Aine's scheduled departure, while he pretended to sleep under a gray, lowering sky, the long-awaited messenger galloped into camp. Conor jumped from his bedroll and raced toward the command tent, shrugging on his sword as he ran. His heart rose into his throat at the standard: not the simple green banner of a Faolanaigh messenger, but Calhoun's crowned wolf.

Aine, Ruarc, and Abban had already arrived, weary but alert. Aine moved to Conor's side, her expression controlled, implacable. But when her hand found his, concealed by the folds of her skirt, he felt a tremor ripple through her.

The messenger handed over a sealed parchment and collapsed into a chair while the commander read the message.

Abban lowered the parchment slowly. "Lisdara's under siege."

Aine sagged against Conor, the brave front slipping. He put a steadying arm around her shoulders and asked, "How is that possible? The wards around the keep still hold."

"The warriors that landed on the eastern coast were not ensorcelled. Calhoun managed to send the message before the attack."

"Gainor predicted this," Aine said. "Fergus made us rely on the wards for protection and then struck once we felt secure. Why didn't Calhoun escape to Dún Eavan while he could?"

"The king wouldn't leave his men, my lady," the messenger said. "Lady Niamh begged him to come with her."

"Niamh's at Dún Eavan?" Aine asked.

"Which is where you are going," Ruarc said. "If it wasn't safe for you before, it's even more dangerous now."

Abban addressed the messenger. "Take some food and rest, young man. We'll find you if we need you."

The messenger departed, and Abban tossed the letter on the table. He sank into the recently vacated chair. "Seaghan can guard the southern front while we move our remaining céads north to Lisdara." He gestured to a servant. "Find Mac Eirhinin."

"I'm here." Mac Eirhinin strode into the tent, holding another message. "This just came."

Abban took the parchment. "The messenger?"

"Dead. Took an arrow as he fled the battlefield. It's a miracle he even reached us. What does it say?"

Abban's scowl deepened as he scanned the message. "The force on the Timhaigh border has been attacked."

"And this time they were ensorcelled," Aine guessed. "There aren't any wards there."

Abban swore sharply. "Fliann's men will be no help now. We'll be lucky if we don't end up fighting them ourselves. All right, Mac Eirhinin. Spread the news. We break camp and move north."

Conor had the eerie sensation of control slipping from their grasp. He couldn't wait for a messenger from the south that might never come, and yet he could hardly run off without direction. He enfolded Aine in his arms and absently brushed away the stray hairs that escaped her braid. As his fingers touched her silver necklace, he realized what he had overlooked. He took her hand and drew her outside the tent.

In the dull gray morning, he tugged the charm on its chain from beneath her bodice. "Can you do something for me?"

Understanding dawned on her face. "You want me to find Meallachán."

Ruarc joined them on their way to Aine's tent and took up a position just inside the entrance. She sank onto her cot and curled her fingers around the charm. Conor clasped her free hand in both of his.

Aine closed her eyes, and Conor waited for sign of a vision. Minutes passed. He had just begun to relinquish hope when her hand tightened on his, and her forehead creased. A tear trickled down her cheek.

"I saw him. He's been tortured." She opened her eyes. "I think he's in a church or a monastery. It had a big stained-glass window of a saint, a man holding a scale and an olive branch. Does that help?"

"Saint Simeon," Conor said immediately. "It has to be the abbey at Cill Rhí. It's a few miles outside of Beancaiseal."

"How do you know?"

"I studied architecture, too." He sent her a sheepish smile. "It's built in the Ciraen style, the only one of its type. I'm sure of it."

Aine didn't return the smile. Her throat worked, and she gripped his hand harder. "I don't want you to go. Please, come with me to Dún Eavan."

Ruarc quietly excused himself, and Conor took Aine's other hand as well. "Did you see something else? Something you're not telling me?"

"No, it's just . . . what if this is it? What if we never see each other again?"

Conor pulled her close, wishing he had some way to reassure her, but he couldn't banish the feeling of dread that had come with the first messenger. If Lisdara fell, Fergus and Diarmuid succeeded. Only Faolán stood between them and total control of the four kingdoms. "We must trust Comdiu will not abandon us, Aine. It's all we have left."

She swiped at her eyes. "If everyone is leaving, I need to see my supplies from the infirmary are properly packed." She touched her forehead to his, as if drawing resolve from his closeness, and then stood. "I'll find you later."

Conor dropped his head into his hands. *Lord, guide me. Help me complete this task set before me. Protect Aine. Let me survive to marry her.* He didn't know what else to say. Their needs were both simple and overwhelming.

Conor found Abban in the command pavilion and emotionlessly outlined his plan. He would take four accomplished riders and swordsmen, a party small enough to slip unnoticed past the enemy. He would form his plan to get inside Cill Rhí once they could survey its defenses. From there, his success would be in Comdiu's hands. Abban's expression turned grim, but he simply nodded.

Mac Eirhinin found him as he left Abban's tent and walked silently beside him for several breaths before he spoke. "I don't like it."

Conor shot him a sidelong glance. "Like what?"

"Aine should go to Dún Eavan now. Our intelligence is at least a week old. By the time a group this large reaches Lisdara, there is no telling where the enemy might be. She's better off with a small, fast party of riders that can slip around Fergus's forces."

"Do you not think she'd be safer in the company of several hundred warriors? A small party is fast, but indefensible."

"Not with men like Ruarc and Lorcan."

Conor stopped and faced Mac Eirhinin, crossing his arms over his chest. "I don't believe this is merely concern for the king's sister."

Mac Eirhinin could not meet his eye. "Come now. Half the men in camp are in love with her, especially those of us who have had the benefit of her care."

"I hadn't realized you knew her so well."

"I've had cause to admire her for some time."

Conor sighed. Aine somehow drew people to her. He could hardly blame Mac Eirhinin for his admiration. "Then what do you recommend?"

"Send her usual escort. Those men have put their lives in danger at her command more than once. Riding hard, they could reach Dún Eavan in five days. She'll be safe at the fortress before we ever engage the enemy."

Everything Mac Eirhinin said was perfectly sensible, and yet the idea unsettled Conor. The other man must have sensed his ambivalence, because he said quietly, "No one would blame you if you chose to escort her there yourself. You could be at Cill Rhí in two weeks. Somehow, I don't think we'll be done fighting by then."

The idea, so appealing when Aine had begged him, sounded even more sensible from Mac Eirhinin's mouth. He could concentrate on his task if he knew she was safe in Dún Eavan.

No, two weeks was too long. "I can't. But I'll speak with Abban and get his opinion."

Abban thought the chieftain's advice to be sensible, and Ruarc agreed. In addition to four men who had escorted Aine to Abban's camp, Ruarc selected six more from the mapping party. The warriors went to make their preparations, and Conor stood alone with Aine outside her tent for what could be the last time.

"I don't want to leave you again," he whispered in her ear.

"All will be as it should." She smiled. "Promise me you'll be careful."

Conor reached for a smile. It felt as false as hers looked. "I have a good reason to come back, don't I?"

He kissed her, but it was a bittersweet farewell, coming so soon after their reunion. When she stepped away, tears pooled in her eyes. "They're ready for me. I have to go."

Conor walked her to her horse and lifted her onto it, his hands lingering on her waist. She caught one of them as he drew away. "Promise me you'll come back."

"I'll do everything within my power." He lifted her hand to his lips. "I love you, Aine."

"And I love you. Go with Comdiu."

Ruarc caught Conor's eye and nodded, a wordless assurance she would be as safe as he could make her. The group moved forward, the men closed around her, and then she was gone from his sight.

Conor didn't expect the crushing sense of loss. He walked amidst the camp in various stages of dismantle and forced down his feelings with each step. He couldn't afford any distractions from his goal now.

When he reached the site where Abban's command tent had once stood, the commander spoke with four men. Abban waved Conor over.

"These are your men. Gair, Darragh, Bram, and Eoin. They'll see you there safely."

Gair and Eoin were the older of the quartet, perhaps five-and-thirty, with the self-assured air of professional warriors. Darragh and Bram weren't much older than Conor, but he had watched them drill and knew they were beyond competent.

"I'm glad to have you," he said. "Has Lord Abban told you the mission?" When they nodded, Conor continued, "We'll travel fast with remounts. Bring only weapons and enough food to get there and back. Rest up, because we'll be moving fast, and if we're successful, we'll be leaving with warriors on our heels."

Darragh and Bram exchanged a grin, just a little too enthusiastic about the scenario.

Lord, preserve us, Conor thought.

Abban and his men left that afternoon, leaving behind only scarred earth as a testament to the camp's existence. Now a mere five warriors crowded around a small fire. Conor tested the edge of his sword and drew a whetstone down its length a few times before he turned his attention to the binding on his staff sling.

"Can you really do what Abban says?" Darragh asked.

Conor looked up at the warrior's skeptical tone. "I hope so. Until I have the harp, I can't know for sure."

"Then we get the harp," Bram said.

Conor met Gair's knowing gaze. It would not likely be that easy.

When morning came, they broke camp silently and efficiently, dousing the embers and packing their few supplies onto the horses. Their planned route would take them along the edge of Rós Dorcha until they broke southeast toward the abbey. Fortunately, his four companions proved to be as good riders as they were swordsmen. Abban had chosen well.

Still, Conor's anxiety increased with each mile. It was not just the knowledge of what awaited them, but the nagging sense he had missed something important. He slept restlessly on the hard ground that first night, chased by half-formed nightmares, until a dream transported him back to Abban's camp.

Aine clung to his arm, her fingers biting into his flesh. "You mustn't go to Cill Rhí. You're in danger."

"You know why I must go. It's our only chance."

Wordlessly, Aine pointed to Mac Eirhinin, standing with Eoin, Bram, and Darragh.

"I don't understand."

"Think," Aine said. "You have felt it from the beginning."

Conor searched his memory, willing the thought that had nagged him all day to materialize.

No one would blame you if you chose to escort her there yourself. You could be at Cill Rhí in two weeks.

Conor's stomach clenched as understanding stole into him. He had never spoken to Mac Eirhinin of his destination, and Abban had agreed to hold back the details from all but his four companions. How else could he have known?

It had been Mac Eirhinin's idea to separate Aine from Abban's forces and send her on to Dún Eavan.

"You know then." Aine shivered, her teeth chattering. "It's time to wake up now."

"But you could be in danger—"

"You mustn't worry about me. Your task is too important. It's time to wake up."

Now, shudders wracked her whole body. Conor grabbed her arms, panic building in his chest. "Aine—"

"Now, Conor. Wake up!"

Wake up!

Conor knocked aside the downward thrust of a blade before he realized his sword was in hand. He rolled to his feet. Blood rushed through his veins, scattering the last remnants of sleep. In the moonlight, his four companions faced him, their weapons in hand.

"Don't do this," Conor said, desperation in his voice. "You're not traitors. You're being manipulated."

"Calhoun is going to lose this war," Darragh said. "We choose the winning side."

The man lunged, expecting to catch him off guard, but Conor parried the thrust and countered with his own. The blade slid into Darragh's midsection with sickening ease. Ten seconds ago, Conor had trusted this man with his life, and now he had killed him.

Eoin came next. Conor knew not to underestimate his skills. Experienced and well-trained, Eoin feinted skillfully, trying to lure him into doing something foolish. Conor kept his breathing measured, his awareness tuned, and when the attack came, he was ready. A short exchange of swordplay, and the warrior lay lifelessly at his feet.

That left him facing Bram. Too late, he realized he had lost track of Gair in the dark. The back of his neck prickled in warning, but before he could act, something slammed into his head. Conor dropped to the ground, and his world slid sideways into blackness.

CHAPTER THIRTY-SEVEN

Aine awoke with a pounding heart. The dream had possessed the same clarity as her other visions, but she couldn't make sense of it until she felt the burn of the wheel charm against her skin.

"Conor," she whispered.

Ruarc's eyes snapped open. "What's wrong?"

"I don't know. I think Conor's in trouble. I had the strangest dream."

You could be in danger, he had said. He had worked something out Aine still didn't understand.

Alarm flashed over Ruarc's face. He drew his sword and leapt to his feet as dozens of men flooded into the camp. The other warriors grasped the danger just a moment later, springing awake to engage the attackers.

Aine scrambled back on the turf, her heart thudding too hard to loose a scream. So many. Her party was fighting valiantly, but they were outnumbered three to one. Two of her guardsmen fell in front of her, one after another.

In the moonlit darkness, she could barely make out individual figures, but the sounds told her all she needed to know: the clash of steel on steel, the whinnies of terrified horses, the cries of dying men.

They were losing.

And she would be taken. Or worse.

Ahead of her, Ruarc was still fighting, still standing. He felled an opponent with a single slash and spun, seeking her.

Their eyes met. "Aine, behind you!" he yelled. He took a step toward her, then jerked to a halt. She followed his gaze down to his chest. The tip of a sword protruded from between the plates in his armor. He found

Aine's face one last time, more startled than pained, then crumpled to the ground.

"Ruarc!" Aine screamed, struggling to her feet. Before she could run to him, a strong arm wrapped around her, pinning her in place.

"Don't call out, or I'll kill you."

The cold bite of a blade against her throat stilled her struggle, as did the steel in her attacker's voice. She fought to think through the wave of grief, her eyes still fixed on Ruarc's lifeless body. Then she realized she knew the man's voice.

Comdiu, help me.

Instantly, a steady presence calmed her nerves. She forced her muscles to relax.

"It's not too late, Keondric," she said beneath the sounds of fighting. "You can still turn from this path."

"You knew me." Keondric's voice held surprising warmth. He swiveled her to face him. "I'm impressed. It's a shame I couldn't steal you away from the Mac Nir boy without having to actually steal you."

Aine dared a glance back toward the skirmish, hoping someone would notice the exchange.

Keondric smiled. "They won't see us. Your intended is not the only one with gifts, you know. I should have gone to Ard Dhaimhin myself, but my father wouldn't hear of it." He held up a length of rope. "Do I need to tie your hands, or will you come peaceably?"

Her mind clicked through the possibilities, even as fear surged through her veins. Keondric seemed to have some real affection for her, however twisted. She could work with that. It was their only chance of survival. She barely stifled her sob. "I'll go with you. Please, just call them off. If it's me you want, my men don't need to die."

Keondric glanced back at the turmoil, then shrugged. "Casualties of war, my dear. You of all people should understand that."

You monster! The words rose in a silent scream in her mind, tears again pricking her eyes, but she forced herself to nod. She followed him meekly to a waiting horse. He lifted her atop it and mounted behind her, clamping one arm around her waist. She resisted the urge to squirm away. Behind them, the fighting still raged, proof that what had seemed like forever had really been only a few seconds. He kicked the horse into a gallop, and Aine squeezed her eyes shut against tears.

She needed time. Time to figure out the pieces of this puzzle, time to discover a way out. Which meant she had to keep him from killing her, no matter what that required.

✦ ✦ ✦

The sun had already crested the horizon when Keondric reined in the horse beside a small stream. He slid off first and helped her down, his manner solicitous, as if he were courting her and not kidnapping her. He walked the horse to the water's edge to drink and filled his skin before handing it to her.

Aine cast a sideways glance at the proffered water bag. "You first, my lord." When he hesitated, she tried to smile, as if her concern were for his welfare. "I insist."

"It's perfectly safe, I assure you." Keondric took a long drink as proof. "It'll be a faster and more pleasant trip if you're conscious."

Aine cautiously sipped from the water skin and handed it back to him. His manner puzzled her. Sometimes, her spirit recoiled from him, as if recognizing something dangerous lurking inside. Other times, like now, he seemed normal. Was he being controlled by the druid or the sidhe? Or was he just mad?

"Why are you doing this?"

Keondric lowered himself to the ground and gestured for Aine to join him. "I thought you would have guessed." He gave her a long look, and for a moment his gaze grew heavy with meaning. She suppressed a shiver, and he looked away, his tone businesslike. "You're bait."

"For Conor? I don't understand—"

"Call it a contingency plan. I can't be sure his escort will kill him. From what I've seen, I'd say it's unlikely. When he realizes I have you, he'll have to choose between you and the harp. Which will he choose, do you think?"

"The harp," Aine said, though it was only an attempt to stall while she worked out the situation. If Keondric was working for Fergus and the druid, it was of his own accord, not because of infection. He would not have been able to move across wards otherwise.

Somehow that was even worse. She could excuse weakness. But this treachery was pure evil. Conor's escort must work for them as well. But why attack so obliquely?

They feared him, she decided, and not just his sword. They thought he was the one with the gift of sight. Keondric had no idea Conor was acting on Aine's visions.

"You'd better hope he chooses you. Otherwise, you're of no more use to us. Strategically, that is." Keondric smiled, and while it was a pleasant smile, it hinted at darker things beneath.

Aine forced herself to maintain a calm exterior. As long as Keondric believed she did not fear him—as long as he believed he could win her—he would refrain from violence. "Why would you betray us? You're the wealthiest man in Faolán besides Calhoun. Your clan has advised the king for generations."

"How long do you think that will last once Faolán falls?" At Aine's shocked expression, Keondric's tone softened. "I know it sounds cold, but given the choice between being an ensorcelled slave and maintaining peace and prosperity for my clan, what else could I do? I cannot condemn them to death."

Aine sighed. She could understand his position, however distasteful. But would Fergus and Diarmuid uphold their end of the bargain once they got what they wanted?

"What's to happen to me, then?"

"That's entirely up to you. I'm taking you to Glenmallaig. As long as you cooperate, you'll be safe. I swear no one will harm you while you're under my protection."

And if she chose to leave his protection by refusing to do what he wanted. . . . Aine heard the warning as clearly as if he'd spoken it aloud.

After they ate a bit of cheese and bread, they mounted up again. This time he did not hold her so tightly. Grateful he had allowed her to keep her cloak, she surreptitiously closed her fingers around the wheel charm. She closed her eyes and tried to see Conor, but minutes passed without result. She tried again, hoping to glimpse Lorcan and the rest of her party, but she was no more successful the second time.

She tucked the charm back into her dress and tried not to let despair overwhelm her. Ruarc—her faithful guard, her trusted friend—was already dead. What made her think the rest weren't as well? Maybe that was why she couldn't see them. She stifled tears before they could rise again.

"Are you all right?"

"No," she snapped. "You're trying to destroy everything I care about in the world. I am definitely not all right."

Keondric had the grace to stay quiet and leave her to her brooding.

CHAPTER THIRTY-EIGHT

Conor's first conscious sensation was searing pain, followed by wild, animal panic. He scrambled in the dark for a weapon to defend himself, but the movement sent waves of agony through him. He doubled over and retched into the grass.

Only when the pain and nausea subsided to a bearable level did he realize he was alone, and the panic did not belong to him.

Mac Eirhinin had betrayed them. He tried to have Conor killed. He separated Aine from Abban's men.

Aine.

Conor jerked upright, only to fall back again, his head spinning. When he regained control of his limbs, he touched his throbbing head. His fingers came away sticky with blood. He gritted his teeth and probed the wound, relieved to find that, though his scalp had been split, his skull was intact. A hand stone, probably. It must have just grazed him. At that range, he was lucky to be alive.

No, not lucky. An experienced fighter would not miss at that distance. He was alive only because Gair hadn't wanted to kill him.

That meant Conor could still complete his mission. With him supposedly dead, the enemy would believe Meallachán and his harp were secure. Unless Mac Eirhinin had sent a warning to Cill Rhí, in which case the messenger would have had a full day's lead on him. But surely his escort would have reported their success? If they were no longer expecting him, he could still slip in unnoticed and retrieve the harp.

Memory of that panic, intense and mindless, stopped him short. He could not explain how he knew it was Aine any more than he could explain the other dreams he'd had over the last three years. He only knew she was in danger.

Conor sank back to the ground. Thinking through the pain felt like wading through molasses. Gair may have spared his life, but he had left him with no way of completing his task. All his resources—the horses, his weapons, even his pack—were gone. Only the patch of blood-stained earth and his throbbing head told Conor he had not dreamed the whole thing.

At least the pouch of hand stones remained on his belt, though they did him little good when he could barely see. The plain dagger was still strapped to his calf. He drew it out with a surge of relief. He was not completely defenseless.

He fumbled with his belt and repeatedly tried to slide the sheath onto the leather, but his fingers seemed to belong to someone else. He flung the weapon to the ground and cradled his head in his hands. No, he was worse than defenseless. He was useless.

The nation's last hope. Conor laughed bitterly. There he was, stranded alone in Siomar, without a horse, without a sword, and he couldn't even buckle his own belt. Some savior he turned out to be.

Who said you were meant to be a savior?

The thought, clear and direct, cut through his self-pity. He could not deny its truth. Fresh from his near-victory against Liam and his timely intervention in the ambush, had he not begun to think of himself as invincible? After all, he was young, well-trained, and he possessed magic that dated back to the Great Kingdom.

All it took was a single, well-placed hand stone to prove how vain his thinking had really been.

"Well, what do I do now, Comdiu?" he said aloud. "I'm helpless here. I don't know where to go or how to get there. Do I go to Cill Rhí? Do I look for Aine?"

Conor considered his choices with as much detachment as he could manage. At Cill Rhí, there lay a harp, which might or might not hold the key to rebuilding the wards. He could possibly shift the tide of the war. That was if he could manage what only one or two others had done since Daimhin's time.

Or he could go after the woman he loved, who was likely a prisoner and moving farther away with each passing second.

He knew what decision he should make. One person, in the scope of this war, could not compare to the lives of thousands.

But he could only picture Aine waiting for a rescue that would never come. If she died, he wouldn't be able to live with himself. If she survived, she would always carry the knowledge he didn't love her enough to save her. Was that how Riordan felt, cast off by his wife, forced to give up his son to another man for the sake of duty? Conor knew the cost all too well.

For right or wrong, he couldn't abandon Aine.

I cannot do this on my own. I need help.

His gaze drifted to the border of Seanrós, just visible in the rapidly spreading morning light. Food, shelter, weapons, information—all lay within the forest's borders. He could not return to Carraigmór, but there were others who might assist him.

He touched the wooden coin he now wore on a leather thong around his wrist and ran through a mental catalog of trackers and sentries. Innis was not far, but he'd be no help in stitching the wound in Conor's head. Corman had barely said a dozen words to him. Odran would be farther north this time of week. That left Beagan, the oddest tracker of the bunch and one who had always made him uncomfortable.

Aye, Beagan would help him, if he could find him. Conor rose slowly, and his legs held. A few experimental steps convinced him, shaky as he was, he wouldn't collapse.

The knife slid onto his belt after only two tries. Conor took a heading from the forest border and the steadily lightening horizon and calculated the distance through his fog. He had at least a full day's walk before he intersected with Beagan's midweek route.

Merciful Balus, You know I'm not equal to this task. Watch over Aine, keep her alive and unharmed. Give me the strength to find her. Put me on the path I need to travel.

Conor's first steps toward Seanrós were halting and unbalanced, but he forced himself onward. He felt as if he were walking underwater, but at least his muscles still worked even if his brain had been scrambled. He crossed into the cool, damp shade of the forest and was taken aback by the absence of the wards. He had never realized how much security he had drawn from the familiar tingle of magic.

He half-expected to encounter Fíréin, but the morning passed without any other sign of humans. Of course. The trackers had relied on the warning of the wards. The famed brotherhood was now blind in its own forest.

He oriented himself on a trap line, but the traps he encountered were empty. He settled for foraging berries and edible fungus for a midmorning meal, though they reminded him only of his empty stomach. When he stopped to drink from a stream, he realized he had wandered too far south on the grid and shifted his route northwest.

By nightfall, Conor could barely stumble forward in a straight line. His head throbbed, his body ached, and a lack of food combined with exertion made his vision dance with flecks of light. He chose a spot beneath a mossy hillock to spend the night and collapsed into an aching heap. He briefly considered gathering berries for his supper, but once his eyes closed, he couldn't pry them open again.

Conor passed the long, uncomfortable night in fits of sleep, broken by terrifying dreams. More than once, he awoke bolt upright, gripping his dagger, only to succumb to the throbbing in his head and sink back to the earth. When the first rays of morning light penetrated the leafy canopy, he felt haggard and achy.

He traveled as quickly as he dared with both his balance and alertness compromised. Morning had passed into midday by the time he neared the first grid markers on Beagan's route. He was making only slightly less noise than a wounded animal in the underbrush. Just as well. Perhaps the tracker would be drawn to him. He only hoped Beagan recognized him before he tried to kill him.

He braced himself against a tree and closed his eyes to summon his last shreds of strength. Beagan could be anywhere. For all he knew, they could have passed each other a quarter mile away and never known it. He heaved a sigh and prepared to move on when the cold point of a dagger jabbed beneath his chin.

"Beagan." Conor opened his eyes, and the pressure of the blade relented slightly.

"Who are you?"

"Brother Conor. Or I was until about a week ago."

Beagan circled to look at him. As well-groomed as any of the kingdoms' lords, the lanky tracker wore his reddish-brown hair braided in Fíréin fashion, his short beard fastidiously trimmed. Yet violence lurked beneath his veneer of civility. Conor had always felt he was the most dangerous of all the trackers.

"It is you," Beagan said in his distinct Timhaigh accent. "What happened? You were making enough noise to wake the dead."

"I had my head split open the night before last."

Beagan squinted at the wound in Conor's blood-matted hair. "You're lucky on that one. I take it you need a sword."

"Aye. I was hoping you might help with that."

"I might. I'm going the opposite way, though."

"Can I convince you otherwise?"

"Tell me why you need a sword. Besides the obvious."

"One of Calhoun's lords betrayed him and tried to have me killed. They kidnapped the woman I love."

Beagan's expression shifted. "Come on then. I want to hear how the man who beat the Ceannaire almost managed to get himself killed."

Thank you, Conor thought, directing the words simultaneously to Comdiu and Beagan. He followed the tracker, who set a deliberately slow pace, and began to tell him the story. He left out the details of his mission, but he told him of the vision that had convinced him Aine was in danger.

"I felt two people with gifts traveling west early this morning. Might it have been your woman?"

"You can sense magic? Even without the wards?"

"How do you think I found you? I've been tracking you for a day and a half."

That was a new one. Most trackers had some sort of affinity for the wards, not for magic itself. "How do you know there were only two?"

"I don't. There could have been more in the party, but two possessed Balus's gifts in a great degree, like you." Beagan began walking again, and Conor hurried to catch up. "Most of the clans have little shreds of it left. I don't even notice them anymore. But ones like you—your magic is a beacon."

Aine was alive. He sent up another silent prayer of thanks. But who had taken her? Mac Eirhinin? He did have royal blood. He could conceivably have a gift.

Beagan glanced back at him at regular intervals as they traveled. "We've got about three more hours. Do you think you can make it? You look pale."

Conor shot him a scathing look. Beagan laughed. "Forget I asked. But if you collapse, you're on your own."

The longer they walked, the harder Conor's head pounded, but he did not collapse. His stamina might have deserted him, but at least his stubborn will had not.

Long after night fell, Beagan stopped and said, "Here we are."

Conor looked around. He saw only the dark silhouette of a rocky outcropping and some trees. "Where?"

"Here." Beagan pushed aside foliage to reveal a large hole in the side of a hillock. "Come on."

Conor crouched down and followed Beagan into the tunnel. Roots brushed his head, and his shoulders scraped the side walls. Ahead, he heard flint striking metal, and then a torch flared to life. He squinted in the sudden glare.

The tunnel opened into a cavern of granite and earth, tall enough in which to stand upright and perhaps ten paces across. It featured all the usual amenities: a straw-stuffed pallet, a small low table with grain-sack cushions, and a wooden chest.

"Sit," Beagan said. "I've some food left over in the basket there. Help yourself."

Conor sank onto a cushion as Beagan started a fire in a small cooking niche that vented upward through the earth, away from the cavern. Conor took a heel of bread from the basket on the table and nibbled at it while Beagan hung a small kettle on a hook to heat. When the tracker at last set a steaming cup of tea before him, Conor drank it gratefully.

"You should probably rest now," Beagan said.

Conor's heavy eyelids drooped down, and the room tilted wildly. Rest sounded like such a good idea when everything swayed so strangely.

His tongue felt thick and clumsy. "You poisoned me!"

"I'm sorry," Beagan said, but Conor was already sliding into oblivion.

✦ ✦ ✦

When Conor awoke, he lay on a straw pallet on the cave floor, half-dressed and feeling like a wrung-out piece of cloth. Light shone dimly from a candle, illuminating the figure of a man bent over a tablet at the low table. Beagan.

Conor remembered his last thought before he had lost consciousness and sat up abruptly. He expected the familiar wave of pain and dizziness, but instead he felt only a distant throb. He touched his head, where a clean line of stitching marked a newly shaved patch of scalp. The lump had diminished drastically.

"What did you do to me?"

Beagan turned. "How do you feel?"

"Better. I don't understand. I thought—"

"I know. I'm sorry. I misjudged how quickly the tea would take effect in your condition. You needed to rest, and I needed you to sleep through your stitches. Are you hungry?"

Conor nodded, pleased to find his brain no longer seemed to rattle in his head with each movement. He joined Beagan at the table, where the tracker pushed a plate of porridge and roasted game toward him.

"How long have I been out?"

"Almost a day. It's sundown."

Conor spooned the porridge into his mouth, forcing himself to fill his empty stomach slowly.

"Did you know I was once a physician?" Beagan asked.

Conor shook his head. It certainly explained the man's skill with a draught and a needle.

"You've already guessed from my accent that I'm your countryman. I was, in my earlier years, the personal physician to Lord Fergus."

"What happened?"

"I was a young man. I had a lovely wife and two daughters. We were wealthy. We lived on Fergus's estate, but we had our own holdings. We were also Balians.

"It was not quite a secret, but I didn't flaunt the fact either. Then the druid came, and suddenly Fergus wanted me to renounce my faith. I refused. He let the matter drop, or so I thought. When I came home one night, my wife and children were missing. We searched all night, but we only found them in the loch the next morning. Lord Fergus wrote it off as an accidental drowning, but everyone knew the truth.

"There were no more Balians there after that day. It's one thing to give your own life for your beliefs, but another to have your family murdered for them."

Conor drew a sharp breath. It hit too close to the fears he'd had about

Labhrás's family, an answer to a question he'd stopped asking. "That's why you're helping me?"

"Fergus and his druid use your loved ones against you. Whatever your mission was, it was threatening enough that they took your young woman from you."

"Are you saying I shouldn't give in?" Conor asked slowly.

"Don't you think I would have saved my family had I been given the chance?" The tracker rose, shedding his introspective demeanor in favor of the cool, calculated exterior Conor remembered. "Come. The last help I can give you." He went to the wooden chest, unlatched the lid, and threw it open.

Weapons glutted the chest: swords, daggers, unstrung short bows with quivers of arrows. So many, in fact, that Conor looked at the tracker uneasily. Odran might be a little too comfortable with his duties, but Conor doubted even he had killed this many men.

"The Timhaigh seem to think the prohibitions don't apply to them lately," Beagan said almost gleefully. "There have been plenty of opportunities to put our training into practice."

So that was what unsettled Conor so much about the tracker. This job was more than just a duty to him. It was revenge. He took out his hatred on the warriors of Tigh under the guise of protecting Ard Dhaimhin.

Conor approached the chest as Beagan rummaged through the weaponry. He drew out a sheathed sword and passed it to him. "See what you think of this one."

Intricately stamped leather covered a steel scabbard, embossed with a complicated knotwork pattern. Conor grasped the plain hilt and drew the sword free, surprised to find the same knotwork design trailing down the blade. It was indeed masterful work. Conor made a few experimental strokes, wondering how it had been made so light.

"Some clan is missing this piece right now."

"Some clan is missing more than that," Beagan said, grinning. He continued to unearth items, one after another: daggers, spearheads, slings, hand stones, practically every weapon imaginable. Conor selected a heavy-bladed knife to replace the one at his belt, which went back at his ankle, as well as a leather sling. He allowed himself a moment's regret over the loss of Riordan's silver dagger, but he had more important concerns now.

"Thank you," Conor said. "I'm indebted to you."

Beagan shrugged. "Knew I might need them with all the unrest. Do you know where you're going next?"

"Glenmallaig." If Fergus and Diarmuid had orchestrated the kidnapping, they would enjoy the irony in making him return home to rescue Aine. "They'll be waiting for me there."

"Are you prepared to do what's necessary to rescue her?"

Dread washed over him again. He had managed to put away the memory of how easily he had taken Eoin's and Darragh's lives, but theirs would not be the only blood on his hands by the end. "I'll do what I must."

Beagan clapped a hand on his shoulder and returned to his reports at the table, leaving Conor to brood over the reality of his mission.

Just know there is a cost.

CHAPTER THIRTY-NINE

In the five days it took to reach Glenmallaig, Aine attempted to establish a rapport with her captor. Keondric already possessed a degree of genuine affection for her, but there was a coldness behind his manner she hadn't been able to thaw.

"Why do we travel alone?" Aine asked when they stopped to rest. "I don't doubt you can protect me, but with all the turmoil . . ."

"We're perfectly safe," Keondric said. He did not elaborate.

But Aine had begun to form her own theory. *Your intended is not the only one with gifts*, he had said. When they passed within shouting distance of several Faolanaigh warriors without even a head turning in their direction, she concluded he must be able to conceal them from sight.

That meant it was most likely a gift of Balus. No wonder he had so easily gained their confidence. They had relied on the wards and forgotten how easily men could be corrupted through conventional methods.

By any standard, hers was a pleasant captivity. Keondric remained solicitous, kind, and attentive. He stopped frequently to allow her to rest and made sure she had enough to eat and drink. He gave her his blanket to sleep beneath, and never did he touch her in a way she could deem inappropriate. Yet beneath it all, Aine sensed a hunger, a lust, the object of which she could not identify. It could have been power or safety or her, but it was overriding.

She had long since lost her sense of direction, so their descent toward Glenmallaig took her by surprise. Her first impression of the fortress chilled her. A murky black moat encircled it, lapping at the bottom of the earthen ramparts. Shreds of mist clung to their tops despite the clear, warm day. Aine shuddered at the evil that skittered across her consciousness: not only the sidhe's magic, but the druid's as well.

The drawbridge groaned down, and Keondric spurred the horse forward. The ivory charm burned white-hot when they broke the veil of sorcery. She swayed, sickened by its stench.

The heavy doors opened, and a pale, haggard man emerged from the structure. Keondric dismounted first and lifted her down, steadying her while her legs adjusted to solid ground.

"This is Glenmallaig's steward," he said. "He'll take care of you. I'll check on you later."

Aine moved toward the gaunt man and then turned impulsively. "Thank you, Keondric. I can't agree with what you are doing, but most men would not have been so kind."

A ghost of a smile lifted Keondric's lips, and for a moment, something like genuine pleasure sparked in his eyes. "I keep my vows, my lady."

Aine forced what she hoped looked like a sincere smile and went with the steward into Glenmallaig's great hall.

"I'm Marcan," the steward said. He gestured for her to follow him down the intersecting corridor. "You are not under guard, because there is no way to escape. You may go wherever you like within the fortress, but if you try to leave the courtyard, the guards have orders to kill you. Do you understand?"

Aine nodded mutely. Inside, the feel of sorcery was not as pronounced, but it still made her skin crawl. Was this the druid's version of the wards? She followed Marcan up a staircase to a circular corridor above.

"This will be your room," he said, opening a door halfway down the hall. "If you need anything, just ask one of the servants."

Aine stepped inside, and Marcan closed the door behind her. Automatically, she put her hand on the latch. It gave easily. She might be a prisoner, but at least she would not be confined to her chamber.

Tears welled up again, but she stuffed them down and locked them away. She couldn't break. Until now, she had harbored hope someone would come after her. But Ruarc was dead, Lorcan most likely along with him. Even if Conor were alive, he didn't know she was in danger.

And if he did come for her? The fortress was filled with warriors. He had trained with the Fíréin, but what could one man do against Glenmallaig's strength?

That meant she could depend only on herself and what few weapons she had at her disposal. Keondric's affection. Her modest beauty. The ivory charm hidden in her bodice.

Aine curled up behind the curtains of her shelf bed, her heart heavy, and lifted up wordless prayers to Comdiu, but the only answer she received was that already spoken. *For your faith, you will be rewarded. Cling to that when the price seems too much to bear.*

The words she had always taken as encouragement chilled her. What exactly would that price be?

+ + +

A knock sounded at the chamber door. Aine pushed herself from the bed and straightened her disheveled dress and hair, determined to put on a brave front for Keondric. She opened the door and lurched back. The chieftain stood there, but he was not alone.

"Come." The druid lifted a finger, and the charm flared hot beneath her dress. Aine didn't move.

His expression shifted, unreadable yet chilling, and she held her breath as he approached. "There's no need to be afraid. I just thought we might take a few moments to get acquainted. My name is Diarmuid."

"I know who you are," Aine said.

He stopped before her and trailed the backs of his fingers across her face as a lover would, as Conor had touched her. Behind him, Keondric stiffened. She clenched her jaw and forced herself to hold the druid's gaze, even though his magic threatened to suffocate her.

"Beautiful," he murmured. "And powerful. I thought Keondric had potential. But you, young one, you have no idea of what you are capable, do you?"

His words made no sense, but Aine would never admit it. She glared at him and pressed her lips tightly together.

Diarmuid's fingers slid down her neck to the silver chain and hovered over the spot where the ivory charm lay. His smile faded. "Don't worry. I'm not going to take it from you."

"Can't take it, you mean." She poured every ounce of defiance she possessed into her stare.

Diarmuid laughed. "I like your fire, little one. I know I promised Keondric he could have you, but I'm sorely tempted. . . . Ah, but that's a discussion for another day. We've still to determine what choice your young man makes. I know you share my anticipation."

Diarmuid turned and exited in a swish of dark robes. Keondric cast an unsettled look in her direction before following the druid from the room. Aine stood her ground until the door closed. Then she fell to the stone floor of her prison, shaking.

✦ ✦ ✦

Aine had composed herself by the time Keondric returned with two servants bearing supper trays. She knew what she had to do.

"I hope you don't mind if I join you," he said.

"Of course not." Inwardly, Aine recoiled at the intimacy of dining with him in her chamber, but she forced a pleasant smile and took her seat. The servants placed the food on the table and quickly departed.

"Has everyone treated you kindly?" Keondric asked.

"Aye, except . . ." Aine set down her spoon and put on a tremulous expression. "I'm frightened. You said you wouldn't let anyone harm me."

Keondric's expression darkened, and his hand tightened around his own spoon. "Has someone hurt you?"

"Not yet. But surely you can see the druid doesn't mean to keep his bargain. He wants me for himself."

Keondric let out a breath and tried to smile. "I can hardly blame him. You are a captivating woman."

"It's more than that. I know when a man desires me." She met his eye, and he shifted uncomfortably, as she knew he would. "But he covets something else. What did he mean when he mentioned your potential?"

Keondric's smile faded. She had struck a nerve. Good. She reached out and rested her hand lightly atop his on the table. "Please, you can trust me with your thoughts."

His eyes flicked down to their hands. When they returned to her face, they were softer, less suspicious. "Diarmuid was the one who first recognized my gifts. My father said they betrayed our blood. But the druid showed me I could be more than my father, groveling before a king who had no more right to the throne than we."

"You learned your skills from Diarmuid? You implied you possess the gifts of Balus, like me."

"I do. Did you know Diarmuid was once Fíréin? He was their leader.

But the brotherhood couldn't see that the High King must once again take the throne."

"You're to be the High King?"

Keondric's enthusiasm dimmed a little. "Of course not."

That had been a mistake. She needed to make him feel powerful if she were to convince him to help her, and he needed to believe they were on the same side. "Then what does he want with people like us? Those with the gifts?"

"I don't know. I was useful because I could cross wards, but now they've all been broken."

"Will he kill us now?" Aine hardly needed to feign the tremor in her voice.

Keondric stood swiftly, then knelt before her and took her hands in his. "The druid may not honor his promises, but I honor mine. I will protect you. I won't let anything happen to you." She lowered her eyes in what she hoped looked like maidenly shyness, and he returned to his seat. "Now, please, eat. It does you no good to waste away."

Aine picked up her spoon again, but she hardly tasted her food. She had just proven how easily Keondric could be manipulated. He had been seduced by promises of power, and he truly believed her affection was real. Now she knew why.

A subtle spell weakened his will, just enough to alter his natural inclinations, but not enough to trigger the wards. In that moment, she actually felt sorry for him. Would he have done any of this if the druid had not changed him, gaining his trust through his insecurities?

Aine did her best to keep up with the inconsequential conversation as they ate, but from Keondric's slight frown, she could tell he knew something was wrong. When he rose to leave, she moved into his path. "May I confide something?"

"Of course, my lady. Anything."

"This may be what the druid wants from me." She drew the charm on its chain from beneath her dress and laid it across her palm.

Keondric touched it with one finger, then jerked as if he had been hit by a bolt of lightning. "What was that?"

"You tell me."

He just shook his head, but she saw doubt forming in his eyes. "Good night, Aine."

"Good night, Keondric." *Comdiu, let it be enough.*

CHAPTER FORTY

Conor followed the trap lines, hoping to come across sentries or trackers who could confirm he was on the right path, but he traveled for days without seeing a single soul. Finally, on the fourth day, he met a young sentry named Pól, who, despite a propensity to ramble, provided him with food and an important bit of information: a man and a woman had passed a few days earlier on horseback, headed west.

Conor nearly collapsed beneath the weight of relief. Aine still lived.

He regained more strength with each passing day, and with it, his stamina and his stealth. His head still felt tender, but at least his balance and vision problems had dissipated. He began to believe he might succeed after all.

On the eighth day after Aine had been taken, Conor reached the margin of Róscomain and stopped short. This was the very road that had taken him to Lisdara three years ago. Even knowing Aine lay at the end of that road, he hesitated. In the forest, he was swift and confident. In the open, he was just another man, a target.

In that case, he might as well work it to his advantage. He unraveled his braid and pulled it back in a more common fashion. These days, tattered clothing drew little interest, and the dirt and blood helped disguise his garments' distinctly old-fashioned cut. Once he was convinced he looked sufficiently unremarkable, he broke free of the tree line and started down the road.

He sorted through his options as he walked. Aine would be at Glenmallaig by now. Was she being treated like a prisoner or a guest? There were dungeons beneath the east walls, but the conditions were so appalling it defeated the purpose of taking her there alive. More likely, she would be under guard in the guest chambers.

You've brought me this far, merciful Comdiu. You'll have to create the opportunities. This won't be easy.

The last time he had prayed that kind of prayer, he had fought Liam to a draw. This time, he had to win.

On the second day, Conor began to see signs of life and commerce: oxcarts carrying goods to and from the fortress or men on horseback. They paid him no attention, other than to avoid him, and sometimes not even then. He smiled to himself, buoyed by the unexpected discovery. If his fading ability worked as well in the open as it did in the forest, he might just have found a way to breach the fortress unnoticed. He still needed physical entry, though.

Late that afternoon, an opportunity presented itself. One of the carts that had passed him earlier now listed dangerously on the side of the road, its cargo of apples partially unloaded. A gray-haired man struggled to lift the cart while a young girl watched.

"Need help?" Conor asked as he approached.

The man jerked his head up and surveyed Conor warily. "Depends. You a wainwright?"

"No, but we might be able to get you to Glenmallaig and have it fixed properly. I assume that's where you're going?"

"Aye," he said slowly. "You?"

"The same. I've a message to deliver, and I'm tired of walking."

The man relaxed. "What happened to your horse?"

"Bandits." Conor pointed to the stitches in his scalp and said, "Villager fixed me up, but horses aren't that easy to come by. Shall we get this wheel off?"

Between the two of them, they lifted the wagon enough to remove the wheel from the axle. Fortunately, nothing was broken. The iron cap had worked free, letting the wheel slide off at an angle.

"You happen to have a hammer?" Conor asked. The man shook his head. "A rock it is then."

In the end, the fix took less than an hour, including loading the apples into the cart. The man and the girl climbed onto the buckboard, and Conor hopped onto the back. "You mind?" he asked, holding up an apple.

"Help yourself. I'm Breck, by the way, and this is my grand-daughter, Airmid."

"Cahan," Conor said.

"Much obliged to you, Cahan."

Conor drew his sword baldric over his head and stashed it out of sight among the bushels. With any luck, the gate guards wouldn't question his presence. Maybe they'd just assume he was another orchard hand.

"Where you coming from?" Breck called over his shoulder. Conor pretended not to hear him, and the man didn't ask again.

Facing backward on the cart, he didn't notice their approach to Glenmallaig until they began to slow. Conor shivered. Three years away had done nothing to diminish the dread the fortress cast over him, and knowing Aine was a prisoner inside only intensified the feeling.

He schooled his expression to boredom as the cart approached the open drawbridge, even though he felt sure the guards could hear the frantic thump of his heart. The cart rattled across and then stopped. While Breck stated his business to the warrior at the gate, another guard walked the length of the cart. Conor concentrated on making himself as uninteresting as possible. For a long moment, the guard paused, then strode back to his partner. Conor let out his breath in a rush when the cart lurched forward again. He'd done it.

He had no intention of testing his anonymity, however. As soon as they entered the courtyard, Conor grabbed his sword from its concealment, hopped off the back of the cart, and faded into the shadows of the inner wall.

From here, he could survey the entire fortress, as well as the armory and the kitchen. Guards stood watch, but there were far fewer than he had expected. With the king campaigning, perhaps there was little to guard. Besides, who would attack? Calhoun was wholly occupied with the siege on Lisdara, and all of Tigh's other enemies had been vanquished.

A servant emerged from the fortress with a wooden tray, headed to the kitchen. Perfect timing. He would be able to slip in unnoticed when the watch changed. Unfortunately, he still had no idea where Aine was being held, and he couldn't search every chamber in the keep.

Conor lounged against the wall and studied the other men while he finished his apple. Their numbers might be fewer than expected, but discipline was as strict as ever. Each man stood at attention, no casual conversations, nothing to eat or drink, their eyes taking in the movements of everyone in the courtyard. Getting into the fortress would be far easier than getting back out.

He closed his eyes and took a long, deep breath. He had come too far to give up because their escape route looked less than ideal. *You brought me here, Comdiu. I'll trust You to make a way.*

True to his estimation, only a half hour passed before men appeared in the courtyard to relieve the day watch. Conor tossed aside the apple core and strode casually toward the keep's back entrance. The guard at the door looked him over as if trying to place him, but he did not stop him as Conor entered the lower corridor.

He concentrated on blending in and followed the man in front of him at a discreet distance.

"Evening, Artagan," his quarry said to a passing guard.

"Better hurry, Naoise," Artagan said with a grin. "It'll be your head if you're late again."

Naoise shot back a particularly colorful oath, which made Artagan laugh. Conor filed away the names as a plan began to form.

The guard made a sharp left turn and started up the stairs to the corridor that encircled the top level of the fortress. Conor waited until he reached the top before he ran up the stairs and burst into the hallway.

"Naoise! Glad I caught you!"

Naoise turned and frowned as Conor approached, pretending to be out of breath. "They want a guard on the girl's chamber tonight. I'm supposed to take your post."

"Under whose orders?" the guard asked, scowling.

Conor stared at him in disbelief. "Whose do you think?" Naoise still looked unconvinced, so he shrugged. "Fine, go ask if you don't believe me. Or I can go back and say you have better things to do."

He surreptitiously sized up the guard as the man considered. Naoise was middle-aged, with a layer of fat covering muscle, but he outweighed Conor by at least a hundred pounds. Regardless of which way this conversation turned, Conor would have to kill him. The idea sickened him, but he had little choice. He only hoped the man would lead him to Aine first.

Naoise swore again. "Fine. Doesn't matter to me if I stand here or there all night. Just tell Sloane to get his assignments straight instead of sending his errand boy." He looked Conor over with a smirk. "Riocárd must be hard up for men if he's drafting from the nursery."

Conor played his role and scowled at him, but inside, he was stunned. Riocárd was still in charge here? That explained the level of discipline from the guards on watch. It also meant they would be as diligent and well-trained as ever. Naoise chuckled at his own joke and ambled down the hallway toward the guest chambers.

Conor waited until he stopped before a room and strode toward him, drawing his dagger. His guts twisted, but it was too late to change his mind. As Naoise turned, Conor drove the dagger under the guard's ribs and into his heart, then eased his bulk to the floor. He couldn't look Naoise in the eye as the man's life ebbed away. He cleaned his hands and blade on the guard's clothes and found he was trembling.

Focus. If he could not overcome his revulsion, he and Aine would die. He couldn't leave the guard here for someone to find. He sheathed his weapon and tried the door latch. It gave easily.

But the room was empty.

So much for his plan. He shouldered open the door and dragged the body inside, then kicked the door shut with his foot.

"Conor?"

His heart leapt into his throat as Aine slid from the shelf bed. Her eyes drifted to the dead man and then back to his face. He steeled himself for her expression of horror, but she only launched herself into his arms. "Thank Comdiu you're alive. I prayed you would come . . ."

Conor buried his face in her hair and allowed himself one blessed moment of relief. She was alive. He had found her. He held her at arm's length, searching her tearful face for some evidence of her ordeal. "Are you all right? Have you been hurt?"

"No, I've been treated kindly. But we have to hurry. Diarmuid may already know you're here."

"Diarmuid's at Glenmallaig?" Conor's blood surged. The sorcerer was so close. He could put an end to this, avenge the deaths of Labhrás and his mother, perhaps even give Calhoun a chance . . .

And if Diarmuid killed him instead? What would happen to Aine?

"Conor, please."

He met Aine's eyes, simultaneously heartened and terrified by the trust he saw there. He kissed her gently. "No matter what happens, remember I love you. Quietly now." He took her hand, opened the door, and stepped out into the empty hallway.

They made it only a few feet before a robed, tattooed man stepped into the corridor. Sorcery, thick and invisible, twined around their legs, halting them in midstep.

"Well, well," the druid said, his booted feet scuffing the floor as he approached. "You chose love over duty after all. Come to rescue your fair maiden, just like a bard's tale." He caressed the word *bard* with a mocking smile. "I certainly hope you're a better musician than rescuer. Seems the Fíréin have been careless in their training since my departure."

Anger flared at the taunt, but Conor forced it back down. "I was about to say the same about your house guard."

Diarmuid chuckled. "Merely for show, my boy. Nothing happens here without my knowledge. I sensed you the moment you broke the perimeter. You Balians are so . . . bright." The druid cocked his head as if listening. "Speaking of which, here comes another one."

Mac Eirhinin rounded the corner on cue. Conor felt rather than heard Aine's sudden intake of breath. He checked another flare of fury against Aine's kidnapper and used the druid's distraction to test the bonds of sorcery that held them. They were as impenetrable as mortar.

The Faolanaigh lord ambled toward them, a slow smile spreading across his face. "You captured them. I'm so pleased. It would have been a shame to let our prize escape so easily." The way Mac Eirhinin's eyes caressed Aine from head to toe uncorked Conor's carefully contained anger once more.

"You're a traitor," Aine hissed, loathing thick in her voice.

Mac Eirhinin's expression hardened, and he turned to the druid. "You've got what you wanted. The boy is here. I hope you mean to honor your agreement now. I have plans for her."

"So do I," Diarmuid said.

Mac Eirhinin's smile faded. He looked at Aine, and his expression softened a degree, giving Conor a glimpse of the feeling he had tried to hide in Abban's camp. Then his gaze traveled to Conor and changed again, but not into hatred or even dislike. Resolve. He gave a barely perceptible nod and flicked his eyes toward the stairwell.

Before Conor could make out his meaning, a dagger appeared in Mac Eirhinin's hands. He spun and plunged the blade into the druid's body.

"Go!" Mac Eirhinin shouted, wrenching the blade free. "Get her out of here!"

The bonds wrapping Conor and Aine evaporated. Conor drew his sword, pulling Aine behind him toward the stairs, but he couldn't help looking back. Mac Eirhinin crumpled to the ground just as the sorcerer sank down beside him in a crimson pool.

They took the steps downward at a breakneck speed and emerged into the lower hallway in time to meet the first guard. Conor ran him through before he had time to draw his weapon and pulled Aine onward.

The warrior at the back exit must have heard the short confrontation, because he was waiting for them. Conor blocked the incoming thrust, then two more. The man was skilled, but compared to the Fíréin, only passably so. A slash to the body took him to the ground.

They burst through the door into the cool night, and for a moment, Conor thought they were free. Then three more guards rushed through the door behind them.

"Do you know where the stable is?" he asked Aine over his shoulder.

She nodded, her eyes wide with fear.

"Go there. Bridle a horse. I'll meet you."

"But—"

"Go!" Conor shouted as the guards charged. He didn't have time to see if she complied before steel clashed against steel and then just as quickly met flesh.

As the first of his three opponents fell before him, he thought he read uncertainty in the others' eyes, but they pressed forward anyway. They too were skilled, but he defeated them without their weapons finding a target.

"Conor!"

Aine tore around the corner of the stable atop a bay mare, bridled with a rope lead. Conor sheathed his bloodstained sword and leapt up behind her. One arm enwrapped her waist, and the other took the lead from her hand as he spurred the horse toward the exit. Abruptly, he reined the mare to a skidding stop.

The drawbridge, open only a few minutes earlier, was closed.

Aine let out a choked cry, but Conor's mind whirred, working out an alternate plan. Glenmallaig had been his home, and foggy as his memories were, he knew the bridge was not the only way out.

He wheeled the horse and kicked her into a full gallop. More guards poured into the courtyard to intercept them and then dove out of the way of flying hooves. Their escape route loomed ahead, nearly invisible in the twilight: narrow steps carved into the inner surface of the battlements.

Conor slid from the horse and helped Aine down. He gave her a push in the direction of the steps. "Up there! I'll be right after you."

She scrambled up the steep stairs, using one hand to clutch her skirts out of the way and the other in front of her to keep her balance. Conor glanced back at the approaching guards, gauging whether he and Aine could reach the top before their enemies caught up to them. Perhaps, but the steps were far too narrow to turn and fight. He would surely end up with a sword in his back. He had no choice but to meet them here on level ground.

Conor counted five in the dim light. When they saw he intended to face them, they spread into a half circle. He drew his sword and took a moment to steady his breathing.

Now would be an excellent time for another miracle.

The peculiar calm settled over him immediately. Time slowed and stretched as it had when he fought Master Liam on the crannog. He circled left, bringing his opponents into line so he could face them one at a time.

They assumed he would take the defensive. Instead, he charged.

The first man was wholly unprepared. One ineffective block, and Conor's blade cut through his middle. He did not even pause before meeting the second, who fell just as quickly. He fought the third and fourth without any conscious thought, carried by instinct and reflex.

The last he underestimated, based on the marginal abilities of the other four warriors. Too late, he realized the man's hesitation came not from intimidation or lack of skill, but careful calculation. Conor barely managed to parry his attack, and the tip of the blade sliced across his upper arm. A warm rush of blood soaked his left sleeve.

The pain broke his focus, and he blinked in recognition. "Riocárd?" Even knowing Galbraith's champion was in command of the fortress, he hadn't expected to meet him here among his guards.

"Do I know you?" Riocárd asked, unwavering.

"Apparently not." Conor launched another attack, but the warrior deflected or avoided the blows altogether. With a pang of dismay, he realized Riocárd's skill matched his own.

They continued to trade offense and defense, both men seeking an opening, the mistake that would lead to a killing blow, and finding none. Riocárd had been among the most proficient of Tigh's swordsmen when Conor was a child, and time had done nothing to diminish his abilities.

Aine now crouched atop the battlements. Archers would pick her off from a distance in mere seconds. He had to end this. He could not leave her unprotected atop the wall.

"I thought you would have recognized me," Conor said tightly as their swords clashed again. "I'm told I resemble my father."

Confusion, followed by recognition, rippled across Riocárd's face. "Conor?"

In that moment of surprise, Riocárd wavered, and Conor seized the opportunity. He feinted, drawing Riocárd's guard open, and delivered a straight thrust to the body. Shock registered on the champion's face.

Conor withdrew his blade, and Riocárd crumpled to the ground. He stared in disbelief for several seconds, breathing hard, until Aine's shout alerted him of still more danger.

Archers rounded the corner, arrows already nocked. Bowstrings twanged as he clambered up the steps toward Aine. The first arrows missed their mark and bounced away at his feet, but they would not be so lucky the next time.

"Where do we go now?" Aine asked.

Conor looked over the side to the moat, at least twenty feet down. "We jump."

"I can't swim!" she cried, but Conor's weight already bore them off the wall to the murky waters below.

CHAPTER FORTY-ONE

The cold water knocked the breath from Aine's lungs, and she plummeted into the moat like an anchor. Shock stunned her into immobility. Then her lungs started to burn, and she flailed against the pressure of the muddy water. Her skirt tangled around her legs, hampering her unschooled attempts to thrust upward.

She broke the surface long enough to suck in a panicked breath before her sodden dress pulled her under again. Then strong hands grabbed her and pulled her back up. An arm encircled her chest, just barely keeping her face out of the water.

"Stop fighting, or you'll drown both of us," Conor said in her ear. She stilled her movements and let him tow her to safety. He pushed her up against the bank, and she scrambled for a handhold while he levered himself up beside her.

She lay on the ground for a moment, panting and blissfully happy to be alive. Shouts rang from Glenmallaig's courtyard, followed by the cranking of the drawbridge's huge gears.

Conor hauled her to her feet. "Can you run?"

"We made it," Aine said, dazed.

"Not yet. Make for the trees. We'll be out of the archers' range."

Conor propelled her forward, but waterlogged wool tangled between her legs. She hauled up handfuls of her skirt and struggled onward. Only a few more yards and they'd be free.

The drawbridge thudded on the outer bank, but she didn't dare look back. When at last they reached the safety of the tree line, she doubled over. "I can't run in this."

Conor glanced back at the men now pouring from the fortress and pulled his knife from his belt. "Stand up."

Aine straightened, still too stunned to question him. He cut the lacings of her bodice and pulled the wet dress from her shoulders. It fell in a sodden heap at her feet. She shivered in her thin linen shift, now plastered to the contours of her body. Her teeth chattered uncontrollably.

"Let's go." Conor took her hand and pulled her deeper into the forest.

The speed with which he moved through the trees astounded her. She struggled to match his pace, afraid she would put a foot wrong in the dark and crash to the ground, but Conor drove her on mercilessly. Her labored lungs began to burn and her muscles cramped from the unaccustomed exertion. She could barely force herself to stay upright.

Conor stopped at last at the bank of a small stream. Aine gasped for breath, palms braced on her knees. "Are they gone?"

"No," he said finally. "A few minutes behind us. And they have dogs."

Despair sapped the last of her strength. She fell to her knees. They couldn't escape. The dogs would follow their tracks until their strength ran out, which judging from her trembling legs, would not be long. A sob escaped her lips.

Conor knelt beside her and gripped her shoulders. "Aine, look at me." When she continued to cry, he shook her and said more forcefully, "Look in my eyes."

She raised her tear-streaked face and saw no fear in his eyes, only determination.

"You can't break down now. We have to keep going. Do you understand?"

She nodded, though her tears continued to fall. He stood and held out a hand again. "Come on."

She followed him, thinking they would cross the stream, but instead he led her up it. The water ran around her calves. She lifted her shift to her knees and pressed forward against the current. Her limbs felt heavy and clumsy, and more than once she fell with a splash. Each time, Conor turned back, helped her to her feet, and started off again.

She lost track of how long they traversed the stream bed, but after a while, she heard the baying of hounds behind them. Conor paused to listen and bit off a frustrated oath.

"They're coming? We didn't lose them?"

"No. Keep moving." He took her hand and pulled her up the opposite bank. He must have seen her fear and weariness, because he gave her a slight smile. "Don't worry. We'll make it. You just have to hold on a little bit longer."

His words heartened her. After everything they had survived, she believed him. He squeezed her hand, and they started into the trees again.

A few minutes later, Conor stopped. "I don't believe it. Look."

Aine followed his gaze. Barely distinguishable in the dim forest was a tiny cottage made of mud and reeds. They tramped through the brush toward the structure. Conor drew his sword and gestured for Aine to wait while he went inside. She heard a rustle, and something thudded to the floor. A moment later, he poked his head out and waved her inside.

Somehow, he had managed to light a candle stub on the single small table. The flame illuminated a musty, cobweb-strewn interior. A blanket covered a small double bedstead, and clothing still hung on pegs.

"What if the owners come back?" she asked.

"They won't." Conor opened the door and pointed to a symbol painted in lime.

The mark Fergus's enforcers left on Balian homes after the owners were executed. She shuddered.

"Rest here," he said. "Collect anything that might be of use. Food, herbs, clothing, whatever you can find."

"Where are you going?" Her heart knocked her ribs. He was leaving her?

"I need to make sure we've lost them." He pulled her tightly to him. "Don't give up now. I'm coming back. Have faith, Aine."

His words and the steady beat of his heart beneath her ear cut through her fear. Conor took the knife from his ankle and pressed it into her hand. "Take this. If anyone comes through the door, wait until they get close enough to use it."

She pulled his head down to kiss him. "Be careful."

He smiled reassuringly and slipped out the door.

✦ ✦ ✦

Conor left the cottage and melted soundlessly into the trees. His brave words aside, they could no longer run. Aine was exhausted to the point of collapse, and his arm had continued to bleed more than it should have.

He cut a strip from the hem of his tunic and bound the wound, then cinched the knot with his teeth. Aine could sew it up later. The dogs had almost certainly picked up their scent by now, and if he didn't end this soon, they would find themselves in a fight they couldn't win.

Fortunately, he was back in his element. The men followed the dogs blindly in the dark, focused on their quarry. They thought only of the pursuit, unaware they were now the pursued.

Conor summoned energy he thought he had already exhausted and moved swiftly into the trees. Hounds bayed in the distance. He would have to eliminate those first. He crossed their original path and headed away from the cottage, hoping the hounds would pick up the newer, stronger trail. Then he hunkered down to wait in a man-sized hollow beneath the roots of an ancient oak.

True to his prediction, the dogs' baying became louder and more insistent as they approached. Their handler crashed along behind them. A single man. Luck was on Conor's side. He gripped his sword as the dogs barked and scrambled toward his hiding place.

He waited until the hounds rounded the tree and silenced them with two quick thrusts of the sword, then faded back into the shadows.

The dog's handler spun, searching the trees wildly, his sword in hand. Conor waited until the man relaxed his guard and sprang from cover. The warrior managed a single inefficient parry, but he only deflected Conor's blade, which opened his abdomen in a gush of blood. He screamed, dropping his sword to clutch at the horrific wound.

Conor silenced him with a second swift blow, pushing down his horror. A messy, ugly death, the last thing he had intended. He would have to deal with the others more efficiently.

It didn't take him long to locate the next two trackers, brought his direction by the commotion only a hundred yards apart. He moved silently through the trees toward them.

The first man remained unaware of his peril until Conor's dagger took him from behind. The second man was more alert. He held his sword at the ready, and his eyes passed over Conor's hiding spot in the scrub several times, as if he sensed his presence. If Conor engaged him now, it would turn into a fight he could ill afford.

Hand stones, then. Conor selected a large stone and crept from the bushes to throw. The projectile cracked into the man's temple. The warrior fell into a patch of ferns and lay motionless.

Conor listened carefully, but he heard only silence. Could he have been mistaken? Were there only three pursuers and not four? His uneasiness mounted. Exhaustion was flowing into the place determination once occupied, and he still didn't know if others still sought them.

He picked his path back to the cottage with care, numbness creeping into his legs. Several times, he staggered and barely caught himself before he fell. "Concentrate," he muttered. "Not much further. You're just tired."

But he could no longer ignore the truth. He'd chosen tactics that didn't require his left arm, which now hung uselessly by his side. His sleeve was bloody, the bandage soaked through, and he left a trail of drops from his dangling fingers. He knew better, but he couldn't lift his arm to cradle it against his body.

The scenery wavered and shifted around him. He was concentrating so hard on staying upright that he almost missed the sound. Not a loud one, merely a crack of a twig that could have been his own misstep. While his pain-fogged mind tried to process the information, instinct screamed at him to draw his sword. He tried, but his right arm obeyed him no better than the left.

The last warrior, a mountain of a man with arms like tree trunks, stepped out from behind a clutch of slender birch. Ordinarily, it would not have been enough to conceal him, even in the dark, but Conor now struggled to focus his vision on a single point. A slow smile spread across the warrior's face. He raised his great sword two-handed and lunged at him with a cry.

Conor sidestepped clumsily, tripped, and hit the ground in a hard roll. He scrambled to his feet and disappeared into the scrub.

"Not so brave when you have to face me one-on-one, are you, boy?"

Conor darted across an open patch to the safety of another group of trees, bent into a crouch. The swordsman whirled at the sound of his now-audible movements, but his eyes passed over the place where Conor knelt.

He had to focus. If he didn't finish this, he would die here. Then the man would take Aine back to Diarmuid.

That thought snapped him out of his stupor. He had to think logically. His aim wasn't worth risking the hand stones. The sword, then.

Conor gathered his strength, forced the fog away by sheer will, and eased his sword from the scabbard. The weapon, usually so light and responsive, now felt like lead in his hand.

He leaned the sword against his leg, point in the dirt, and took one of the stones from his pouch. He drew a deep breath and lobbed it as far as he could into the trees. The man whirled. With one last burst of energy, Conor took up the sword, threw himself into a staggering run, and drove the blade through his foe's back.

The momentum carried him forward even as his strength gave out, and he crashed to the ground onto his wounded arm. Pain burst in his shoulder and spread like fire through his body, blanking his vision and stilling his breath. He recognized, somewhere beyond the pain, he might not have killed the brute, but he could only writhe in agony.

Then the pain faded into numbness. Conor turned his head and looked directly into the sightless eyes of the dead giant. The sword still impaled him, a lucky strike through the heart. An inch to either side, and the man would have lived long enough to kill him.

I have to get back to Aine. Conor tried to push himself up, but his muscles refused to respond. In the corner of his vision, a man emerged from the trees. His mind screamed at him to defend himself. With every bit of strength left in his body, he wrenched the weapon free from the dead man beside him.

Before he could think about what he planned to do with the sword, the world went dark.

CHAPTER FORTY-TWO

Aine huddled in the corner of the cottage, shivering with cold and fatigue. She could scarcely process what had happened. Whether it was her manipulation or his own conscience, Keondric had sacrificed himself for them. He had kept his vow after all.

He was not the only one. Ruarc. Lorcan. Even now, Calhoun held off the dark forces that threatened Lisdara. Tears slid down her cheeks as she considered all the people she loved now in danger, perhaps already dead.

Then there was Conor. Even the Fíréin's renown had not hinted at the extent of his abilities. She had always sensed he was capable of far more than even he suspected, but the brotherhood had honed his raw talent and determination into something remarkable.

He would come back to her. He had to. He could not live through all that just to die now.

Please, Lord, just bring him back safely.

The answering certainty that washed over her gave her strength and purpose. She forced herself to rise, pushing away the bone-deep weariness that gripped her limbs. When he came back, they would probably not linger long. She rifled through the contents of the cottage, silently thanking Comdiu that He had turned these poor people's misfortune into a blessing.

A single dress hung on a peg with a linen shift. She discarded her wet underdress and slipped into the borrowed clothing. She had to overlap the eyelets of the dress's lacing and cut off excess fabric at the hem, but at least it was warm and dry. Her shivering slowly subsided. She set aside a few pieces of men's clothing for Conor, then continued to search the cottage.

Anything edible had already been carried off by rats, but she did find a sharp bone needle, some gut thread, and a few tallow candle stubs.

Time crawled, minutes turning into an hour, then two. The sick feeling seeped back in. Conor should be back by now. Had something happened to him?

Still, she made herself wait. Blundering around in the dark would only worsen the situation. If he returned and she wasn't there, they could end up wandering around the forest all night or worse.

Just when she could bear the wait no longer, the door burst open. A large man filled the doorway, Conor's body slung over his shoulder like a life-sized rag doll. She backed away, clutching the dagger in the folds of her skirt.

"You have nothing to fear from me, Lady Aine. He's hurt."

Aine surveyed the dark-haired man uneasily. He looked to be carved from rock, all muscle and sinew, and he moved with a particular grace she had unconsciously come to associate with Conor. Fírein. She nodded jerkily and gestured to the bed, though she still gripped the knife.

"Who are you?"

"Brother Eoghan, my lady. I'm a friend of Conor's. I'm told you have . . . certain gifts?"

She just nodded again. Eoghan laid Conor gently on the bed and stepped back. Her insides twisted. He looked so pale that had it not been for the barely perceptible rise and fall of his chest, she would have thought he was dead. And the blood . . . the left side of his tunic was soaked, his hands smeared with it. Which was worse? That it was all his? Or that it wasn't?

She sat down beside Conor and placed her hand against his cheek. Sensations instantly flooded her mind, and she exhaled in relief. "He's exhausted, and he's lost blood, but he'll recover. He just needs rest."

"Something neither of you will get much of," Eoghan said. "Can you fix his arm?"

Aine nodded. The man's posture said he was far more concerned for Conor than his calm tone suggested. She retrieved the needle and thread and said hopefully, "I don't suppose there's fresh water nearby?"

Eoghan passed her the water skin slung over his shoulder. She unbuckled Conor's belt and sword baldric and set them aside, then slit his tunic from cuff to hem. "Help me get this off him."

Eoghan lifted him while she gingerly removed the garment. Purple bruises mottled Conor's torso, but he otherwise seemed whole. Aine washed the sword wound and surveyed the damage. The gash was deep, and it bled as she manipulated it, but at least it was a clean cut from a sharp blade. She threaded the needle clumsily in the candlelight and began her delicate work, aware of Eoghan's scrutiny as she made a row of even, tiny stitches. Conor stirred in his sleep, but he did not wake.

When she finished, she bound his arm with linen scraps left over from her hasty alterations and turned to cleaning the rest of the blood and grime from his body.

"You've done this more than once, I can see," Eoghan said.

Aine brushed a piece of damp hair from Conor's eyes. "I spent two years on the Siomaigh front. There were plenty of opportunities for practice." She glanced back at Eoghan. "I don't mean to seem ungrateful, but what are you doing here? I thought the Fíréin stayed out of this sort of thing. He's no longer one of you."

"Conor has won the respect of a number of brothers. When I heard what he was planning, I thought he could use some help."

"We're indebted to you," Aine said softly.

Eoghan looked embarrassed. "Not at all, my lady. For now, sleep. I'll keep watch outside."

"Thank you."

Eoghan bowed and stepped out the door.

Aine stretched out on the mattress beside Conor and pulled the blanket over them. After a moment's hesitation, she laid her head on his uninjured shoulder and wrapped her arms around him, as if she could force strength back into his body through sheer will. She managed a few incoherent words of prayer, and then she succumbed to her exhaustion.

CHAPTER FORTY-THREE

Conor awoke with a start in the dimly lit room, disoriented. After several moments, he recognized the cottage in which he had left Aine, but the events afterward remained fuzzy. How had he gotten here?

He quickly realized he was not alone on the mattress. Aine slept beside him, her body pressed alongside his, her head resting on his bare chest. He caught his breath, allowing himself a moment of pure pleasure at the feel of her beside him and the peaceful expression on her lovely face as she slept.

Where was the pain? By all rights, he should be in agony from the injuries to his arm and head and the overexertion of the last few weeks. The newly stitched wounds itched and stung, but he recognized those sensations as signs of healing. The rest of his body felt as if he had just completed a day's labor at Ard Dhaimhin, a bearable feeling, pleasant even. How was that possible?

Carefully, he eased himself from beneath Aine's head. Her eyes fluttered open, and she jerked upright, her face flaming. "Oh! I didn't realize—"

Conor silenced her apology with his mouth. Her hand slid behind his neck and twined through his tangled hair, and he shivered with an entirely different sort of pleasure.

"I hope I'm not interrupting anything?"

Conor jerked away from Aine, and his hand closed on the sword beside him before he recognized the man standing in the doorway. "Eoghan?"

Eoghan shut the door behind himself, doing a poor job of hiding his smile. "It didn't take you long to recover."

"Can you blame me?" Conor retorted. Aine blushed an even deeper shade of pink. "What are you doing here?"

Eoghan folded himself into a chair as Conor untangled himself from the blankets. "The trackers passed word back to me. I thought you might need help. Looks like I was too late, though. It took me some time to procure the horses. In a few hours, there won't be any safe place for you in Seare."

Conor nodded. "We have to go to Aron. Lisdara was our last option, and it's under siege."

"It's worse than that, I'm afraid." Eoghan's expression sobered. "Lisdara has already fallen."

Aine let out a strangled cry, and Conor put his arm around her. "I'm sorry," he whispered in her ear. "I'd hoped with Diarmuid dead . . ."

"The druid's dead?" Eoghan asked. "When?"

"Mac Eirhinin killed him last night. Or at least, I assume he killed him. No one could survive a wound like that. But the wards are already broken, and Meallachán's harp is probably gone." He stroked Aine's hair as she pressed her face to his shoulder, gripped by the sorrow of another loss. Eoghan watched them with a wistful look on his face.

"I'm surprised Master Liam let you leave," Conor said.

"Master Liam doesn't know."

Aine lifted her head. "Will you be punished? Surely when he learns you were helping us . . ."

"Perhaps," Eoghan said, but his expression left no doubt as to what he thought awaited him in Ard Dhaimhin. "It's three days to Port an Tuaisceart. If you've any chance of beating the blockade, we must leave now."

Conor brushed tears from Aine's cheek, silently questioning. She nodded. "Give me a few minutes to gather our things." She pushed herself to her feet and began to fold supplies into the blanket.

Eoghan drew Conor off a few paces and pitched his voice low. "They sent trackers after you. I took care of them, but they'll send more. We'll have to make haste."

"Aine's a good rider. She can handle the pace."

"I understand why you moved heaven and earth to come back to her," Eoghan said, his eyes returning to Aine. "She's quite a woman."

"That she is." Conor clasped Eoghan's arm firmly. "Thank you. I owe you more than I can ever repay."

"You have a second chance. Don't waste it."

+ + +

They traveled briskly north, Aine riding behind Conor on a large gelding, Eoghan on a chestnut mare. Aine said little, but from time to time, her arms tightened around his waist, and her body shook with silent sobs. He simply held her hand and locked away his own disturbing memories. He would have time to deal with those later. Right now, she needed his strength.

Eoghan and Conor remained alert for pursuing riders, but none appeared. They could only conclude Glenmallaig's new commander had decided to cut his losses in the druid's absence.

That evening, they talked quietly by the fire about the dire situation in which Seare now found itself.

"I wouldn't yet consider Ard Dhaimhin to be safe," Conor said. "We presume Diarmuid is gone, but with the wards broken, there would be nothing stopping Fergus from attempting to take the city. He'd have ten thousand men at his disposal. From his perspective, those are good odds."

"We'll be ready if he does. The Conclave has been considering the possibility they will have to defend the city. Nothing I said would sway them to send men to Faolán, though it probably wouldn't have helped. Fergus struck Lisdara more quickly than anyone expected."

Conor glanced at Aine, who studied her ragged nails with more interest than they warranted. He took her hand, and she squeezed it tightly. "There's only one thing that might have made a difference, but there's no telling where the harp is now."

"I could try—" Aine began.

"No. If I hadn't left you to pursue the harp, you would have never been in danger. I won't repeat that mistake."

Aine didn't respond. Instead, she excused herself, claiming the need for privacy. When she was out of earshot, Eoghan said, "I know you. You're not going to give up that easily."

"How can I? The harp is the key to retaking Seare, and I may be the only person left alive who can use it. I just won't sacrifice Aine again in the process." Conor's voice caught. "I came too close to losing her."

Eoghan poked at the fire, then fixed him with a solemn look. "What happened at Glenmallaig?"

Conor studied his hands. They were clean now, but he couldn't forget the sight of them covered in other men's blood. Nothing could have prepared him for the horror that pressed at the back of his mind like water behind a dam. Every time he opened his mouth, it threatened to rush out of him in a terrifying howl. He steadied his voice and said, "Treasach warned me there was a cost. I just didn't know how high it would be."

"It will take time."

"And what happens when Aine realizes what I'm capable of? Right now, she's just relieved to be alive, but in time . . . she'll never look at me the same again."

"You do her a disservice," Eoghan said. "She loves you, Conor, truly. I think she's far wiser than you give her credit for. Would you do it any differently, knowing the cost?"

Foliage crunched underfoot as Aine returned, looking small and vulnerable in her borrowed clothing. His love for her struck him like a blow to the chest, painful in its intensity.

"No. I wouldn't change a thing."

Their third day on the road stretched into night, and they entered Port an Tuaisceart as the sky lightened to gray. The sleepy village on the Faolanaigh border was little more than an inlet for the fishing boats and coastal skiffs that brought supplies to Faolán's northern coast, but Eoghan seemed remarkably assured they would find what they were seeking.

They left the horses and followed Eoghan down to the harbor. Seabirds called overhead as they circled in search of food, and a few fishermen stood on the docks, loading their nets onto the boats for the day's work. A single-masted cog, out of place in the tiny port, floated at anchor a few hundred yards offshore, its draft too deep for the shallow harbor. When they neared the dock, Conor could just make out the name *Resolute* and a pair of familiar shield knots emblazoned on the side.

A rowboat separated from the ship and glided toward the docks, carrying two men. Eoghan caught the rope they tossed up to him and fastened it securely before offering a hand to the older of the two. Despite his graying hair, the man still possessed a strong body and a particular quality of movement that bespoke Fíréin training. Conor then understood Eoghan had done far more than arrange a few horses to bring them from the forest.

"Brother Eoghan, I presume?" the man said.

"Captain Ui Brolláchin. I wasn't sure you had gotten my message."

"Barely," he replied. "But one doesn't refuse a favor of the Ceannaire himself."

Conor's heart beat faster as he comprehended the significance. Eoghan shot him a bleak smile before he turned back to the captain. "This is Brother Conor and Lady Aine. They'll be your passengers."

Ui Brollacháin bowed to Aine and offered his hand to Conor. "Welcome. We'd best be getting to the ship. We'll be chancing the blockades as it is." He bowed to Eoghan. "Give my regards to Master Liam."

Eoghan nodded. Conor waited until the captain climbed back into the boat before he spoke. "You shouldn't have risked so much. You know the penalty for such a thing. You could come with us."

"No. If I leave, all those who helped me will pay because I engaged them under false pretenses. I knew the price when I started out."

Conor blinked back tears. He'd thought after all that had happened, he'd be immune to the effect of yet another sacrifice. He gripped Eoghan's arm and then clapped him into an embrace. "Thank you, my friend. I don't know what to say."

"I'm fully expecting your firstborn son to be named after me," Eoghan said with a grin.

Conor laughed, hoping it didn't sound as forced as it felt. "You can count on it."

Eoghan turned to Aine and bowed. "My lady. Conor is truly a fortunate man."

"Thank you, Eoghan." Aine put her arms around him and squeezed him tightly. "You are a true friend. We won't forget this."

Eoghan disentangled himself, looking moved by her spontaneous thanks. "Go now, you two. Your ship awaits."

Conor took Aine's pack and helped her into the rowboat. Eoghan loosened the tether and tossed the rope back down. As they rowed away from the dock, Conor lifted a hand in farewell and saw his friend's answering wave.

Once aboard the *Resolute*, they found an out-of-the-way spot at the rail, and Conor held Aine protectively in front of him while the crewmen drew the sail up the mast and hauled in the anchor. As the ship sailed from port under its billowing canvas, he strained for one last glimpse of Eoghan, standing with the two horses near the dock.

"What will happen to him when he returns to Ard Dhaimhin?" Aine asked.

"Fíréin discipline is harsh. If he's lucky, flogging."

"If not?"

Conor hesitated. "Execution."

Aine stifled a cry. Tears slid down her face, and Conor could not keep his own from welling in his eyes again.

"So many sacrifices," she whispered. "How many people died so we could live?"

They stood at the rail until the ship picked up speed and began to track northeast toward Aron, the shoreline fading into an expanse of green-blue.

"What will Lady Macha say when I show up with you in Forrais unannounced?" Conor asked.

"She won't be able to say anything when I introduce you as my husband." Aine turned toward him expectantly.

"Aine . . ." Conor began, but she silenced him with a finger on his lips.

"Do you love me?"

"Of course I do. I've never loved anyone else. But—"

She shook her head. "I don't know what tomorrow will bring, Conor. I don't know if we will have a tomorrow. But I don't want to live in fear any longer."

He looked into her eyes and saw the truth. She had known all along. Known he would have to leave again, known this time he might not return. Still, she wanted to be his wife. His heart swelled. He took her face in his hands and kissed her until she was breathless and laughing.

"I'll find the captain," he said with a smile.

They said their vows on deck at sunset before Comdiu and the sea, with a dozen amused crewmen as their witnesses. Conor barely heard the words through his surge of joy when the captain joined their hands and declared them husband and wife. He could not even find the words for prayer, but he knew Comdiu would understand his gratitude for bringing them together on this path, despite all the heartaches and sacrifices they had endured along the way.

Aine smiled as Conor bent to seal their union with a kiss. The crew whistled and stomped the deck in approval, and she laughed as he led her to the low-slung passenger cabin beneath the forecastle that would be their bridal chamber.

Still, Conor could not help looking back at the ominous storm clouds gathering on the horizon. He felt a brief pang of unease, a warning their troubles could not be escaped so easily. Then he put his worries aside. If he had learned a single lesson from all that had happened, it was that Comdiu was faithful. Whatever their future path held, they did not walk it alone.

BEHIND THE STORY:

THE FÍRÉIN BROTHERHOOD

When I created the setting for the Song of Seare, I drew heavily on the true history and culture of Ireland between the third and the eighth centuries A.D. Many of the unusual details that set the story apart from other English- or continental-inspired medieval fantasy—such as the election of the kings and their successors (tanists)—come directly from the pages of Irish history, as do many of the fashions, customs, and laws.

But when it came to creating the Fíréin Brotherhood, I had a more difficult task at hand. I wanted the warrior-brotherhood to feel both realistic to the setting, but also have a magical, mysterious quality about it. After all, when the book opens, Conor is most definitely not the typical fantasy hero, and it was going to take more than a simple mentor to turn him from a bookish scholar into the reluctant but proficient warrior he becomes by the end of the book.

THE HISTORICAL ORIGIN OF THE FÍRÉIN

I drew on the real-life existence of two groups for the basis of the Fíréin. The first is a group known as the Red Branch Knights (even though "red" is thought to be a mistranslation of the Gaelic word for "royal.") This was a militia who, according to the heroic stories, were loyal to the King of Ulster. Every summer, they would come to Emain, the seat of the king, to drill and train in military skills and arms. Other stories of the Red Branch Knights speak of their medical prowess, including an entire medical corps that traveled with the Ulster Army. These accounts imply that though they were essentially mercenaries, they were not uneducated nor unintelligent; they were renowned for their knowledge and healing abilities long before the first mention of what we'd consider "proper" physicians in Ireland.

Another group was known as the Fianna, or the Fena of Erin. This fighting force was loyal to the High King of Ireland, most notably in the late 200s AD. I was most interested in the fact that in addition to their fighting ability, candidates had to prove they were educated men by their ability to recite a large amount of poetry and stories, one of the markers of learning of the era. Another account speaks of how the men had to be able to run swiftly through the forest without snagging their long, unbound hair on branches (something that inspired my conception of the trackers and runners of the Fíréin brotherhood). Interestingly, the Fena's loyalties remained uncertain: sometimes they fought with the High King and sometimes against. The histories don't tell us why, leaving me to imagine that their loyalties were based on some internal criteria other than loyalty to title, clan, or bloodline.

Still, while archaeological and contemporary sources tell us that these two groups did exist, the historical fact has been so well folded into myth and legend that it's hard to tell what's true and what's fiction. That suited me just fine when using them as a basis for the Fíréin: in the tales, both groups perform feats that call upon supernatural skills and knowledge that go well beyond the abilities of the typical historical Irish warrior. These otherworldly myths gave me the foundation for a brotherhood that would be spoken about in Seare with a mixture of admiration and apprehension.

THE FÍRÉIN TRAINING
AND FIGHTING STYLE

In the Song of Seare, the Fíréin warriors have been awarded an almost mythological stature by the warriors of the kingdoms, reinforced by the fact that brothers who return to the kingdoms do so quietly and without drawing attention to their training at Ard Dhaimhin, adding to the perception that many may enter, but few may leave. I wanted their status as incomparable fighters to be rooted in truth—they really were better trained than the kingdom's men, even those professional warriors who did nothing but prepare for battle—but I also wanted those reasons to be perceived as supernatural ability.

The solution to that problem was presented by the history of High King Daimhin, who formed the personal guard from which the Fíréin were descended. I described him as a mercenary living in the east, where he ostensibly worked with and fought alongside men of different origins and traditions. I theorized that he could have learned different regions' fighting systems, which he would have internalized and brought back to Seare, then taught later to his personal guard. The unfamiliar methods would have not only taken opponents off guard and made them easier to subdue, but would also have conferred upon Daimhin's men an almost heroic status.

This is why the training methods of Ard Dhaimhin utilize the traditional weapons of Seare (hand stones, slings, staff, spear, bow, and sword) but use a more formalized, codified system of training that is similar to both Roman Gladiatorial schools and the Chinese Shaolin Temple, birthplace of Shaolin Kung Fu. From the Roman accounts, I took the use of wooden practice swords and the graded levels of training. From the Chinese side, I drew on my own martial arts experience, which spans both Korean and Chinese arts. Kung fu in particular focuses heavily on conditioning and strength training as well as cultivating a sense of family within the school. (In fact, in addition to traditional Chinese forms of address used in my school, we referred to each other as brother and sister.) It was this stratified and yet communal feel that I adopted for the Fíréin brotherhood, layered with its obvious monastic overtones.

Additionally, I conceived of the Fíréin-made swords as being thinner and lighter—more consistent with a Chinese-style weapon and technique. Were this set in an environment with medieval-style plate armor, this would be a disadvantage, but in an era where armor was a combination of padded clothing, boiled leather, and small metal plates sewn to other materials, the fast, nimble Fíréin fighting style would have been devastating and difficult to defend against.

ARD DHAIMHIN
AND THE MONASTIC LIFE

We learn in later books how Ard Dhaimhin went from being the seat of the High King and a thriving city to a cloistered society whose borders cannot be breached upon threat of death. In part, this is a nod to Ireland's existing centers of learning and worship in the form of the nemetons—groves, shrines, and temples that served as the center of ancient Celtic paganism. But there is also the monastic tradition that grew up after the coming of Christianity to the isle, or in the case of this story, when Daimhin brought Balianism back to his homeland.

While Irish monasteries were known for welcoming students of all origins for varying periods of time without requiring them to make a life-long commitment (known as a permeable monasticism), they were also protected by great walls, and for good reason. As a center of learning, they were also known as centers of great wealth, something that drew later incursions from the Vikings, who wanted to pillage the monasteries' riches. Irish monasticism is less reclusive than forms practiced elsewhere in Europe and no doubt benefited from the flow of information and out of settlement walls, while preserving a degree of separation from secular concerns.

But both Irish and continental monasteries found that over time, they had to leave the walls of their cloisters to both spread the gospel and the knowledge that was lost over centuries of conquests by "barbarians." It's this argument that Conor brings at the end of *Oath of the Brotherhood* and which permeates the other two books in the series: what good is their knowledge and prowess if they're going to remain completely separated from the world around them? What purpose is there in possessing the light if they're not going to use it to fight the darkness?

All these questions—and the Fíréin's dedication to isolationism—feel real and plausible because it taps into the human impulse to protect ourselves, to resist change, to fear the unknown and therefore avoid action. Conor's entrance into the Fíréin brotherhood is not merely a decision to learn to fight or to flee danger in the kingdoms: it's a symbol of his willingness to commit himself to the unknown, even death, on the strength of his trust in Comdiu. His arrival in Ard Dhaimhin, as we see in *Oath of the Brotherhood* and will see on a much larger scale in future books, challenges the very principles of the brotherhood and asks whether inaction is truly a sign of faith or merely fear of an uncertain future.

Q & A

WITH AUTHOR CARLA LAUREANO

You're best known for writing romance. Why did you decide to write fantasy?

I was actually a fantasy writer long before I wrote romance, though my books have always included love stories in some format. I wrote my first fantasy manuscript at the age of twenty, when I discovered that the genre was much larger than C.S. Lewis and J.R.R. Tolkein, the only fantasy writers I was familiar with as a child. (I can thank a college friend who dropped off his favorite fantasy paperback at my apartment during graduation week.) I loved that I could easily explore themes such as heroism, sacrifice, duty, and purpose in a natural way.

You can't discount the vagaries of publishing, though, and it was a romance novel I wrote during a break from editing this book that sold first, launching me along a path of writing contemporary romance and surprising me by the fact I *was* able to touch on those themes, albeit in a different way.

You can see both of those influences in *Oath of the Brotherhood*, where the love story is a catalyst for some of the larger actions in the story. It wasn't until writing this series that I realized that all stories are in some way a love story, whether they're about love of God, love of country, or love of another person. Even "unredeemable" anti-heroes display an underlying love of independence, justice, money, or self. The worthiness of the object of love has a huge influence on the tone and scope of the story.

Why did you choose a recognizable historical setting for your book rather than starting from scratch?

I love Ireland and Scotland, and I've always been fascinated by the Celtic history and myth of those countries. I've also read fantasy for decades, but most of my favorite books were set in a generically medieval continental European or British setting. Then I discovered two historical fantasy writers, Guy Gavriel Kay and Juliet Marillier, and my eyes were opened to how much historical settings—whether they used the actual historical context or just one that was heavily influenced by it—could become a character and a driving force in a story. Ireland is a culture that is inextricably linked to its land and its myths, so having felt an instant affinity for Eire when I first visited at the age of nineteen, it seemed natural to build my fantasy world based on that country.

How long did it take you to write Oath of the Brotherhood?

Almost a decade.... though not continuously. I came up with the idea while I was still working full time and toyed with it on free weekends and evenings... building the world, trying out different plot ideas, swapping out characters. Then it got put on a shelf for a long period of time after I had my first son. It was when I was pregnant with my second son and was put on bedrest that I pulled out the idea again and started daydreaming what it could be. It was only once I decided that this was meant to be a Christian fantasy novel that it finally found its heart and soul. I worked on it on and off for about two more years before I was ready to pitch it at conferences.

The other books in the series were written much more quickly—in less than a year—because the world was already established. I'd like to say that I'd had the entire story plotted out from the beginning, but a lot of it I figured out as I went along. And the ending of the series surprised even me.

What's your writing process like?

I used to write in successive drafts, and books would have six or seven versions before they were ready to be seen by anyone. Over time, I've been able to streamline that into two or three.

I tend to be pretty disciplined about the writing process, especially when I'm under a deadline: I sit down at the same time each day and write for a certain number of words (which I determine based on how many work days I have to complete a draft). These books, which were written several years ago, were largely completed in three-hour chunks while my youngest son was in preschool. I'd set up my "office" at a coffee shop nearby (so I didn't waste part of that work time driving home) and write as fast as I could with a cup of coffee and an epic soundtrack playing through headphones. If I finished my 3300 words, I was done for the day. If I wasn't, I had to sneak minutes in the carpool pickup line or during nap times or after everyone went to bed. I spent driving time working through setting ideas or the plot for the next chapter so I was prepared for the next chance I had to get it down on paper.

These days the process is easier because my kids are older and in school full time, and I can sit at my own desk. But the structure is more or less the same.

How did you develop the magic system for your series?

Ireland in the Dark Ages was a highly religious place, first in pagan beliefs and later with the coming of Christianity, so I wanted magic to be interwoven into those beliefs. Since this was to be a Christian fantasy, it made sense for magic to be a gift similar to spiritual gifts, only available to believers, through the influence of the Holy Spirit (if you look closely, you can see His presence in this book, even if He's not explicitly described). Conversely, any other magic had to be rooted in pagan folk beliefs or something darker. Since early Christian scholars denounced the *sidhe* of Irish paganism as demons, it was natural to position my fictional *sidhe* as enemies of the good. But it would be simplistic to paint all druids with the same brush, especially considering the real druids of Ireland maintained their status as poets, historians, and judges after the coming of Christianity. Therefore I invented the class of the Red Druid, practitioners of blood magic whose power issues from a dark source. Even though this is a fantasy version of Ireland, I wanted it to feel plausible enough within a real historic framework.

Did you intend for the book to be read as a Christian allegory?

The Song of Seare isn't meant to be an allegory. As a secondary world fantasy, Seare and its environs exists completely separate from our own world. However, I had to address a question that comes up every time Christians talk about the possibility of the existence of other worlds or a multiverse: if God created everything, then He created the other worlds; if those other worlds were fallen and sin existed, then He would provide a Savior. Considering Seare is so closely based on real-world Ireland, it made sense to make the salvation story in this universe similar to our own. But because the fictional world is different—and magic exists—I only intended to draw attention to a broader spiritual message and not finer points of theology.

What can we expect from future books in the series?

Although *Oath of the Brotherhood* ends with a nominal victory, there's some ominous foreshadowing that things might not have been as neatly concluded as it might seem. There's still evil brewing, there's still the question of war in Seare and the Fíréin's involvement in it, and there's still uncertainty about Conor's unconventional path. Was he educated and trained merely to save Aine's life... or does a greater purpose still lie ahead of him? Those questions and more will be answered in the remaining books, *Beneath the Forsaken City* and *The Sword and the Song*.

ACKNOWLEDGMENTS

When I began writing *Oath of the Brotherhood*, I hoped that it would somehow find its way into print, but I didn't dream that it would be given not one, but two lives: first as a paperback release with NavPress and later as a hardcover with Enclave Publishing. It's been a long journey from the book's inception to holding this iteration in hand, and it never would have happened without a distinguished list of enthusiastic publishing professionals to help it on its way. My deepest gratitude goes to:

Reagen Reed, the only person I've ever met who has read more fantasy than me. I am grateful for both your sharp insight and your ability to keep me from embarrassing myself. I couldn't have asked for a better editor for this project.

The crew at NavPress who edited and shaped this book the first time around, particularly Meg Wallin and Brian Thomasson.

The crew at Enclave Publishing, who embraced this book as their own and have given it a second chance to reach readers in this beautiful new format.

My agent (and now publisher), Steve Laube. I've said it before and I'll say it again: I wouldn't be doing this if it weren't for you. I'm forever grateful for both your insight and your friendship.

My husband, Rey, for your constant support, encouragement, and willingness to share your wife with imaginary people. I love you now and always.

Nathan and Preston: in the time since this book was first written, you've grown into two amazing young men. I'm proud to call you my sons.

Mom and Dad, for being my early readers, cheerleaders, and encouragers. You told me I could do anything with hard work, determination, and prayer, and you made sure I believed it. Thank you.

ABOUT THE AUTHOR

Carla Laureano is the two-time RITA® award-winning author of over a dozen books, spanning the genres of contemporary romance and Celtic fantasy. A graduate of Pepperdine University, she worked in sales and marketing for more than a decade before leaving corporate life behind to write full-time. She currently lives in Denver, Colorado with her husband, two sons, and an opinionated tortoiseshell cat named Willow.